JAN 3 1 2012

ELK GROVE VILLAGE PUBLIC LIBRARY

3 1250 00980 3325

DISCARDED BY
ELK GROVE VILLAGE PUBLIC LIBRARY

P9-ELW-520

DISCARDED BY
ELK GROVE VILLAGE PUBLIC LIBRARY

ELK GROVE VILLAGE PUBLIC LIBRARY
1001 WELLINGTON AVE
ELK GROVE VILLAGE, IL 60007
(847) 439-0447

ELK GROVE VILLAGE PUBLIC LIBRARY
1001 WELLINGTON AVE
ELK GROVE VILLAGE, IL 60007
(847) 439-0447

Gillespie and I

ALSO BY JANE HARRIS

The Observations

Gillespie and I

A NOVEL

JANE
HARRIS

HARPER PERENNIAL

NEW YORK • LONDON • TORONTO • SYDNEY • NEW DELHI • AUCKLAND

HARPER ● PERENNIAL

First published in Great Britain in 2011 by Faber & Faber.

GILLESPIE AND I. Copyright © 2012 by Jane Harris. All rights reserved. Printed in the United States of America. No part of this book may be used or reproduced in any manner whatsoever without written permission except in the case of brief quotations embodied in critical articles and reviews. For information address HarperCollins Publishers, 10 East 53rd Street, New York, NY 10022.

HarperCollins books may be purchased for educational, business, or sales promotional use. For information please write: Special Markets Department, HarperCollins Publishers, 10 East 53rd Street, New York, NY 10022.

FIRST U.S. EDITION

Library of Congress Cataloging-in-Publication Data is available upon request.

ISBN 978-0-06-210320-8

12 13 14 15 16   RRD   10 9 8 7 6 5 4 3 2 1

FOR TOM

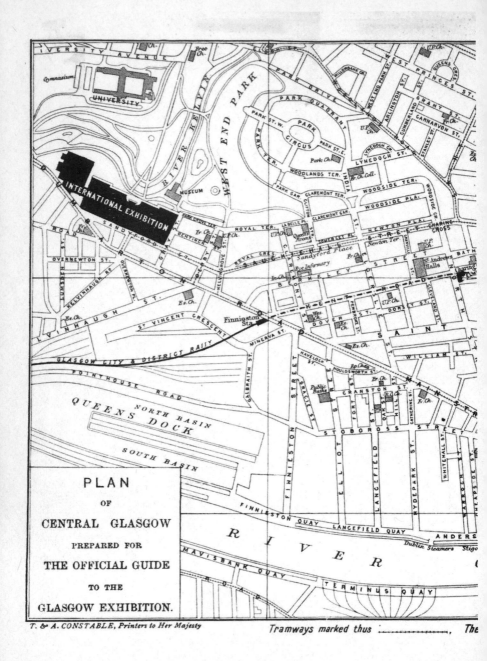

PLAN OF CENTRAL GLASGOW PREPARED FOR THE OFFICIAL GUIDE TO THE GLASGOW EXHIBITION.

T. & A. CONSTABLE, Printers to Her Majesty

Tramways marked thus ·············· , The

COPYRIGHT

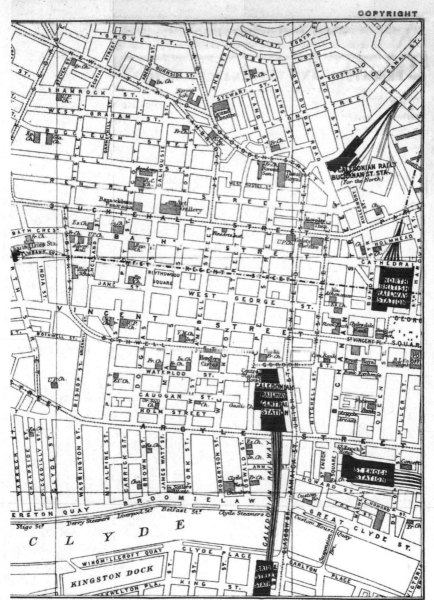

The Plan is divided into Half-Mile squares

J. BARTHOLOMEW, EDIN?

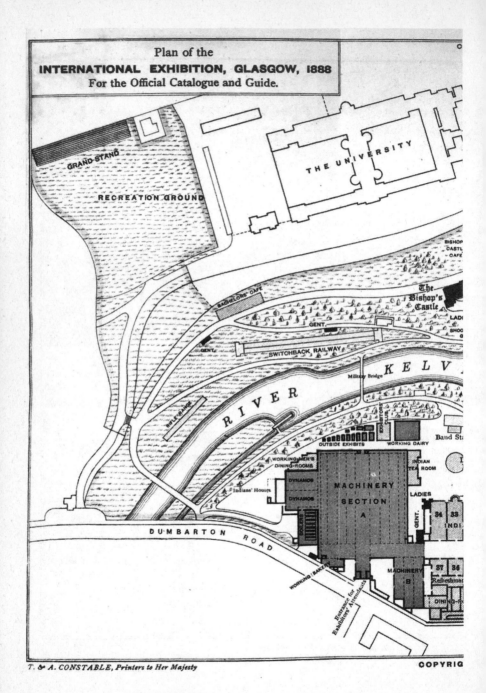

Plan of the
INTERNATIONAL EXHIBITION, GLASGOW, 1888
For the Official Catalogue and Guide.

T. & A. CONSTABLE, Printers to Her Majesty

COPYRIG

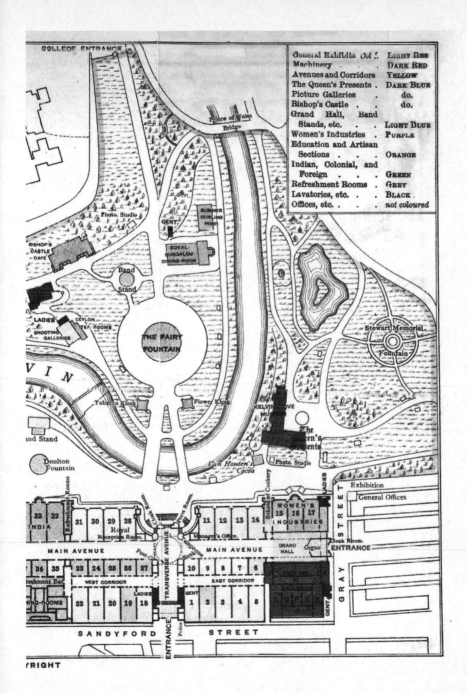

COLLEGE ENTRANCE

Prince of Wales
Bridge

General Exhibits *vol 1* . . LIGHT RED
Machinery . . . . . DARK RED
Avenues and Corridors . . YELLOW
The Queen's Presents . . DARK BLUE
Picture Galleries . . . do.
Bishop's Castle . . . do.
Grand Hall, Band
  Stands, etc. . . . LIGHT BLUE
Women's Industries . . PURPLE
Education and Artisan
  Sections . . . . ORANGE
Indian, Colonial, and
  Foreign . . . . GREEN
Refreshment Rooms . . GREY
Lavatories, etc. . . . BLACK
Offices, etc. . . . *not coloured*

Photo. Studio

GENT

SUMMER
CURLING
POND

BISHOP'S
CASTLE
~ CAFE

ROYAL
BUNGALOW
DINING-ROOM

Band
Stand

LADIES
SHOOTING
GALLERIES

CEYLON
TEA ROOMS

THE FAIRY
FOUNTAIN

Stewart Memorial
Fountain

VIN

Tobacco Kiosk

Flower Kiosk

and Stand

Doulton
Fountain

KELVIN GROVE
MUSEUM

The
Queen's
Presents

Van Houten's
Cocoa

Photo. Studio

School of Cookery

LADIES

Exhibition

General Offices

33 32
INDIA

31 30 29 28

Cloak Room

Press Room

11 12 13 14

WOMEN'S

15 16 17

INDUSTRIES

Royal
Reception Room

Manager's Office

Cloak Room.

GRAY STREET

ENTRANCE

MAIN AVENUE

Post Office

Banking

MAIN AVENUE

GRAND
HALL

Organ

34 35

Refreshment Bar

23 24 25 26 27

WEST CORRIDOR

TRANSVERSE AVENUE

10 9 8 7 6

EAST CORRIDOR

ING-ROOMS

22 21 20 19 18

LADIES

GENT

1 2 3 4 5

GENT

SANDYFORD

ENTRANCE

Police

STREET

YRIGHT

[ix]

PREFACE

Tuesday, 11 April 1933

LONDON

It would appear that I am to be the first to write a book on Gillespie. Who, if not me, was dealt that hand? Indeed, one might say, who else is left to tell the tale? Ned Gillespie: artist, innovator, and forgotten genius; my dear friend and soul mate. I first became acquainted with Gillespie in the spring of 1888 and during the course of several years thereafter we were connected through the most intimate of friendships. During this time, I learned to understand Ned – not simply through what he said – but also through his merest glance. So profound was our rapport that I was, on occasion, the first to behold his completed paintings, sometimes before his wife Annie had cast her gaze upon them. Ned and I had even agreed to co-author a volume on his life and work; but, unfortunately, that book was never written, due to his tragic and premature death at the age of thirty-six, just as (in my humble opinion) he was about to reach the very zenith of his creative powers.

Reader, if you wonder – as I suspect you may – why you have never heard of Gillespie, this supposed genius, then be aware of one thing: that, before he died, Ned burned almost all of his work, save for a handful of paintings which were in private ownership and thus inaccessible to him. I believe that he attempted to recover some of these canvases, and to my certain knowledge, one moonlit night, would have stolen back a portrait of Mrs Euphemia Urquart of Woodside Terrace, Glasgow, had not he been interrupted in the act of forcing a water-closet window by the Urquarts' butler, who (apparently cut short in solitary labours of his own) had been sitting in the dark; and who – despite the handicap of having his trousers at his ankles – grasped the intruder's shoulders as they emerged beneath the sash. A momentary struggle ensued, but soon thereafter Ned wriggled free and bounded away across the back green, chuckling (perhaps in relief at his escape?), and the butler was left holding only a tweed jacket, aromatic with pipe tobacco. A few bills in the pockets revealed Ned's identity but, happily, the police were not minded to pursue any investigation.

The Urquart portrait therefore survives, along with a few others, but most of the paintings were reduced to ashes. It is to my everlasting regret that amongst those ruined canvases were Gillespie's most recent and finest – if bleakest – works. I have no doubt that those precious masterpieces marked a new departure for him and would have given us a glimpse – yes! of the future! – and also of Ned's struggles, both within himself and with his ill-fated wife and family, a group of persons who, sadly, were a burdensome factor in his life as much as they were a source of inspiration to him.

You may also wonder why I have been silent for so long, and why it has taken me all these years to put pen to paper. Perhaps I needed to gain some distance from a sequence of profoundly affecting events, not least of which was that Ned, in addition to wiping out his artistic legacy, also took his own life. By that time, I was thousands of miles away, and powerless to help him. Confident of an eventual reconciliation, I never suspected that we were moving towards such a rapid unravelling, not only of our relationship (what with all that silly white-slavery business and the trial) but also of his entire fate. However, let us not get ahead of ourselves. I will come to all that in due course.

Do you know: there are times when the past is so vivid in my mind that it seems more tangible to me even than my real life? Perhaps the act of committing this narrative to paper will free me of certain recurring dreams and (God willing!) diminish my eternal aching sadness about Ned Gillespie.

Gillespie and I

I

May 1888

GLASGOW

I

In the spring of 1888, it so happened that I moved from London to Glasgow, following the decease, at Christmas, of my aunt, whom I had nursed all through the autumn and early winter. During those cold, dark months of sickbed vigil, London had become oppressive to me and I grew to associate the place with death and dying. After several months of mourning had elapsed, I began to yearn for a change of scene, and so I decided to undertake a trip of some description, using a portion of the funds conferred upon me by my maternal grandfather, who had died several years previously, leaving me a lump sum and a small annuity.

It was to Scotland that I turned my sights. I had never visited there, but my mother was Scottish, in origin, if not inclination, and my stepfather — also a Scot — resided near Helensburgh. I rather suspect that, in going north, I nurtured some romantic notion of discovering my Caledonian heritage. Perhaps it might be considered callous to undertake such an apparently carefree, touristic trip so soon after one's close relative has passed away, but please understand that neither my mind nor my heart were carefree. Fresh air was what I craved: fresh air and distraction, to escape the odour of hothouse funeral flowers, and to purge my mind of bad memories.

As you may remember, the first Glasgow International Exhibition was staged in the year '88. For several months, the newspapers had talked of little else, and it occurred to me that some solace might be found in a sojourn to the magnificent spectacle that was said to bestraddle both banks of the River Kelvin. Thus, in the second week of May, having closed up my aunt's little house in Clerkenwell, I took the train to Scotland. Travelling alone held no fears for me. I was thirty-five years old, and quite accustomed to making my own way in the world. Of course, in those days, the very idea of going hither and thither, unaccompanied, would have been viewed by many as unbecoming, or as a symptom of lowliness or poverty – which was not, in fact, the case. I was young, independent and modern, and although I was deeply affected by the death of Aunt Miriam, I certainly never saw myself as helpless, which is why I always took advantage of my own vigour. Admittedly, one had to be careful: gazing neither left nor right, and never (Heaven forfend!) looking any man, gentle or otherwise, in the eye.

The journey from the south seemed never ending, and dusk was falling as we approached our destination, the train rattling on through the landscape of hills and fields, with the sound of cinders pelting the roof of the carriage. We passed village after village – some fringed by heaps of waste, others by stagnant pools – then more fields, blanched in the smoke from our engine. Soon, the fields disappeared, swallowed by the night and the lamp-lit suburbs. At last, our speed slackened; the buildings shot up higher on each side, plunging us into darkness, and my travelling companions began to gather their belongings, as the train rumbled, canting from side to side, out onto a bridge. When the gloom lifted, I glimpsed, through silvery girders, a stretch of copper-coloured water: the Clyde. The river teemed with vessels and, all along the quays, lights were blinking, whilst, above us, the reflected glow of countless furnaces turned the clouds sulphurous yellow.

That summer, the Exhibition in Glasgow was to create an influx of visitors from all over the world. By chance, my arrival was well timed: early enough in the year to secure half-decent lodgings, yet just a few days after the brouhaha of the opening ceremony with its crowds (large, enthusiastic) and royal visit (dumpy, indifferent). Once I had settled into my accommodation – two rooms in the attic floor of a terraced house not far from the West End Park – I spent a moderately distracting week strolling around the exhibits: the Fine Art and Sculpture Rooms in the Eastern Palace; the thrilling assault to the senses, both aural and nasal, in the Dynamo Shed; the Queen's Jubilee gifts (dull but, presumably, for those that need it, *terribly* reassuring); a reproduction of the Bishop's Palace which, upon investigation with the tip of my umbrella, revealed itself to be made entirely of painted canvas; and – my favourite, illicit haunt – Howell's tobacco kiosk with its wondrous international selection of cigarettes: Piccadilly Puffs; Shantung Silks; Dinard Dainties; *Tiffy Loos*! Oh, how I longed to stretch out on one of those divans up in the lounge and partake of nicotinic delights! However, this was many years ago; the world was a less tolerant place than it is now, and thus I had to content myself with ladylike forays to the front counter 'on behalf of my father' to purchase little darlings that I would later enjoy in private.

Not all my time was spent in the park. I found that walking seemed to alleviate my spirits, and so, once the novelty of the Exhibition had begun to fade, I started to explore the centre of Glasgow, to familiarise myself with this Second City of the Empire, this place of many hills – and it was on one of these invigorating excursions that I first encountered two ladies who, as it transpired, turned out to be close relatives of Ned Gillespie.

This would have been, perhaps, in late May. I cannot recall the precise date but do remember that it was an unusually hot day and, feeling too stuffy in my accommodation, I had taken myself for a walk into town. The streets – with their pearly awnings and gay bustle of hats and parasols – were all a-shimmer in the heat, and swarming with 'foreigners', with the result that Glasgow had assumed the air of a cosmopolis, resembling, perhaps, Seville, Paris or even Naples, on a fête day. In places, the city appeared to be a building site, with offices, tenements and churches under construction on all sides. The silhouettes of wooden cranes jutted skywards and, on almost every street, there appeared patches of waste-ground, piled high with planks and mounds of stone, or gable ends of half-built tenements, with hearths already provided for persons yet unborn. Whilst walking along the busy thoroughfares, I was delighted to overhear snatches of conversation in a dozen different accents and languages: there were the Scots, of course, and the English, and the Americans, but I also encountered French, German and Dutch, and another tongue, which, at first, I could not identify, until it dawned upon me that what I was hearing was the language of the Gaels, the Highlanders of Scotland and, from across the water, the Irish.

In Buchanan Street, I had paused to inspect a display of table linen in the window of Wylie and Lochhead, when something incongruous came to my attention. The pavement upon which I found myself was in shade, but the opposite side of the street was awash with sunshine and, brightly mirrored in the glass before me, I saw a woman in a black capote bonnet, stretched out on the ground, whilst a girl crouched beside her. At first I took this for some impromptu piece of street entertainment: not at all a far-fetched conclusion, given that, as a result of the Exhibition, the city was bristling with *plein-air* theatricals of one sort or another. I turned to gain a better view. There, indeed, was a lady, perhaps in her early sixties, lying on the pavement near the entrance to the Argyle Arcade. However, now that I could see clearly, I ascertained that she was not a 'comedienne', but that she had suffered some kind of collapse. This was evident from the genuine dismay on the face of the girl at her side, a pretty golden-haired creature in print frock and tall-crowned straw hat. The girl gazed around wildly and then hailed a youth in dusty clothes who happened to be passing. I could not overhear what was said because at that moment a cab sped by, but after a few words were spoken on both sides, the boy turned and dashed up Buchanan Street, no doubt in search of help.

Meanwhile, the scene on the pavement had attracted the attention of passers-by, and a small crowd began to assemble. A bossy-looking dowager swooped in with a vial of smelling salts, but when the application of these beneath the victim's nose had no effect, our beldam was obliged to fall back, defeated. Thereafter, a tall gentleman bent down and thrust the collapsed matron's discarded tapestry bag beneath her neck: no doubt a chivalrous act designed to keep her head off the ground, but one that forced her chin towards her chest and tipped the capote bonnet askew. The girl tightened its ribbons and then fastened her companion's collar, which had come undone.

Evidently, the rougher elements of the throng were treating the emergency as part of the day's entertainment. They called out to the girl and to each other, and their comments ranged from the well intentioned ('Pinch her cheeks!' and 'Sumdy away and fetch a doactor!') to the rather less altruistic: 'Anybody got any sengwiches?' – a question that seemed, to me, to typify the gallows humour of the Glaswegian.

It was at this point that I decided to see if I could be of any assistance. Over the previous few years, I had attended several lectures run by the St John Ambulance Association, and was very familiar with its textbook, *First Aid to the Injured*. My interest in the subject was partly that of the casual enthusiast and partly prompted by my poor aunt's failing health. I will not claim to have been an expert, but I knew enough to see that the fumbling ministrations of those gathered around the victim might do more harm than good.

Without further ado, I hurried across the road, stepping between bystanders until I had reached the figure on the ground, whereupon I crouched down and commenced to inspect her stout person. Her lips were parted; her eyes closed, as though in sleep. Her young companion was fanning the air, uselessly, and weeping. From a distance, this girl had looked to be about fifteen years old, but I saw now, as she glanced up, that she was a young woman, perhaps in her early or middle twenties. When I asked what had happened, she shook her head.

'I don't know! She fell down. But she won't wake up!'

'Please don't worry,' I told her. 'I'm sure she'll be quite fine.'

And so saying, I began to feel for a pulse. Perhaps I was looking in the wrong place, or perhaps the matron's wrist was too plump, but I could detect nothing. The young woman was staring at me with great anxiety.

'Are you a nurse, madam?' she asked.

Not wishing to disappoint her by replying in the negative, I simply ignored her question and addressed the crowd sternly. (They had been leaning in for a better view of proceedings.)

'Stand back please! Give us air!'

There was a modicum of rearward shuffling, but I saw at once that it would be impossible to make them retreat to any distance. Therefore, I returned to my examination of the patient. I had already decided the most likely possibility: that she had fainted in the unaccustomed heat. There was, furthermore, a chance that she might have banged her head upon falling, and rendered herself unconscious. However, as I peered down at her face, I saw that matters were graver still, for her lips had turned blue. A bad sign, I knew, but – I will admit now – for the life of me, I could not remember what, exactly, this indicated. Was there something amiss with her heart, perhaps? Or was it the lungs?

The poor fair-haired woman was clearly on the verge of panic and so, rather than appear at a loss, and thereby frighten her, I began to carry out procedures that would have been advisable in any case, trusting that a diagnosis would come to me ere long. Firstly, I unfastened the capote bonnet; this, I passed to the young woman, to give her something to do, other than flap her hands and weep. Next, I unbuttoned the lady's collar. Then, supporting the back of the skull, I removed the carpet-bag 'pillow' from beneath her neck. This prompted some rumbling objections from the gentleman who had so recently thrust it there, but I silenced him with a look.

The matron's head was clammy. I ran my fingers through her pale, thinning hair, to check for injuries, but could detect no sign of blood or swellings. I pressed my ear to her chest and perceived a faint heartbeat. That, at least, was good news. And yet, those blue lips, still darkening!

As a last resort, I held my hand and ear to her mouth and discovered, to my surprise, that the patient was not breathing. She was alive – but not breathing. How could that be? And then it came to me. Almost certainly, there must be some sort of obstruction in her mouth. I had once witnessed a practical demonstration in which my friend Esther Watson, a lady lecturer from St John, had checked the oral cavity of a supposedly unconscious person (in fact, her husband Henry, who had sportingly volunteered to recline on the carpet). Esther had explained that such a procedure was necessary in case the tongue or vomitus had blocked the throat. Remembering her example, I pressed down on the matron's chin, thereby causing her jaw to drop and her lips to part. Then I leaned forwards to peer inside her mouth.

Perhaps I should point out that I was not relishing any of these developments. Upon rising that morning, I had hoped to spend the day in quiet contemplation of shop windows, with, perhaps, the addition of a visit to a tea room. It did not occur to me for a second that I might, by mid-afternoon, be considering at close quarters the orifices of an elderly citizen. However, having embarked upon my physical examination, I found myself compelled to proceed. Annie (that is to say, the fair-haired young woman, as I was later to find out her name) had fixed me with a tearful gaze. The crowd had already dubbed me 'Florence Nightingale', and were calling out words of encouragement. I felt compelled to live up to my name.

However, peer as I might, I could detect nothing in the lady's mouth. Why, there was not even a tooth in her head! The recess of her throat was too dark to see, but her tongue lay flat and was not sagging back to block her air passage, and there was no sign of any vomitus. I remembered, then, that, during the St John lecture, Esther had, as a final precaution, inserted a finger and thumb inside her husband's oral cavity and felt around for obstructions. Could I bring myself to do such a thing? It seemed I could, for my fingertips were already sliding between the woman's lips, prompting a collective intake of breath from the crowd, and one or two moans of distaste. Admittedly, it was not a pleasant sensation. She was hot inside and sticky. My fingers probed beneath the tongue and behind the gums, edging towards her gullet.

Nothing. I was just about to withdraw my hand when one of my fingernails brushed against something right at the very back of her mouth, something slimy, but hard to the touch, and which, unmistakably, did not belong in a person's throat.

With the utmost caution, I stretched my finger further, perhaps by a quarter of an inch. There! I could feel it now with my fingertip: a solid object, as unyielding to the touch as ebony. No time to consider what this thing might be. I knew only that it must be removed at once, for undoubtedly this was what prevented her from breathing. Her lips were already darker blue: if I did not act quickly, she would soon be dead. I would have to get enough purchase on the obstruction without pushing it further down her throat, which could prove fatal.

Gently, gently, I extended my arm. The crowd moaned once more as my hand disappeared, beyond the knuckles, into the woman's face. Hidden from view, deep in her gorge, my fingertips investigated the slippery edge of the mysterious item. It was almost impossible to get a grip on it. Then, abruptly, my middle finger slid behind some sort of ridge, and hooked there. I gave a soft tug. The thing shifted, moved upwards slightly, so that I was able to press my thumb against it. Much encouraged, I pulled again, this time with more urgency and – to my great surprise – my fist came flying out of her mouth with the great sucking whoosh of a Kilner jar as the seal is broken. The crowd gasped and lurched backwards, staring with obvious distaste at my hand. I followed their gaze. And there, clutched between my thumb and fingers, was a full upper set of false teeth, in Vulcanite and porcelain! Presumably, the woman had fainted, and the dentures had slipped back to seal her gullet like a stopper. I gazed down and saw – for the first time – the rise and fall of her bosom as she breathed once more. Her eyelids fluttered, then opened. The crowd forgot their disgust and cheered. Laughing through her tears, the pretty young woman cried out: 'Elspeth! Elspeth! Oh! You're awake!'

The lady gave me a rather distrustful glance, then turned her head towards her companion and whispered hoarsely: 'Annie! Where's my handbag?'

(As if I might have stolen it!)

The young woman picked up the bag to show her. Another ragged cheer went up, but now that the crisis had ended and – alas – nobody was dying, people had begun to drift away. I gazed at the teeth in my hand, wondering what to do with them. Elspeth herself was too confused to take them from me, so I held them out to Annie, who gazed at me blankly for a moment and then, emptying her own bag onto the pavement, began to sift through its contents, finally producing a rather grubby handkerchief, in which she wrapped the denture.

I thanked her, and she nodded. 'Aye, you're welcome.'

What a delightful local accent she had! I had imagined that, since she was reasonably well dressed, she might be rather differently spoken. But it was quite charming to hear such a pretty Glaswegian brogue.

From her prone position, Elspeth squinted at me. 'Have we been introduced, madam?' she asked, faintly.

'This lady's a nurse,' Annie explained. 'She made you better.'

At this, I felt shamefaced. The time had come to tell the truth. After all, my intervention had been a success. I had saved a life! I stood up, brushing the dust from my skirts, saying: 'To be perfectly honest, I'm not exactly a nurse. I simply know a little about how to tend to the injured.'

Annie frowned. 'Oh?' she said, examining me afresh, apparently disconcerted. Her reaction caused me to wonder whether she would have been so trusting of me had she known the truth all along.

Elspeth was gazing at me, still befuddled.

'I've seen her before,' she said.

'No,' sighed Annie. 'This is the lady that made you better. Just rest now.'

At that moment, the dustily clad youth returned, accompanied by a gentleman whose leather bag and general air of imperious, bad-tempered conceit revealed him to be a doctor. In fact, I was relieved to yield authority to him. The strain of the past few minutes had begun to catch up with me, and I felt a little light-headed. I gave him a brief account of what had taken place, and he raised an eyebrow when he heard how long Elspeth had been unconscious, without breathing.

'Perhaps two minutes, you say?' He looked me up and down as he tried to get my measure. 'You are medically trained, madam?'

'Not exactly. Not medically trained, no, but – '

'I thought not,' he said, distinctly unimpressed. 'None the less, I'd wager you've saved this lady's life.'

Then he knelt down to tend to Elspeth, who submitted, like a child, to his examination. Annie – having gathered up her scattered belongings – had stood up, and was skittishly untying and retying the ribbon strings of her hat. I decided to absent myself quietly and politely.

'Well, I must go now. I'm so glad to have been of some use to you today.'

'Och, thanks for your help,' said Annie, and I was about to take my leave when she added: 'By the bye, how *do* you know all those things? Listening for a heartbeat and all the rest?'

I hesitated.

'Well, you see, I was looking after someone who was ill, and in the interest of being more useful, I attended some lectures by the St John Ambulance Association. The instructors demonstrated all sorts of procedures and techniques – '

'Oh well, that's good.'

'Yes – but sadly, what I learned was not enough to save my poor aunt. She died, just before Christmas.'

'Och, I'm sorry!' said Annie. 'I didn't realise.'

'Please – don't apologise. Sometimes, I do still dress in mourning – except that I had the misfortune, the other day, to be caught in that dreadful thunderstorm without my umbrella. There was not a cab in sight, and – well – I had to walk all the way back to Queen's Crescent in the pouring rain. Crape is such a difficult fabric, I find: it just shrivels and rusts in the slightest shower.'

Elspeth, who had sat up to accept a glass of water from one of the shopkeepers, croaked: 'Queen's Crescent? At George's Cross?'

I admitted that this was, indeed, where I lodged.

'That's just around the corner from us,' said Annie.

'Invite her to call,' whispered Elspeth. 'Tomorrow.'

'Perhaps the lady's too busy.' Annie turned to me. 'I'm sorry, I don't know your name. I'm Annie – Annie Gillespie.'

'Nonsense,' came the matron's husky voice. 'She's not too busy.'

'And that's my mother-in-law, Elspeth – Mrs Gillespie.'

'How do you do?' I said. 'My name's Harriet – Miss Harriet Baxter. But, as for tea – I couldn't possibly –'

'Annie! Tell her!'

The young woman raised an eyebrow, and gazed at me, without enthusiasm. 'I'm afraid we have no choice in the matter,' she said.

And so it was that I was invited for tea, the very next day, at Stanley Street.

Momentous occasion!

Or was it? Upon reflection, I believe that I did feel rather pleased, but only in the way that one does when invited to break bread with a Native. Suddenly one feels an entirely new connection to the place where one finds oneself. It no longer feels like such foreign soil. And a world of hitherto unknown possibilities seems to open up.

2

On the following day – promptly, at three o'clock – I presented myself at the door of number 11 Stanley Street, and rang the top bell. I had found the address with no difficulty since it was, as Annie had said, just around the corner from my lodgings. Indeed, when she described the location of her residence to me, I realised that I had already walked along Stanley Street a number of times, because it was on one of my routes to the park. Apparently, her mother-in-law occupied a main-door house across the road, but it was to Annie's home at number 11 that I had been invited.

In contrast to Queen's Crescent (a well-kept terrace of houses set behind a pretty communal garden) Stanley Street was rather less attractive: a short thoroughfare, flanked by spiked iron railings behind which lay tenements, handsome but much blackened by carbonic deposits, the whole vista made all the more sombre by a lack of open spaces or greenery. These were still respectable dwellings: indeed, it seemed that a well-known composer resided across the landing from the Gillespies. However, most of the inhabitants of Stanley Street were much less affluent than their neighbours in some of the very grand terraces nearby.

Annie herself threw open the door. She looked surprised – and possibly slightly irritated – when she saw me.

'Miss Baxter – oh dear, you're on time.'

'Ah – I do apologise. Shall I come back later?'

'Oh no – come in, come in. It's just that we're not quite ready.'

She shut the door behind me, then turned and began to make her way up the long close towards the stairs. Now that she was hatless, I could see the full glory of her hair, a tangle of golden tresses worn about her shoulders in half-hearted plaits.

'It's the maid's afternoon off,' she called out. 'So we're fending for ourselves . . . hope you don't mind.'

'Not at all.'

Glancing upwards, I decided to conserve my breath for the ascent. We climbed several flights of stone steps, passing, on each landing, the entrances to other apartments. The stairwell was clean, but the air was stuffy, and redolent of many gravies. Annie bounded ahead of me and, upon reaching the topmost storey, she stepped through an open door on the right, saying: 'Here we are.'

By the time that I entered the apartment, a few moments later, she had disappeared. The hall in which I found myself was furnished attractively but simply, with a coat stand and a few framed photographs. A narrow flight of stairs at the far end provided access, presumably, to an upper floor. Several doors led off the hallway, but only one – that which faced the little staircase – lay fully open, and so I headed towards it. A glance across the threshold confirmed that here, indeed, was the parlour: a modestly furnished room, with a threadbare carpet.

Annie had already made herself comfortable on a faded sofa by the hearth. The only other occupants of the room were Elspeth – who, apparently fully recovered, was stuffing envelopes at the central table – and two small girls, one of about seven years of age, the other perhaps four years younger. As I stepped across the threshold, these children ran to Annie's side and clutched at her skirts, staring at me with suspicion. Meanwhile, Elspeth had risen to greet me.

'Ahh! Come in, dear friend! My Angel of Mercy!' She came towards me, grinning from ear to ear. This ebullient mood was quite in contrast to her subdued, whispering demeanour of the previous day. (I was relieved to note that she had also put her teeth back in; as far as I am aware, she only ever wore the top set.) 'How lovely to see you, Miss Bexter. We're absolutely delighted that you're here.'

Now that she was no longer hoarse, I realised that she had a rather distinctive accent, which flattened the vowels. This supposedly Anglified pronunciation was, as I had already noted from my encounters with certain other Glaswegians, an artifice deployed – mainly by ladies – who believed that it made them sound more *refained*. Although her words themselves were unequivocally welcoming, I have to admit that I felt myself slightly overborne, since Elspeth's intonation was a mite shrill and jarring. Of course, we cannot all have pleasant voices, and it is certainly not *essential* in life to speak in mellifluous tones; no doubt, this lady had many redeeming qualities, but Orphean elocution was not one of them.

She guided me towards an easy chair, opposite the sofa.

'I wasn't *compos mentis* yesterday, after fainting. But Annie has told me what happened. My dear friend, I owe my life to you – *my very life*!' At this, she chuckled hard – and at such proximity that I feared for the integrity of my eardrum. I took a faltering step backwards (narrowly avoiding a collision with an old what-not) and sank down onto the chair. 'You just make yourself at home, Miss Bexter.'

'Please, do call me Harriet.'

'Yes indeed. Herriet! And you must call me Elspeth.' She smiled at the children, who were casting wary glances at me, as though I were the Boneyman. Then her gaze fell upon the heap of papers on the table. 'Dearie me, look at this guddle.' She hurried over to tidy the mess. 'You must excuse us, Herriet. We are just now in the process of sending out the newsletter for my dear church, Free St John's on George Street. It's that time of the month again. I must tell you, this edition has a particularly interesting article on the Jewish mission on the south of the river. I don't know if you're familiar with the mission?'

'No, I'm not.'

'Well – you *must* read this article. I'm sure you'd find it of interest. You are Jewish, are you not?'

I gazed at her, somewhat taken aback. 'No,' I said, after a moment.

'Ah – do forgive me. I thought for some reason . . . although

[16]

now I reflect on it your name isn't particularly Jewish, is it? Oh well, never mind. It is a most interesting article none the less.' Learning that I was not, in fact, Jewish seemed, momentarily, to have knocked the wind out of her sails. She paused to draw breath, beaming hard (for some reason) at Annie, who smiled vaguely back at her. I was on the point of saying something myself, but before I could utter a syllable, Elspeth was off again. 'There's also an extremely good piece on Reverend Johnson in this edition. You'll have heard of Jacob Johnson, our wonderful Negro revivalist who arrived last week? What an inspiring sermon he gave us! He and his family were my guests on Wednesday evening, you know. It is quite charming to look around the table and see such an array of happy brown faces: I find them so soothing to look at and attractive. Do you know, Herriet, sometimes I find myself wishing that all Glasgow were filled with Negroes, singing and chuckling in that infectious way they have, rather than miserable peely-wally Scottish folk. Would that not be far superior?'

She chortled merrily and, not wishing to be thought impolite, I joined in the mirth. Annie, I noticed, did not laugh, but there was a glazed smile on her lips as she stared out of the window, apparently lost in thought.

'Now, Miss Bexter,' cried Elspeth. 'If you'll excuse me, I shall hold my wheesht – as we say here in Scotland – and go and hurry along our tea.'

Elspeth swept out of the room, still chuckling, and then began humming a strident tune, which remained audible until she entered another room and closed the door behind her. For a moment, silence fell. It was broken only when Annie breathed in deeply and then gave vent to an enormous sigh, rather as though oxygen had just flooded back into the parlour. Perhaps Elspeth's cheerful volubility was a source of some vexation to her daughter-in-law, but when I turned to look at Annie, she was gazing down at the child who lay in her lap: the three-year-old, who had scrambled there whilst Elspeth had been holding forth. The girl was now curled up, like a baby. Annie stroked her hair.

[17]

'There, Rose, that's right,' she murmured and it all made quite a charming picture, until one realised that Annie (having made some adjustment to the bodice of her dress) was quite openly nursing the girl. I believe that, momentarily, I was taken unawares, having never before witnessed this intimate maternal procedure. Perhaps the surprise was evident in my face, because when Annie glanced up, she said: 'Oh, you don't mind, do you? Only I can't get this wee one to leave me alone – you'd think she wanted to crawl inside my skin.'

Just then, the seven-year-old climbed up beside them. This child had fussed and fretted since my arrival. Having failed to force herself onto her mother's lap, she now stood up and commenced to bang her hip against Annie's shoulder, until Annie was forced to remonstrate with her, whereupon the child threw herself down upon the sofa and began to wail.

I cannot tell you how fervent was my hope that this display of ill temper was not caused by an impatience to be fed in the same manner as her sister.

'Shh,' said Annie. 'Don't cry, Sibyl.'

But the girl continued to wail. Since her mother seemed content to ignore me, I was obliged to make conversation, and had to raise my voice over Sibyl's din.

'Will anyone be joining us?' I called out brightly.

'I don't expect so,' said Annie, vaguely. 'Shhh, Sibyl – please, be quiet.'

'What about your husband?' I enquired, in the hope of kindling at least an ember of conversation. 'I suppose he is out at work?'

However, Annie did not answer, perhaps because she was once again preoccupied with her younger daughter, chatting to her whilst switching her from one side to the other. It was hard to tell whether she was being rude, or not. I glanced away, and my gaze fell upon the older girl who was now merely snivelling. To be honest, even on this first acquaintance, I found Sibyl's feverish intensity somewhat unnerving. She was a pretty little thing, although her top lip might be considered a shade too thin, and her complexion a shade too sallow. She scrutinised me, sulkily.

'*You've* got a big nose,' she said. 'Like a *witch*.'

I laughed, gaily. 'Why yes – I dare say I do.'

'Si-byl,' said Annie wearily.

In response, Sibyl leapt off the couch and began to skip noisily around the room, darting between the furnishings in a frantic way that looked most hazardous.

Annie turned to me. 'I do apologise for Sibyl. She's awful tired.'

'Indeed,' said I, watching the child whirl around the table like an agitated Dervish. 'Poor mite.'

At that moment, a slender young woman entered the room, bearing a heavily laden tea tray. She wore an elegant lace blouse and slim-fitting skirt and her chestnut-coloured hair was piled on her head. I smiled, ready to greet this newcomer, but she failed to return my gaze. From certain angles, she might have been considered a great beauty. The neck was graceful; the features fine. Her eyes were deep blue, almost violet. But there was a hard quality in her face – and something in the breadth and tilt of her jaw – that (unfortunately) put one in mind of a frying pan. She set the tray on the table, and then flitted across to the window, where she proceeded to fold her arms and frown out at the clouds as though they had offended her. Assuming that this person must be another member of the family, I turned to Annie, expecting some sort of introduction, but Annie gave no sign that she had even noticed the woman's entrance. Instead, she busied herself by setting Rose on the floor and encouraging her to play with a small wooden horse, just as Elspeth sailed back into the room, bearing a teapot, and a plate of little pastries.

'Here we are!' cried Elspeth, then shrieked with laughter, for reasons that I could not, at the time, fathom. (However, I came to realise that Elspeth preferred her entrances and exits to be accompanied by the sound of merriment.)

'Elspeth, please – shh,' pleaded Annie, and gestured at the ceiling.

[19]

Still laughing gleefully, Elspeth crossed to the table, narrowly avoiding a collision, as Sibyl darted past her. The child skipped on and, arriving at the battered old piano, threw up its lid and began to bang on the keys. Annie leapt to her feet, saying again: 'Shh – remember Papa,' and she closed the parlour door, whilst Elspeth set down the plate and teapot and turned to me.

'Sibyl is learning a new song,' she cried. 'A Negro Spiritual. She'll play it for the Reverend Johnson once it's perfected. Wouldn't it be very *fine*, Herriet, if she were to sing it for us, as practice?'

Annie wrung her hands together, saying: 'But perhaps, Elspeth, not until later – please. We don't want to make too much noise with the piano, do we?'

'Och now,' said Elspeth. 'She'll play quietly – won't you, dear?'

Sibyl nodded, and Annie sank back down, with a sigh. 'Well, I suppose – '

Elspeth beamed at her granddaughter who, in need of no encouragement, had already begun to fumble and peep her way through a rudimentary hymn. I do not claim to know its title, but like most of its kind it expressed, over and over, naught but patience for this life and triumph in the next. From time to time, amongst the wrong notes, Sibyl cast intense glances at us, over her shoulder, to check that we were paying heed. Annie appeared to be listening with her head on one side, as she rebuttoned her bodice. Rose leaned against her mother's skirts, watching her older sister, wide-eyed, as though she were a specimen. The young woman at the window had taken out a mirror and was rearranging her hair, while Elspeth smiled proudly at her granddaughter and hummed along, here and there, with the melody.

As the hymn progressed, I took the opportunity to glance around the room. This was not exactly a household of paupers, but judging from the shabby, faded look of the furnishings, the Gillespie family was not, by any means, flourishing. The children's clothes were clean, but ill-fitting, and oft-mended; the oilcloth on the table was worn thin in places; the cups and saucers were chipped and cracked. Atop the piano, next to the stack of sheet music, I noticed, for the first time, a gentleman's straw boater, with a narrow brim, and the low crown wrapped around with a glossy striped ribbon in shades of blue and green: a rather lovely hat, which, presumably, belonged to Annie's husband. He had left it there the last time he had been in this room, perhaps. Had he removed it in order to sit down and play? Or had he set it on top of the piano only in passing?

Such were the idle thoughts that occupied my mind until – at last – the hymn came to a faltering conclusion. We applauded, and Sibyl grinned, baring recently acquired little teeth so gap-ridden and misaligned that the effect was somewhat eerie and vampirish.

'Bravo!' cried Elspeth. I braced myself against the possibility that she might suggest we hear another but, thankfully, she began to lay out cups and saucers, saying: 'That's enough now, Sibyl, Granny's tea will be stewed.' The child continued to tinkle at the keys, while Elspeth picked up the teapot and addressed me. 'Now, dear Herriet! You must tell us all about yourself. I want to know *every single detail* about the person who *saved my life*. Milk? Sugar?'

'Yes, milk please. And sugar.'

'Ah – a sweet tooth, like myself. But you are so slender, Herriet, so elegant. Do you avoid starchy foods at all? They are *my* downfall. Rock cake? Shortbread?'

'Shortbread, if you please. As for starchy foods, I certainly don't avoid them. If the truth were known, just between ourselves, I practically *exist* on biscuits.'

Elspeth admonished me with a wag of her finger. 'That sweet tooth of yours! Now, in that case, I do hope you'll have a lemon-curd tart. Rose and I baked them *especially* for your visit.'

Something must have gone amiss in the preparation, because the tarts were so blistered and misshapen that they bore closer resemblance to a cluster of purulent sores than to a selection of *pâtisserie*. However, since I had no desire to hurt anyone's feelings,

I selected the least alarming tart, and pronounced it 'delicious'.

Elspeth smiled at the young woman, who had approached the table, and was helping to serve tea. 'You and Mabel have been introduced, I presume? This is Mabel, my daughter, recently returned from America.'

'Ah – America,' I said and – quickly grasping this straw before it could be whisked away in Elspeth's beak – I turned to Mabel. 'How fascinating. Do tell me all about it. What was the climate like over there?'

Mabel smiled at me with what seemed like pity and then explained: 'Well, it can be hot, of course, but if you stay in the shade it doesn't matter. And I'd rather have the heat than twelve full months of rain, as happens here in Scotland.'

'Och, shtoosh-shtoosh,' said Elspeth, with a smile at me, as she sank down into her chair. 'Not quite twelve months, dear.'

'Well, *practically* twelve months!' cried Mabel – and when Annie motioned her to lower her voice, she continued, in a mutter: 'I don't see why you have to contradict every *single* thing I say.'

Elspeth took a breath, but before she could speak – and in order to forestall what looked like a disagreement – I leapt in with the first question that came to mind: 'Have you all been enjoying the International Exhibition?'

'Ah – our wonderful Ex!' cried Elspeth. 'We are season-ticket holders, of course, and I'm partial to a real Indian curry, and they do a marvellous one at the General Gordon Buffet. You'll have been round the Palace yourself, then, Herriet?'

'Yes,' I said. 'In fact, that's one of the reasons I came to Glasgow – to see the Exhibition and take my mind off . . . well . . . recent events.'

'I know, dear,' said Elspeth, with a sympathetic look. 'Annie told me you'd lost your aunt. I'm so sorry.'

'Well, Aunt Miriam was terribly kind – like a mother to me, really. My own mother passed away some years ago.'

Elspeth nodded. 'I know *exactly* what you're going through.'

'You do?'

'Well, I'm a widow, you see, and Our Heavenly Father took my own dear mother to himself many years ago. And Annie's mother was taken when she was quite young. We've all been through the passing of our mothers, you know.'

'Not all of us,' said Mabel. 'Not yet.'

Elspeth blinked, once, but gave no other sign that she had heard, or been wounded, by this comment. In hindsight, there was a reason for Mabel's prickly demeanour: I later learned that her fiancé, an American, had recently broken off their engagement, resulting in her unexpected and solitary return to Scotland. Dear Mabel was never one to conceal her moods, and, for the time being, the family was treating her with kid gloves, tolerating her more melodramatic outbursts, and ignoring any bad-tempered remarks.

To dispel this moment of awkwardness, I spoke up again: 'Mabel, I've heard it said that America is a very vibrant country. Did you find it so?'

With a shrug of her shoulders, she sat down at the table.

'Well, naturally – that goes without saying. Everything is so much better over there than it is here. American coffee, for instance, is wonderful. Do you prefer tea or coffee, Miss Baxter?'

'Usually, I have tea.'

'Really?' Once again, she gave me the look of pity. 'I prefer coffee. But you can't get decent coffee in Glasgow. It's tea rooms, everywhere you look. Tea rooms!' And she hooted with laughter, at the absurdity of it all.

'Well they do serve coffee,' muttered Elspeth, and then, turning to me, with a shriek, she banged the table (making Annie wince). 'Which reminds me, Herriet, I've remembered where I've seen you before.'

'I have indeed walked along this street many times, it's on my route to the – '

'No, no – it was outside Assafrey's, last week. I went in, with my son, but the place was full, so we left, and that was when we bumped into you: you were going *in*, as we came *out*.'

'Goodness, I've been to so many tea rooms – I'm afraid I don't recall seeing you, Elspeth. Although, who knows – if your son joins us, I might recognise him.'

I smiled at Mabel, who had been eyeing the cakes, without taking one. Now, she fixed me with a regretful, pained expression. 'My brother is working,' she explained, as though I were a child. 'I doubt he'll come down. When I left him he said he didn't want to be disturbed.'

Upon hearing this, Sibyl suddenly ceased to tinkle at the piano. She arranged her features into a sugary little smile, then sidled up to Mabel and began to stroke her skirts, with fluttery fingers, in an ingratiating fashion.

'Did you go into Papa's room?' she lisped.

'For a wee while,' replied Mabel, lightly, but in a way that suggested that she was rather pleased with herself.

As Sibyl cast a wistful glance at the door, Elspeth leaned towards me. 'My son is an artist. I don't know if you may have heard of him, down south. Ned Gillespie? He's quite "weel kent" up here, among the art crowd.'

'Is he a painter?' I asked.

'Yes, indeed – a very fine one too,' said Elspeth and then there was a pause, as she took a bite from her scone.

I turned to Annie. 'There's a picture by a Gillespie in the International Exhibition – a little girl, with some ducks.'

Annie nodded. 'Aye – that's his – *By the Pond*.'

I had seen the painting, a few times. In fact, I was almost certain that I had, albeit briefly, met the man who had painted it.

'I was forever sketching when I was a girl,' Elspeth announced, having despatched with her scone. 'And I often came second in the class for my artwork. Such a marvellous teacher I had – I shall *never* forget her. What was her name again? Miss Niven! She was so encouraging to my youthful talent. But Ned, you see, has taken after me in every respect: he is a *genius*.'

Fortunately, it was appropriate to smile. 'How proud you must be,' I said, and turned to Annie. 'Has your husband ever been to London? I did meet a Scottish artist named Gillespie, in the autumn, at the Grosvenor Gallery.'

He and I had spoken only for a few moments and I had, more or less, forgotten about him until my arrival in Glasgow when I noticed a Gillespie listed among the artists in the catalogue of the Exhibition, and wondered, vaguely, whether this could be the same man.

Mabel turned to her sister-in-law. 'He went down to that exhibition, remember?'

Annie nodded.

'Ah – the Grosvenor!' exclaimed Elspeth. 'The wonderful Grosvenor – such a fine gallery, I believe. They were extremely enthusiastic in London about his paintings – and quite right too.'

While we had been speaking, I could not help but notice that Sibyl had edged, silently, towards the closed door, and now, she put her hand to the door knob, and turned it slowly. At the creak of the latch, Mabel swivelled in her seat.

'Sibyl? Where are you going?'

The girl tittered, guiltily. 'Nowhere,' she piped, sidling out of the room.

'You see?' Mabel admonished Annie. 'Yesterday I had to bring her down about six times. She simply won't leave him alone.'

With a sigh, Annie rose to her feet. One of her plaits had come undone, and she had fastened up her bodice wrongly, leaving a spare button at the top. She trailed out of the room, calling wearily: 'Sibyl – please come back!'

But Sibyl, it seemed, had no intention of returning. Footsteps thudded up the stairs; there was the sound of a brief scuffle, and then the child began to scream. The screaming grew louder – and more disturbed – until one might have thought that she was being murdered. Moments later, Annie reappeared, dragging her daughter by the hand. The child scrabbled and clutched at the door jamb, but she lost her grip when Annie prised her fingers free. We all leapt to our feet, and Mabel slammed the door shut, then tried to help Annie restrain the girl, who was still wriggling and writhing. As they crossed the room, supporting her between them, Sibyl tried to hang onto a chair, and then, before anyone could stop her, she reached out and grabbed at the oilcloth, with the unfortunate result that it came flying off the table. Down came the cups and saucers, the tarts and cakes, the dull teaspoons, the tarnished tray, the teapot, an old lamp (which, thankfully, since it was daylight, was not lit), a dish of dented wax fruit, a water-stained sewing box, various odds and ends, and all the church newsletters and envelopes. Everything fell to the floor with a sudden, startling crash – which made Rose take fright, and then she too burst into tears. Annie immediately hurried over to comfort her younger daughter, leaving Sibyl to sink to the floor, scarlet-cheeked, and screaming, with Mabel chiding her to behave herself and stop bothering Ned, and Elspeth, in between apologetic glances at me, trying to soothe one and all, whilst – up, up – from the pile of cloths and debris on the carpet went a great rolling cloud of dust.

Just audible, over this bedlam, were some noises from the floor above. I heard a few impatient footsteps, and then, after a pause, a rhythmic banging, as though – in protest at the racket from the parlour – somebody was rapping the floorboards sharply with a cane or stick. The artist – in his garret! Six or seven times the floor was struck and then, it seemed, he gave up, for there was a clatter and then a rattling sound, as though he had flung down the cane and let it roll across the floorboards.

Meanwhile, Sibyl stretched herself out on the carpet, stiffly, her little arms rigid at her sides, wailing for her 'Papa-aa!' until, at length, her fit of temper became so prolonged and unbearable that Annie relented, and told her that she *could* go upstairs to the studio and see her father, after all. At once, the child's shrieks subsided to shuddering little sobs. Then, she picked herself up and stalked, slowly, out of the room, casting dark, accusing looks at one and all.

I listened to her footsteps as they faltered on the first few stairs, and then increased in speed as she ascended, until she could be heard positively skipping along the upper floor, her misery forgotten. Moments later, there was the sound of a door opening and closing – presumably the door to the studio, wherein worked the girl's father – the artist, Ned Gillespie.

Ah yes: Ned Gillespie. You may be wondering, dear Reader, when he is going to make an actual appearance in this overwhelmingly feminine account. On this occasion, I must disappoint you, because once Sibyl had disappeared inside the studio, the door remained closed: Ned did not come down to tea, at all, that day; he showed the parlour not so much as a whisker.

Personally speaking, I suppose that I was now quite curious to meet Elspeth's son, to see if he was, indeed, the young artist whom I had encountered in London. Life is full of strange coincidences. In fact, it was sheer chance that I had even gone to that exhibition at the Grosvenor back in the autumn: left to my own devices, I would never have left Aunt Miriam's side. As I have already mentioned, she was ill and, by late September, my duties as nurse had caused me to be virtually housebound, for several weeks. A few concerned friends, who had noted my pallor and exhaustion, eventually suggested that I relinquish the sickroom for one night, and accompany them, first to the Grosvenor, and then on to supper. Opening nights of exhibitions always attract a large and fashionable throng and – right up until the very last minute – I was in two minds about whether to go. Not only was I loath to leave my aunt, but I also dreaded the prospect of spending several hours, forced to make conversation, in noisy rooms. However, in the end, my friends persuaded me.

Just as I had feared, the gallery was so crammed that even the large West Room felt overcrowded. My friends formed a merry party, having come from a late luncheon; my own mood, by contrast, was sombre, and such was my state of mind that I soon tired of their jollity, and so contrived to drift away from them, and wander about, alone, gazing at the various artworks.

At one point, I found myself in a relatively tranquil corner of the East Gallery, lingering in front of a small canvas, a domestic interior, entitled *The Studio*. The colours of this picture were particularly striking against the scarlet damask of the wall. The painting depicted an elegant lady in a black frock. She was standing in what appeared to be an attic room, an easel in the background the only suggestion that this loft belonged to an artist. A shaft of light fell from a skylight window, illuminating the woman's figure. Her hat was trimmed with a short, diaphanous veil. In one hand, she held a little bag of seed, which she was feeding to a canary in a cage. Although she seemed to be a guest in the house, one formed the impression – simply from the way that she fed the bird – that she was a frequent visitor. The expression on her face was intriguing: she looked so placid and content, lost in thought, perhaps – even – in love.

Of course, I would like to be able to say that, upon first viewing, I was seized by the genius in the conception and execution of this painting, *The Studio*. However, knowing little about art, I did not, at the time, single it out as exceptional. Indeed, I lingered in front of it – in what the Scots might call a 'dwam' – primarily because that corner of the room happened, just at that moment, to be less crowded.

My reverie was suddenly interrupted when a pair of hands grasped me by the shoulders and began to draw me away from the painting. For a second, I assumed that my friends had found me, and were dragging me off to Romano's but, as I turned, I realised that I was simply being moved to one side by a complete stranger: a bearded gentleman, in evening dress.

'Madam, if you would,' he said, and deposited me a few feet away, next to a gilded table. Then he turned to his companions, a group of important-looking gentlemen. 'Now, as I said, this picture may be of interest. Note if you will . . .'

As he went on speaking, I continued to stand where I had been placed, somewhat stunned at having been shoved aside as though I were no more than an irksome piece of furniture. The bearded fellow, I deduced, was a guide, or curator of the exhibition; his companions – a group of be-whiskered gents – were, presumably, potential buyers of the work.

One man, younger than the rest, stood at the back of the group. In comparison to the others, his evening dress was not quite so impeccable, and he was clean shaven, except for a small moustache. While the other men followed the curator's every word, this young fellow stared, rather crossly, at the floor. His face was flushed, and I wondered, at first, whether he had taken too much sherry.

At that moment, the curator beckoned to him, calling out: 'Sir – would you care to add a few words – perhaps about your intentions in painting this work?'

The young man frowned at him. 'No, sir, I would not,' he said, in a rich, Scottish brogue. 'First of all, a picture should speak for itself – '

'Indeed,' said the bearded guide, with a smile, and then he nodded, indulgently, at the other men. 'So say many of our young artists.'

The painter stepped forward. 'But that's beside the point,' he said, and then he extended his arm, to indicate me. 'I think you should apologise to this lady here.'

The curator gave a short laugh. 'What?'

'Right enough, her hat is tall,' the painter continued, 'and it obscured our view, but that's no excuse. We could have waited, or you could simply have asked her to step aside – instead of acting like a damn brute.'

The gentlemen in the group exchanged shocked glances. I looked at the curator: the smile on his face had vanished.

'Oh, please,' I said, hoping to forestall an argument. 'It doesn't matter.'

Ignoring me, the curator addressed the artist, hotly: 'I *beg* your pardon?'

'It's not my pardon you should be begging,' said the painter. 'Now will you please apologise to the lady?'

Wide eyed with outrage, the curator turned to me. 'Madam,' he snarled and, with a click of his heels, he gave me a sharp bow. Then, he marched off into the crowd, saying: 'This way, gentlemen. Follow me – I believe there's something more interesting in the next room.'

Some of the group scurried off in his wake, whilst others turned away more hesitantly, offering me the odd apologetic smile or nod as they departed. In the interim, the young artist had come to my side.

'I do beg your pardon,' he said. 'That fellow is insufferably rude. Allow me to apologise properly on his behalf.'

'Oh, please – I don't mind.'

The young Scot scowled after the departing curator, who was guiding his charges towards the doorway. 'That wasn't a real apology, not by any means. But don't you worry – I'll drag him back here and get him to say he's sorry.'

'No, don't,' I begged him, before he could charge off across the room. 'Please don't make a scene on my account. You mustn't cause a fuss. After all, you could have sold your painting to one of those men, if you hadn't spoken out.'

'Ach, no – they wouldnae have bought it.'

I barely remember what remarks we exchanged thereafter – simple pleasantries, no doubt. We spoke for no more than a few moments. Reading between the lines, I gained the impression that the young man was slightly overwhelmed by the grandeur of the occasion. While we talked, he kept pulling at his collar, as though he was unaccustomed to wearing one so high, and he fiddled so much with one of his brass collar-studs that it fell to the floor, bounced out of sight, and was lost. We both bent down to search for it, but before it could be found, a different curator appeared and ushered the artist away, into the next room, in order to present him to another group of gentlemen; and soon, thereafter, my friends descended upon me, and persuaded me to join them for supper.

That, in brief, was my encounter with the Scottish artist named

Gillespie. Upon reflection, it seemed very possible that he and Annie's husband were one and the same person. An interesting coincidence, I thought to myself — and there it might have rested, had not Elspeth invited me to meet the family again, the following Saturday, outside the quaint Cocoa House in the park.

3

On the appointed day, finding that I had arrived at the park a little early, I decided to while away some time in the Fine Art Section. This would have been, I dare say, the last Saturday in May and, due to a spell of fine weather (before those terrible rains at the end of the month), the entire Exhibition was teeming with crowds. As I battled my way through the British and Foreign Loan Collections, I was, as ever, reminded that galleries do attract a disproportionate number of wiseacres: those persons who like to show off to their companions, and give anyone within earshot the benefit of their wisdom about the pictures on display. At one point, I even witnessed a man crouching down in order to *sniff* a canvas, before declaring to his companions that it was '*most definitely, wi'oot a doot, an oil painting*'.

Weary of the crowds, I headed for the British Sale Room, which was always a little quieter, although, as usual, it had attracted that other unfortunate breed of citizen: those who possess no real interest in Art, but who hurtle around in groups, barely glancing at the paintings, in their search for that with the heftiest price tag:

'*There's one at forty-two pound!*'

'*Never mind that, Archie, here's a six-hundred-pounder!*'

Eight pounds and ten shillings was the price of *By the Pond*, the only one of Ned Gillespie's works to be included in the Exhibition. Now that I had become acquainted with the artist's family, I paused to examine it with fresh eyes. *By the Pond* was a large canvas, in the *plein-air* style of Ned's contemporaries: a rural, naturalistic scene of a little girl chasing ducks. I realised, now, that he had used his older daughter as a model. However, the child in the picture wore an angelic expression: either Sibyl had stopped glowering for a few minutes, or Ned had used his imagination.

The painting had an undeniable charm and was fashionable at the time, which would explain its inclusion in the Exhibition. I cannot pretend to be an expert in Art but, in my opinion, the subject matter was too slight to merit its imposing scale: Sibyl and her ducks would have been far better reduced to half the size. None the less, the composition and use of colour were pleasing, and I believed that I would be able to compliment Annie's husband on his exhibit, should we happen to meet.

Regrettably, it was impossible to ignore that *By the Pond* had been terribly badly hung, in the worst spot in all the Fine Art Section: an ill-lit, lofty position, above a doorway, at the eastern end of the British Sale Room, and at unfortunate proximity to an oft-blocked and malodorous drain. This situation gave rise to much hilarity on the part of visitors, who were wont to hasten beneath Ned's painting whilst wafting their hands in front of their faces and uttering various ribald comments. I myself was aware of the jokes regarding the picture's aromatic location – albeit vaguely, as an outsider. The general consensus was that the pond in question must have been a 'right stinky stank' (stank being a Scots word for a pool of stagnant water or drain). For a time, there was a danger that this phrase might even become a nickname for the artist himself, when a certain satirical drawing, which caricatured Ned unkindly, and appeared above the name 'Stinky Stank', would doubtless – if published, as planned, in an issue of *The Thistle* – have stoked the flames of mockery. Fortunately, the caricaturist withdrew it at the last moment and thereafter the nickname fell into disuse.

But I am getting ahead of myself.

Towards four o'clock, the hour appointed for our meeting, I made my way outside, into the sunshine, and strolled over towards Van Houten's Cocoa House. The exterior tables were all fully occupied, and so I found a place on the grass, from which vantage point to watch for the approach of Annie and Elspeth.

From where I stood, I could see Kelvingrove Mansion, and the stream of visitors, emerging – benumbed and replete – having just gorged themselves on the sight of Her Majesty's many gifts: the silver caskets, battleaxes, bejewelled slippers, and so on; an array of useless, opulent articles which (to my mind) struck a vulgar note when contrasted with the poverty evident elsewhere in Glasgow, a city that teemed with beggars, many of whom were children – an inequity to which these day-trippers seemed oblivious. Is it only me who is tempted, in such circumstances, to shout insults, such as 'Imbeciles! Fools! Pudding-heads!'? Of course, one resists these urges, and tries not to feel too much in common with the ragged, drunken little men who often seem to crop up in public places, shaking grubby fists at the throng, and uttering oaths and imprecations; I do sometimes wonder whether I myself – by sheer force of will and dint of imagination – have not conjured up these little fellows to berate the multitude on my own behalf: the very daemons of my psyche.

My daydreams were interrupted by the hoot of the little steam launch on the Kelvin. So lost had I become in my thoughts, as I stood there on the grass, that I had failed to notice the passing of time. Now, glancing at my watch, I saw with surprise that it was half past four o'clock, long after the hour that Elspeth had proposed that we meet; of course, I had no idea, then, that the Gillespies were *always* late, for *every* occasion. I hurried into Van Houten's and peered into each salon, but my new friends were nowhere to be seen. Thereafter, feeling disappointed, I gave up, and decided to return to my rooms, by way of the lake and the Hillhead exit.

Beyond the Mansion, I took the path towards a crossroads where several routes converged, just south of the lake. It was at this point that I heard a strange yelping sound. Thinking that perhaps some poor dog was in pain, I glanced in the direction of the noise, only to see Elspeth Gillespie bearing down upon me. The high-pitched cry that I had mistaken for a canine yap was, in fact, emanating from her throat, apparently as a means of attracting my attention. 'Youp!' she cried. 'Youp! Miss Bexter! Youp! Youp! Herriet!'

In her wake came Mabel, walking closely with a gentleman in a straw boater (he had, at that moment, bent his head to light his pipe); and, behind them, Annie and the children, trailing along with a younger man, who was staring off, towards the river. Just then, the gentleman in the boater looked up, exhaling a mouthful of smoke. He was a broad-shouldered individual of about the middle height, with even, handsome features, his eyes perhaps a little sad. I recognised him, at once, as the artist whom I had met those several months previously in London.

Here, then, was Ned Gillespie: the man himself, walking towards me. Of course, I feel a thrill now in describing this moment but, at the time, I cannot think that it meant terribly much to me to see him there in the park, especially since I was obliged to direct my attention to his mother, who already had me in her clutches.

'Miss Bexter! Lovely to see you! We are a little late, but it took some time to get organised. Allow me to introduce you to . . .' – she peered over her left shoulder; Mabel and Ned had just drawn abreast of us, behind her, and Annie had paused to admonish Sibyl for some misdemeanour, so that Elspeth's gaze fell instead upon the young man, who was fast approaching – '. . . to my son, Kenneth. Kenny, dear, this is Miss Herriet Bexter, the lady I told you about, who saved my life!'

The young man greeted me, briefly. I judged him to be about twenty-four years of age, and handsome enough, notwithstanding a slight puggish cast to his nose, and his hair, which one might, in all politeness, describe as 'auburn'. He was dressed in checked trousers, cutaway coat, and fob watch and, despite the studied nonchalance with which his bowler was perched upon his head, he emanated mild discomfort and impatience. This, I interpreted (perhaps wrongly, as later events might suggest) as youthful shame at having to be seen *passeggiare* with his mama. We exchanged a few pleasantries, and then he turned to Elspeth, saying: 'I'm away to the refreshment bar, mother', and, without further ado, he strode off down the path.

'Don't stay out too late, dear!'

Elspeth frowned anxiously after his retreating figure, leaving me to exchange greetings with her daughter-in-law. Compared with the last time that we had met, Annie's face appeared a little tired and pale. Diplomacy was required and, since she had clearly made an effort to dress smartly – in a narrow-skirted plaid frock, and jade velvet tam o' shanter – I paid her a compliment. 'What a delightful costume, Annie!'

She looked surprised. 'Thank you, Harriet. Did we keep you waiting?'

'Oh, on such a day as this, one doesn't mind a little wait.'

I turned to her girls, whom good manners required that I also acknowledge. With their shining cheeks and stiff, short dresses, Sibyl and Rose had the scrubbed, chastened look of children who have been soundly bathed and fastened into their finest clothes. 'What a pretty dress, Rose! How smart you look, Sibyl!'

The younger girl grew bashful, and attempted to hide her face, while Sibyl raised a coy shoulder and gave me an affected grin across it, displaying her little fangs. Seconds later, however, the smile vanished, and I found myself, once more, unsettled by her dull-eyed, unflinching gaze: it was not malicious, exactly, yet neither was it pleasant.

Meanwhile, Mabel had linked arms with Ned and – somewhat impolitely, I felt – steered him off down the path, rather than stopping to say good afternoon. It was of no consequence, but I daresay that I was mildly curious to be reacquainted with the artist. However, Mabel was possessive of her brother to a degree that might almost be regarded as – one hesitates to say *unnatural* – but all her actions concerning him were coloured by an anomalous proprietary instinct. I noticed that Kenneth caught up with them and appeared to borrow money from his brother before hurrying off, and then Ned and Mabel paused to converse with some acquaintances.

Our little group, consisting of Elspeth, Annie, the children and myself, began to move in their direction. Unfortunately, Elspeth hampered our progress somewhat by stopping in her tracks, every so often, the better to speak. She began to tell me about a person that an acquaintance of hers had once encountered; somebody whom I was never likely to meet, and whom, moreover, Elspeth *herself* had never met – but apparently none of these particulars prevented her from expounding at length on the subject of this complete stranger.

I could have wished for some moral support under this torrent of verbiage, but Annie, exhibiting no fellow feeling, soon wandered off the path to pick up a leaf, and then became lost in contemplation of its form, thereby falling behind. Sibyl and Rose skipped on ahead. As Elspeth continued to chatter, my gaze drifted over to where Ned stood with the others. He had turned away from his companions in order to gaze across the park at the Waterbury Watches balloon, which was just visible above the trees, over by the Machinery Section. His arm was half raised, and he appeared to be fiddling with something at his wrist – a cufflink, perhaps, or a timepiece. I found myself wondering whether or not he would remember our previous encounter in London.

Just at that moment, he happened to glance in our direction and, almost without thinking, I waved to him, as one might to an old friend. To my surprise, he instantly broke away from Mabel and the others, and hurried towards us, tapping his pipe to dispose of the cinders. I felt sure that he must have recognised me. At the very least, his approach interrupted Elspeth's monologue.

'Come and meet Miss Baxter, Ned dear! Herriet, this is Ned, my other son.'

The artist doffed his hat and then, turning to his mother, said simply: 'Well?'

'No sign yet, dear,' replied Elspeth. 'But we must wait until we get to the Palace. That's where we're most likely to see him.'

'Aye,' said Ned, and gazed off towards Annie, who was still standing on the grass, some distance away, examining the leaf that she had found. As he considered his wife, his expression softened, and he smiled.

Clearly, he had not recognised me – not at all – but why should he have? A professional artist might well be introduced to dozens of strangers during an opening at a gallery like the Grosvenor, and if his work appears in several other shows over the course of a year, the number of new faces that he encounters must mount into the hundreds. I would have been extremely silly to be hurt that he had not remembered me.

'What's she doing?' said Ned – fondly, to himself – and then he called out: 'Annie, dearest! Keep up!'

He beckoned to her, but she simply waved back, smiling very prettily: I suspect that she was too far away to hear him. Ned laughed, and blew her a kiss, and then he gave a happy sigh, and set off down the path, swinging his cane. Elspeth and I fell into step with him, and the children began to dart amongst and between the three of us, singing a nursery rhyme, something about bluebells. A passer-by might have taken us for a family, on a day out, with myself as the mother figure: the thought of it rather amused me.

'So, Herriet!' cried Elspeth. 'You don't mind if we make haste, do you? Only we're looking for Mr Hamilton, of the Fine Art Committee. We're hoping to get Ned's picture moved and we've had an idea of how it might be achieved.'

She went on to explain that the poor location of *By the Pond* had been a source of concern since the start of the Exhibition. Indeed, in the opening week, Ned had taken the measure of writing to Horatio Hamilton, politely requesting that the painting be moved. Hamilton (now long forgotten) was then a well-established painter of the old-fashioned 'gluepot school': artists so called because of the dark, sticky nature of their preferred medium, megilp, and also, perhaps, because of their subject matter, which was often gooey, mawkish, and overly moralistic. As such, Hamilton was probably not one of Ned's natural allies, but he was a leading light of the Fine Art Committee for the Exhibition, he ran a well-respected gallery in Bath Street and, crucially, he had been one of Ned's tutors at the Art School. Without Hamilton's support, Ned felt that he would have little chance of persuading the organisers to shift his painting. Thus, according to Elspeth, he had sent the man a letter, but received no reply. A second letter had also been ignored.

This was all fascinating information, and I was flattered to be taken into their confidence, although I noticed that Ned did not join in the telling of the story. Indeed, in the beginning, he tried to dissuade his mother from divulging too much, but he might as well have been a newborn kitten in the path of a runaway bull. He soon gave up attempting to change the subject and concentrated on beseeching his mother to walk while she talked. Meanwhile, the little girls continued to run rings around us. Sibyl, in particular, seemed to barge into us almost every time that she hurtled past and, once or twice, I did wonder whether she had jostled me deliberately.

'It's a well-known fact', Elspeth was saying, 'that Hamilton always takes a wee tour round the park between five and six o'clock. Now, Herriet, our plan is that we bump into him, as though by chance, and then, in the course of conversation, we can talk him into making sure that Ned's painting is shifted. We won't let him leave the park until he's agreed to do what we want. I shall *sit* on him, if necessary!' Although this did not strike me as an advisable course of action, it would have been impolite to suggest as much, and so I simply looked thoughtful, as though giving full consideration to what she had outlined. 'If all else fails,' cried Elspeth, to her son, 'you must put the man in his place. Tell him he's an old fool. Tell him he's a pompous over-rated fat bald-pated snobbish old nincompoop!'

'Yes,' said Ned, with a smile. 'That would certainly win him over.'

'And while you're at it, dear, should you not *insist* that your pond picture be displayed somewhere that *everyone* will see it? Why not move it out of that gallery altogether? Hardly anybody goes in there.'

'That is the British Sale Gallery,' said Ned, kindly. 'The painting has to be in there, Mother, since it's on sale, not on loan, and it's classified as British.'

Elspeth dismissed these trifling details with a wave of her arm. 'But it *hasn't* sold, dear, because it's in such a terrible location. They should put it next to that picture of Balaclava! Everybody stops to look at that one. If your pond painting were beside it, then all the visitors queuing to see Balaclava would be *forced* to stare at your picture while they waited in line!'

'How gratifying,' said Ned, evenly, 'to think of them being *forced.*'

'Or – what about the main hall? It could be hung there. Then it would be the very first thing that visitors saw as they entered the building.'

'Now, Mother dear, that would be neither feasible, nor permitted.'

His words made excellent sense, and yet Elspeth persisted. Her cheerful loyalty to her son was to be admired, even if her suggestions were impractical.

'Could they not construct *another* gallery,' she continued, 'to display just a few of the best paintings? And your work could be given a prominent position.'

Ned appeared to consider this.

'Perhaps they could call it "The Gillespie Wing",' he said, drily.

'Ebbsolutely!' squawked Elspeth, having failed to note the twinkle in his eye. She clapped her hands together. 'What a brilliant, brilliant idea.'

Suddenly, just to my right, Sibyl tripped and tumbled to the ground, landing on her hands and knees. There was a hiatus, for a few seconds, while she took in what had happened, and then, unsurprisingly, she began to wail. Elspeth swooped in to the rescue, and Annie hurried over to comfort her daughter, and thus it was that – by a quirk of fate – the artist and I ended up walking ahead together, just the two of us, alone. Ned was clearly preoccupied: he kept looking this way and that, scanning the groups of visitors, presumably in search of Hamilton. Hoping to distract him from his anxiety, I broke the silence.

'Your mother has recovered very well, it seems.'

He gave me a puzzled smile. 'Recovered?' he said. 'Forgive me, but – recovered from what?'

I stared at him, surprised. Surely they had told him what had happened? 'From her accident, last week, in town – when she fainted.'

'Oh aye – that. Aye, yes, she has indeed. You're quite right.'

Another moment passed. Ned scrutinised the queue outside Kelvingrove Mansion as we approached. Presently, since he said nothing further, I spoke again: 'Thank goodness I happened to be passing, in town that day, and saw her.'

He peered at me through narrowed eyes. 'Oh, so *you're* the lady. I do beg your pardon. Yes, thank *you*. Thank you very much. We're most grateful for what you did.' He smiled at me, warmly. 'It's turned out a lovely day, has it not?'

It was, indeed, a beautiful afternoon. There was not a cloud in the sky but, thanks to a light breeze, the air was not too hot. The trees were in their best and freshest garniture, and all around us the grass grew, lush and green. We might almost have been two figures promenading in a verdant landscape painting. The Blue Hungarians were playing at the bandstand, and the boisterous sound of their music floated across the park. I felt, suddenly, elated. Perhaps it was this jubilation that caused me to be rather impertinent in my next remarks. I felt carefree and bold: what did it matter if I showed an interest?

'I believe you're an artist, sir. Pray tell what you've been working on of late.'

Ned gestured, rather bashfully, at the landscape. 'Well – this,' he said. 'The Exhibition, artisans. That sort of thing.'

'Artisans – how fascinating,' I said, and then added (a little mischievously perhaps): 'Quite a departure from your painting *The Studio* – the lady in the black frock and veil, with the bird-cage?'

He turned to look at me, in surprise. 'But – what? You've seen that, then?'

'Oh yes.'

'But – that picture was shown only the once.'

'I know – I was there, at the Grosvenor. Did someone buy it, then?'

'Yes – an anonymous collector, no less.'

I clapped my hands together. 'Anonymous? How thrilling!'

However, Ned had stopped in his tracks. 'Excuse me – I've just realised, I've been terribly rude. I remember your face now, from that night. I beg your pardon.'

'Oh, not at all – you've no reason to remember me.'

'Ah, but I do remember,' he insisted. 'You were wearing an elaborate hat – a very tall, nice hat – and a – a very striking blue dress. Yes, I remember now – there was that dreadful curator – your hat annoyed him, it was in the way – and then I lost a collar-stud. Forgive me for not recognising you at first. You see, when my mother introduced us, I just assumed you were one of the ladies from her church.'

'Ah – not I! To tell the truth, I'm what you might call a free-thinker.'

Ned glanced over his shoulder, and then gave me a light-hearted, conspiratorial look. 'Aye, well, just between ourselves,' he said, in a low voice, 'I'm not a great one for the Kirk either.'

I laughed, and he smiled at me. 'Sorry, miss, but what was your name again? Those openings are such a trial to the nerves: I never remember what anybody says.'

'No need to apologise – we weren't actually introduced. My name is Harriet Baxter. But – please – call me Harriet.'

'Harriet, it is. How d'you do?'

He shook my hand. Such a lovely moment: the first time that I had ever heard my name upon his lips, and then, that shy, endearing smile that he gave me, after he had spoken. His eyes, although sad, were of a rare and startling blue: at that instant, I could not have named the colour, but with the hindsight of years, I would describe their shade, that afternoon, as ultramarine.

I glanced down as he released my hand, noticing first the muscular span of his wrist, and then I saw, scribbled all across the back of his cuff, a pencil sketch of the hot-air balloon, which must have been what he was doing earlier, when I had assumed that he was winding his watch or fiddling with a shirt fastener. It may sound silly, but I found this quite thrilling: that he would spoil his cuffs by drawing on them showed a refreshing lack of vanity, not to mention an appealing, devil-may-care attitude to convention.

We fell back into step and, moments later, came into view of the multitudes swarming in front of the main building. The place was busy, even for a Saturday. Ned's glance darted here and there as we headed towards the Eastern Palace.

'I'm interested to hear you're sketching the Exhibition,' I told him. 'Such an inspiring subject. The urban landscape! The smoke! The city dweller! The crowds!'

'Aye,' he said, doubtfully. 'But nobody wants to buy paintings of the city. They'd far rather hang haystacks and cottar's gardens on their walls. And a man has to make a living, Miss Baxter, especially with a family to support.'

I recalled the little scene that I had witnessed earlier: Ned's brother, borrowing money. Was that a regular occurrence, I wondered? Certainly, to judge from his clothing, Kenneth Gillespie had expensive tastes to maintain. And how many of the others did Ned have to provide for? His mother was a widow, it seemed; Mabel remained unmarried; and there were also Annie and the children to feed and clothe.

'I expect there are many demands on your purse,' I remarked.

When Ned made no reply, I glanced at him and found that he was staring at a gentleman who was seated behind an easel, on the grass near Van Houten's, in the very same spot where I had, only recently, been standing. The artist – a squat, balding character – appeared to be sketching the crowds as they milled about in front of the Palace. A white umbrella shaded him from the sun. Several people stood at a respectful distance on either side, admiring his work.

Ned glared at him, as though thunderstruck.

'Would that be Mr Hamilton?' I ventured.

'Not at all,' muttered Ned. 'It's Lavery – confound him!'

And, so saying, he charged across the concourse with great fierceness of purpose. I half suspected that he was about to attack the artist, or overturn and stamp upon his easel and, fearing something of the sort, I hurried after him; but, in the event, Ned did neither of these things (of course not – violence was not in his nature). He simply stared coolly at the man as he strode past, and bade him a stiff and pointed: 'Afternoon, John.'

By way of greeting, Lavery waved a stick of charcoal in mid-air, and carried on sketching, apparently oblivious to Ned's barbed tone. No introductions were made; Ned marched on, without pause, until we reached the bridges, then he came to a halt, and began scowling around him at the passing crowds. It was easy to guess the reason for this change of humour: he was simply annoyed to find another artist recording the Exhibition. Indeed, as I later learned, Ned had been busy, a few weeks earlier, making studies of Muratti's tobacco girls, rolling their Turkish cigarettes, when Lavery – who, heretofore, had not been seen in the park with so much as a pencil in his hand – happened to wander past and, spying Ned, had paused to comment upon his sketches. It was from this encounter (or so Ned suspected), that Lavery borrowed the idea to draw some Exhibition scenes of his own.

Sad to see my new friend downcast, I ventured to suggest a distraction. 'Perhaps we could go inside the Palace, Mr Gillespie. I'd be most interested to hear your opinions on the exhibits. And you could show me the location to which you wish your painting to be moved.'

He glanced at his watch and then looked disappointed. 'I'm afraid that won't be possible today,' he said. 'I must, as you know, locate Hamilton – and after that I'm obliged to meet a friend. Some other time, perhaps. It would be a pleasure.'

Just then, amongst the scattered hordes outside the Women's Industries Section, I spotted Mabel's wraith like figure bearing down upon us, followed, at some little distance, by the rest of the family. Inevitable though this intrusion was, I had enjoyed my private time with the artist, and was most disappointed that it was now drawing to a close. However, an excellent idea had just occurred to me: perhaps I could help out the family purse by buying one of Ned's paintings. I wondered how to broach the subject, and said, at last: 'As it happens, I should very much like to own a painting by an up-and-coming Scottish artist – perhaps even more than one.'

Ned nodded, thoughtfully. 'Well, if I can be of any help,' he said. 'I do know Lavery – he's not a bad chap, really. Of course, there's Guthrie and MacGregor; and some of my friends are making quite a name for themselves: Walter Peden, for instance. But MacGregor or Guthrie might be the ones to approach first. I could certainly get you the introductions, if you like.'

'Oh – but I'm afraid you misunderstand me. What I mean is that, to begin with, I should like to buy some of *your* work.'

Ned swept off his boater and dragged his fingers through his hair, his outstretched arm exposing, once again, the scribbled drawing on his cuff. 'Good Heavens!' he said. 'Well, I'm – extremely flattered.'

And so it was agreed that I would call upon him at his studio, later that week. We were just finalising the details of my visit when Mabel arrived and linked arms with her brother. She whispered something in his ear and then turned to me.

'Afternoon, Harriet. Are you having a frightfully spiffing time?'

'Yes, thank you.'

'I think people *should* have spiffing times, don't you, Ned?' Mabel jogged his elbow. 'What d'you think, brother mine? Eh, what?'

She was making some kind of joke, I gathered, and possibly at my expense. I felt awkward, since there was nothing, really, that could be said, under the circumstances. Ned laughed, of course; no doubt, he would have missed Mabel's mocking undertones, oblivious, as ever, to her bad manners: dear Ned always saw the best in people, and he was often completely blind to their faults.

In extremis, I fell back upon that old friend, flattery. 'Why, Mabel, that's a lovely frock you're wearing.'

'Thank you,' she trilled, mechanically, and – although she looked me up and down – failed to return any compliment. All at once, the others descended upon us, and Elspeth began, immediately, to screech in my ear. Glancing down, I was unnerved to see Sibyl glowering at me and at my parasol. The sight of a child's face transformed by such a baleful stare was most disquieting. I was beginning to realise that being cornered by Elspeth made one feel rather like a fly, trapped in the web of a spider: an irrepressibly cheerful and loquacious spider, but a spider nonetheless. Hypnotised by the movements of her mouth as she chattered on, I had almost convinced myself that I would soon be bound in silken threads and left – dangling – to be devoured later, when Annie bustled over, interrupting her mother-in-law with the words: 'Where's Rose?'

'I don't know,' said Elspeth. 'Was she not with Sibyl?'

We all looked down at the child. The baleful stare had gone, only to be replaced by a look of injured innocence.

'Where's your sister?' Annie asked.

Sibyl widened her eyes, as though she had been insulted. 'I don't know.'

I glanced over towards the main building. Outside the entrance, Ned and Mabel had just accosted a prosperous-looking gentleman, perhaps the person that they sought to meet. Elspeth had followed my gaze and, as though to confirm my thoughts, exclaimed: 'Hamilton!', and sailed off to join ranks with her son and daughter. I watched on, in the hope that Ned might be successful in his mission to have his canvas relocated. The gallery owner gave every appearance of listening intently to his former student. Unfortunately, Mabel had not had the sense to absent herself. Instead, she had adopted a rather superior stance, her eyes half closed, her chin upturned, a condescending and confrontational pose, which I hoped that the man would not find too off-putting. Beside me, Annie was scolding Sibyl.

'How many times do I have to tell you not to let her out your sight?'

The girl pouted, and kicked at the ground.

At that moment, from the vicinity of the stone bridge, the disembodied wail of a small child could be heard. Annie spun around with a loud cry:

'Rose? Where are you?'

She hurried off in the direction of the river. I glanced back towards the entrance. Having heard Annie's yell, Ned broke off from his conversation with Hamilton, and stared, with some concern, towards his wife. As I watched, he muttered something to Elspeth, who had just joined their little group, and then, leaving her with Hamilton and Mabel, he ran across the concourse, darting between the crowds, yelling as he went.

'Annie! What's the matter?'

'It's Rose!' I heard her shout in reply. 'Rose, dear — where are you?'

And then the littlest Gillespie came into view. She was sitting on a path, near the Fire Engine, bawling, her fat apple cheeks dirty and tear-stained. As soon as she saw her mother and father approaching, she ceased to cry, realising that she was no longer lost. Annie descended upon the child, and swept her up.

'There you are, my wee poppet.'

Elspeth, Mabel and the gallery owner were all staring over at the little scene by the river, but as soon as it became clear that Rose was in no danger, the two women turned back to Hamilton and both of them began to harangue him, at once. Elspeth's lips moved, nineteen to the dozen, and although I was unable to distinguish any individual words from where I stood, I could hear her shrill, overbearing tones. Meanwhile, apparently oblivious to the ruination of his plans, Ned had joined Annie and both of them were fussing over Rose. I stole a glance at Sibyl, who was staring across the concourse at her sister and parents. The expression on her face was downcast, perhaps more miserable than sullen. Annie, in particular, appeared to dote on her youngest child: it seemed clear to me, even then, that Rose was her favourite. I wondered whether Sibyl ever felt excluded.

In an effort to cheer her up, I said: 'It must be hard being the eldest, looking after your sister all the time.'

No doubt, I was also attempting to endear myself to the child, having, thus far, struggled to befriend her, but Sibyl was unimpressed. She flicked her eyes at me, askance – another strange look that seemed, somehow, too mature for her years.

'Rose is always getting lost,' she lisped, and then she turned and skipped away, in the direction of the Doulton Fountain.

When I think of that moment now, I shiver.

By the time that Ned rejoined his mother and sister at the entrance, Horatio Hamilton of the Fine Art Committee had endured enough of the two women and, having made his excuses, he had disappeared into some private office within the main building, not to be seen again, that day. Nobody could be sure of exactly what had passed between Elspeth, Mabel, and the gallery owner, but according to them, despite their most charming and persuasive efforts, he had assured them that he was unable to help Ned with the relocation of his picture. It seemed that the Committee had drawn up careful plans, several weeks previously; paintings could not just be moved about the place at the whim of artists and their relatives. Thus, *By the Pond* remained where it was, for the duration of the Exhibition, with the result that Ned's public profile was not what it might have been.

Perhaps a picture is beginning to emerge: a picture of an artist, a man of indisputable talent, but a man hampered by circumstance and responsibility. Poor Ned! Is it any wonder that he was struggling to make his name? It would not have surprised me in the least to learn that he envied his peers, especially those without domestic entanglements. Moreover, he was forced to contend with the inequities of an artistic establishment that was (then, as now) notoriously prone to snobbism, and nowhere more cliquish than Scotland, wherein most established artists were possessed of wealth, an Edinburgh heritage, and a first-rate education. Even the avant-garde of the 'new school' – that loose alliance of painters who became known, eventually, as 'The Glasgow Boys' – were, in the main, sons of the manse, of merchants, or of shipping magnates, who, with financial support from their families and patrons, were not obliged to sell pictures in order to live. Some of these men were so established, by then, that not only had their work been included in the Exhibition, but they had also been asked to paint various decorative frescos in the Exhibition buildings. Ned Gillespie, on the other hand, was not part of this charmed inner circle, and had not been asked to contribute so much as a scribble.

Strictly speaking, the Gillespies were respectable enough, but despite Elspeth's valiant attempts to sound well bred, there was neither wealth nor *noblesse* on her side. And yet, here Ned was, striving to create works of art, despite his unfavourable circumstances and background. I was prompted to wonder how many others there were, like him: gifted young men, whose talents were left to rot for want of money and opportunity. I also could not help but reflect on others of my acquaintance who, despite wealth and every advantage, had accomplished nothing meaningful. Ned, at least, was creating something of worth with his talent. My heart went out to him and, that evening, as I sat alone in my rooms, I found myself reflecting on the terrible unfairness of the world.

4

Having given the matter some thought, I decided to see what could be done to help this Ned Gillespie, this talented young man. It was the least I could do, and would involve little or no hardship on my part. Clearly, a number of factors stood between him and real success. From our conversation in the park, I had deduced that, for financial reasons, he was forced to churn out 'popular' pictures, instead of indulging his own, more interesting, creativity. I also suspected that he was rather at the mercy of his charming, but unruly, family, who must surely have been a great distraction from his craft, especially since his studio was in the attic of his home. Lastly, it was obvious that he lacked a circle of influence: the friends in high places that tend to make life easier for many artists. Poor Ned had no such advantage, and I had an inkling that he was neither mercenary nor calculating enough to cultivate influential or moneyed acquaintances.

Before retiring that evening, I composed a letter to my step-father, Ramsay Dalrymple, who resided just north of Helens-burgh, a town not far from Glasgow. My feeling was that I ought, at least, to bring Ned to his attention. As far as I was aware, Ramsay was not particularly interested in Fine Art, but he was a wealthy man, and there was always the chance that he might be persuaded to buy a painting or two. Moreover, I felt that he was bound to be acquainted with some of the West of Scotland's 'Establishment' figures, perhaps even from within the art world itself, connections the like of which might prove useful to a young painter.

In my letter, I proposed to visit him on Wednesday, provided that this met with his approval. No reply was forthcoming, but this was no surprise, as I was well aware that Ramsay disliked letter writing. Indeed, since he had moved away from London, after separating from my mother – and although I had written to him, several times, every year – he had sent me only a handful of brief notes in reply. These days, he rarely left his estate, and I myself had been so busy in the previous few weeks (what with the Exhibition, and my new friends, and so on), that I had yet to inform him of my arrival in Glasgow. Notwithstanding his dislike of correspondence, had he not wished me to call upon him at home, I presumed that he would have conveyed as much to me, if only by telegraph. Therefore, on Wednesday morning, having heard nothing to the contrary, I took the train to Helensburgh.

Perhaps I should explain that Ramsay was my mother's second husband. My real father, a captain in the Fusiliers, was killed at the Battle of Alma, in 1854, the year after I was born. A year later, my mother remarried and – perhaps because I was so young at the time – I had always thought of Ramsay as my 'papa', even though he was often a rather distant figure.

But that is by the bye. As I was explaining, on Wednesday, I set out to visit my father – that is to say, my stepfather (perhaps, for the sake of clarity, I should refer to him thus, from now on). The day was wet, and cold for late May. Unfortunately, I must have been sickening for something, because I began to feel light-headed at the railway station, and became so queasy on the train that I thought that I might even have to disembark a few stops early. I managed to control myself until we arrived at Helensburgh, where I made haste to the sea-front, and breathed in fresh air for ten minutes or so. Then I hired a man with a pony trap for the afternoon. I did fear for my stomach on the ride to the estate, but the road was excellent and, thankfully, I was not bounced around too much.

My stepfather's house – which I saw, that day, for the first time – can be described only as a fortress: a castellated mansion, grim and grey, which overlooked the Gare Loch (grimmer, greyer). Upon arrival, I was shown into a drawing room to wait. The room was cavernous and chilly. In one corner stood a familiar display cabinet: I did not even need to glance inside to know that it was full of my stepfather's kaleidoscope collection. Nearby, on a dusty plinth, lay what might have been a gyroscope. A sewing machine sat on a table and, propped against an open crate, was a strange-looking contraption: a low, wooden box, on wheels, with a long broom-like handle. Clearly, my stepfather's obsessions had not changed. He had always been fanatical about the acquisition of new gadgets, perhaps because he was suspicious of the modern world and its exigencies, and, therefore, terrified of being left behind. As a child, I can remember him scanning the newspapers and periodicals for any reference to recent inventions, and he bought all the newfangled devices as soon as they became available. Alas, when these purchases arrived, he often found that he had no idea how to operate them, and his horror of appearing ill-informed made him far too proud to request further instruction from the manufacturer, with the result that the rooms of our house in Eaton Square were always littered with the carcases of useless contraptions that nobody could work. Indeed, Ramsay would not permit us or the servants even to touch the machines until he had used them himself, and if he was unable to work them, then he insisted that nobody could.

There were no fires in any of the grates and, since movement seemed to quell my nausea, I began to walk around the room to keep warm. After about ten minutes, the door flew open, and my stepfather strode in, rubbing his hands together in an athletic fashion. He looked me up and down, with a tight grin on his face.

'Aye, lassie! You've hardly changed – I'd know that beak any-where!'

For some reason, I cannot remember what exactly was said in the next few minutes. Perhaps I was shocked to see how much he had aged since I had last seen him, over ten years previously, at a family funeral – although, in truth, I should not have been surprised: after all, by then, he was almost seventy years old. Physically, he seemed robust enough, but his hair and whiskers had turned silvery white, and his skin was as pale as tallow. He had always possessed a ghostly complexion – but, in my memory, his hair and beard were black, and only lightly flecked with grey.

Eager to engage him in conversation and, noticing that his gaze kept straying to the contraption beside the crate, I asked: 'Is this a recent acquisition, sir? What is it?'

'A carpet sweeper,' he replied, then asked, idly: 'Any idea how it works?' When I informed him that I had not the slightest notion how to operate such a thing, he frowned, and prodded the box with his foot. 'Ach, I think it's broke, in any case,' he said. 'These rods won't turn. Had it shipped all the way from America, too, at great expense – typical!'

While our tea was being made, we undertook a tour of the mansion, at my request. It seemed that my stepfather was greatly exercised by the notion of burglars, for the premises were fastened up with more padlocks than a bridewell. I noticed a watchman patrolling the grounds, with dogs; all the windows appeared to be nailed shut; the outer doors were secured with iron bars at top and bottom; and every internal door could be bolted from the adjacent hall or corridor, thus, in the unlikely event that an intruder did gain access to one of the rooms, he would find ingress to the rest of the house thwarted, unless he was possessed of several rods of dynamite.

Despite this, and Ramsay's wealth, there did not seem to be much that was worth stealing. Most of the rooms were unfurnished and simply functioned as store places for his various gadgets. On the one hand, my stepfather appeared to be frustrated by his malfunctioning machines, but he also seemed to gloat at their failure, as though this confirmed that the modern world, for all its baffling contrivances and precocity, was not so clever after all. In the morning room, he encouraged me to admire a mechanical graphophone: a talking machine, which had apparently never uttered so much as a syllable. Next to the scullery, he showed me a refrigerator; this object not only never got cold, but also (according to the cook) intermittently leaked poisonous gases. Outside, on the carriage drive, we paused to gaze into a shrubbery, at a half-concealed, steam-powered lawnmower. Sadly, the machine was out of puff, and crumbling with rust, since the gardener had refused to use it. We arrived, eventually, at the study, the tiny room in which my stepfather seemed to spend most of his time. He sat down and, picking up a pile of murky glass negatives, he began to shuffle through them. I was about to bring up the subject of Ned when he enquired, abruptly, whether I knew how to operate a camera (or, as he called it, a 'photographic apparatus'), and when I replied that I did not, he raised an eyebrow. 'But you are young,' he cried. 'As a female, you can be excused an ignorance of photographics – but you don't know the first thing, either, about these new carpet sweepers? Dearie me.'

I smiled at him, graciously, and said, 'I know that they are very useful, sir. And – come to think of it – I do know a person who *has* a carpet sweeper in his home: the artist Ned Gillespie.' I will admit that this last was not entirely true: as far as I was aware, the Gillespies owned nothing more sophisticated than a broom, but I was keen to get my stepfather off the subject of his contraptions. I went on, quickly: 'Do you know his work?'

Ignoring my question, Ramsay waggled his hands at me. 'Your friend's machine – where is it manufactured?'

'I think you misunderstand me, sir. He's an artist, not an inventor.'

'Yes, but you said he had a carpet sweeper, did you not? What I really want to know is – can his machine wash the carpet as well as sweep it?'

'I'm fairly confident that it doesn't wash the carpet, sir. But what I wanted to say was that Mr Gillespie –'

'Ah-hah!' said my stepfather. 'In that case, tell me this, young lady, do you know of any device that washes as well as sweeps? Does such a machine exist?'

This was an exhausting conversation, hostile and full of dead ends. I had forgotten that such was the only type of discussion in which my stepfather engaged; his interlocutors were always his adversaries; indeed he did not feel that he was engaged in a real dialogue unless one participant ended by triumphing over the other. I will admit to feeling frustrated. We had not seen each other for many years; it seemed hard to believe that we were embroiled in such a pointless, combative exchange about nothing more meaningful than gadgets.

'No, sir,' I said, shortly. 'I know of no such device.'

His lip curled, and he gazed at me, askance: if I were a representative of the modern world, then it would appear that I was distinctly below par in his estimation. Immediately, I was filled with regret and anxiety: I had let him down! As a child, I had learned all about kaleidoscopes, in the hope of pleasing him. If only I was better informed, now, about carpet sweepers.

At that moment, our tea arrived. Ramsay sat bolt upright and became, of a sudden, quietly vigilant. I soon saw the reason. The room was so small, and his aged housekeeper had such terrible tremors, that the action of laying out the tea was quite perilous, especially whenever scalding liquids were involved. The old woman shook; the china rattled; the milk and water splashed, and my stepfather seemed ready to leap forward to her assistance at any moment. Once she had gone, I brought up the subject of Ned once more. 'You may have seen his painting at the Exhibition,' I told my stepfather. 'You've been to the Exhibition, I dare say?'

'Not at all!' he said, dismissively. 'It's all sideshows and sweeties.'

'Well, sir, there is more to it than that. We should go, one day. There are some very attractive buildings – and the machinery! Not to mention the inventions. They're selling a very clever self-pouring teapot.' A flicker of interest crossed his face. 'I could also show you Ned's painting, although the one at the Exhibition isn't really his best.'

My stepfather gave me a hard stare. 'Have you got your hooks dug into this man Dobbin's flesh?'

'My – I beg your pardon?'

'Are you set to marry him? Is that what this is all about?'

I laughed. 'No, no! His name is Gillespie, sir, and he's already married. No, I simply believe that he's extremely talented.'

How typical of my stepfather to associate marriage with an image of female 'hooks' digging into masculine flesh. He was very devoted to my mother, of course, at least before they separated but, in general, he seemed to have a low opinion of the feminine sex. He would certainly never have been a suffragist! In fact, he was to die long before *that* campaign got under way: the victim, alas, of a bizarre explosion, caused by a newly acquired and unpatented gas-powered shower-bath.

'Why don't you come to town next week, sir? We could visit the Exhibition – make a day of it. I could invite Mr Gillespie and his wife. Or, I could bring Ned here, perhaps, next time I come?' The look of alarm on Ramsay's face was such that I added, immediately: 'But perhaps not; it might be better if you yourself came to town. More tea?'

He gave his head a little shake.

'I was wondering, sir, if you – perhaps – have some friends who are collectors, or gallery owners?'

'Friends,' said Ramsay, bitterly, and gave the sugar bowl a little push. Perhaps, these days, he was rather more reclusive than I had previously thought.

Not knowing what else to do, I smiled, and then glanced out of the study at the draughty room beyond. 'You have such a wonderful home here, sir,' I said. 'It might be nice to hang something on these walls – some paintings, for instance.'

'Hmmph,' said my stepfather. Then he leaned forwards and looked at me, with a glint in his eye. 'You're wanting me to recommend this Gillespie, are you, to all and sundry?'

'Oh, well – that would be very helpful. He's not at the forefront, yet, but he's as good as any of these fellows, like Guthrie, or Walton.' The expression on Ramsay's face did not change: it was conceivable that he might not even have heard of these artists. 'If we fixed a date for you to come to town,' I added, 'then I could arrange for you to view his work –'

'Aye, well – we'll see.' He held up one of the misty glass negatives to the light and peered at it. 'Fog in the drawing room!' he croaked. 'Useless!'

Whether my stepfather would buy any of Gillespie's work, or even recommend him to his associates, remained to be seen. However, before I left that day, Ramsay did make a surprising offer: to pay for me to have my portrait painted, so that he could hang the finished product on his drawing-room wall. Of course, I was flattered and pleased, but I must also admit that, initially, I found the notion a little embarrassing. For one thing, it seemed a vanity to sit for one's own portrait. Moreover, even in my youth, I had no illusions about my appearance, and I certainly did not possess the kind of beauty that might make one relish the thought of being scrutinised, at close quarters, and at length. Nevertheless, such a commission would pay well, and I decided to offer it to Ned Gillespie, certain that it would be of great financial benefit to him. Having my portrait painted might prolong my stay in Glasgow, but I had no objections to extending my trip, even for a few months, and there was nothing pressing in London that required my attention.

The following day, as arranged, I called at Stanley Street, to look at Ned's paintings. After ringing the bell, I was admitted into the building by a person in carpet slippers and apron: clearly, this was the Gillespies' servant, Christina. On my previous visit, it had crossed my mind that Annie, with her protestations about the maid's day off, might have been attempting to conceal a genteel poverty, *sans serveuse* – but here the girl was, blue of eye, dark of lash, and pretty, in a pert, snub-nosed way. She preceded me upstairs, her slippers flapping at her heels. Her appearance lacked polish, perhaps; none the less, she seemed (at least on first acquaintance) a capable enough creature.

Inside the apartment, Christina led me directly upstairs. An attic is an unusual feature for a tenement, but Stanley Street had been built to a rare design. For instance, each apartment had the luxury of an interior water closet, and residents of the top floor, like the Gillespies, had this second storey in the loft. Ned's family had made full use of the extra space. Besides three tiny bedrooms (one each, for Sibyl, Rose and Christina), there was a linen press, and – my destination that afternoon – the artist's studio: a narrow, dingy garret, with one skylight. I recognised it, at once, as the attic depicted in the painting that I had seen at the Grosvenor Gallery.

It was a surprise, and something of a disappointment, to discover that I was not the only guest that day. Ned's friend Walter Peden was already there when I arrived and – 'by coincidence' – happened to have brought along his portfolio. Although of Scottish descent, Peden was born in London and had studied Classics at Cambridge, circumstances that had blessed him both with an English accent and with the attitude that, no matter where he found himself, he was always the most intelligent person in the room. Peden prided himself on his bookishness and wore it conspicuously, like a badge. Alas, he had confounded intellect with pedantry, two separate qualities that are, by no means, the same thing. He was a balding, bespectacled, hen-toed fellow of average height, and his supercilious air was amplified by an inability to address anyone without closing over his little eyes, rather as though he did not care to soil his gaze by letting it fall upon you. So incapable was he of dealing with his fellow humans that he could not, in conversation, face anyone directly, and instead kept finding ways of placing himself at oblique angles to his interlocutor. Equally disconcerting was his tendency, without warning, to dance around like a Native, whilst smiling to himself in a self-satisfied manner. In general, he cut rather a tragic figure, but perhaps this 'happy dance' was his way of protesting otherwise to the world, and pretending that, deep inside, he was actually a jubilant and well-contented individual.

It was quite obvious to me that Ned had invited Peden along in the expectation that I might purchase some of his work. Indeed,

I had barely set down my basket when Ned very generously suggested that we go through Walter's portfolio first, before we considered any of his own paintings. A few of Peden's efforts were on display at the Exhibition, and they had not exactly taken my breath away. However, to oblige my host, I gave my cheerful consent, and was rewarded when I saw how pleased Ned looked.

'Walter's work is outstanding,' he told me. 'I don't think I'd be faulted for saying that he's one of our finest artists.'

Certainly, Peden himself did not appear to dispute this assertion. He proceeded to produce a series of watercolours, tossing the pages upon the table, one after the other, as though they were of little consequence to him. The pictures were executed competently enough but, much as I had expected, the majority were flatly representational portraits of animals: cows, sheep, ducks, a basket of kittens, a pony, a pigeon, some *gosses des riches* with their puppy, etcetera. I suppose that *somebody* has to paint livestock and pets, but such subject matter has never been of great interest to me. It was all that I could do to stop my gaze from wandering off, towards the stacks of canvases that leaned, here and there, against the wall, and at the painting on Ned's easel – which was angled away from us, at the far end of the room. Even though the skylight had been propped open, the garret was stuffy, and seemed unsuitable for use as a studio. The light quality was dim and, since the window faced more west than north, presumably it was also inconsistent. The ceiling, which slanted almost to the floor, presented a hazard for anyone of the normal height. I could only imagine that my host must often bang his head.

'*Psittacus erithacus erithacus*,' announced Peden, throwing down a picture of a grey parrot. 'Extremely intelligent birds, originally native to Africa and, as I'm sure you know, Miss Baxter, much prized by the ancient Greeks and Romans, for their ability to talk, sometimes in complete sentences.'

'Yes, indeed,' I replied. 'And pray tell, what did this magnificent bird communicate to you?'

'As it happens,' Peden sniffed, 'he was mute.'

'He spoke not at all?'

'No – the owner had recently had him stuffed.'

A somewhat undignified admission, perhaps, but to demonstrate that he suffered no discomfiture, Peden danced about on the spot with his eyelids sealed shut, and a smile of rapture upon his face.

'Remarkable!' I said. 'Well, in that case, may I congratulate you, sir. You've done a wonderful job of bringing him back to life. If I'm not mistaken, you've even put a gleam in his eye.'

I smiled at Ned, who nodded, happily, in agreement, and then gestured at the other pages on the table, saying: 'Do you see any painting you like, in particular?'

'Oh no, they're all equally good,' I said. 'And if one were a devotee of animal portraiture, and had money to spend, then I'm convinced that one would be hard pressed to find better than these marvellous pictures.'

As I had hoped, this made it quite plain that I had no intention of purchasing any, and Peden began, a little crossly, to gather up his work.

'I quite agree, Harriet,' said Ned. 'Walter's pictures will be worth a fortune, one day. He's such a talent.'

'I am now aware of Mr Peden,' I said, 'and of his work. Thank you so much for the introduction. But I'm most curious to see your *own* recent endeavours.'

Ned gave a fretful glance towards his easel, and I felt a tingle of anticipation, but just then, footsteps clattered on the landing, and Sibyl burst in, looking hot and over-excited. She ran to Ned, and tugged at his hand.

'Papa! Papa!' she squeaked. 'Come and see what I done!'

'Come and see what?'

'My fern! I planted it in a pot! Come and look!'

She clung to him like a little tick, dragging, with surprising strength, not only at his hand, but also at the hem of his jacket, straining the material at the seams.

'No, Sibyl,' he said. 'We have visitors', and I was about to throw my hat in the air and give three cheers (metaphorically, of course), when he added, 'Bring your ferns up here if you must. But be quick. Papa's busy.'

Instantly, Sibyl fled back downstairs. Ned chortled and gave his head an exasperated little shake. 'My apologies – they're planting those blasted ferns.'

'Pteridomania!' exclaimed Peden. 'That dreaded disease.' He angled his body away from me, in order to address me, sideways, over his shoulder. 'It seems that when you ladies are weary of novels and gossip and crochet, you find much entertainment in ferns. No doubt you preside over a fern collection, Miss Baxter?'

'Sadly, no!' I replied. 'What with all my novels and gossip and crochet, there's no time left over for ferns.'

The astute reader will, of course, realise that I was employing irony; but Mr Peden gave a self-satisfied nod – as though I had proven his point.

Just then, footsteps thundered once again on the landing, and Sibyl returned, followed by Rose, who sidled into the room, more shyly. Each child bore a fern in a coloured pot (yellow for Sibyl, blue for Rose), which they set down upon the table for us to admire. Sibyl pushed her plant towards Ned, causing Peden to leap forward and rescue his portfolio. 'Careful!' he muttered, and began, fussily, to tie the strings.

'That's my one, Papa!' cried Sibyl, ignoring him. 'Look at mine!'

'My one is the nicest,' said Rose, quietly.

Sibyl turned on her. 'No, it *isn't*!' she hissed. 'And you're just a big fat *baby*!'

'Now then, my wee beauty,' said Ned, with a laugh. He scooped Sibyl into his arms, and smothered her in kisses. Just then, another footstep was heard on the landing, and Annie appeared at the threshold, in outdoor clothes.

'Here you are!' she cried, unfastening her bonnet. 'Good afternoon, Harriet. Walter. Ned, dear.' And she smiled at us, hazily, as though through a pretty fog.

Peden gave her a little bow and flourish. Sibyl jumped down from Ned's arms, and the children ran to their mother, their voices clamouring as they struggled to be heard, one above the other.

'Come in, dearest,' said Ned. 'How wonderful to see you.'

It occurred to me to wonder whether there might have been an edge of sarcasm to this remark, but apparently not: he was regarding her with genuine affection. In return, Annie lowered her head and gazed at him through her eyelashes, a look that smouldered sufficiently to make any witness feel *de trop*.

'How was your class, dear?' asked Ned. 'Did you enjoy it?'

'Yes,' she replied, examining the ribbon string of her bonnet, which had just fallen off in her hand, and would require stitching. 'But we had a model this afternoon, and it was awful difficult. I did some *horrible* drawings. I need practice.'

'My wife is being modest,' Ned told me, and then smiled at her. 'She's a far better painter than I am.'

Annie widened her eyes, in mock horror. 'Och, away!' she said. 'Now you're just being silly. But here – why don't we all go down and have some tea? It's a bit crowded in here, is it not? Ned?'

'Oh no,' I found myself saying, and they all turned to look at me. I cleared my throat. 'I mean – I'm afraid – I only have an hour to spare and I was rather hoping to have at least that amount of time to look at Ned's work. I'm sure Mr Peden here would welcome a cup of tea, but perhaps Ned and I might . . .' I glanced at my host, hoping for support, and to my relief, he agreed.

'Yes, you go down, Walter; I'll have tea later, my sweet.' This last was addressed not to the balding Mr Peden, of course, but to Annie, of the bewitching golden locks. She frowned at her husband, and then turned to his friend.

'Well, Walter, it seems you'll have to suffer my company.'

Peden closed his eyes, and danced at her.

'That would be charming, but I'm sorry – Mrs G. – I must be off.'

'What a pity,' said Annie, and turned to Sibyl and Rose. 'Take your ferns downstairs, like good girls. Put them in the dining room. And go and tell Christina to bring up tea.'

The children grabbed their plants and departed, followed by Peden, who jigged across the room, bobbing his head and punching at the air with his fists, much as though he were a member of the Zulu tribe, and not the Glasgow Chess Club. '*Exit, pursued by bear*,' he intoned, as he went. 'Miss Baxter, you will, of course, recognise the quote.'

Deciding that the best policy was to ignore him, I simply smiled and stepped out of his way. He paused at the threshold. '*Winter's Tale*,' he said. 'In case you are completely bemused.'

'I beg your pardon?'

'Shakespeare, Miss Baxter. Shakespeare.'

And so saying, he scuttled off down the stairs.

Annie had thrown herself down on the old, battered chaise, and was unfastening her shoes. I had hoped to have some time with the artist, alone, to view his paintings, and to ask him whether he might be interested in undertaking a portrait commission. However, in the presence of a third party, I felt a little self-conscious and constrained.

Ned stood with his hands in his pockets, staring out of the skylight, across the rooftops, towards the tower of St Jude's. He seemed ill at ease, and I wondered why. Of course, in hindsight, it seems likely that he was embarrassed at having someone examine his work, which always made him uncomfortable. At the time, I simply sensed his awkwardness and – since he was making no move to show me his canvases – I brought up the subject of my stepfather, and his request that I have my portrait painted.

'I wondered, Ned, whether you'd be so kind as to consider taking the commission? I can assure you it will pay well.'

He and Annie exchanged a look. Then the artist turned to me, with a sigh. 'It's very good of you to consider me, Harriet, but I'm afraid I can't take on any more work, not for the moment.'

Annie dropped her shoes to the floor, with a clatter. 'He's under consideration to paint Her Majesty, in August.'

I looked at them both, in astonishment. 'The Queen? Really?'

Ned appeared to blush, saying: 'Well, it's by no means definite.'

'But she's coming up to inaugurate the Exhibition,' said Annie. 'And they want a painting to commemorate the day.'

'Oh, my goodness!' I said. 'How thrilling. But – forgive me for saying – if the visit isn't until August, then don't you have some time, before then –'

'Aye, but it's not that simple,' said Annie. 'There's six artists being considered, four of them well established, and a couple of newer names, like Ned. They've each to put in some paintings, as examples, and the Committee make their decision based on that.'

Ned cleared his throat. 'A portrait commission would be useful, financially, Harriet, but I'm having to work, full time, on my picture submissions. I'm so sorry.'

'Oh, I completely understand. You must think of the longer term. No doubt, the man who is chosen to paint the Queen will never again want for money.'

'Aye.' He scratched his head, thoughtfully, and then his face cleared. 'But what about Walter?'

Annie made a sad face. 'Walter isn't one of the six,' she confided.

'No,' said Ned. 'But I'm sure he'd be happy to paint Harriet's portrait.'

'Mr Peden?' I said. 'Yes – that's certainly another option to consider. Now, excuse me, Annie, would you be so kind – if you don't mind – as to direct me to your facilities? I'd very much like to wash my hands.'

'Oh, go right ahead,' she said, swinging her feet up onto the chaise. 'They're downstairs, just on the left as you come in the front door.'

I hurried out, and descended to the hallway. Apparently, the children were in the kitchen with Christina, for I could hear their girlish prattle above the clatter of pots and pans. I stepped inside the little water closet beneath the stairs, and ran the tap. In fact, my hands were perfectly clean; I had simply wanted to avoid an awkward situation, given that I had no desire, whatsoever, to have my portrait painted by Walter Peden, and I needed a moment to compose myself, in order to find a polite excuse. Watching the water trickle down the plughole, I decided to tell Ned that – if he himself was unable to paint the portrait – then I would ask my stepfather to choose an artist.

And, so it might have been, had I not, on my way back to the studio, caught sight of a pile of drawings on the floor by a chair in the hallway. Annie must have dropped them onto the seat, upon returning from her class, and perhaps the children had knocked them off, in passing. I crouched down to tidy them up, idly glancing through them as I did so. The uppermost sketch depicted a woman, costumed and posed rather in the mode of a Russian princess. I was struck, at once, by how well executed this portrait was, and paused to take a better look. The lines were bold, the composition pleasing. To my untrained eyes, it seemed a very stylish and confident piece of work. Favourably impressed, I gathered up the other pictures, studying them as I went. Annie had been dismissive of her own talent, but I saw now that she was, without question, a very capable artist in her own right. What a talented pair, I thought to myself. And it was while I was replacing the drawings, and making my way back to the attic, that it came to me.

Upstairs, there was silence, although Ned and Annie were still in the studio. As I crossed the landing, I caught a glimpse of them, through the doorway. In my absence, the artist had moved behind the chaise, and was leaning down to embrace his wife, from behind. Her head was thrown back, and her eyes were closed, as he nuzzled at her neck. The first few buttons of her frock had come undone, I noticed, and then I saw that his hands had slipped down inside the bodice, to cup her bosom.

I froze to the spot, and was just wondering whether I should tiptoe away, when a floorboard creaked beneath my foot. Suddenly aware of my approach, Ned pulled away from his wife, and began to inspect a paintbrush, while Annie fumbled with her buttons. Deciding to brazen it out, and pretend that I had seen nothing, I breezed into the room.

'There you are, Harriet!' said Ned. 'You're light on your feet.'

'Yes – but – unlucky at cards!' I trilled, saying the first idiotic thing that came into my head, since I was flustered at having witnessed so intimate an embrace. Unable to stop myself, I babbled on: 'I hope you don't mind, Annie, but your drawings fell off the chair, and I just stopped to pick them up, out of harm's way. I couldn't help but notice – they're extremely good indeed.'

'Oh, well, thank you,' said Annie, calmly smoothing down her hair.

And then, I told them my idea: that *she,* instead of Ned, should paint my portrait. Annie gazed at me, in disbelief.

'What – me?'

'Why not?' I said. 'You're very talented – and you were just saying that you need practice. I'd be more than happy to sit for you.'

'Ach, no.' Annie shook her head. 'I can't practise on *you.* I mean, on somebody who'd be *paying* for it. That wouldn't be right.'

'Well, my stepfather will pay, and he left the choice of artist up to me. Oh, please, *do* say yes.'

'I don't think so,' she said, shortly. 'It's not necessary.'

Perhaps I had given the wrong impression. She seemed on guard, apparently having decided that I viewed her as a needy case. Ned smiled.

'Why not, dear?' he said. 'It's an excellent idea, a great opportunity. I really think it would be foolish to turn it down.'

'Really?' said his wife, and began to look doubtful. 'Well, it would be good to do some sustained work with a model.'

Thus, after a little further discussion, it was decided that my commission should go to Annie. I would sit for her once or twice a week – her household obligations, and art classes, permitting. Fortunately, my time was my own, and I was happy to fit in around the family's domestic requirements. Once the details were finalised, Annie settled on an old armchair in the corner and, taking needle and thread from her bag, she mended her bonnet, whilst Ned and I looked at his work. The artist paced the floor, pulling out canvases and drawings of various sizes for me to examine, whilst he stood back, puffing on his pipe. From time to time, the children ran in and out of the studio. Christina brought in the tea, and left. At one point, Sibyl marched into the centre of the room, stretched out her arms, and screamed at the top of her lungs, before marching out again. Neither of her parents seemed at all perturbed by this behaviour: Annie simply carried on sewing, while Ned continued to browse through a stack of canvases.

It seemed that Gillespie spent rather a lot of time painting his relatives, when he could persuade them to sit. Annie featured heavily, as did Sibyl and Mabel. Recalling the picture that I had seen at the Grosvenor, it dawned on me that I was standing at the very spot where it had been painted, and also, that it had been Annie who had posed, veiled, as the woman feeding the canary. I glanced around the attic, in search of a birdcage, but saw none; later, I learned that they had borrowed the cage, to create a focal point for the painting.

The selection of canvases that Ned showed me that afternoon also included some views of the Exhibition: his unsentimental sketches of Muratti's girls; a portrait of the two Venetian gondoliers who had been hired to row visitors up and down the River Kelvin; and several vibrant crowd scenes, at the bandstand, beside the Switchback Railway, and outside the Eastern Palace. In the end, however, I chose a small canvas that had nothing to do with the Exhibition, or with his family. *Stanley Street* was, simply, a view from the parlour window, showing a winter's day, and a few people hurrying along with umbrellas. Here was a picture with an arresting, urban quality, and it leapt out at me as honest, original and modern. Ned had all but forgotten the canvas, which had been propped against the wall, at the far end of the studio, but, having examined it for a few moments, I lifted it onto the table, saying: 'I do like this one.'

The artist laughed. 'That thing? Just an exercise I set myself one morning. I'm going to use that canvas for something else – scrape it off and paint over it.'

'Oh no!' I cried. 'You mustn't. This is a wonderful painting.'

Ned peered at it, sceptically, his head cocked to one side, to avoid the low roof. He was standing not a foot away from me, panting slightly from the exertion of hefting the larger frames (he was, it seemed, a little asthmatic). A few of the canvases were still damp, and the heady scent of poppy-seed oil rose up and joined with the lingering pipe smoke to envelop us, like a fragrant mist. I ran my fingers down the edge of the stretcher frame, the rough fabric tickling my flesh.

'This is my favourite,' I told him.

Annie glanced up, from her corner, and gave a tinkling little laugh. 'Who wants to look at a rainy day in Stanley Street?'

'Oh, I'm no connoisseur,' I told her. 'But I think this is a wonderful painting. And it would always be a reminder to me, of my time here, in Glasgow.' I turned to Ned. 'Presumably, this isn't one of the pictures you're working on for your submission to the Committee?'

'No-o,' he chortled.

'Then – please may I buy it? How much would you want for it?'

He shook his head. 'You're giving us quite enough, already, for the portrait. Take that one, for nothing – please. I'm just glad you like it.'

I realised that he was looking at me, with a quizzical smile on his face. Perhaps he was just amused at my choice of picture, but I like to think that there was also a certain amount of nascent camaraderie in that gaze.

The time for departure came all too soon. One moment we were absorbed in our discussion of his work, and the next Ned was glancing at his watch and exclaiming: 'Dear God! Ten past! Did you not have an appointment, Harriet?'

'What a pity – I was enjoying myself so much. I suppose I *could* be late . . .'

'Not at all, I won't hear of it. Now, do you have far to go?'

'Oh – no – just the park. I'm meeting someone.'

'Well, you'll not be wanting to lug that painting with you, will you – but if you're at home tomorrow, I'll wrap it up and send it round with the neighbour's boy – he's quite reliable.'

'Oh yes, that might be for the best – thank you, Ned! I'm at number 13.'

'Don't forget your hat and basket, there. Annie – are you coming, dear?'

As I gathered up my belongings, his wife slipped past us onto the landing and headed down. Ned and I followed, and we had just reached the turn of the staircase, when there was a shriek from the hallway, followed by the sound of juvenile lamentation. Ned peered over the banister.

'What now?' he muttered.

The reason for the fracas soon became clear: it was simply a continuation of the children's squabble about their ferns. The door to the dining room lay open, and Christina and the two girls stood inside the room. Sibyl was weeping, while Rose glared at her, accusingly, her face also begrimed with tears. The cause of their despair lay on the dining-room floor: Rose's blue pot smashed to smithereens, the earth scattered across the rug, her fern in shreds – while Sibyl's plant sat, pristine, on the dining table.

'Sibyl broke my pot!' cried Rose, as her parents and I came into view.

'I didn't!' shrieked the older girl.

Annie sighed. 'Oh, Sibyl – did you drop it by accident?

The child jumped up and down, wailing: 'NO! It wasn't me! I didn't do it!'

'Oh dear,' sighed Annie, putting her head in her hands. 'Whatever next?'

Clearly, she found her children – especially Sibyl – difficult to control. Ned went to his wife's side, and slipped his arm around her. She leaned against him, giving him a grateful, watery smile, and he kissed her, once, on the top of the head, and then on the cheek. After a moment, he gave Sibyl a kindly wink.

'It doesn't matter, Sibyl,' he told her. 'It's only a pot.'

The child ran to him, throwing her arms around his legs, and he swung her up into his arms, to embrace her.

I turned to little Rose. 'Your fern is beyond saving, dear. But I'm sure someone can find you another, tomorrow – no need to despair.' She gave me a winsome nod. I peered down at the mess on the rug. 'That china does look sharp,' I said. 'Be careful, Christina, when you pick it up. Perhaps, if I might suggest, a pair of gloves to protect your fingers.'

And so, by degrees, the household returned to a calmer state. Ned wandered back up to his studio, with Sibyl in his arms and Rose climbing the stairs in their wake, while Christina cleared up the mess, and Annie came with me to the door, where we said our farewells, and confirmed that our first portrait sitting should take place on the following Wednesday afternoon.

This incident with the fern might have been passed off as an accident, except for what happened later that evening. As the youngest person in the house, Rose slept in the smallest attic room, a little cupboard of a place, just next to the studio. There was only enough space for a child's mattress, a small chest of drawers, and a few toys. Apparently, at bedtime, a shard of blue china was discovered between Rose's sheets, just below her bolster. The fragment was sharp-edged and triangular, with three cruel, jagged points, and had it not been spotted (by the lynx-eyed Mabel, who had offered to read her niece a bedtime story), the child might have been lacerated, perhaps seriously injured, in the night.

It was only with the passing of time, and the unfolding of other, more horrible events, that the family began to wonder in earnest whether Sibyl might, in a rage, have smashed her sister's potted fern and then tiptoed upstairs to hide the nasty surprise in her bed. Admittedly, nobody had heard any disturbance that afternoon, which was mysterious, since the plant pot would have made quite a racket, were it thrown to the dining-room floor. But then, of course, everyone was otherwise engaged, and the culprit might easily have muffled any noise, perhaps by wrapping the pot in one end of the rug and then stamping hard upon it. The resulting sound would surely have been only a faint thud with – perhaps – a dim, ringing crack as the vessel came apart and fell into pieces. Shredding the fern itself would have been the business of a moment, conducted in silence. She must then have slipped out of the dining room, unnoticed, and crept upstairs to her sister's tiny room, where she tucked the vicious fragment between the bedclothes.

At least, such was how we supposed it might have happened, in retrospect.

Wednesday, 12 April 1933

LONDON

It occurs to me that I should, perhaps, say a few words about my current situation. For the past twenty years, I have resided, quietly and modestly, in the Bloomsbury area of London, on the fourth floor of a mansion block, within sight of a large garden square. I am not wealthy: a small inheritance – invested in things that would neither smash nor flourish – provides me with a moderate income. Forty years ago, my accountant informed me that, if I chose so to do, I could dine on chateaubriand and champagne, every day, from then, until my last gasp. However, I rather suspect that he did not envisage me surviving quite this long, and, for the past decade, I have been obliged to make a few economies.

Back in 1888, I remember bounding up and down to the Gillespies' apartment like a mountain goat but, these days, staircases are a challenge, and I am none too fond of the lift in this building, which is prone to breakdowns. Thus, life is lived, for the most part, within these walls. I venture out only infrequently, and tend to rely upon others to bring in what is needed. The local tradesmen deliver, and I have a regular order with Lockwood's, the grocer, across the street. In any case, my needs are few: although my health is generally good, and I am in possession of all my faculties, I am increasingly prone to heartburn, with the result that I eat like a bird. Thus, very little mess is generated, which cuts down on the housework, and means that I have no need for a maid. In any case, I have never been keen on maids; a good one is hard to find, and there is much truth in the old adage about domestic staff: 'seven years my servant, seven years my equal, seven years my master' – although, from experience and observation, I would reduce the cited seven years to three.

Alas, I am no longer quite able to deal with everything myself and so, as a compromise, I have been in the habit of employing a companion or assistant. Young girls have proved themselves to be unreliable and so, this time, I requested the employment agency to provide a person with a little more maturity. My current girl, Sarah, has been with me now for just over a month. I have tried to make her comfortable. She has her own bedroom, of course, and the use of a little sitting room at the end of the kitchen, overlooking the rear courtyard. In addition to keeping me company, and a few light household chores, she has, very kindly, undertaken to do some research, to help with my memoir: nothing too onerous, just a little checking of facts at the library. She spends one or two afternoons a week there, looking up references for me, and copying passages from various books and documents. Of course, in writing this account, I must rely upon my own recollections, for the most part. However, I find Sarah's notes useful for checking dates and so on. This kind of paperwork is, really, above and beyond her stated duties, but she seems not to mind – at least, as far as I can tell. So far, she has proved sturdily reliable, if a mite taciturn.

Companions tend to come and go, but the true fellow travellers of my twilight years are my lovely birds, a pair of oriental greenfinches. They live in a boxwood birdcage, which was bought, in Glasgow, many years ago; I am delighted to be able to put it to good use these days, and the sight of the bamboo slats and netsuke-type carvings are a constant reminder of my old friend Ned. The cage came from one of his favourite places: a little *japonais* curio shop on Sauchiehall Street, not far from where he resided. Ned had a great fondness for the exotic – hence he always paused to look in at the window of that shop. I cannot but think it a shame that, due to everything that happened, he never had the opportunity to see the cage complete with songbirds.

No doubt, he would have loved my greenfinches. They are petite, lively creatures, and very affectionate to each other, which is why I named them Layla and Majnun (or Maj, for short), after the lovers in the Arabic legend. They have been with me now for six or seven years. Maj, the male, is more brightly coloured, and his song is much sweeter. He sings all day long to his lady love, but mostly in the mornings and towards dusk. Indeed, I can hear him now, chirping away, as the light fades. Much as I adore Maj, he has been known to start singing before dawn, and so the cage is kept in the dining room, which is far enough along the corridor from my bedroom to minimise the early-morning disturbance. Other than that negligible problem, the finches are only a joy to behold. One often sees them preening each other and, occasionally, Maj will feed Layla as she begs, open mouthed, and flutters her wings, as though she were a chick. Quaint though it may sound, having observed them, closely, for several years, it is my belief that these two birds are truly in love. Sadly, they will insist, from time to time, on building a nest, using their own feathers, or any other materials gathered up from the floor of the cage (old apple peel gone leathery, or shreds of newspaper, and so on). I have to discourage them from breeding, as I have no desire to care for fledglings, and so, unfortunately, these little nests must be deconstructed as soon as they are built, otherwise the female will lay.

Last week, having given it some thought, I decided to allocate care of the greenfinches to Sarah. From now on, she is in charge of the daily feeding of the birds, the change of water, the cleaning, and so on. I am perfectly capable of doing that kind of thing by myself, but I can see that the finches give Sarah pleasure, and it is my surmise that her life has, thus far, been short on that very commodity. Moreover, I have become absorbed in the writing of this memoir, and I wish to devote all my energy to it. Of course, I will still look in on my avian friends, for half an hour, each afternoon, when it is my habit to shut the windows and allow them out of the cage to flit about the apartment. Layla likes to investigate corners, and hide behind things, whilst Maj is much more adventuresome and bold: I have even taught him to sit on my finger!

I am pleased to say that, so far, Sarah has responded well to caring for the birds. Indeed, she takes great pleasure in it. One would have to have a heart of stone not to empathise with this girl (I say 'girl': she must be fifty – and yet despite her years, there is something childlike about her). Admittedly, she has not, thus far, been very forthcoming; but one can tell, from her face – the lines between her brows, the set of her mouth, and an occasional flintiness about the eyes – that she has not had an easy life. In view of this, I am attempting to make her employment here as enjoyable as possible. She has plenty of time off: on Tuesday, she takes a half-day, and I have also given her Saturday evening and all of Sunday to do as she pleases. Since the museum is a short walk away, I encourage her to spend time there, and to take fresh air, en route, in the gardens. If I were her age, I would spend any spare hours at the cinema, but she seems to go only once a week, and prefers to stay in her little sitting room, sewing: she smokes Kensitas, and is making up a flowered quilt from the free silks. One of our daily rituals has evolved around the opening of each new packet of cigarettes, to see what flower is inside; I believe that we are still awaiting several species, including Petunia, Tea Rose and Violet.

This afternoon, she brought me a cup of tea in the sitting room, as usual, but instead of letting her go immediately, I asked her to stay for a moment, and indicated that she should sit down in the armchair that faces mine. Sarah gave the chair a glance and then looked at me. Her expression was difficult to read, but, sensing that she was apprehensive, I was quick to reassure her: 'Don't worry! I'm very happy with your work. I just thought we might have a little talk.'

'Oh.' She perched on the chair, and sat there, rigidly, with her hands clasped together. 'Only, will it take long?'

'No, no!' I told her, with a laugh. 'Not long at all. Would you care for some tea? Do fetch yourself a cup, if you so desire.'

'No, thank you.'

She was not frowning, exactly, but her brow was heavy. Despite the heat, she wore a long-sleeved cardigan, buttoned to the throat. Her top lip was beaded with perspiration, the result of her efforts in the kitchen.

'I'd just like to know how you're settling in.'

'Well enough, I suppose.'

'Your room is comfortable? Not too stuffy? The mattress – it's not too hard?'

'No, it's fine.'

'And your duties – how are you coping with them?'

'Not too bad.'

'You don't find them onerous?'

'Can't say as I do.'

'Well, that's good.'

There was a pause. I smiled at her, even though I myself was now quite ill at ease. She had voiced no complaints, and yet something about her responses gave me the impression that she was not entirely happy. She also made me feel that – by asking these questions – I was fussing too much. I tried again.

'Sarah, is there something, perhaps, that you might want to ask me?'

She gazed at me, blankly, and then, at length, said: 'No, I don't think so. Excepting . . . well, shouldn't I change the birds' water now? Only I ought to do it before I make a start on the supper.'

'Ah – yes, of course. Do – do go ahead.'

With that, she surged to her feet and plodded out of the room. There seems to be rather a lot going on, under the surface, but I suppose that I should take her at her word, and accept that she is getting on well enough. Sometimes, I get the distinct impression that she disapproves of me. I suspect that she might be less pleasant to me were I not so advanced in years. However, she is obliged to be nice: I have diplomatic immunity; I am almost eighty years of age!

II

June – August 1888

GLASGOW

5

Perhaps here is as good a place as any to say something of Ned Gillespie's early life, about which I learned as I became acquainted with his family. The artist was born in 1856, and grew up in a tiny cottage in the village of Maryhill. His childhood was dominated by the financial problems of his father, Cecil, the son of a tenant farmer, who struggled for many years to pay off debtors while he established his store on Great Western Road: 'Gillespie's Wool and Hosiery'. As a small boy, Ned shared a cramped bedroom with his siblings, and although he demonstrated an early talent for drawing and painting, there was no money for him to study art, or to enrol in an *atelier*; indeed, I suspect that such a thing would have been unthinkable, back then, to his penny-plain parents – simple folk, with (it must be said) conventional opinions about what might be a fitting occupation for their son. Thus, Ned began his working life at the age of fifteen, in the shop, as his father's assistant. Once Cecil's debts were finally paid off, he was able to move his family out of the cottage (which was soon to be demolished), and into a main-door house in Stanley Street.

With a room of his own for the first time (albeit in a dingy basement), Ned started to paint in earnest, whenever he could, and later, aged twenty-one, he enrolled at the School of Art, in early-morning classes that had been laid on for working men who were unable to study full-time. On six days a week, this courageous young man would rise before dawn to attend the Art School, after which he would put in a full day's work, lugging crates, and selling pincushions and hose. A few years later, he met Annie when she sat for one of his classes (having been orphaned at the age of sixteen, she had been obliged to seek work as a life model). They married when Ned was twenty-five, and she was eighteen.

Annie gave up modelling, and they set up home at number 11, just across the street from Ned's family. The following year, Sibyl was born, and a year after that, Cecil Gillespie passed away. By this time, Kenneth was at work in the store, alongside Ned. After their father's death, the brothers decided to diversify, and began to sell a wider range of stock: alongside the wool and hose, they introduced fancy goods, small tools, and a few gardening implements.

In the interim, Ned painted and worked, and worked and painted. At last, in the mid-1880s, at about the time of Rose's birth, he had a minor artistic breakthrough: a few of his canvases were chosen for local exhibitions, and one or two were sold. Having accumulated a modicum of savings, in case of emergencies, he decided to risk surviving by his art alone; and so, in early 1887, Ned Gillespie employed an assistant, Miss MacHaffie, to take his place, and he quit working in the family shop – although he maintained control of the finances. Thus, when we first met, he had been a full-time artist for scarcely a year.

Ned's background could scarcely have been more different from mine, and yet he and I had an enormous amount in common, in matters of Taste and Aesthetics, and in our outlook on Society. He and I were nearly the same age; only a few years separated us: moreover, I was born on the 20th of April, and he on the 21st of May, and the relationship of these numbers has always appealed to me, since I feel that there is something significant in the progression of both day and month of our births.

Initially, it was from Elspeth and Mabel that I learned about Ned and the rest of the family, since Annie was, by nature, less forthcoming. In the early days of my portrait sittings with her, I did attempt to pass the time by making conversation. However, her monosyllabic replies to my questions, and her apparent lack of desire to initiate any discussion, soon deterred me.

Having decided to extend my stay in Glasgow, I had made various arrangements, opening an account with the National Bank of Scotland, and committing to rent my rooms for a further three months, with the option to remain for longer, should I choose so to do. I ended up spending a good deal of time at the Gillespie residence over the course of that summer, sitting for my portrait once or twice a week, provided that Annie's other commitments would allow. The area in front of the parlour windows was fairly bright, and so that is where we set up our little makeshift studio. Annie's husband could usually be found upstairs, working on his paintings for presentation to the Committee members who would award the Royal Commission. Apparently, these gentlemen wished to see three canvases from each of the artists under consideration, and would make their decision after a private view, some time in August. Ned was concentrating on a large-scale picture of the Eastern Palace, which he hoped to finish in time. There was something cosy about having him so close at hand, painting away, whilst Annie and I were similarly engaged, down in the parlour, as she made some early sketches of me: we were quite the little Fine Art factory. However, I never felt entirely at ease, particularly since Annie worked in silence, with a scowl on her face, and her charcoal often made angry, scratching noises against the paper.

Now and again, the artist would call his wife upstairs to consult her opinion on some aspect of his work and, whenever – on his way in or out of the apartment – he happened to pop his head around the door to ask a question, or to let us know the hour of his return, he was always kind and encouraging about her progress with my portrait. He would give me a cheerful 'good afternoon', and, on occasion, pause to chat with us, and with whoever else happened to be in the parlour at the time. As the weeks progressed, I became familiar with his various quirks of character. His little sniff, for instance (he always forgot his handkerchief); his full-throated laugh; and his lack of personal vanity. I do believe that every single cuff in his possession was scribbled upon, as a result of those occasions when he had found himself without a notebook; he was always paint-speckled, of course, and the children left their sticky traces on him, on his clothes, in the form of various unsavoury smears and stains.

I suspect that Ned would never have shaved or trimmed his moustaches, or even eaten a meal, were he not prompted to do so by one or other of the Gillespie women. Such worldly matters hardly seemed to occur to him. Like many men, he had an enviable ability to become absorbed in his work, to the exclusion of all else. Usually, he was so involved in painting that he forgot to notice the passage of time, with the result that he was rarely punctual for engagements. He would, absent-mindedly, set out to walk to his destination at the very hour when he was meant to *arrive* there, and yet he always expressed astonishment at being late.

Number 11 was, without doubt, a very lively home, and we were not often left to our own devices. Several front-door keys were in circulation, which meant that the rest of the family – who resided across the street – were constantly breezing in and out, unannounced. Elspeth seemed to treat the apartment as an annexe of her own parlour, and would descend upon us, full of chatter, after church or en route to Duke Street gaol, where she was a member of the Visit Committee. Mabel's visits to see her brother were also frequent. That summer, she was at a loose end, tormented by the dissolution of her engagement, and needy, which meant that Ned – a sympathetic listener – would have to put aside his work to hear her tales of woe. Ned's brother Kenneth tended to call in on his way back from the Wool and Hosiery – expressly, it seemed, to over-stimulate his nieces before bed-time – and Walter Peden was a regular afternoon guest, scuttling upstairs to the studio with such frequency that he might as well have built himself a nest in the linen cupboard.

Of course, Annie was required to accommodate these callers, in the parlour, if necessary, and she had to set aside her paint-brush in order to provide refreshments, whenever her maid was nowhere to be found: an all-too-frequent occurrence. Christina usually claimed, upon return, to have 'just dashed out to the grocer's'. However, a moment's observation of the girl's conduct was enough to confirm that she never 'dashed' anywhere. On the contrary, she was frequently to be seen dawdling about the neighbourhood, talking with other women in the street, and – although I made no mention of it to Annie – I myself had witnessed her, on more than one occasion, emerging from a squalid public house on St George's Road. Annie was afraid of Christina, I believe, which is why the girl had never been taken to task or dismissed.

With this feckless maid, and a demanding, extended family, it was small wonder that Annie made slow progress on my portrait. Indeed, for the first few weeks, she did nothing more than make sketches of me in different poses until she found one that she liked. Only then – and only gradually – did she progress to painting on canvas. Mercifully, we took frequent breaks, and the pose was not too difficult to maintain: I was seated, with my elbows resting on the arms of the chair, and my hands clasped together in my lap. Annie positioned herself so that I was in three-quarter profile. She asked me to refrain from smiling, and requested that, so far as possible, I think of nothing. Of course, I have an active mind – even now! But I tried not to let my thoughts affect my expression, and I believe that I became quite skilled at this. Annie had no qualms about showing me her work and, as the weeks went by, I found it intriguing to watch the progress of the portrait, from charcoal sketch, to vague blocks of colour, until a recognisable figure finally began to emerge from the shadows.

Although she would never have admitted it, I could tell that Ned's wife longed to be an artist of merit. She was always disappointed if forced, for some domestic reason, to miss her drawing class, and I believe that she would have attended more lessons, had she not been so busy looking after house and home. I am a great supporter of females who try to do something out of the ordinary, and felt nothing but sympathy for Annie in her artistic ambitions. However, I do not scruple to say that, at times, she was abrupt with me; not to mention all that scowling while she worked, and the way that she sometimes slashed at the canvas with her brush. I did wonder, for a while, whether there was some unflattering explanation for her lack of warmth: was I proving to be too difficult a subject, for instance? However, in the end, I came to the conclusion that Annie simply preferred to be quiet while she worked, and thereafter, I gave up trying to engage her interest and contented myself with observing the comings and goings of the household.

On the surface, the Gillespies did seem like a fairly stable family. However, ere long, I began to see beneath the façade, and to realise that, particularly with regard to Sibyl, cracks were beginning to show.

Perhaps it should be no surprise that the children were the cause of most disruption in the household. Unless Elspeth or Mabel had been kind enough to take the girls for the afternoon, their mother and I were obliged to watch over them during our sittings. I believe that Annie would have been quite happy to send her daughters out every day, to roam around the neighbourhood, as all the local children did, and much as she herself had done, as a child. Given what happened, in the end, I am ashamed to say that I was always rather grateful when, patience exhausted, she shooed the girls outside. However, Ned was never very keen on sending his daughters into the street, unsupervised. He preferred that his wife (or someone else) accompany them if they ever ventured into the back green, or around the corner, to their favourite spot, the little gardens in front of my lodgings in Queen's Crescent, the gates of which were usually left open. Annie did not always have time to set aside her housework in order to take the children out to play, with the result that her husband's wishes were only infrequently carried out.

Besides, the little girls were a nosy pair, and whenever visitors such as myself were present, they showed scant inclination to leave the apartment for fear that they might miss something. Annie usually tried to persuade them to play in other rooms, or asked Christina to keep an eye on them, but they never stayed away for long. All too soon, Sibyl would come mincing back into the parlour, and I confess that my heart would sink as she slid onto the piano stool. For a moment or two, she would make a pretence of idly tinkling at the keys, but this was only ever a preamble to a prolonged session of showing off. Alas, Elspeth kept discovering more Spirituals with which to impress her American pastor, and so – trapped, immobile, in my seated pose, a few feet away from the piano – I became very familiar with these never-ending hymns and others, such as 'I Wish I Were an Angel' and 'Where is Now the Prophet Daniel?' I am not sure which I grew to dread more: the disquieting, gloomy looks that Sibyl would cast at me, intermittently, over her shoulder, or the requirement, every so often, to make appreciative noises in response to her playing.

At some point, Rose would come tottering back to the parlour in her sister's wake, and – since the two children could not be together for long without ending up at loggerheads – the squabbling would soon commence. Despite being the older child, Sibyl was usually the initiator of trouble. I soon grew to realise that Rose was, in many ways, a more lovable, less troublesome child. Sadly, the fact that her sister had a sunnier disposition only made Sibyl's antics worse.

Plainly, the Gillespies' elder daughter had always been a problem, but as the summer weeks drew on, it became evident that her behaviour was beginning to escalate beyond control. Back in May, there had been signs of this – for example, in the incident with the broken plant pot. Then, one day, Annie mislaid her straw hat, which reappeared the following morning, shredded, in the coal scuttle. A few days later, several pieces of Rose's miniature china tea service turned up, under the parlour sofa, smashed to bits. And, a week after that, when the water closet flooded, Annie's apron was found, stuffed down the trap of the lavatory.

Pity the poor parents of such a wayward child! Admittedly, Sibyl's outrages were usually directed against the females of the household, and – although Rose's and Christina's belongings sometimes came under attack – thus far, it was Annie who had borne the brunt of her daughter's wickedness. Perhaps some feminine Oedipus attitude was in operation. Sibyl envied her mother's relationship with dear Papa, of that I have no doubt: Mama slept in his bed, and carried out the wifely duties, and brought him his slippers, and was his everyday companion, and so on – and this, I imagine, drove the little girl mad with jealousy.

Matters only grew worse, in July, when Sibyl's school closed for the summer and her teachers, the Misses Walkinshaw, left on their annual trip to Florence. With the child at home all day long, it was even harder to keep her out of mischief. That same week, scribbled drawings began to appear on the walls of number 11. Then, one morning, Annie picked up Rose's shoes, only to discover that the entire contents of the pin box had been tipped inside them: thank goodness that the child was too young to dress herself, otherwise she might have pricked her wee foot.

The following evening, Elspeth was on her way to visit the apartment when she noticed several unopened tubes of paint lying in the street. Assuming that these belonged to her son, she gathered them up and brought them inside. In fact, the paints had been a gift, from myself to Annie: I had only recently presented them to her. According to Elspeth, they were scattered on the pavement outside the building, as though they had been hurled, in a temper, from the parlour window. I happened to be there when Annie confronted Sibyl with this latest misdemeanour, sitting her on the piano stool to question her. In response to Annie's accusations, the child's eyes narrowed, and I must admit that I found it disquieting to see the horrid change that came over her face. She hunched her shoulders, clenched her jaw, and adopted an expression of such extreme malevolence as she gazed back at her poor mother that I found myself getting quite cross, on Annie's behalf.

'Please tell the truth, dear,' she pleaded with her daughter. 'Tell the truth and shame the Devil. Did you throw the paints out the window?'

But come what may, Sibyl refused to admit her guilt, and she grew increasingly hostile until, eventually, she threw herself down upon the floor and erupted into a screaming tantrum that was almost frightening to behold.

Later that week, in another, more sinister development, the scribbles on the wall began to change. To begin with, they had been simple childish doodles. However, as time went on, the drawings became more disturbing. Both girls had access to crayons, but Sibyl was the more likely culprit since she was known as the troublemaker, and the drawings were apparently too sophisticated to have been executed by her sister. On one memorable occasion, when Annie had gone to fetch something from the kitchen, I heard her gasp and, upon her return to the parlour, she did admit that she had come across something horrible that one of the children had scribbled on the wall. Whatever it was, she must have washed it away immediately, for when I took our teacups through to the sink only a few minutes later, I saw no drawing, only a damp patch on the plaster where one might have been, and I was left to wonder what form this horrid scribble might have taken.

It so happened that, towards the end of the month, I did witness one such scrawl, during a portrait session with Annie. The weather had been cold and damp for a few days, but we had heaped up the fire and made ourselves quite cosy in the parlour. Upstairs in the studio, Ned was working on his *Eastern Palace*, which he hoped would be finished in time to submit to the Selection Committee. My portrait had also made some progress: Annie had begun to tackle the complicated folds of my skirts. Now that she had settled down to working in oils, she seemed more focused and self-assured, but she did look tired, perhaps because of the problems with Sibyl. That afternoon was dull and cloudy. I seem to remember that we had just gone back to work, after one of our rest breaks, and Annie was pacing back and forth, glancing over at my position, as she usually did, to check that my skirts were correctly draped, when, of a sudden, the sun came out, and a blast of light illuminated one side of the room. Annie paused, in the act of wiping her brush, and a strange expression transformed her face. I realised that, instead of studying my pose, she was gazing beyond me, at the corner, near the window. She looked positively alarmed.

As I turned to see what had caught her attention, she swept past my chair and, crouching down at the skirting board, began to rub at the wall with her cloth.

'What is it?' I asked.

'Nothing,' she said, sharply. 'Just a mark on the wall.'

The 'mark', as she called it, was executed in red and black pastel crayon. Presumably, to avoid alarming me, Annie had endeavoured to shield it from my view, but I caught a glimpse of it, over her shoulder. What I saw can only be described as obscene. It was a crude drawing, about the size of a small marrow, boldly executed, and yet, clearly, the work of a child. I found myself chilled to the bone at the thought that a little girl could have produced such an explicit image.

Perhaps, up to that point, I had failed to realise how grave the situation with Sibyl had become. Although I had overheard Elspeth and Mabel discussing Sibyl's new habit of defacing the walls, I had not realised that what she scribbled would be so brutish and disturbing. However, the sight of that drawing convinced me that the child ought to be brought under control, as quickly as possible.

I suspected that Mabel would have disciplined Sibyl more severely than either of the parents, since she pulled disapproving faces whenever her niece misbehaved – or, indeed, when Annie nursed Rose – and she was the only person who really insisted on keeping the children out of the studio, although, paradoxically, Mabel herself was always up there, talking to her brother. On several occasions, when we had been left alone in the parlour at number 11, she had wasted no time in speaking with me, quite openly, about herself, her broken engagement, and her family. Initially, I had found it hard to warm to Ned's sister, with her puzzling blend of personality traits: she seemed well intentioned, yet pugnacious; sanctimonious, yet confiding. Although she was often abrupt, one could not help but admire her forthright attitude. I soon came to the conclusion that her self-righteous demeanour was the result of having been ignored as a child. Not only did Elspeth, like many mothers, prefer her sons, but her every waking hour was devoted to the coming of God's Kingdom on Earth; to charitable works; and to the various waifs, strays and exotic personages that she collected from around the globe, her particular favourite being the Jews, whom she believed ought to be first in line for conversion to Christianity, which accounted for her initial interest in *me*, when she had assumed that I was Jewish. It did not take much imagination to picture Ned's sister as a child, overshadowed by her brothers, neglected, whilst her mother entertained a multi-hued houseful of guests: Negro evangelists, pallid Polish Jews, olive-skinned Rajahs, dusky Moslem pedlars and all manner of Western missionaries. I had concluded that what Mabel lacked was attention, she yearned to be listened to, and taken seriously. With this in mind, I made it my habit to consult her advice on all things. I sought her counsel on where to find the finest grocer's, and on how I should best pin my hair. She was, at first, I believe, a trifle suspicious; but ultimately, much too opinionated to refrain from giving me the benefit of her wisdom. I made sure to act promptly upon her recommendations, and always congratulated her excellent taste or admirable sense – and, in this way, she began to warm to me.

One afternoon, she joined me at Queen's Crescent, for coffee, which I had taken up drinking on her recommendation. Although Mabel and I had been in the same company together on several previous occasions, this was, I believe, the first time that we had arranged to meet, alone: a crucial milestone in female friendship, as you may be aware, and one at which all might be forever lost, should the general atmosphere not achieve a correct and harmonious (yet somehow indefinable) balance of warmth and mutual respect. Regrettably, I was obliged to maintain a sense of humour that afternoon, since Ned's sister was in a sniffy mood to begin with, and made little effort to endear herself. As soon as she arrived, she found fault with the fabric of the curtains in my sitting room; and then she implied that the view from my window was not quite as attractive as one might have expected; my choice of coffee beans failed to meet with her unmitigated approval; and at the table, she made a great performance of selecting a biscuit, which she then scrutinised, doubtfully, before finally discarding it onto her plate, uneaten.

'I see you don't share Elspeth's sweet tooth,' I said, in an effort to engage her. 'You're so slender in comparison. I'd never take you for mother and daughter.'

'Really?'

'Not at all! And besides, you and Elspeth seem so different.'

'Do we?'

The scowl disappeared; her face brightened: it was as if the sun had peeked through the scullery window, unexpectedly, to put a gleam on the pots and pans.

'Yes indeed!' I cried, sensing that I was onto something. (Of course, poor dear, she loved her mama, but this love was combined, as is so often the case in daughters, with a deep-seated desire to be as different from her as possible.) 'Presumably you and she do not have the same tendency to gain weight; and as for character – well, in some respects, you and your mother are like night and day!'

'Oh, I do gain weight,' said Mabel, unable to resist contradicting me. 'Unless I'm very careful about what I eat. But I have indeed often thought that Mother and I are quite different, temperamentally.'

'Exactly! And is that not often the case? Annie and Sibyl, for instance –'

'Och, Sibyl!' said Mabel, and cast her eyes towards the ceiling.

'She is a handful,' I agreed. 'These terrible drawings . . .'

Mabel shook her head in disgust. As it transpired, she was of the opinion that an investigation should be conducted at Sibyl's school, to see if any of the other children might be leading her astray. It was a mixed school, with (according to Mabel) a very rough set of boys. However, since all the pupils and teachers had dispersed for the summer, any enquiry in that arena would have to wait.

'How on earth does Ned concentrate on his work?' I asked her. 'Sibyl is up in the studio bothering him most of the time now she's on holiday.'

'Och, I know! We do try to keep her out, myself especially.'

'When I was a child, I wasn't allowed to set foot in my step-father's study.'

'Of course not!' said Mabel. 'A man needs somewhere quiet to do his work.'

'I remember once, when I was about Sibyl's age, I crept in there, while he was upstairs with my mother. He had a collection of kaleidoscopes, you see, that I was curious about. I tiptoed in, and picked one up, and then – suddenly – I heard him coming back downstairs and heading towards the study.'

'Oh dear!' said Mabel.

'Yes, I got such a fright, I dropped the kaleidoscope with a clatter, and some of the paint chipped off. My stepfather came bounding in and when he saw what I'd done, he drew back his fist and punched me in the stomach, as though he might have punched a grown man – so hard, in fact, that he lifted me clean off my feet, and I flew into the air and – rather comically, I think – bounced right off the windowpane.'

'Mercy me!'

'Oh, the glass didn't break, thankfully, I just bounced off. Landed on my own two feet and scampered out of the room as fast as my little legs would carry me.'

We both laughed.

'That was that,' I said. 'Not that I ever minded being hit, and I forgot all about what happened that day, for years, so it can't have done me any harm. But, as you can imagine, I never went near his study again. He could smoke his cigars in there in peace, and think great thoughts about business, without being bothered.'

'Quite.'

'Talking of cigarettes . . .'

I produced one, and proceeded to light it, an act that caused Mabel to hoot with laughter, since I had never previously smoked in her presence. She was shocked, of course, but too proud to show it, hence her forced amusement.

'Harriet – you're *smoking*?'

'Oh yes, I've done it for years. Recently, I've found it goes very well with coffee. And it allows one to skip meals, without ever going hungry.'

'Is that so?' said Mabel, and her gaze fell, with a certain amount of fresh interest, upon the cigarette box.

I blew out a long stream of smoke.

'Of course, I wouldn't suggest that they box Sibyl's ears, not for a moment, but perhaps she needs to be discouraged, more firmly.'

'Yes, indeed,' agreed Mabel. 'I've always maintained they ought to discipline her in some way, so that she knows the difference between right and wrong.'

Unlike Mabel, Ned's mother – no doubt relishing her role as sole grandparent – was inclined to spoil the children. Of course, Elspeth herself required veneration and attention much as others require air to breathe, but she liked to be seen to dote on the girls, particularly Sibyl who, as the firstborn – and, arguably, the prettier child – was her favourite. Perhaps she also felt some guilt at having ignored her own offspring while they were growing up, and compensated for this by being an over-indulgent grand-mama. She fussed over Sibyl, with hugs, kisses, and shrieks of delight – perhaps in the knowledge that such a charming 'tableau of the generations' was bound to attract admiring glances from anyone present. Naturally, most of the admiration was directed at the child, but Elspeth was more than content to bask in the reflected glow. Needless to say, she never scolded Sibyl, and did all that she could to remain in the child's favour.

By contrast, Annie did try to be firm with her daughter, but Sibyl merely had to throw a prolonged and terrifying tantrum in order to get her own way. Ned tended to be even more indulgent than his wife, so that, unfortunately, the two parents often contradicted each other. For instance, Annie might spend all afternoon denying Sibyl more sweet things to eat, only for Ned to give her some Coulter's Candy, in an attempt to stop her whining. Annie did *try* to keep the girl out of his studio, but the artist himself would often crumble before Sibyl's pleading, and invite her in, and then we would hear her leaping around up there like a little flea, pestering him, and keeping him from his work. No matter how great Ned's powers of concentration, his darling Sibyl always found it easy to distract him.

As for Ned's brother Kenneth, he seemed blithely unaware that Sibyl was a problem. Indeed, her behaviour was worse whenever he was involved. I suspect that she had a childish infatuation with him. She always became very unruly during his visits, and if he failed to focus on her at all times, or made the mistake of trying to talk to anybody else, she would jump up and down, feverishly, calling out his name, over and over: 'Kenneth! Uncle Kenneth! Kenneth!' until he gave her his full attention. She always looked forward to seeing him, but Ned's brother was not the most reliable character. When not at work, he frequented the bars and cafeterias in the park and, sometimes, he made promises to visit Sibyl that he failed to keep. On these occasions, she would wait for him, impatiently, before slumping into melancholy when she realised that he was not going to put in an appearance. Then, she would become fractious and tearful, and it was only a matter of time before she would resort to mischief, out of spite.

If only we had known then what the future held in store, then one of us might have acted more promptly. After our conversation over coffee, Mabel did try to persuade Annie to take a harder line with Sibyl, even suggesting that they might bring in some sort of expert in nervous diseases to examine the child. However, Annie seemed to take fright at this notion, and told her sister-in-law to say no more on the subject, particularly to Ned. He would have been alarmed to hear Mabel's idea about consulting a doctor, and Annie did not wish him to be upset in any way while he was working on his submissions for the Fine Art Committee. Thus, the question of addressing Sibyl's misbehaviour was brushed under the carpet.

Of course, as a recent acquaintance, it would have been inappropriate for me to pass comment to the Gillespies on how they dealt with their daughter, and so I kept my thoughts to myself but, as far as I could see, Kenneth was one of the worst influences on Sibyl. Such was the pleasure he took in over-exciting the child that it occurred to me that he might even have taught her to execute those nasty drawings.

6

My curiosity about Kenneth began to be aroused, one fine afternoon, whilst I was sitting for my portrait. Ned was upstairs in
his studio, still working on his *Eastern Palace,* and Annie had
sent the children to play around the corner, in the gardens of
Queen's Crescent. The portrait was nearing completion: my
skirts were done, and Annie had begun the difficult work on the
fine detail of face and hands. We were taking advantage of the
unaccustomed tranquillity to work in peace, when the doorbell
rang. Miraculously, Christina, the maid, was in evidence, and
she ran downstairs to admit the visitor, who turned out to be
Walter Peden, calling to see Ned. As was his wont, he stopped
off in the parlour on his way up to the studio, and – in the course
of conversation with Annie – he happened to mention a rumour
that he had heard.

Apparently, the artist and caricaturist Mungo Findlay was at
work on a vignette of Ned. Over the past few months, to coincide
with the Exhibition, Findlay had produced a series of irreverent
sketches depicting local painters, and these had been published in
The Thistle, a Glasgow weekly paper, rival to *The Bailie* and *Quiz.*
For the most part, Findlay's caricatures were harmless enough.
However, the less well disposed he was to his subject, the more
mocking the portrayal. For instance, his drawing of Lavery had
been particularly merciless, not so much in any exaggeration of
the man's features, but in the way that his self-importance was
satirised. According to Peden, the vignette of Ned was, as yet,
unfinished, but was due to be published in a mid-August edition
of the magazine. In some respects, inclusion in this *Thistle* series
was flattering, since it meant that the featured artist had, to a certain extent, made his mark upon the world of Scottish Art. The

fact that Ned was considered important enough to be depicted ought to have been a cause for celebration. None the less, much depended upon how he was portrayed. The timing was hardly fortuitous, since the caricature would be published just before the Committee met to make its decision about the Royal Commission, and if Findlay's portrayal was unflattering, it could be an embarrassment to Ned.

Peden had heard these rumours from a friend who was vaguely acquainted with Mungo Findlay – or 'Old Findlaypops' as Peden insisted upon calling him – though it is my surmise that they had never met, since it was Walter's habit to concoct jolly soubriquets for persons he barely knew, in order to imply a social intimacy that did not, in fact, exist. For instance, he insisted upon calling me Hetty.

'It's not just Ned in the vignette,' Peden told us. 'Kenneth also features.'

'Kenneth!' exclaimed Annie. 'I thought these were sketches of artists?'

'This time, it's something different: an artist and his brother.'

Annie frowned. 'Is there a caption? What does it say?'

I suspect that Peden would have danced at her, except that he was stretched out on the sofa, where he had thrown himself upon his arrival. Instead, he moved his shoulders from side to side and gave his nose a knowing tap. He was clearly enjoying his role as bearer of important news.

'Ah-ha! Old Findlaypops is keeping very quiet about it.'

'But why is Kenneth in it, at all?'

Despite her questions, Peden was unable to provide us with further details. His friend had not seen the caricature, having simply overheard Findlay bragging, dropping hints that his depiction of Kenneth would throw light on something scandalous. I wondered what sort of scandal Ned's brother could be involved in. All manner of worrying alternatives passed through my mind: an *affaire de cœur* – perhaps with a married lady? Was he a gambler? An eater of opium?

Annie also seemed apprehensive. 'Can't we see it before it appears?'

'I doubt it. He tends not to show his sketches until publication. We must just wait and see, Mrs G. All will be revealed next month.'

'How very mysterious,' I said.

'Yes, indeed, Hetty! You see – that's just what Findlaypops is like. You never know what the old scoundrel will come up with next.'

Annie sighed, and chewed her lip. She was already worn down by Sibyl's misbehaviour, and all this cryptic nonsense was clearly unsettling her. If only Peden would be quiet. I gazed at him.

'Would I be correct in saying, Walter, that – normally, if it weren't for the Exhibition – you would be spending the entire summer far away from here, and that you wouldn't return to Glasgow until the winter?'

'Indeed. It's my habit to spend the summer at Cockburnspath, or Kirkcudbright. Why do you ask?'

'Oh – no reason,' said I, lightly.

Clearly, the man was bored out of his wits, which made him more tiresome and gossipy than he might ordinarily have been. It occurred to me that what he really needed was a wife: but he was so awkward in his dealings with women that the prospect of matrimony seemed unlikely. Thank goodness, he soon went upstairs to see Ned, leaving me alone with Annie, whose forehead was still puckered by the frown that had settled there ever since Peden had mentioned Kenneth. She took up her brush and began to move it up and down as though applying colour to the canvas, although I suspected that she was only pretending to paint.

Since becoming acquainted with the family, I had noticed that Annie and her brother-in-law were quite close. She was nearer to him in age than she was to her husband: only three months separated Annie's birthday from Kenneth's. They were always in cahoots together. One would, on occasion, catch them exchanging 'significant' glances, and I had seen them, a few times, laughing behind their hands at jokes that were rarely shared with the general company. Obviously, this news about Kenneth and the caricature had upset Annie. But why should that be? Did she know something that the rest of us did not?

Hoping to draw her out, I mentioned that I had recently encountered Kenneth at the Exhibition, looking troubled. This was not exactly accurate: I had seen him on the river path, but, in truth, he had been walking along with great insouciance, hurling stones into the water. However, by suggesting that he seemed unhappy, I was hoping to make her more conversable.

'It was very strange,' I told her. 'He walked straight past, without even noticing me. I wonder what was on his mind; he seemed so lost in thought.'

'He probably didn't see you,' said Annie.

'He looked almost haunted. Is he terribly prone to mood swings?'

'Not really.'

'I saw him go into the Cocoa House – he seems to spend a lot of time there, chatting with the waitresses.'

Annie gave a shrug of her shoulders.

'Good gracious!' I cried. 'I think we may have touched on his secret!'

She looked startled. 'What do you mean?'

'A clandestine romance – with a Van Houten's girl!' Annie laughed, and then, blushing slightly, leaned in to peer more closely at her canvas, thereby concealing her face. I persevered, somewhat clumsily. 'Perhaps they've been careless and she's in trouble . . .'

'Oh, I don't think it's any of our business, do you?' said Annie, and then, rather abruptly, she ended our session, claiming that she was too tired, that afternoon, to continue any longer.

Next day, as previously arranged, I accompanied Elspeth to the General Gordon Buffet, where she bought me an Indian curry luncheon, a treat with which she had been threatening me ever since I had rescued her from suffocation by her teeth. During our meal of many fiery dishes, I made a few discreet enquiries about Kenneth and his habits; but, on that particular afternoon, it was difficult to steer Ned's mother away from the subject of the state visit and the Queen's portrait. Elspeth had heard a rumour that the commissioners desired the painting to depict not only Her Majesty but also two hundred and fifty local dignitaries and officials, amongst whom the Fine Art Committee themselves would, no doubt, prominently feature. The widow Gillespie enjoyed getting hot and bothered, and here was something to get hot and bothered about.

'Over two hundred faces, Herriot! And they must all be painted accurately!'

'That is rather a lot,' I agreed. 'If Ned gets the commission, perhaps Kenneth could help him. Can Kenneth paint? What are his talents? Do tell me about him.'

'Kenneth? Och, he's no artist. No, Ned would have to do it by himself; he'd still be at it on his deathbed. Of course, painting Her Majesty would be an honour – but two hundred and fifty sets of whiskers, all got up in their sporrans and robes, all desperate to be in the picture!'

We were both in agreement that such grand-scale portraits are often more interesting for their topicality than for any contribution towards great Art. However, a commission to paint royalty was not to be sniffed at, since everyone from butchers' wives to baronets would pay through the nose to have their likeness painted by Her Majesty's portraitist; and with (say) half-a-dozen such lucrative canvases per year, Ned would be able to pursue his own, more interesting work, in between. Elspeth was sensible enough to realise that such a commission could be a turning point in her son's career and she was, as ever, admirably enthusiastic in her support of him, but, in the absence of any real knowledge of the way things are achieved in the Art World, her suggestions as to how he should go about being selected by the Committee struck me as rather fanciful.

'He must get his bank manager to recommend him. Or some-body more important should write a letter on his behalf – the Lord Provost! Sir James – no – I have it! Not James King, but the Queen!' She banged her fist on the table. 'He must show the Queen his paintings, and she *herself* will recommend him for the job!'

'Yes,' I said. 'But, perhaps, meeting the Queen might be diffi-cult to orchestrate. What about Kenneth? Does he know anyone of importance, who could help – perhaps one of his customers at the shop?'

Elspeth shook her head. 'Och, Kenneth doesn't know anybody. No, I think Ned should write a nice letter to the Queen. Or – no! Perhaps we can get the Provost to write to the Queen, on his behalf! Yes, that's it!'

And so on and so forth – at any rate, I learned no more about Kenneth from his mother.

After we had finished our luncheon, Elspeth bustled off and – finding myself at a loose end – I decided, on the spur of the moment, to take up knitting. In search of the requisites of my new avocation, I called in at the Wool and Hosiery on Great Western Road. Of course, this was the Gillespies' store, where Ned's brother worked, and although I was indeed eager to begin my new knitting adventure, I must admit that there was a sec-ondary motive for my visit. I was interested to see Kenneth on his own territory, as it were, outside the family circle. Unfortunately, when I went into the shop that day, there was no sign of him, and I found myself discussing needles and yarn, at great length, with the other assistant, Miss MacHaffie, a lethally helpful old lady. I had hoped that Kenneth might emerge, at some point, from behind the scenes, but he did not and, eventually, I made a few purchases and left, realising that it must be his afternoon off.

However, it occurred to me that by keeping an eye on Ned's brother, I might see where he went, and perhaps discover his secret, whatever it might be. *Praemonitus, praemunitus*, as they say.

Thus, for a few days, whenever I was able, and without altering my own habits too much, I observed his movements. His routine hardly varied. At half past eight o'clock, he walked to work and opened the shop at nine; he took a meal break, usually at half past two, and usually in the Bachelor's Café in the park; at six o'clock sharp, he closed the shop, and returned to Stanley Street, sometimes calling at number 11 for a while, to play with Sibyl and Rose, before heading across the road, to his mother's house, for his evening meal; thereafter, more often than not, he went back to the park, to drink in the Bodega. He seemed to have befriended various Exhibition employees and, once the park had shut for the night, he and assorted friends usually disappeared into the Caledonian Tavern. There was nothing particularly untoward in his behaviour, as far as I could tell. He frequented public houses, not opium dens. He drank, certainly, but no more than other men of his age and class. After a few days, I began to wonder whether Kenneth's secret, whatever form it took, was something that had happened in the past. However, as it transpired, I did not have to speculate for much longer.

On Saturday evening, having spent a pleasant few hours at the Exhibition, I turned my steps homewards, intending to follow the river north and head over the Prince of Wales Bridge, thence up and around the dramatic skyline of Woodland Hill – a magnificent circular arrangement of residential terraces, pavilions, and jutting towers and spires, Glasgow's veritable crown, from which is to be had a commanding view of the whole city – and finally, downhill to Queen's Crescent: a humble tiara, by comparison. Dusk was gathering, but thanks to all the wonderful electrification, one could see quite clearly. Several great windows of the Eastern Palace glowed brightly, whilst over to the east and south lay the twinkling lights of the city and its factories and shipyards. A smell of chimney smoke was in the air, drifting across the park from the Machinery Section, and the din of the dynamos was still audible, since they would not be shut down until the Exhibition closed for the day. That hour was still distant, and people were flocking, as usual, towards the Fairy Fountain, the magical rainbow tints of which illuminated the sky and reflected prettily in the river.

It was as I approached the central bridges that I happened to notice Kenneth Gillespie. This was a coincidence, since I had just been thinking about him, wondering whether he might be in the park. He was leaving Howell's Smoking Lounge, in the company of a tall individual in a dark, broad-brimmed hat, a man whom I recognised, at once, as the younger of the gondoliers. The two men were within hailing distance and I could easily have greeted Kenneth, but I was tired, and it was getting late, and thus, I pretended to look in at Howell's window, so that they might walk ahead without noticing me. No doubt they were bound for the Caledonian. They wandered along the path and crossed over to the riverside, in front of the Chocolate Kiosk, where they paused for a moment, in conversation, although I was now too far away to hear what they said. It was my understanding that the gondolier had few words of English, and I wondered how he managed to converse with the locals.

Just then, a flaring match caught my attention, as a fat man paused to light a cigar in Howell's doorway before setting off across the bridge, leaving behind him a sour and tantalising whiff of smoke. I myself was perishing for a cigarette, but *that* would have to wait until I got back to my lodgings. In the meantime, I peered through Howell's window at the well-stocked shelves and ornamental mirrors. It all looked very bright and cosy inside, and I could almost smell the tobacco through the glass. Two serving girls came downstairs from the lounge, very pretty in their starched pinafores and white caps. A gentleman propped his elbow on the counter as he flirted with another girl. My thoughts drifted to the gondolier. The locals had dubbed the two Venetians 'Signors Hokey and Pokey' since, in the mind of the Glaswegian, any Italian is irredeemably associated with ice-cream, or hokey-pokey. Ned had painted these gondoliers, several times. In my opinion, the pictures were too quaint, but Peden kept encouraging him to produce more in the same vein, to be sold as souvenirs of the Exhibition. Personally speaking, I had no high regard for Walter's opinions on Art; in my mind, I had reduced him to a tongue-twister (*Peden the Pedant, painter of pets; postulates, prances and pirouettes*), and I wished that Ned was not quite so easily influenced.

Thus, my thoughts meandered. When I glanced around again, only a few moments had passed, and so I was surprised to find that Kenneth and the gondolier had vanished. I looked in all directions, but they were not to be seen on any of the nearby paths. I made my way to the spot where they had been standing, but although I peered into the undergrowth, there was no trace of them. I began to worry that some misfortune might have befallen them: night was falling, after all; and so I ventured a little way down the riverbank. The slope was steep in places, and I had to proceed with caution. Having established that there was no one on the easterly side, I made my way towards the first bridge, thinking that they might have gone under there, perhaps to throw stones, or to smoke, or for some other masculine reason.

I wonder can you imagine what sight greeted my eyes as I peered into the shadows under that low bridge? To begin with, I myself did not know quite what to make of it. At first, I was surprised to see that they were wrestling. Signor Pokey seemed to have pounced from behind and got the better of his opponent, since he was on top of Ned's brother, with an arm around his neck, and he was thrusting him into the dirt, causing Kenneth to grunt. Harm was being done, I was sure; and I was about to cry out when suddenly it came to me that the two young men were not, in fact, engaged in mortal combat; rather, they were committing an act of another kind altogether; and it seemed that the oarsman was (in a phrase that I have since heard said) giving Kenneth quite a tail.

Please, do not misunderstand me: I am not easily shocked, and I have no objection to acts of love, Greek or otherwise. My immediate and only concern at the time was for my new friend, the artist Ned Gillespie. Clearly, it was *not* the Cocoa House girls that his brother was interested in, after all; Kenneth was ploughing a rather different furrow. If this was the scandalous matter that 'Old Findlaypops' was about to reveal in his caricature, we were indeed facing a catastrophe. You see, the good burghers of Glasgow have never been renowned for their tolerance, especially when it comes to *patapoufs* or *Mary-Anns* or inverts (or whatever the current terminology might be). What on earth would it do to Ned's promising reputation, to his prospects, and to his chances of winning the commission to paint the state visit, if the reckless and inappropriate behaviour of his brother were to be made public in an issue of *The Thistle*?

Next day, at Stanley Street, the main door was lying open when I arrived for my portrait sitting, and on my way upstairs, on one of the landings, I bumped into Ned, who was heading out, with his easel under his arm. Apparently, he had just heard from the Fine Art Committee, which had, at last, announced a submission date for canvases. There was to be a small private view and, thereafter, the members would retire to choose which artist they would commission to paint the Queen. The viewing was planned for the 15th of August, just a few days after Findlay's caricature was due to appear. I dreaded to think what scurrilous image the gentlemen of the Committee might have in their minds whilst they cast their eyes over Gillespie's work.

'I'm not sure I'll finish my *Eastern Palace* in time,' Ned was saying, as he set down his easel to rest his arm. 'So I'll probably submit one of my *Gondolier* pictures.'

'*The Gondoliers*?' I replied, in alarm. 'Oh no, but surely your *Eastern Palace* would be a more appropriate subject.' I disguised my misgivings with a smile. 'When does that dreadful piece of tosh come out?'

Ned looked at me, blankly. 'What do you mean?'

'You know – Findlay's caricature, in *The Thistle*.'

'Oh – that!' He laughed. 'I haven't a notion.'

'Have you any idea of how he has drawn you?'

'No – none at all,' he said, and shook his head, smiling. 'Although Peden says Kenneth is in it, which might be amusing.'

From his reaction, it seemed perfectly plain that he was entirely ignorant of his brother's proclivities.

'Well – you must concentrate on your submissions,' I told him. 'If the Committee see your *Eastern Palace*, I wager they'll be forcing a cheque into your hands before the sherry gets warm. It's such a wonderful picture, very appropriate, a large building with all those figures, fabulous colours – proof positive that you're the right man for the state portrait.'

Ned chuckled, a little puzzled. 'But – forgive me, Harriet, I don't believe you've *seen* the painting.'

'Indeed, I haven't, but Annie told me it's one of your finest.'

'Och, I don't know about that . . .'

'Of course, your *Gondoliers* are pleasant enough, but they don't show the full breadth of your talent.'

'Well – we'll see,' he said. 'Anyway, I'm just going down there now to make some more sketches in the park.'

'But surely you've enough sketches? You could complete your *Eastern Palace* in a few days, if you put your mind to it.'

He looked so doubtful of this prospect, that I gave a light laugh. Just then, Annie appeared on the top landing. Perhaps she had heard the echo of our voices in the stairwell. She leaned on the banister, looking down upon us, unsmiling.

'Oh, it's you, Harriet,' she said. 'Are you coming in at all?'

'Yes,' I said. 'Ned and I were just talking about his paintings.'

'Well, we should get on with ours, don't you think? You'll be pleased to hear we're almost finished.'

'Really? I thought there was rather more to do, on the hands –'

'No,' said Annie, shortly. 'I think I'm nearly done. A few more sessions should suffice.' She glanced at Ned, who was standing beside me, lost in thought. 'Are you going out, dear, or what are you doing?'

The artist hesitated. 'I don't know — as a matter of fact, I've changed my mind. I think I'll go back up to the studio.' And, so saying, he lifted his easel, and gave me a nod. 'Thank you, Harriet,' he said. 'I do believe you're right. I probably should press on and, at least, try to finish my *Eastern Palace*. Shall we?'

And he held out his hand, to guide me up the stairs ahead of him. I must admit to feeling rather pleased, and not a little relieved, that he seemed to have heeded my advice.

However, there was still the problem of the vignette. I knew that there must be a way out of this ghastly situation, but temporarily, I was at a loss. The Gillespies were already struggling, financially. If Ned's commissions and sales were to diminish as a result of the publication of a seedy caricature, the family would suffer even more. I had to blink away some horrible images of Ned and the children, dressed in rags, begging on Buchanan Street. Of course, it would never come to that, I hoped. But how was Mungo Findlay to be stopped?

Having racked my brains, overnight, I decided that it was imperative to see exactly what the caricaturist had drawn. Thus, I wrote to him and introduced myself with the claim that I wished to engage him as portrait painter and, marking the note 'Urgent', I delivered it, by hand, to the handsome new Italianate offices of *The Thistle*, in West George Street, on Sunday morning. This, I hoped, might result in an invitation to his studio. As yet, I had no clear notion of what I might do once I was there. For some reason, I had imagined Findlay to be an untidy sort of fellow, who left his work lying about the place, and I suppose that I had envisaged a scenario in which the drawing of Ned and Kenneth might be found, in plain view; one glance would tell me whether or not it was damaging, and, if necessary, I was prepared to use all my powers of persuasion in order to protect my friends from scandal.

As it transpired, Findlay must have called in at the *Thistle* building at some point on Sunday, for I received his reply, promptly, on Monday morning. He provided his home address, and invited me to visit him, on Tuesday, at three o'clock. Personally, I would have preferred to see him sooner. I already had an arrangement to sit for Annie on Tuesday afternoon. Moreover, it worried me that Findlay had gone to the offices of the paper on the Sabbath: quite conceivably, he could have been delivering the finished caricature. Having no wish to appear over-eager, I simply wrote to him, accepting his invitation, and resolved to wait another day.

There is no need to dwell at any length upon my encounter with 'Old Findlaypops'. His house, on Smith Street South, although fair-sized, was filthy, damp and odoriferous; his servant had the ruddy, unkempt look of a man who had been lying, drunk, in a field for several days, and the artist himself turned out to be a thoroughly unpleasant fellow. His studio was situated at the back of the house, in a large-windowed room. To my surprise, it was unexpectedly bare and tidy, with a portfolio on a desk, and about a dozen canvases stacked against the wall, and no sign of any vignettes, anywhere. I am afraid that I could scarcely disguise my impatience whilst Findlay paraded his paintings, which were, for the most part, mediocre renditions of fruit and dead pheasants: perfect for the decoration of tea trays, but fit for little else.

Getting hold of the caricature, thereafter, proved to be less than straightforward. In order to persuade Findlay to leave the room, I had to insist that I had heard someone falling, or dropping something, in the hallway, so that when he went off, sceptically, to investigate, I could sneak a look inside his portfolio. Knowing that I would have no more than a few moments alone, I tugged at the ribbon strings, and flipped open the folder. There – fortuitously, at the very top of the pile of drawings – was the vignette of Ned and Kenneth.

I dare say that there can be no harm in describing it now, after all these years. Findlay had depicted the Gillespie brothers in what appeared to be an artist's studio. Ned was at an easel, upon which stood his painting, *By the Pond*. He looked rather miserable, possibly because Kenneth was at his side, dressed in petticoats and bonnet. There was a large pot of flowers in the foreground, the inclusion of which confused me, at first, until I realised that they were pansies. Kenneth's cheek appeared to have been rouged; there was a beauty spot above his lip. With one hand he was holding up a frock, whilst the other tugged at the hem of Ned's jacket. The drawing was entitled '*Stinky Stank et Frère*' and the dialogue beneath, which rhymed with the caption, had Kenneth exclaiming: '*Oh Neddy, dear, whatever shall I wear?*'

A crowning touch, you will no doubt agree.

Upon his return to the room, Findlay affected a great weariness.

'You appear to be hearing things, madam. I can find –' But there, he paused, noticing the open portfolio on the desk, and the caricature, which I had not bothered to hide, since I needed to bring it to his attention, and I could see no point in further subterfuge. His expression underwent an adjustment, from mild irritation, to outrage. 'Excuse me!' he bristled. 'What the blazes – ?'

There and then, although it pained me to do so, I pleaded with him not to submit such a ridiculous item for publication. I told him that it was libellous and could only harm his own reputation, to which he replied that he was happy to face the consequences. When I suggested that the drawing was, in any case, far too risqué for *The Thistle*, he retorted that he already had a verbal agreement with the editor, and that, once he had added a few final details, the vignette would be ready for submission, to be published on the 13th of August, which was, as he said, 'unlucky for Stinky'. Thereafter, in the face of his indifference, I was forced to appeal to the man's conscience, citing Ned's poor infants and their dependence on his income, et cetera, but to my dismay, nothing that I said would dissuade Findlay. Moreover, now that he had ascertained that I was not really interested in engaging him to paint my portrait, he accused me of trespassing, and threatened me with the police (a hysterical over-reaction under the circumstances).

I did only what any good friend might have done. At all costs,

I was determined to ensure that Ned was saved, if only from public humiliation. Reading between the lines, I had surmised that Findlay was impoverished, and not about to relinquish any income that this series of caricatures might bring him. It seemed that financial compensation might be the only way to his heart. And so it was that, after some considerable negotiation, the caricaturist agreed to destroy his dratted vignette. There and then, as I watched over him, he put his drawing on the fire, and I saw it reduced to ashes.

Suffice to say: money can buy anything.

Old Findlay was not so bad, I suppose. Despite his general reptilian tendencies, when interviewed, in later years, by the 'journalist' Mr Bruce Kemp, he said nothing untoward about me, personally, except that I was a 'nosy pest', when he might, instead, have told any number of elaborate untruths (as did others!). I suppose that one ought to feel, in some ways, grateful to him, and yet, he remains unredeemed in my eyes, for his attempt to harm Ned and family.

Old Findlaypops.

Come to think of it, he probably died *long* ago. Sometimes, one cannot help but feel like the very last sturdy old tree of an extremely ancient forest – still standing, enduring, indomitable – whilst, all around, the weaker ones have rotted and dropped into the stinking mire.

I saw no reason to mention what had happened to anyone of my acquaintance. As far as I was concerned, the matter was closed. For the next two weeks, however, my every waking hour was underscored by mild anxiety, since I could not get it out of my head that Findlay might double-cross me, in some way. How, exactly, he could achieve this, I could not imagine, but the possibility was there, looming. As for Ned, so far as I am aware, apart from a slight embarrassment at the notion of being put in the spotlight, he barely gave a thought to the prospect that he might be lampooned in an issue of *The Thistle*. All his attention was concentrated on finishing his *Eastern Palace* in time to be inspected by the Selection Committee. Annie, on the other hand, seemed tense, and although she made no mention of the caricature during this period, it is my belief that she was living in dread of its publication. I would gladly have reassured her, but in order to do so, I would have had to admit that I had stumbled upon Kenneth's secret, and I was hardly about to bring up *that* subject in polite conversation.

In addition to Annie's concerns about Findlay's vignette, was the constant strain of looking after her children, all day long. Sibyl had recently ripped up some of Mabel's precious Berlin work, and this act of sabotage seemed to have upset Annie more than any other thus far. Poor dear! Her hair was more carelessly pinned than ever, and there was something wary in her gaze, almost as though she was awaiting the next disaster.

With my portrait almost complete, she was using our sessions to add a few finishing touches to the hands and face, but I could tell that her mind was often elsewhere, partly because she kept making mistakes, and having to correct what she had done. To be honest, I was almost glad whenever this happened, since it meant that the painting would take longer to finish. I had very much enjoyed my time in the Gillespie home, getting to know the family, and I realised that I would miss them all once these portrait sessions came to an end.

Very early on the morning of the 13th of August, in the dead hours, I jolted awake, the blood pounding in my veins. I had no memory of any dreams or nightmares, but as I lay there, a dreadful thought came to me, all at once: what if Findlay had drawn *another* caricature of Ned and Kenneth, one that was identical to the first in every way? He could, simply, have submitted such a thing to the editor, as planned. This notion crystallised and accreted in my brain, and – by the time that the dawn light had crept into my room – I was certain that such treachery had always been the man's intention. He had gone along with my request, and destroyed his drawing, but it was all a charade simply to get rid of me. I could just imagine him, sniggering to himself, as he redrafted exactly the same image!

The Thistle was to appear on shop counters that morning. Assuming that the paper would be delivered first to any shops near its offices, I decided to walk into town, to buy a copy. Without any real knowledge of what time the journal might go on sale, I waited, anxiously, until ten o'clock, and then set out along Sauchiehall Street, prepared to walk all the way to the Central Station, if necessary. As luck would have it, however, I soon passed a confectioner's that sold newspapers and, peering into the shadowy depths of the shop, I saw a small pile of *Thistles*, sitting on the counter. Having bought a copy, I hurried outside, and turned the pages, with trembling fingers.

One could, of course, ignore the pompous parochialism of 'Our Crabby Critic', but I did pause to glance at 'Megilp', the Fine Art column (thank goodness, no mention of Ned or Kenneth there), and then flicking forwards, I located page 9, where Findlay's caricature usually appeared. And there it was, this week's illustration: a sketch of Mr Crawhall, depicted as a scrawny scarecrow, dour of countenance, and sat upon by numerous pigeons and crows. I flicked back and forth through the newspaper, unable to believe that Findlay had, indeed, kept his word; but I could find no other vignettes, and no reference, anywhere, to Ned Gillespie or his brother.

I suppose that I should have felt relieved. However, my mind simply leapt to the next possibility: that the caricature might appear in some future issue of *The Thistle* or some other journal. Besides, if Findlay knew about Kenneth's secret, then there was every chance that others might also have heard rumours.

I had arranged to sit for Annie, that afternoon, but was in two minds about honouring the appointment. Whether or not the Gillespies had seen *The Thistle*, there might be speculation about the vignette, and I had no real desire to be present, should there be any discussion of the subject: I knew not whether I would be able to sit through such a conversation without blushing. However, I was disinclined to cancel with so little notice, and so – resolving to say nothing, should Findlay be mentioned – I walked round the corner to number 11, at two o'clock, as planned. It was a warm and sunny afternoon, not a cloud in the sky. I found Annie at home, alone, with the children. Ned had gone to the Art Club to supervise the hanging of his submissions for the private view, which would take place that week, and Christina, the maid, had begged some time off, in order to visit her mother, who (apparently) was unwell.

Someone else was also claiming ill health, that afternoon. When I arrived, Rose was upstairs taking a nap, while Sibyl lay on the parlour sofa, under a blanket, with an empty bowl on the floor beside her. She wore a thin shift, and held a small mirror in her hand. Her face was even paler than usual, and there were dark mauve shadows beneath her eyes. As I entered, she gave me one of her malefic stares, and then turned her back to the room.

'Poor love,' said Annie. 'She's been feeling sick again.'

These tummy aches, along with headaches, were the most recent development in Sibyl's disruptive, attention-seeking conduct. Over the past few weeks, she had grown yet more tearful and moody. She no longer reacted with hysterics when faced with evidence of her destructive behaviour; instead, she had become withdrawn, silent and guarded. It was almost as though she was plotting something: watching, and waiting. Little by little, over the course of the summer, this child had become an ever more menacing presence. Even now, as her mother and I crossed the room, Sibyl was observing us: although her back was turned, I noticed that she was holding up her mirror at an angle, in order to capture our reflections. Framed in the oval of silvered glass, I could see one of her eyes, staring at me. Was it my imagination, or did even her flimsy shoulder blades seem to bristle with malice?

In the interim, Annie had turned her easel around to show

me my portrait. There I was, displayed, on the canvas. She had painted me in shades of purple and grey. The colours were harmonious, the brushwork fluid and assured. Of course, I would never be beautiful, or even comely, but Annie had made me almost presentable. If nothing else, I was very thin!

'How close are we to finishing?' I asked her.

'Oh – I'll be done today. I just want to touch up the hands, but it shouldn't take long. Shall we begin?'

I crossed to the window, and took my seat, the contours of which were, by then, very familiar. I felt rather melancholy and dejected. Our last session! I would miss spending time at Stanley Street, even if Sibyl did make me feel uncomfortable, from time to time. Mercifully, she was not in my line of sight whilst I posed, since our makeshift studio was in a corner of the room. And yet, as we worked, I could not help but be aware of the child's brooding presence, nearby. From time to time, she spied on our reflections, by poking her looking-glass beyond the upholstered arm of the sofa. At least she was quiet, for once.

As for Annie, she seemed even frostier than she had been for the past few weeks. Ever since the day when I had bumped into Ned on the staircase, and she had seen us talking together, from the top landing, her attitude to me had been cold. I wondered whether I had done something to annoy her: she had no reason to feel jealous, of course, but perhaps she disliked that I had been giving her husband advice. It was also possible (I told myself) that she had not yet seen *The Thistle*: she might simply be on edge about the dreaded caricature.

We had been working steadily for about half an hour, when I heard footsteps on the communal stairs, and recognised the sound of Peden, pontificating, his voice reverberating off the walls of the close, as he approached the top landing. My assumption was that he had come in with Ned, until the key turned in the lock, and the front door flew open, accompanied by a burst of female giggling. Nosy as ever, Sibyl sat up on the sofa, and peered into the hall, and Annie glanced towards the door, just as Christina and Peden came into view. The maid was more dishevelled than usual, and as she approached the threshold of the parlour, I had the distinct impression that she was a little unsteady on her feet.

'That's me back,' she said, shortly, and then pursed her lips.

Annie stared at her maid, without speaking. In response to this silence, Christina's pretty face took on a very serious look. She leaned into the room, and breathed heavily at us, through her nose. 'My mother isnae well,' said she. 'Not at all. She's took terrible – very sick. Misser Peden's here – a lemon, s'at right?'

In fact, she was not calling Peden a lemon, as I first thought, but telling Annie that she had 'let him in'. There could be no doubt that Christina had been drinking. Indeed, the sweet smell of liquor had begun to waft across the room towards us. As far as I could tell, she was not pie-eyed, but she was certainly squiffy. Walter hovered behind her, making a great pantomime of hopping around, biting his fist with anxiety, like a character in a play. Presumably, he hoped not only to over-dramatise the situation, but also to convey that he was not to blame for the maid's condition. Of course, he was being ridiculous, since neither Annie nor I thought for a moment that he was responsible. My hostess was clearly furious with her maid, but it was not in her nature to cause a fuss, in front of guests.

'Go back to work, Christina,' she said quietly. 'I'll speak to you later.'

The girl marched off. A moment later, there was the sound of the kitchen door banging shut. Peden came tiptoeing into the parlour, still gnawing at his fist. 'Yoicks!' cried he, rolling his eyes. 'I was about to ring the bell when she came up the steps behind me. It's not my fault – I wasn't with her.'

'Of course not,' said Annie. 'Now, Walter, Ned's at the Art Club.'

'Oh, I know,' said Peden, and then he turned and gave me a strange, piercing look. 'I'm just on my way there myself. Afternoon, Hetty.'

Then, with a flourish, he produced a copy of *The Thistle* from his pocket. Annie gasped and, rushing forwards, she grabbed the journal from him even as he was opening it at the appropriate page. I watched the relief spread across her face, when Peden pointed out Findlay's cartoon of Mr Crawhall.

'Oh thank goodness!' she cried.

Meanwhile, I was unsettled to realise that Walter was winking at me, in conspiratorial fashion.

'What a relief,' said Annie. 'He's not even drawn Ned at all – or Kenneth!'

'Well, as it happens,' Peden announced. 'I heard something very interesting over luncheon, about Old Findlaypops and his sketch of the brothers Gillespie.'

I braced myself: perhaps Findlay had gone ahead and published a caricature in one of the other weeklies: *Quiz*, perhaps, or *The Bailie*. Annie began to bite her lip, a sure sign that she, too, was nervous. Sibyl had thrown herself down on the sofa, out of sight, but there could be no doubt that she was all ears.

'He didn't even submit it to *The Thistle*,' said Peden. 'And – seemingly – the reason is, that somebody persuaded him not to. In fact, they made him *destroy* it.'

'Really?' said Annie.

Peden turned to me. 'Seemingly,' he said (how I hated the word: seemingly this and seemingly that; he was such an old gossip!), 'according to what I heard, it was a lady who made him destroy it: an English lady – by the name of Miss Baxter.'

Out of the corner of my eye, I was aware of Annie, turning to stare at me. Indeed, all eyes were upon me, because Sibyl's spyglass was inching silently into view, beyond the arm of the sofa, in a way that I would have found almost comical, had I not been in such a tight spot.

'What on earth are you suggesting, Walter?' said Annie.

'Yes, what?' I added, with as much composure as I could muster.

'Oh, come now, Hetty, don't act innocent. A lady with an English accent –'

'There must be five thousand of those in Glasgow this summer,' I told him. 'What with the Exhibition.'

'Yes, but how many of them are named Baxter?'

Annie was frowning at me, lack of comprehension writ large across her face. After a moment, she turned to Peden.

'What was in Findlay's drawing?' she asked him. 'How were Ned and Kenneth depicted?'

Walter shook his head. 'I don't know,' he replied, then gave me a scolding look. 'Come on, Hetty – admit it was you. Miss Baxter? From London?'

I laughed. 'You're barking up the wrong tree,' I told him. 'Why would I stop Findlay publishing his silly doodles? Why should I interfere?'

'I have no idea,' said Peden. 'But it seems evident that you did. I have it on good authority, right down to your physical description.'

At that moment, a strange sound made us both turn to look at Annie. I was surprised to realise that she was sobbing. And then, to my astonishment, she stepped forwards, with a tearful smile, and threw her arms around me.

'Oh, thank you!' she murmured, in my ear. 'I was so worried about that stupid man and his drawing. Thank you so much for stopping him.'

Her neck smelt faintly of her favourite 'Crab Apple' scent. I could see Peden, over her shoulder, staring at me.

'What I don't understand', he said, 'is why you made him destroy it, Hetty. What on earth was in it? Findlay won't say a word: claims he's sworn to secrecy.'

Annie released me from her warm embrace, and stepped back to face Peden, as she wiped her eyes. 'Never mind,' she said. 'Perhaps we'll never know what was in that vignette. The main thing is it wasn't published. Now, Walter, if you don't mind, we must get on with our work.'

'Oh! Of course – the Great Portrait!' he said, and danced at her. 'I'll be off then. Good day, dear Mrs. G – and farewell, Hetty, you sly dog.'

He gave me one last narrow-eyed look, and then sauntered, pigeon-toed, across the hall, and out of the apartment.

Annie addressed her daughter, who was still lying, eavesdropping, on the sofa. 'Sibyl – go to your room for a nap.'

An interval of whining ensued, but, eventually, the child shuffled out of the room, trailing her blanket behind her. Annie waited until Sibyl had gone upstairs, and then she closed the parlour door, quietly. I expected her to return to her easel, but instead, she sat down in one of the chairs by the hearth and, propping her head up on one hand, she gave me a long, inquisitive look. I thought, at first, that she was studying me, for the purposes of the painting, but eventually she spoke.

'Now then, Harriet – whatever have you been up to?'

As it turned out, I had been correct in my assumptions about Annie: she *did* know all about her brother-in-law's secret. A few weeks later, I heard the full, unexpurgated story of how she had become his confidante, several months previously, after he had confessed all. Suffice to say, her suspicions about him had first been aroused on a family outing to Edinburgh in late December. Kenneth and Annie had been seated together in a busy train, the rest of the family having been obliged to occupy another carriage. It seemed that, during the journey – and unbeknownst to Annie – Ned's brother had become intimate with an Argyll and Sutherland Highlander who had taken the seat at his other side. The encounter began with the pressure of one man's thigh against the other, at first – apparently – accidental, and then (at Bishopbriggs, following the departure from the carriage of the remaining passengers) more deliberate; and it progressed, by furtive, fumbling degrees, to a concluding act which I will not elucidate here, but which Kenneth performed manually upon the soldier as the train entered Haymarket Station; his actions cunningly concealed by the military cape draped across the stranger's lap. (This aspect of the tale, Annie alluded to only in the most vague of terms, but there was no mistaking what she meant.)

I gathered that what she found most unnerving was that all of this wanton activity had occurred right beside her, whilst she was deeply absorbed in reading a book, her beloved *David Copperfield* and, at the very moment when Kenneth had been applying himself with the greatest fervour to the Highlander, on the approach to Haymarket, she had just reached the saddest part of the story: the deaths of Jip, the adorable miniature dog, and also of the hero's wife, poor little Dora. These combined tragedies (all within a single page!) had reduced Annie to tears; and it upset her to think that – whilst she wept, quietly oblivious, and moved by masterful storytelling – Kenneth had been at her side, fiddling about in the clammy netherworld of a soldier's kilt (not her words but mine). It was only afterwards – when the soldier had disembarked at Haymarket, and Kenneth had acted strangely, running after him, and then refusing to say why – that Annie grew suspicious.

'So I asked him about it, at Hogmanay, when he was drunk. He wouldn't tell me at first, just kept hinting there was something about him I didn't know. But later, he got more drunk and then – well – he said what had happened on the train.'

Despite any reservations that she might have harboured, Annie had since been careful not to show Kenneth her disapproval. She was, I think, flattered that he had confided in her. As for Kenneth, once he realised that his brother's wife would not only keep his secrets, but also allow him to talk about them without condemning his actions, he acquired a taste for confession and abandoned all modesty, even seeming quite thrilled to provide her with unexpurgated accounts of his exploits.

'After that, he told me everything,' she said. 'About all the other men that he'd been with, in all sorts of places. I used to tell him he should be careful, but he never pays a blind bit of notice. And then the Exhibition started, and he met Carmine – the gondola man – and *that* was a blessing, believe me, Harriet, because it calmed him down. He's not going off with strangers any more, one after the other, like he used to. Whatever he and Carmine do, it happens in private.'

'Alas, not *always*,' I reminded her. 'Lucky for them that it was only me who saw them under the bridge. Imagine had I been a policeman!'

Annie looked crestfallen. Poor girl (for she really was no more than a girl): carrying the burden of this secret for so many months had been a strain, and I believe it was a huge relief for her to confide in me.

But there I go again, rushing ahead. I did not hear all of the above until – perhaps – September, by which time Annie and I had developed a closer friendship, and were able to talk about such things, albeit in euphemistic terms.

On the day in question, of course, very little was said. Although Annie pressed me, I continued to deny any involvement in the destruction of Findlay's caricature, for several minutes. Then, I will admit, I gave in. She was so desperate to know how Ned and Kenneth had been depicted, and begged me so hard that, eventually, I described it for her. Thereafter, she insisted upon knowing why on earth I had gone to Findlay's house in the first place and so, in the most delicate way possible, I told her that I had witnessed Kenneth, in the park, in the company of the gondolier. 'They didn't see me – it was quite dark by that time – but I saw them; I saw – what they were doing.'

Annie had clamped her lips together so tightly, that they had all but disappeared. Eager to reassure her, I clasped her hands in both of mine.

'Please don't fret, dear. Why, I know quite a few men of the same sort, down in London. It's more common than you'd think. I won't tell a soul, I promise.'

She gazed into my eyes, trying to determine whether or not I could be trusted, until, at last, something inside her seemed to yield, and she gave a sigh. 'Oh, Harriet! Ned doesn't know about it, and I've been almost going mad, thinking that this drawing might come out, and ruin everything – Kenneth, and Ned – all of us.'

'Well, hopefully we don't have to worry about it any more.'

She shook her head; there were tears in her eyes. 'I don't know how to thank you. I won't forget what you've done to help us – ever.'

Just at that moment, the front door flew open and, a second or two later, Ned bounded into the parlour.

'Afternoon, ladies,' he cried. 'What are you doing in here, all cooped up? We should be out in the park, in the fresh air.'

'You seem in good form, dear,' said Annie, recovering herself with admirable grace. 'Have you seen Walter?'

'Should I have?'

'He's away to find you at the Club. You must've missed him in the street.'

'Not to worry,' said Ned, and then turned to me, with a smile. 'Harriet, I'm sure you'll be glad to know that my *Eastern Palace* is finished, and is now up on the wall at the Art Club, awaiting the verdict of the Fine Art Committee.'

'Wonderful – how does it look?'

'I'm not entirely happy with it, of course, but –'

'Ach,' said Annie, scathingly. 'Don't listen to him. It's magnificent.'

Ned gave a modest laugh. 'Well, I wouldn't go that far. But Horatio Hamilton was there, and he did tell me he thought it was my best work yet.'

'Oh, that's simply marvellous,' I told him.

'Now Ned, dearest,' said Annie. 'Don't be disappointed, but that thing wasn't in *The Thistle* after all.'

Ned looked blank. 'What thing?'

Remarkably, given the straits that the rest of us had been in, he seemed to have forgotten altogether about the vignette.

'Findlay's sketch, dear. He put Mr Crawhall in *The Thistle* instead of you.'

Ned laughed. 'Good old Crawhall! Aye, he'd be a much better subject than me, anyway. Now –' He clapped his hands together, the caricature already forgotten. 'Why don't we all go to the park, and celebrate that I finished my painting? Thanks to your good advice, Harriet, I think I might even stand half a chance of this commission. I do hope I can find some way to repay you.'

'Oh, good gracious –' I said, more than a little embarrassed. 'I was just so sure that your *Eastern Palace* would be something special.'

'Well, you were right – from now on, I shall consult you before I do anything. Annie, where are the girls? Let's get out of here. Come on, Harriet, let me buy you a hokey-pokey or a cold drink.'

'Oh, that would be wonderful but –' I glanced at his wife, doubtfully. 'We ought to get on with my portrait. Annie's keen to finish.'

To my great surprise, she shook her head.

'Och, never mind that, now. We can work on it some other day. Ned's right. We all deserve some fresh air, and some fun, in the park.' She smiled at me and, reaching out, took my hand in hers. 'Would you mind coming upstairs with me, Harriet dear, and helping me to get the girls ready to go out?'

My face grew warm with pleasure at this unaccustomed display of affection.

'Not at all,' I told her. 'I'd be delighted.'

And thus began a wonderful new phase in my friendship with the Gillespies.

Thursday, 8 June 1933

LONDON

How ironic that just as I am writing about improved relations with Annie and the Gillespies, matters with Sarah have taken a turn for the worse. It all began with the finches. The unfortunate thing about keeping any kind of pet – be it dog or cat or bird – is that one can get very attached to an animal and then, when something goes wrong, there can be great heartache and sorrow. Such has been the case with Maj and Layla. They are not sick, thank heavens; despite being mature, in bird years, they seem healthy enough. However, I have had to intervene of late, in a way that always causes me great anguish. Moreover, the incident has created a rift between my new assistant and myself.

Sarah did seem to have been settling in fairly well, despite her inscrutability and a general dearth of cheer. There is a slightly mournful quality to her, a sense of something lacking. She is also inclined to overeat. Indeed, she has gained weight since she arrived here; her waist has thickened; her arms, like two plump sausages, seem ready to burst out of her sleeves. I myself have never had much of an appetite, and, these days, it is an effort to eat enough, in order not to become too frail; none the less, I can understand that it must be uncomfortable to carry around all that extra bulk, especially this summer, which has, thus far, been quite too horribly warm. Sarah is clearly conscious of her size, since – no matter what the temperature – she swathes herself in old-fashioned, wide-beamed skirts, long sleeves, and thick stockings. It is perhaps unfortunate that her sitting room is in the kitchen, adjacent to the larder: in the evenings, there are rustlings, and munchings.

She has not eaten the birds, of course. That would be silly. Why I even mention her weight, I do not know. She has perfectly pleasant features, and one can see that – beyond the frown lines and dewlaps – she must have been pretty when she was young. I do find myself wondering why she never wed. Perhaps she was once married and is now a widow; but there has been no mention of a husband, and she calls herself 'Miss Whittle'. Without prying, I have tried, on several occasions, to ask about her life, and her family background, and so on, but she continues to be reticent. I do suspect that she would have had children, had she been able.

It is unsettling to hear her chatting away to Maj and Layla, as if they could understand her. She checks on their feed and water with a frequency that borders on the obsessive and, recently, I became aware that – even though I had asked her not to – sometimes, when she believed me to be taking my nap, she was shutting the dining-room window and letting the birds out of the cage. At any rate, she has tended to fuss over them too much, and is preoccupied with them in a way that seems not quite healthy. One cannot help but draw certain conclusions, particularly after our recent upset.

It all began about ten days ago, when Sarah came to the threshold of my sitting room and uttered the following words: 'Well, you'll not believe what those birds have gone and done now!'

Patiently, I put down my book. Having owned Maj and Layla for seven years, I am familiar with all their little quirks, but Sarah, as a newcomer, still has the capacity to be surprised by them.

'What have they done?' I asked.

Instead of replying, she bustled off down the hall, and I was obliged to set aside my book, and follow her to the dining room. When I got there, the birds were in their cage, as usual; Maj was preening under his wing, whilst Layla alternately shook her little head, and pecked at seed. Sarah had taken up a position at the end of the sideboard, which had been pulled a few inches away from the wall. She was smiling.

'Look,' she said, pointing into the shadows.

My spirits sank: I already had a good idea of what she might have found, but just to be sure, I stood next to her and peered down behind the sideboard. There, next to the skirting, was a small nest made from some horsehair stuffing, newspaper shreds, and a few sweet papers. In the centre lay three bluish white, speckled eggs.

'Oh dear,' I said.

'Aren't they tiny?' Sarah whispered. I could feel the heat rising from her body. Her pullover gave off a sharp, damp smell.

'Yes, they are indeed.'

'Those are my toffee papers she's used, you know, and I only got those toffees once, a few weeks back; they weren't very good. She must have been building this for ages, out of all the things we've dropped or put in the wastepaper basket. I did wonder what she was doing behind here, every afternoon.'

This, for Sarah, was a very long speech. She was more animated than I had ever seen her before. I sighed.

'Oh, Sarah! Didn't I ask you not to let them out, unless I was here?'

She frowned, and looked a little guilty. 'Sorry, I've only done it a few times. I do shut the window if I open the cage – sorry.'

Feeling quite miserable, I picked up the nest and put it on the sideboard. It really was a too poignantly comic little object. Poor Layla-bird! Presumably, she had pecked the horsehair stuffing out of a chair. She had also utilised, in the nest's construction, an old shoelace, and some cigarette stubs, which she must have stolen from the ashtrays. 'Oh dear,' I said again. 'They will build nests, you see, if you don't keep an eye on them. She's done it before.'

'Really?'

'Oh, yes, quite a few times, here, behind the sideboard, and once or twice behind the sofa. You can't let Layla out of your sight, I'm afraid. This breaks my heart. They're probably no good anyway, but we have to do this, dear, just in case.'

And then, I did the decent thing – as I have done, on a few previous occasions – according to the vet's advice. I took the little eggs, one by one and, feeling dreadfully squeamish, I shook them until I heard a tiny, sloshing sound. 'There,' I said, despondently, restoring them to the nest. 'They won't hatch now. We can put it back on the floor for a while. She'll sit on them when she can, poor thing, and then, when they don't hatch, she'll grow bored of them, and we can quietly tidy the nest away.' I turned to Sarah. Her face had fallen. 'I know, it's awful,' I said. 'Frightful! When the vet first told me what to do, I was appalled. But it does have to be done, and I suppose I'm used to it now. We can't possibly have any more birds, dear. They're the most awful breeders. We'd be overrun in no time. Two is quite enough.'

Sarah said not a word; she simply gave me a very reproachful look, and then marched out of the dining room.

Since then, I hear her, from time to time, talking to the birds in soothing tones, as though they are the victims of some atrocity. She fails to realise that finches are hardy little souls; I would not be surprised if they had already forgotten about those eggs. What I did was no more than standard practice; most bird owners do something of the sort. Not only that, but the eggs were, in all likelihood, already dead, since Layla can have sat on them only for a matter of minutes.

I did try to explain all this to Sarah but, for the moment, she continues to brood: a most apt word that – brood – for I suspect that all this upset over the birds is linked in some way to Sarah's own sorrows about having never brought a child into the world. Consequently, I cannot be cross with her and, to be perfectly honest, I now utterly regret having done the vet's bidding – or at least, having done it in front of Sarah, without warning. Personally speaking, I have not even been able to look at a boiled egg, since.

Perhaps, if the birds ever lay again, I might let Sarah keep one of the chicks. There is no reason why she should not have a caged bird of her own; she could keep him in the kitchen. I tend to doubt, however, that there will be much more laying of eggs. Maj and Layla are getting rather too elderly for that sort of thing. I suspect that this clutch of three was one last moribund attempt at breeding.

Ever since the egg incident, relations between Sarah and myself have been strained. I am still rather cross that she was letting the birds out, against my specific instructions. Indeed, I have begun to wonder whether she has been entirely honest with me in other respects. Is she, in fact, trustworthy? For instance – although, up until now, I have thought nothing of it – I have noticed a number of inconsistencies in the way that she speaks. Admittedly, when first she came to live here, I scarcely noticed her accent. She is not a Cockney, certainly. To my ears, she initially sounded like many other women of her sort: born and raised – not in London – but in the Home Counties or somewhere in the South. She attempts to speak well, but the end result is that her pronunciation is only rather bland; at times, a little strained. However, as the weeks have gone by, I have begun to notice that there is something amiss with her vowels. The word 'bird', for instance, never sounds quite right.

On Friday afternoon, I was having a nap in my room when she tapped on the door and asked my permission to give some fruit to the finches. Their mainstay is seed, but they do love fruit. Lockwood, the grocer, was kind enough to store a crate of Coxes for me this winter. Even though the remaining apples are now wrinkled, they are still edible and, once or twice a week, we pop half of one in the cage, and Maj and Layla peck out the pulp. At any rate, there was Sarah in the doorway, saying: 'Would you be bothered if I gave the birds some apple?'

Quite apart from the phrasing of this sentence (which does not strike me as pertaining particularly to the South of England), there – again – was her strange pronunciation of the word 'bird', with the oddly shortened vowel sound, and perhaps even a slight roll of the 'r'. Ignoring her question, for the moment, I said: 'Your accent, Sarah, I can't quite place it – where is it from?'

'Around about,' she said and then clamped her teeth down on her lower lip.

'But where, exactly? You're not from London, are you?'

'Originally West Country, miss, like I've told you, but I've moved around, London, Colchester, Sevenoaks, Woking...'

'I see – was that with your family?'

'For work.'

I sat up, yawning, and put my feet into my slippers. 'Where, originally, in the West Country, dear?'

'Dorset.'

'Ah! Such a pretty county – what part? I do know Swanage.'

'It's nearer Weymouth – a small place – you won't have heard of it.'

'And your village was called . . .?'

She paused, and then said: 'Langton Herring.'

A preposterous name, and it occurred to me that, perhaps, she had made it up. I went on to ask a few questions about her family, and her reactions continued to be guarded. She told me that her parents were dead. I did manage to get a little more out of her. To my mind, it all sounds far too much like something out of a fairy tale. She claims to have grown up in a tiny cottage beside a well; her father was a shoemaker, and her mother, a washerwoman. Tempted to ask: 'And your grandparents – were they elves?' I managed to restrain myself, just in time.

Admittedly, while we were talking about Dorset and her family, her pronunciation did veer towards the West Country; but before long she seemed to forget, and resumed her old, bland accent, with its puzzling vowels. I am still not quite sure what to make of this. The way she looks at me, of late, is also rather unsettling. There is a certain flinty cast to her gaze.

On Saturday, while Sarah was out shopping, I telephoned to Burridge's, the employment agency, and asked them to send me, once again, her letters of recommendation in a plain envelope, one that made no mention of Burridge's or its address. I stipulated this, since Sarah is often the first to see the post when it arrives, and I had no desire to alarm her, unnecessarily. I merely wished to follow up her references, something that I ought to have done before I hired her, but, at the time, I was busy, and took it for granted that the letters were to be trusted.

Mrs Clinch, the principal of the agency, possesses a drawling, affected, nasal voice, and evidently has a low opinion of the elderly, for she habitually speaks to me, very slowly and loudly, as though I were both half-witted and deaf. 'What seems to be the problem?' she shouted, in answer to my request for the references.

'No problem,' I replied. 'I simply wish to be sent the letters in a plain envelope, with no return address, and no mention of your office.'

'Miss Baxter, I'm just looking at the red chester here –'

'The what?'

'The red chester!'

I had heard her perfectly well; I simply cannot believe that anyone imagines a register to be called a 'red chester'. Clinch is very fond of her 'red chester'. Whenever she is being particularly superior, I take pleasure in making her refer to it.

'– and I can see from what's written here, you've already had the references, I believe. We sent them to you some weeks ago, didn't we – and you sent them back to us, dear, remember? I have them in front of me. They're good references. Are you having a problem with Miss Whittle?'

'No,' I said. 'No problem.'

'Then why d'you need the references for, might I enquire?'

'I'd simply like to have another look at them. I believe I'm perfectly entitled to do so. I really fail to see why it should be so complicated.'

'Well, provided Miss Whittle is happy – and you're happy –'

'We're both quite content, thanks most awfully.'

'Rightie-o, I'll put them in the post directly, dear.'

'Oh, good – and you'll mark that in your – in your – eh –'

'Yes, I'll mark it in the red chester. They should be with you soon.'

In fact, they arrived on Monday. As luck would have it, Sarah was out again, this time at the tobacconist's, but I was glad to see that, apart from my address, the envelope was blank. There were two letters of recommendation: one from a Miss Barnes, of Chepworth Villas, London, and another from a Miss Clay, of Greenstead, Essex. Just as I remembered, from when I looked at them back in April, both ladies praised Sarah's many qualities and did not hesitate to recommend her (et cetera). Only the Chepworth Villas address included a telephone number. I was tempted to dial it straight away, but Sarah was due to return at any moment and, since I wished to make the call undisturbed, I waited until the afternoon, when I sent Sarah back out, with a long list of questions about the economy of Scotland in the last century, and asked her not to return until she had found out the answers. In fact, I have no interest in the Scottish economy. There are, of course, some genuine facts that I would like her to check, but my main purpose in sending her to the library was to ensure that she was out of the apartment for a few hours.

Once she had gone, I waited, just in case she might come back to retrieve something that she had forgotten, until – after twenty minutes or so – it seemed certain that she would not return. Then, I placed a call to Chepworth Villas.

Miss Barnes was younger than I had expected. I had thought that she might be a lady of around my own age, but she sounded as though she was in her forties, or even younger. She also answered the telephone herself.

'Hello?'

'Is that Miss Barnes – Miss Clara Barnes?'

'Yes, speaking.'

Her voice was light and high, and she was breathless, almost as though she had just been engaged in some vigorous activity.

'I'm telephoning about Sarah Whittle. I'm thinking of employing her.'

There was a long pause, and then the woman said (rather carefully, I thought): 'Sarah is – looking for work then, is she?'

'Yes. Would you recommend her?'

'Oh, indeed, I would,' she said, very quickly. 'She's a terrific girl.' Something about that phrase bothered me: 'terrific girl'. Is that how one talks about employees these days? She went on: 'I'd have no hesitation in recommending her.'

'Forgive me for asking, but might I enquire why she left you?'

At once, Miss Barnes became awkward. 'I'm afraid I – I'm sorry, I didn't catch your name.'

The words 'Harriet Baxter' almost leapt out of my mouth – and then I thought better of it. Just then, there was a lively twittering from the birds next door, and I had an idea. 'My name is Gillespie,' I said. 'Mrs Madge Gillespie.'

'Mrs Gillespie, you must understand that it was not through any fault of Sarah's that she had to leave here – I can assure you of that.'

'Can't you be more – specific?'

'No, I'm afraid I can't.'

'I take it, then, you didn't find her accent disconcerting – the way it roams?'

'Not in the least.'

'And you think she's trustworthy?'

'Oh yes! One of the most honest people I've ever met. I did write a character letter for her. I think I kept a copy – I could send it to you, if you like.'

'Oh no, thank you – I have it, from the registry. Yes, most impressive.'

Certain aspects of this conversation trouble me. Miss Barnes's relative youth, for example, is surprising. Her reactions to my questions were also puzzling: she was surprised to hear that Sarah was looking for work (almost as though she knew very well that this was not the case). Then there was her strange response when asked why Sarah had left her employ. Her other replies had seemed prepared, but this question, clearly, took her unawares.

All in all, I am not sure what to make of this Miss Barnes.

Recent events have made me think that it might be worth writing to Sarah's other previous employer, at the Essex address, to see what kind of reply I receive. However, sending the letter will be bothersome, because Sarah usually goes to the pillar box, and I cannot, at this stage, give her an envelope addressed to 'Miss Clay' of Greenstead, since she will wonder why, after all these weeks, I am following up her references.

And now, as it transpires, I have made a rather interesting discovery. Of late, I rarely leave the apartment on my own. However, on Tuesday, I had an appointment to see the doctor. I hasten to add that there is nothing whatsoever wrong with me; I simply needed to pick up more of my little miracle pills, to help me sleep. Sarah wanted to accompany me, but I told her that I preferred to go in a cab, alone, and that I intended to spend the rest of the afternoon at the museum.

Dr Derrett was as brusque and Lilliputian as ever. In fact, come to think of it, I will describe, briefly, what happened at the surgery. Forgive me if this incident is, in any way, shocking or unpleasant. I would not, usually, dwell on such things, but it is worth mentioning, if only to record somewhere how one is treated. We may have the vote now, and win Pulitzer prizes, and fly solo across the Atlantic and, these days, a female artist with a family might well earn a good living from painting, but in the privacy of the doctor's surgery, we are still made to feel insignificant, aberrant, even unnatural.

When I happened to mention, in passing, my heartburn, Derrett insisted that I take off my blouse, and lie down on the couch. My health has always been good, on the whole, and, therefore, it is a long time since I have bared my skin and bones for inspection by a doctor. I felt somewhat self-conscious, and my mood was not helped when Derrett, taking one glance at my torso, cried: 'Ha! Polythelia!'

'Polly who?'

He pointed, gleefully, at various places along my upper body.

'Here, here, here. To be blunt: accessory nipples. You're probably under the misapprehension that they are moles; in fact, they are supernumeraries along the milk lines.'

'*Milk* lines?'

'Mammalian milk lines. Pigs have them – sows, also cats, rats – and you.'

'Oh dear,' I said. 'How revolting!'

'Nothing to worry about. They're not connected in any way to heartburn or lack of appetite. They simply – exist – for no reason. They'll do you no harm.'

'How reassuring,' I said.

All the same, I was more than a little disturbed at having been categorised along with pigs, cats and rats. Derrett was still in his element. 'Mind you,' he mused, 'a few hundred years ago, you'd probably have been burned at the stake.'

'Oh!'

'The sign of a witch, you see – moles.' He flicked one of them, with his finger, and then commenced to prod and knead my abdomen with both hands. 'Now, let's see about this indigestion . . . just relax . . .'

I cannot say that any of his comments had made me in the least relaxed. On the contrary, I felt very hot and bothered, and his poking at my stomach was anything but gentle. He seemed altogether too pleased with himself. In conclusion, he told me: 'I'll book a blood test for you, but poor digestion is only to be expected at your age. You're lucky you can eat at all – lucky you even have teeth. You seem a bit bloated, round the midriff.'

That was the final straw. 'Now you're being silly,' I told him. 'I ate a bread roll this morning. Bread makes me swell up like a football.'

He is very against smoking and drinking, for some reason, but one never pays any attention to that, since what would life be without cigarettes and the odd *tira mi sù*? Besides, I believe that I might never sleep, were it not for my little nightcap of Scotch and veronal (of which Derrett gave me another three months' supply). The ache in my hips (he assures me) is due, simply, to arthritis, and might be helped by exercise. Afterwards, exhausted by this appointment, I decided to skip the museum and return home, directly. The lift in the mansions is such a temperamental contraption – with oak walls, and as cramped as a coffin – that I am always a reluctant passenger, and so I resolved to walk upstairs. At only five storeys, this is hardly the Chrysler Building; one is able to rest and recover on the landings. Besides, Derrett said I should exercise.

It was during the ascent that I became aware of a melodious tinkling emanating from above: someone, somewhere, was playing a piano. To my surprise, as I approached the fourth floor, I realised that the music was coming from inside my own apartment, from the piano in the hall. I would recognise the tones of that old Bechstein anywhere; it has always been boomy, ever since moths ate the felts. There could be no doubt: Sarah was at the keyboard – playing Bach, no less. She had never touched the piano in the past, but then, she had never before been alone in the apartment. I must admit that her playing was not at all bad.

Since I had eschewed the lift – with its groaning, ticking machinery, and the screech of its folding metal gates – my approach, thus far, had been relatively quiet. However, as soon as I put my key in the front door, the music stopped. There was a thunderous scuttle of footsteps as I entered, and I saw my assistant disappearing into the kitchen with such haste that she careened off the doorjamb. Deciding not to speak to her, just then, I turned on my heel, and departed, without a word. For the next half an hour or so, I sat on a bench in the garden square, watching the populace come and go, and thinking about Sarah.

Not once had she mentioned that she could play the piano. The more I thought about it, the more it struck me as strange or, at least, secretive. Surely any normal person might have dashed out a few chords in passing? She ran the duster over the instrument, once or twice a week, when we tackled the housework: was she never tempted to practise? Apparently not, except for when I vacated the building. Was it mere shyness that stopped her from displaying her talent at the keyboard?

It was very warm there, on the bench, beneath the trees and, at some point, I must have fallen asleep. The next thing I knew, there was a tapping on my shoulder, and I awoke to find two young men, in overalls, peering at me. Their faces looked vaguely familiar, and I realised that they worked in the new garage at the rear of the mansions. I had seen them from my bedroom window – on numerous occasions – down in the back yard, washing cars. One of them had bulging brown eyes, like brandy balls. The other sported a downy moustache and curls. As I came to my senses, brandy balls sniggered.

'She's right as ninepence,' he muttered. 'Told you.'

His companion, who had a kinder face, nodded, and gave me a smile. 'Excuse us, madam,' he said. 'You give us quite a turn then – sat there ever so still, with your mouth open – we thought you was a goner.'

Bestowing upon them my most imperial look, I announced: 'I have no intention of going anywhere.'

They laughed, as I had hoped, and then they wandered away, across the square, idly kicking out at each other's shins.

Later, upon my return to the mansions, Sarah served me supper. She looked rather shamefaced, but made no mention of what had happened earlier, and so I, too, said nothing. However, this business with the piano has troubled me, for reasons that I cannot quite put my finger on, or explain.

But here I am, fretting over trivia, like a doddering fool. Age is a terrible thing. Never grow old, my dears: that is my advice to you. Never grow old.

III

September 1888 – March 1889

GLASGOW

7

As you may be aware, despite working hard at his submissions, Ned was not fortunate enough to receive the Royal Commission. Following the private view, it was announced that John Lavery had prevailed over his peers, and was chosen, by the esteemed gentlemen of the Fine Art Committee, to paint the Queen. Muttonheads! It serves them right that he cheated and took photographs from which to work: believe it or not, I saw him, with my own eyes. On Inauguration Day, once the good and great had surged out of the Grand Hall in Her Majesty's wake, I simply popped my head around the door to have a peek at the dais, and saw Lavery himself, emerging, squatly, from a curtained alcove, and what did he have with him? A sketchbook? Charcoal? Paints? No, sir! I beg to differ: he had with him a man – a lugubrious, balding man – who might have resembled an undertaker were he not carrying a bellows camera and tripod. 'The Great Master' had hired a photographer to do his work!

But enough of that chump Lavery; plenty has been written about *him*.

Naturally, Ned was disappointed not to have won, but in some respects, perhaps, it was a relief. After all, the painting would have dominated his life for the foreseeable future. In the meantime, his reputation had been greatly enhanced: the Committee had been particularly impressed with his picture of the *Eastern Palace*, and rumour was that he had been the unofficial silver medallist. I was greatly surprised and flattered when – a few days later, in the parlour at number 11 – Ned consulted my opinion on how he should try to take advantage of this small breakthrough. Having given his question some consideration, it seemed to me that his best course would be to seek out a handful of lucrative portrait commissions. Of course, now that Lavery had the royal seal of approval, many wealthy Glaswegians dreamed only of being immortalised in paint by the Great Man himself. However, they would have to wait until Lavery had finished his 'Victoria', which might take months – even years. This being the case, Ned could take advantage of the delay and then, with a few commissions under his belt, devote some time to his own, more interesting, work. Thus, at my suggestion, he made it known that he was interested in undertaking a small number of select portraits. Within weeks, he had received several commissions, including one from Mrs Euphemia Urquart, who resided nearby, in one of the very grand houses on Woodside Crescent. As the wife of an eminent surgeon and university professor, Mrs Urquart had a natural air of command suitable to her elevated station, and rivalled even the Queen for embonpoint and loftiness, to the extent that we came to refer to her, in private, as 'The Duchess'.

I believe that Annie might have been slightly peeved that Ned had consulted my advice about his career, but if she did have any reservations she kept them to herself, particularly when she realised that these portrait commissions would secure the family's finances for months. Generally speaking, Annie's attitude to me had undergone a complete transformation, ever since she had learned about my intervention regarding Findlay's caricature. She was eminently more welcoming, and in less of a hurry to finish my portrait, eventually taking another four sessions to complete it to her satisfaction. Even then, she encouraged me to visit number 11, so that it became second nature for me to call upon the family, a few times a week, without even an invitation. As I grew to know her better, I came to realise that – due to the difficult circumstances of her impoverished childhood – Annie found it hard to trust new acquaintances. However, once her confidence had been gained, she was extremely warm and loyal and soon she began to treat me like an old and trusted friend. Perhaps it was an indication of how welcome I now was at Stanley Street that the

Gillespies spent part of the fee from my portrait on a new arm-chair for the parlour, which became known as 'Harriet's chair' and was reserved for me to sit upon, during my visits.

Our time was not often spent at leisure, however. Since Ned's preferred remedy for Sybil's 'nerves' was fresh air and activity, I began to keep Annie company while she took the girls for long walks, in an attempt to tire them out. Vigorous exercise, indeed! There is a saying that the Clyde is the only level highway in Glasgow, and the West End, in particular, is built upon a set of drumlins, producing the curious effect that – no matter which direction one takes – one always seems to be trudging uphill. On fine days, in late summer, these walks were pleasant enough. However, as soon as true autumn set in, there was scant pleasure to be had in tramping the streets of Kelvinside, battered by horizontal rain.

Knowing how much Annie yearned to improve her painting, I tried to help out around the house, whenever I could, so that she could devote more time to her Art. Personally, I have never had much talent for any of life's accomplishments. I certainly cannot draw or paint and, despite the early-morning childhood drill of scales and exercises, my piano playing was always indifferent – but any fool can do housework. Thus, I lent a hand with the mending, which led, first, to the reorganisation of the upstairs linen press and, thence, to the creation of new curtains for the dining room, to replace the old ones which had, mysteriously, developed great rips and holes. Arithmetic was not Annie's strong point, whereas I like nothing better than addition and subtraction, marshalling columns of figures, the fact that there is always, but always, an incontrovertible solution, and – seeing her, one day, struggling over her accounts, I offered to help. As it transpired, both she and Ned were so pleased with the result of my efforts, that they persuaded me to continue balancing the family's books, something that I did, most willingly, for several months thereafter.

Accounting aside, there was always plenty to do at number 11, because – despite being employed as maid – Christina appeared to have no initiative or inclination in that respect. Annie knew that she ought to get rid of the girl, but could never quite pluck up the courage. However, the final straw came, in late October, when Christina failed to return from her afternoon off until the following day. Yet again, she was the worse of drink, and this time, giving no credible excuse for her lateness, promptly fell asleep on a chair in the kitchen. At long last, Annie dismissed her – much to the outrage of Christina, who left in high dudgeon (although we will hear more of her, later). Jessie, her replacement, could not have been more different: where Christina had been flighty and fair, this new girl was dull and plain. Unfortunately, she too was not without her flaws, as we were to learn, in time.

As for the business of the caricature, I kept an eye on every issue of *The Thistle* until Findlay's series reached an end in November, but no risqué vignette of Ned and his brother ever appeared. Nowadays, when it comes to such matters, one cannot help but think of Oscar Wilde (a marvellous writer, but a dreadful show-off). Of course, all this took place several years before the Wilde trials, but there had been other high-profile scandals, and Kenneth Gillespie can have had few illusions about what events might have been set in train, had a revealing sketch been published.

Down at the river, Kenneth's Venetian friend continued to occupy his usual position, aft of the gondola, steering on, po-faced, whilst his older compatriot laughed and sang as he leaned to his oar. Thankfully, in the immediate aftermath of the Findlay business, Kenneth did curtail his illicit activities. He avoided the park, whereas, previously, he had been a regular visitor, and began to take luncheon in the shop, or nearby, at Assafrey's. In the evenings, he either stayed at home, in his mother's house, or called at number 11 to see his nieces. According to Annie, there was a new air of melancholy in his demeanour. Apparently, he blamed himself that Ned had not triumphed over Lavery. Even though Findlay's caricature had never seen the light of day, Kenneth was convinced that the Fine Art Committee must have heard rumours.

About a fortnight after the scarecrow-like figure of Mr Crawhall had appeared in *The Thistle*, I was on my way up Great Western Road, en route to some engagement, when I realised that I was about to pass the Wool and Hosiery. Having not seen Ned's brother for a few weeks, I was mildly curious to know how his narrow escape had affected him, and so I decided to glance inside the shop, in the hope of catching a glimpse of him. My plan was to give the appearance of casually examining the window display in passing. To this end, I approached at a brisk pace and, drawing near to the glass, fixed my gaze, first, upon a pyramid of cotton reels, and then, on a garden squirt. Glancing up, I was startled to find myself staring, at close proximity, into Kenneth's face, for he had been loitering just behind the display, daydreaming, as he looked out into the street. Here was a moment of social awkwardness, neatly partitioned by a pane of glass. Ned's brother flinched like a startled cat, and then, recovering himself, gave me a curt nod. Previously, I might have gone in to offer him 'good day', but such an encounter, now, would prove embarrassing. Thus, I simply waved, cheerfully, and strolled on past. As I departed, I saw Kenneth shrink away from the window and walk, rather stiff-legged, towards the counter. He looked utterly miserable.

Whenever he and I met, subsequently, we were perfectly polite to each other, but he was unable to look at me directly, his gaze tending to slide away to the floor. He seemed perfectly wretched, and I believe that Annie was right in her view that he was punishing himself for what he saw as his role in Ned's failure.

Alas, as summer turned to autumn – and despite Annie's repeated pleas for caution – Kenneth resumed his old ways. Apparently driven by a reckless melancholy, he began, once again, to indulge in venereal activities with the gondolier, now conducted in ever more daring locations: at night, on an empty bandstand; at dusk, behind a mausoleum in the Necropolis; and once (I was reliably informed, by Annie) in broad daylight, on the top deck of a half-empty tramway car. Ned and the rest of the family remained ignorant of his exploits, but it seemed that it would only be a matter of time before he was caught.

And then, in November, something happened that took us all by surprise.

Following a successful summer, the Exhibition came to an end on the 10th of the month: the exhibitors packed up their wares, and left the city; many of the buildings began to be deconstructed, and the pleasure boats ceased to plough up and down the River Kelvin. A few days later, Mabel put her head around Kenneth's door to call him to breakfast, only to find his bed empty, and a note upon his pillow. At some point during the night, he had packed a bag of clothes and crept out of the house. The note – addressed to his mother – explained that he had decided to leave Glasgow. He made no mention of his destination, but begged Elspeth not to worry about him, and promised to contact her when he 'got settled'.

In the days that followed, Ned took time off from portrait painting, and attempted to persuade the police to investigate his brother's disappearance, but they refused to treat the matter as worthy of inquiry. After all, Kenneth had left a letter; he was over twenty-one; and had gone, apparently, of his own volition. With no police help forthcoming, Ned undertook some investigations of his own: he advertised in newspapers, both north and south of the border, and questioned Kenneth's acquaintances, but nobody was able to enlighten him.

Ned was hurt, of course, that his brother had chosen to leave without informing him, and greatly inconvenienced, since he himself was obliged to work in the shop for two days, until some-one was found to take Kenneth's place. The artist's reaction to this latest crisis was admirably level-headed. For the sake of his mother, he put a brave face on things, and assured us all that, no doubt, Kenneth had gone to seek a new life for himself; next time we heard of him, he would have made his name in some important field. Unaware of Kenneth's secret, Gillespie had a straight-forward view of the situation: in his eyes, his brother had simply fled town to escape the drudgery of life as a shop assistant.

Privately, Annie had her own suspicions about where her brother-in-law might have gone. It was, perhaps, no coincidence that he had vanished just a few days after the closure of the Exhibition. The gondoliers' employment had come to an end, and they had, presumably, returned to their native country.

'I think he's gone to Venice, with Carmine,' she confided, one unexpectedly fine afternoon, a few days after his departure, as we were paying our pennies at the gate of the Botanic Gardens. 'Either that, or he's followed him there.'

'Really?' I said. 'Kenneth doesn't strike me as particularly adventurous, in that way. Travelling to Italy alone, for instance. He doesn't speak Italian, does he?'

'Only a little, from Carmine. But if they've gone together . . . Sibyl! Wait!'

The child had raced ahead at such speed that she was already almost out of earshot, beyond Kibble Palace. Rose, who had gone tottering after her, retraced her steps towards us, but naughty Sibyl had to be summoned, several times, before she came to a reluctant standstill, and began kicking, disconsolately, at the edge of the grass. As yet, she had not been informed that her cherished Uncle Kenneth had left town. Ned was still hoping that his brother might have second thoughts, and return home, and nobody wished to upset Sibyl, unnecessarily, by giving her bad news.

Annie sighed as she put away her purse.

'Presumably, he has no money?' I asked.

She shook her head. 'But I expect he'll manage. He couldn't be any more miserable than he was here. Perhaps Carmine might get him work, on a gondola.'

A vision of Kenneth poling up and down the Venetian canals flashed into my mind, and I almost laughed, so incongruous was the image. Never let it be said that I was pleased that Ned's brother had fled Glasgow, so mysteriously. However, there was, perhaps, a slight sense of relief, on my part, and (I suspect) also on the part of Annie. At the very least, we were able to comfort each other, and the thought that Kenneth was, in all likelihood, safely ensconced somewhere, far from Glasgow, with his gondolier friend, allowed us both to be optimistic about his welfare.

The rest of the family had reacted to his departure in their own individual ways. Mabel was certainly capable of histrionics but, from time to time, she was just as likely to take everybody by surprise, and shrug off a situation that might have upset any other mortal – and so it was, concerning Kenneth.

'He's a grown man,' she told me, one afternoon. 'He can look after himself fine. He's probably gone chasing after some girl.' Perhaps this subdued response was due, in part, to a change in her own circumstances: she and Walter Peden had recently embarked upon an unlikely flirtation. The romance was only in its early stages but, rather than moping at home, or bothering Ned in his studio, as she had been doing all year, Mabel was spending the autumn out and about, with Walter and various friends from the Art School, where he tutored an evening class. These chums were a group of impoverished painters, and arts and crafts tutors, both male and female, who tended to entertain themselves cheaply, dining in each other's rooms, and taking sixpenny seats at the Gaiety: a bohemian, forgiving crowd, and even prickly Mabel was welcome amongst their number, her beauty a passport into this circle of aesthetes. Peden had made it his mission to distract her, which meant that she was less inclined to fret about Kenneth.

Unfortunately, the same could not be said for Elspeth. As the weeks went by, and there was no word of her son, and no letter, she became increasingly hipped. Naturally, she knew nothing of his secret life, and Annie and I were unable to reassure her by revealing what we suspected: indeed, I imagine that Ned's mother would have found the news that Kenneth was a homosexual considerably more alarming than his disappearance. Poor Elspeth! She took it badly, no matter how much we tried to reassure her.

Nevertheless, without a doubt, the person most affected by Kenneth's departure was his niece. There came a point when Sibyl had to be told the truth: Kenneth had gone away and nobody knew when he might return. She was utterly inconsolable at this news, and spent much of November moping around in sulks. Her head and tummy aches suddenly increased in frequency, and she got little rest, being almost incapable of falling asleep, and then waking, frequently, in the night. These symptoms always seemed to be at their worst after she had found herself in trouble, yet again, for her various acts of wilful and malicious destruction. Vile drawings continued to appear on the walls of the apartment, but she also developed some new and troubling habits. For instance, she took to rearranging the objects in a room, in secret, like a little living poltergeist, and although this was not exactly hazardous behaviour, it was inconvenient and frustrating. Rather more ominously, however, Sibyl developed a fascination with matches, and the 'Bryant & May's' from the parlour and kitchen would often go missing, only to turn up in one of her pockets. Mabel's Berlin work was found scorched, as was Rose's wooden horse.

Even Ned's mother finally lost patience with the child. On the last day of November, the entire batch of her church newsletter, *Let God Arise*, was discovered, burned to ashes on the parlour fire. Elspeth was horrified that Sibyl could have committed such an unchristian act. Sensing that the child had gone too far, this time, Annie came down hard, and locked her in her room, a punishment that sent Sibyl into a filthy, inconsolable rage.

Early one afternoon, Annie and I were sewing in the parlour when the new maid, Jessie, came running upstairs from the washhouse and presented herself at the threshold, huffing and puffing, and holding out for inspection what appeared to be a soggy, half-burnt sack or rag, which she claimed to have found amongst the ash pile in the corner of the back green. Initially, we failed to fathom why she was so animated, since any amount of rubbish was to be found in the ash pits.

However, when Jessie unfolded the cloth for us to examine, we saw that one side of the fabric was coated in oil paint, and realised, with dismay, that it was not a filthy rag at all, but one of Ned's paintings. The canvas had been cut clean away from the frame, and then slashed with a knife or razor, and scorched, until it was almost unrecognisable. Nevertheless, Annie knew the painting, at once, because it was an old, small-scale portrait of herself, depicted against a blue background, a picture that usually sat in the studio, against the wall, amongst a stack of other unsold works. Now, it was ruined.

'I thought it was one of they paintings,' said Jessie. 'I just didnae know if Mr Gillespie might have thrown it out hisself.'

At that time, it was unthinkable that Ned would ever have destroyed a canvas, although he might have reused one, by overpainting. There was no telling how long the portrait of Annie had lain, undetected, in the ash pit: perhaps several days. Ned had completely failed to notice that it was missing, and so he cannot have valued it too highly. Admittedly, it was not a recent picture, nor one that was of any commercial value. None the less, the violence of what had happened, and the potential threat that such a fate might befall a more saleable painting, shocked us to the core. Annie told me that when she showed Ned the shredded portrait, that evening, he was devastated. Unable to bring himself to put it on the fire, he took it out to the back green and reburied it in the ash pit. Apparently, he stood staring down at the heaps of ashes for almost ten minutes before returning inside.

Our worst fears were confirmed, that night, when Ned and Annie searched Sibyl's room. Hidden beneath the bed, they found one of Ned's Kropp razors, and a stretcher frame, with – as incontrovertible proof – the remaining edges of the blue-painted canvas still attached. Apparently, Sibyl was present during the search, and went into hysterics as soon as Ned leaned down to peer under her bed.

From that day forth, the child was forbidden to enter the studio, at any time. As far as punishment was concerned, the Gillespies threatened to cancel their Hogmanay celebration, an annual *soirée* that was, by all accounts, legendary. Usually, the children enjoyed the privilege of being allowed to stay up later than usual, and they had looked forward to the party all year. The threat of cancellation – unless there was, in the interim, a dramatic improvement in her conduct was Sibyl's only real punishment, and so, as might be expected, she promised to be good.

In the aftermath of these latest incidents, Ned's wife began to worry that she had failed as a mother. Once again, when Mabel proposed that an expert in nervous disorders be brought in to examine Sibyl, Annie brushed aside her suggestion, knowing that Ned would be appalled at the mere suggestion that his daughter was not right in the mind. Perhaps out of desperation, Annie seized on the idea that living in the city was entirely to blame for Sibyl's bad behaviour.

'It can't be good for her, Harriet,' she kept telling me. 'All this smoke and grime, being cooped up indoors all winter.' She began to talk about the possibility of taking the girls to the coast, believing that seaside air, away from Glasgow, might cure the child. 'We just need to get her out of town.'

It so happened that Walter Peden had inherited a tiny cottage at Cockburnspath and he invited the Gillespies to spend a few weeks with him there, over Christmas. Ned, Annie and the children were to have the only proper bedroom, whilst Mabel (who was also invited) would sleep in a little adjacent room that had once housed geese. Peden himself claimed that he was happy to doss down in front of the parlour fire, on a mattress.

Sadly, there was no space for me to join them. When the trip was first mooted, Ned did suggest that Mabel and I could share the goose house, but after Peden had described its tiny dimensions, the idea was quickly overruled as impractical. I dare say, had I wanted, I could have taken a room in a guesthouse, nearby. However, I was quite happy with the prospect of remaining in Glasgow. My landlady and her daughters had invited me to spend

Christmas Day in their company, and there was the possibility, in the evening, of calling upon Elspeth, who did not celebrate Christmas, a festival that she viewed as entirely heathen.

Having resolved to spend my Yuletide thus, I was surprised, (on the 16th of December, a few days after Peden and the Gillespies had left for Co'path), to hear from my stepfather, who invited me to join him for Christmas dinner at the Grand Hotel. Given his aversion to correspondence, it was extraordinary that Ramsay had even written me a letter. I was delighted to reflect that, not only had I been in his thoughts, but he also desired to spend Christmas with me. As the day approached, I grew increasingly excited, and also, perhaps, nervous, about the occasion.

The 25th of December dawned, frosty and bright. Our table at the Grand was booked for the afternoon, and Ramsay had arranged to meet me, in the tea room, at one o'clock, before we went upstairs for dinner. Having dressed carefully, I arrived in plenty of time and was shown to a table in the corner. There, I remained for almost thirty minutes, and I began to wonder whether my stepfather had forgotten our appointment but, as it transpired, there had been a misunderstanding, and he was waiting for me, with increasing impatience, up in the restaurant. This setback started us off on a bad footing and Ramsay's sour mood endured throughout most of dinner: he was rude to the waiters and impatient with me; the wine was too cold; his beef too stringy. Only when dessert had been served did he mellow somewhat, and offered to take me back to my lodgings in his carriage.

'How kind of you, sir. If you wouldn't mind, I'd be most grateful.'

In fact, it had just occurred to me that, if my stepfather had an hour to spare, I could show him my rooms. To my mind, Queen's Crescent was a charming terrace, with its central gardens, and stone fountain; my landlady, Mrs Alexander, kept a tidy house; my sitting room caught the morning light; I had sewed my own curtains, and brightened up an old screen, by pasting on scraps and dried flowers. My abode may not have amounted to much, but it was the first place where I had resided that I could call my very own. In hindsight, I suppose that I craved parental approval of my choices. On second thoughts, it was perhaps not approval that I sought; I simply hoped that Ramsay would be glad to know more about my circumstances, and curious to see where I now resided.

The journey to Queen's Crescent took us only a few minutes in the carriage. In my enthusiasm, forgetting that Ramsay knew Glasgow well, I drew his attention to a few local landmarks, and when – having forgotten his customary disdain for 'sweeties' – I pointed to the chocolate factory in passing, he gave the façade a sideways glance and intoned: 'Aye', a single word which he imbued with maximum possible West of Scotland scepticism.

The afternoon light was fading as we drew up outside my lodgings. I began to feel rather nervous about inviting my step-father inside, fearing a refusal. Before I could speak, however, he climbed from the carriage and stood, one arm outstretched, to assist me onto the pavement. As I climbed down, he was casting a critical gaze at the terrace behind him.

'Is this it?' he asked, and then continued: 'Listen here, Harriet, I own a house at Bardowie – unoccupied. You'd be welcome to stay there. 'Merlinsfield', it's called. It's by the loch, very pretty. There's an old couple, Deuchars and his wife, live in the cottage, and they look after the place for me. They'd help you settle in.'

This offer came so abruptly, out of the blue, that I was dumb-founded. 'I – that's kind of you, sir. I don't know what to say. Where is Bardowie, exactly?'

'Oh, only six miles out of town. What does your rent cost you here?'

When I told him what I paid, he frowned. 'For the whole house?'

'No – just two rooms, in the attic.'

He looked shocked. 'By Jove! Well – you'd have the run of Merlinsfield – it's a fair-sized house with grounds, mind, and as for rent – well . . .' He smiled. 'I'm sure we could reach an agreement to suit your purse.'

At this, I felt confused, and a little deflated: did that mean, then, that he would charge me rent? Or was this comment about my purse an attempt at joviality?

'Will you be moving back down south?' he asked.

In fact, I had not really thought, on any conscious level, about when – or even whether – I might return to London. There was no pressing reason for me to leave Scotland. At any rate, I was happy where I was, for the present.

'No,' I told him. 'I hadn't planned –'

Nodding, he went on: 'One thing to mention, there's a builder at Merlinsfield, working on the roof and suchlike. You could just keep an eye on him, if you wouldn't mind. He's taken too long already. It's just a few repairs, and there's no real problem with damp – only in a few rooms. At any rate, I'm beginning to suspect the man's a swindler, and old Deuchars is getting on in years; he's got no authority. But now, if I had somebody young on hand, to hurry this builder along . . . And there's other jobs about the place need done, if you've time.' Ramsay tilted back his head and stared at me down the length of his nose, a look that I remembered well from childhood. 'Would you be able to manage that, do you think?'

'I – I don't know, sir. It sounds rather as though you need some sort of building manager.'

He laughed. 'A building manager, is it, eh? Have you any idea how much that would cost? No, no, I need somebody I can trust.' He dug into his pocket and produced several sheets of paper, folded together, which he handed to me. 'That's a list of what needs doing to the house. Rooms painted, furniture restored, curtains mended, that kind of thing. Some of it should wait until the roof's done but you could tackle a fair few jobs in the meantime. I expect you can manage most of it yourself, but you could hire a decorator, provided he's cheap and we agree costs.'

Of a sudden, I felt very muddled. It was flattering to be entrusted with the house, of course, and I wanted him to think that I was capable of dealing with builders, and so on. But, on the other hand, I was not sure that I wanted to live six miles away from my new friends.

'Your offer's kind, sir, but I wonder whether I might prefer to remain in town. If you don't mind, I'd just like to think on it, and let you know in a day or two . . .'

'Aye, if you must,' he said, stiffly. 'Let me know what you decide.'

'Yes, indeed – and thank you again for your kind offer. Now, would you care to come in for me – I mean, for tea! For tea! Do – please – come in, come in, for tea.'

I told myself to stop repeating every word that I said, but Ramsay was too busy peering at his watch to notice my stammers. 'No – no,' he said, briskly. 'I'd best be away. I bid you good day, Harriet.'

Something in his tone made me suspect that I had disappointed him, as though my lack of decisiveness over the matter of the house had confirmed an already low opinion of me. He shook my hand, and climbed into the carriage.

'Good day, sir,' I called out. 'I'll certainly give your offer serious consideration and let you know as soon as possible – thank you!'

However, just at that moment, Ramsay was giving instructions to the driver and appeared not to hear me. At a flick of the reins, the horses lurched into motion and the carriage set off around the Crescent.

When I opened the door of my lodgings, I could hear the Alexanders playing parlour games in the sitting room. Although I had been invited to join them upon my return, I was no longer in the mood and so went directly upstairs. My own room seemed very silent and still. Shutting myself away, I went over the events of the past few hours, in my mind. Disappointed that Ramsay had hurried off, so abruptly, I tried to convince myself that he was keen to be on the road before night fell, but I did feel slighted. Clearly, he had not a modicum of curiosity about me.

Moreover, although it was kind of him to have offered the use of his house at Bardowie, I began to wonder whether, in fact, I would be doing *him* a favour by taking up residence, if Merlinsfield was damp, and I was tasked with overseeing the work of a lazy builder. It appeared that I might even be charged rent for the privilege. Not to mention the forty-seven jobs of renovation that required attention around the premises (Ramsay had numbered the items on his list). His proposition had seemed spontaneous — and yet, could it really be a coincidence that, on Christmas Day, he had been carrying around in his pocket this inventory of tasks?

The more I thought about it, the more dejected I became. Disillusioned, I glanced around the sitting room, which looked, suddenly, shabby, as I saw it through my stepfather's eyes. Since it was Christmas, Mrs Alexander's daughter, Lily, had not been in to clean, and everything was exactly as I had left it that morning, with a dirty cup and saucer on the table, a frock draped over a chair, and, on the linoleum, in the kitchen corner, a dark stain of coffee that I must have spilled that morning, without noticing.

But all this bosh about Ramsay is by the bye. There I go again, like the bibulous butler, forever stumbling up the wrong passage.

8

The following week, on the evening of the 31st of December, I bade Mrs Alexander and her daughters 'Happy New Year', and stepped into the night. Outside, the air tasted of sulphur. A heavy rain had cleared in the afternoon, giving way to a drop in temperature. The cold was magisterial. It had turned the streets to icy metal, and robed the buildings in freezing fog so thick that the gardens at the centre of the Crescent were barely visible. However, I rather enjoy the mystery of fog, and was in fine spirits. Ned and Annie had just returned from Co'path. Sibyl had been as good as gold for the past few weeks, with the result that the Gillespies had decided to go ahead with their New Year's celebrations. I was quite thrilled that I was about to experience my first ever Caledonian 'Hogmanay' in their company.

Perhaps I should have seen the fog as an omen. Crossing West Princes Street, I passed a cab that was creeping along at the rate of twenty yards a minute, the driver carrying a torch and leading his horse by its bridle, in case of collisions. Further on, I found a small, sobbing boy clinging to the railings of the Academy: he was lost in the fog, yet probably within a stone's throw of home. As I leaned down to offer assistance, a sharp-visaged girl, a few years his senior, appeared.

'There ye are!' she cried, scooping up the child and scolding him as they disappeared into the swirling mist: 'Now, dinnae greet no more, you're found.'

A few workmen loitered at the top of Stanley Street, smoking their pipes, and talking, beneath the sooty yellow light of a lamp-post. Another man passed by, calling out to them: 'How was the day, lads?', and one of their number spat into the gutter before replying, impassively: 'Mondayish.' My coat soon grew moist with fog and – despite my *tricot*, scarf, gloves and boots – my feet and face were numb by the time that I reached my destination.

In answer to my ring, Jessie, the maid, came downstairs. She had been with the Gillespies for several weeks by this time and, thus far, gave the impression of being honest enough. I found her rather dour but, as we climbed towards the apartment, I took a stab at conversation:

'Now, Jessie, did you have a wonderful Christmas?'

'We don't go in for Christmas, Miss Baxter, as much as you do, down south.'

Ah yes, 'down south': as far as Jessie was concerned, any person or thing from 'down south' was to be viewed with suspicion.

'Of course!' I replied. 'Well, in that case, a very Happy New Year to you!'

'It's not even eight o'clock yet,' said Jessie, as she sailed inside the apartment, leaving me to infer that, in addition to being a Sassenach, I had committed the sin of prematurity. When I entered the hall, she was nowhere to be seen, but a clatter of chairs suggested that she had repaired to the dining room. Annie emerged from the kitchen, in her apron, to greet me. Her hair was tumbling down, and there was flour on her face and hands. She looked flustered, but happy.

'Harriet!' she cried and, careful not to get flour on my clothes, she embraced me, and kissed my cheek. 'I'm so glad you're here.'

Only a small group of family and friends was expected before midnight. Most of the guests would arrive after the bells: local artists, the younger teaching staff from the Art School, a few well-liked neighbours, the Wool and Hosiery assistants, various of Elspeth's waifs and strays, and several valued customers who used the shop ('but nobody too stuffy', according to Annie). While she hung up my coat, she explained that Mrs Calthrop from downstairs had taken the children, to allow us to get on with the preparations for the party.

'No doubt, they'll be back any minute, though,' said Annie. 'She can only ever thole them for half an hour.'

In the kitchen, a scene of devastation greeted us. All manner of dishes lay scattered about, in various stages of completion, and everything seemed to be coated in a thin layer of flour. I set to clearing some space on the table, so that I could make a start on the shortbread.

'And how was Co'path?' I enquired.

'Wonderful! It did miracles for Sibyl, anyway, and that had a good effect on the rest of us. We went on lots of walks and Ned did some sketching. The sea air did us the world of good. None of this reeking smoke! I wish we could live out there.'

'I believe it's very pretty, with the harbour, and so on.'

'Yes, it is.' She looked embarrassed. 'Well, you must – you really must come with us next time. It's just the cottage is so small . . .'

'Oh, gracious! That's very kind of you.' Of a sudden, I felt hot. The kitchen was steamy, but also, I had glimpsed something in Annie's expression that I found disconcerting. It had never entered my head that they should have taken me, rather than Mabel. After all, she was a family member – and there was the budding romance to consider.

'Would you go back again?' I asked, quickly.

'Och, Ned would live there, if he could – but he's got so much to do here, now, with the Duchess to finish.'

'Ah yes – Her Grace. How is she progressing? Presumably, he'll soon be able to get back to his own work, at last.'

But before Annie could reply, there was a knock at the front door. She sighed and hurried into the hall, calling out: 'I'll get it, Jessie! It's probably just the girls.'

So ended our peace and quiet. I heard Annie talking to that Calthrop woman on the doorstep. Meanwhile, Sibyl slipped into the kitchen. Ignoring me, she went straight to the cake box and plucked at its strings.

'What's this?'

'It's a cake, dear, for your mother. Did you have a nice holiday?'

She gazed at me, balefully. Perhaps she had gained a little weight in Cockburnspath, though her complexion was still sallow.

'Can I see the cake?'

'Not just at the moment.'

Sibyl twisted her arms and hands into little begging gestures, a feverish, beseeching look on her face.

'Oh, please can I? Let me see it, please, Harriet, please!'

'No, dear,' I said firmly. 'Your mother shall see it first, since it is her cake.'

'Is it a chocolate cake?'

'No, it is not.'

'Is it a cherry cake?'

'No.'

'Is it a currant cake?'

We might have continued in the same vein, indefinitely, but just then Annie reappeared with Rose, and so I turned away from Sibyl and addressed her mother. I knew that Annie never put up a Christmas tree, but was not exactly sure where she and Ned stood on the subject of giving and receiving festive gifts. 'I hope you don't mind, Annie, but I've brought you all Christmas presents.'

'Hurrah!' cried Sibyl. She began to jump up and down, jabbering nonsense, and Rose, who always liked to emulate her sister, joined in.

'How kind,' said Annie. 'Don't worry, we gave each other presents this year. I even put some holly on the mantel at the cottage – oh, but don't tell Elspeth that!' For a second, she looked as alarmed as a naughty schoolgirl, and then we both dissolved into laughter. 'We've got a gift for you as well,' said Annie, recovering.

'How lovely! Is Ned in? Why don't we open our presents together?'

She gave her head a brief shake. 'He'll be back later, let's do it then.'

To keep the children out of mischief while we worked, I gave them some flour and water in a bowl, with which to make a paste, and, for a while, they applied themselves to this game with subdued industry. Their mother made punch, by boiling up oranges with wine, sugar, and spices. The air soon filled with the scents of warm cloves and cinnamon, and although the kitchen was still untidy, it occurred to me what a pretty domestic scene we would make for Ned, whenever he returned. Once the punch was ready, Annie set it aside, and began to stuff the vol-au-vents. I rolled out the shortbread, whilst Sibyl, having abandoned her flour paste, stood at the table, staring, as though hypnotised, at the clove-studded oranges, now afloat and gleaming in the pan of red wine.

Not for the first time, I was drawn to wonder what went on in that strange little head of hers. Now, as I watched her, Sibyl passed her hand over the pan of punch and would have poked the oranges with her finger had I not coughed pointedly, and given her a mock-warning look, in response to which she giggled, and scampered out of the room. At the same moment, the front door opened. 'Papa!' came Sibyl's cry, and then, the sound of a groaning sigh, presumably as Ned lifted her into his arms.

'There's my lovely girl,' I heard him murmur. Then, silence fell. Although Sibyl had left the door ajar, I could not see them from where I was standing, and, as the silence continued, I began to wonder what they could be doing. I glanced towards the hearth. Annie had sat down and was gazing into the fire, with a faraway expression on her face, while Rose played at her feet. And still, there was no sound from beyond the kitchen door. It occurred to me that, perhaps, Ned was leafing through his mail, at the hall-stand, but then I wondered why I had heard no sound of paper rustling, or letter-opening. At any rate, it was time for the shortbread to go into the range. As I stepped around the table, I happened to glance through the doorway, and there, I saw them. Ned stood quietly, holding Sibyl in his arms. She had wrapped her legs around his waist. Her head rested on his shoulder, and he was rocking her, gently, from side to side. Neither of them noticed me; they both simply gazed off into space, with an air of quiet contentment. Here was a private moment, I realised, a moment of tenderness, between father and daughter. I felt that I was witnessing something intimate and strange, something beyond words or understanding. Discomfited, and embarrassed, lest one of them might suddenly turn and see me, I hurried across the kitchen, and bent down to put the petticoat tails in to bake. Against my face, the scorching breath of the range felt as hot as a furnace. I shut the metal door with a clang and, when I turned around, Annie was lifting her youngest daughter to her feet, saying: 'Why don't you show Harriet your Christmas present, Rosie?'

The child became bashful, as she often did, when thrust into the limelight. With Sibyl acknowledged as the black sheep of the family, Rose tended, these days, to enjoy improved status. She had always been her mother's favourite, of course, and lately, Elspeth – still smarting over the destruction of her newsletters – was prone to ignore Sibyl, whilst lavishing attention on her sister.

No doubt to prevent arguments, the girls had been given exactly the same Christmas present: a silver chain upon which hung a delicate pendant of mother-of-pearl, set in silver. Apart from a few natural ripples, the necklaces were identical, and the girls' names had been engraved on the silver backings, to distinguish them. With some encouragement, Rose very sweetly lifted her chin, and held out her pendant for me to admire.

'My name on the back, look,' she said, in lilting tones.

'Aren't you a lucky girl?'

And she nodded. I remember, distinctly, the iridescence of that fragment of nacre, the way it shimmered, blue and pink and green, between her little fingers, and the soft down on her cheek as she gazed at her Christmas gift, a proud smile lifting the corners of her rosebud lips.

And there I must stop, for these recollections have made me rather too upset to continue.

As far as Ned's mother was concerned, Christmas gifts symbolised a reprehensible voluptuousness and wanton display of excess. It was unfortunate, therefore, that when she arrived that night, we had all just opened our presents. I had bought books for the girls, gloves for Annie, and a soft comforter for Ned. They, in turn, gave me a pincushion, which I was in the process of unwrapping when we heard the front door open, and Elspeth let herself in, exclaiming to Jessie about the cold.

At the sound of his mother's voice in the hall, Ned swore softly, under his breath, and shoved his comforter under a cushion. He shooed the girls into a corner with their books, while Annie and I snatched up the discarded wrapping papers, and fed them to the fire, hoping to avoid any awkwardness.

'Thank you, thank you both,' I murmured, dropping my new pincushion into my bag, just as Elspeth surged across the threshold, with her usual screech of laughter. Glancing at the hearth, I was dismayed to see that the wrapping paper was still smouldering but, mercifully, Ned's mother was oblivious, being very taken up with a description of the fog.

'You can barely see your hend in front of your face!' she exclaimed. 'And the cold! When I think of poor Kenneth, out in this weather!'

'I doubt he's out in the cold,' said Ned, sensible as ever.

'But where is he?' Elspeth continued. 'And why has he not written to let us know? There are all these ghestly murders in London. To think of him – he might be wandering the streets of Whitechapel, lost and alone!'

'Mother, we've no reason to think he's in London,' said Ned. 'He might be in Timbuktu, for all we know. But wherever he is, I'm sure he's fine.'

'Well, we can but hope,' said Elspeth, clasping her hands and raising them, in supplication, to the ceiling.

'Yes, indeed,' I said. 'And even if he is in London, you needn't worry about those murders. I think you'll find that they're being perpetrated only upon the female sex. Kenneth is in no danger – unless he's taken to wearing skirts.'

What a silly thing to say, but it was out of my mouth before I could stop myself, perhaps because a vision of Findlay's drawing had flashed into my mind: Kenneth in petticoats and rouge. Annie's gaze – a little alarmed – locked with mine, and something passed between us. She had not seen the caricature, of course, but

I had described it to her and perhaps she was imagining a similar picture. She raised an eyebrow, and sucked in her cheeks, as though she might be overcome with mirth. Fortunately, nobody else seemed to have noticed, but I, too, had a sudden urge to laugh, and so I stood up and, to give myself time to recover, grabbed the teapot and headed for the kitchen, in search of more hot water.

On my way past the dining room, I glanced in and saw Rose, clutching at the maid's apron strings, and swinging from side to side, whilst Jessie attempted to polish the glasses. The kitchen door was half closed and so I backed in, with the teapot in both hands and turned – just in time to see Sibyl – with a strange, guilty expression on her face – stepping away from the table, where all manner of tempting dishes were laid out, ready to be taken through to the buffet in the dining room.

'Shoo!' I told her, and she put down her head and ran from the room.

Perhaps I *did* notice her stuff something into her apron pocket – or perhaps the intervening years have simply played tricks with my memory. In any case, I thought little of the incident at the time.

Mabel turned up at half past nine, scurrying into the apartment, very pink in the face, which I attributed, at first, to the cold. However, moments later, when the doorbell rang, Jessie ran down and returned with Walter Peden, which made me suspect that, perhaps, Mabel's high colour was due to something else, and that she and Walter had been together until their arrival, but had chosen to make separate entrances. Apparently, matters had progressed in Cockburnspath but, according to Annie, Elspeth had yet to be told of her daughter's romance.

A handful of guests arrived before midnight. Apart from a few stolid-looking types from the Art School (no doubt the real bohemians would make a late entrance), most of the early guests had been invited by Ned's mother. There was a group of Jewish gentlemen, who looked bewildered upon arrival, but became very animated when they spied Ned's chessboard and, ere long, they had set up a miniature tournament at the dining-room table. The Reverend Johnson, Elspeth's American pastor, strayed from her side only to fetch her refreshments. Elspeth was never so ebullient as she was in Johnson's company, and the two of them cackled loud and long, at the slightest excuse, until the racket bounced off the walls and ceiling, and one's ears positively rang, and people were driven from the room.

It was just as well that the remaining guests were not due to arrive until after the bells, since Ned and Annie disappeared behind the door of their room to change their clothes and did not re-emerge for an hour, leaving the rest of us to look after the children and organise the refreshments. Nobody seemed to be taking responsibility for this party, but I suppose that, by that stage, I should not have been surprised: such was the ever-relaxed Gillespie modus operandi. I helped Jessie to set out the buffet, while Mabel read to the children from the books that I had given them for Christmas, (*The Fairy Shop* for Rose, and, for Sibyl, *Struwwelpeter*), and Peden, very graciously, surrendered himself to conversation with Elspeth and the Reverend, on the condition that we keep him supplied with punch.

At long last, Ned reappeared, looking very smart – not in evening clothes, which he abhorred – but in his favourite old dark tweed jacket, and a low-collared shirt. He set about making 'het pint' for consumption by those who, like himself, could not abide wine. Annie eventually emerged, having changed into an eau-de-Nil dress. Pinned at her throat was her Christmas gift from her husband: a silver bar-brooch, with a heart-shaped pendant, set with a small baroque pearl, green pastes and tourmalines. (At the time, I wondered how Ned had been able to afford all these relatively costly gifts, but some time later, while tallying the accounts, I saw that Professor Urquart had paid his wife's fee, in advance). Mabel also looked very elegant that evening, in a charcoal frock, with leg-of-mutton sleeves and cinched waist. She had lost weight, perhaps, in part, because of her nascent romance with Peden, but also because she had taken up cigarettes, another matter that we were obliged to keep secret. Personally, I suspect that she could have smoked an entire box of Turkish Trophies in her mother's face, one after the other, and Elspeth would not have noticed. None the less, this was fifty years ago, you must remember, and few ladies dared to smoke in public. Moreover, Mabel was rather daunted by her mother, and desperate for her approval, and so she always made sure to cover the smell of her cigarettes with cologne and peppermints.

As a special treat, the children were permitted to stay up later than usual. Sibyl gave a piano recital, during which she played some of the mawkish hymns and Spirituals with which I had become all too familiar. I believe that this was a bid to regain favour with her granny, and although the widow applauded along with the rest of us, she was less ebullient and fulsome in her praise than she once might have been, and I could see that Sibyl was disappointed. Thereafter, Elspeth attached herself to a chair by the buffet, in the dining room, where she maintained an incessant prattle whilst grabbing at any choice morsels within reach.

At some point between eleven o'clock and midnight, during that stultifying final gasp of the Old Year (a single hour which always seems, inexplicably, to last the course of ages), the girls were finally sent to bed. Initially, Sibyl moaned at having to quit the party and then, I remember, at the time, finding it strange that, when Annie reminded her to behave herself, the child ran upstairs, giggling, in an odd, secretive fashion. Ned followed her, intending to read to the girls from their new books.

Thereafter, excusing myself from the dining room, I headed for the empty parlour, where I sank down on the sofa, grateful for a few minutes alone. I wondered whether to make my excuses and go home, but I had hoped to steal a moment with Ned before I left. There would be no chance of *that* in the dining room, but at least, from the parlour sofa, I might be able to hail him as he returned downstairs. Almost immediately, rather to my dismay,

Walter Peden came bouncing in to join me. Over the preceding few months, I had warmed to Walter, somewhat. He was a terrible prig (rather like Mabel, in fact) but beneath his awkward manner, he meant no harm. To my surprise and delight, he confided in me: earlier that evening, he had proposed to Mabel, and she had accepted him. He intended to announce the engagement, later, after the bells.

'Most heartfelt congratulations,' I told him. 'I'm so happy for you both.'

'Thank you, Hetty. Mabel has already planned the seating arrangement for the wedding breakfast – you, of course, are at the top table. She wants to invite half of Glasgow. Her only worry is that there'll be room for us all in the dining room at number 14.' He drained his glass, and then surged to his feet, pasty-faced, his forehead beaded with sweat. 'You've been most kind, Harriet, most kind.'

He seemed to have got it into his head that I was responsible for bringing him and Mabel together: quite frankly, an over-exaggeration. All that I had done was to arrange to meet them both on an 'open day' at the Botanic Gardens and then, through no fault of my own, was unable to make the appointment, which had the effect of throwing them together, alone, in the moist and fecund atmosphere of the Kibble Palace.

'Allow me to fetch you a drink,' said Walter. 'This punch is rather good.'

I myself had found it too bitter, and had drunk only one glass.

'No, thank you,' I told him. 'I've had ample sufficiency. Perhaps later.'

He bobbed around, unsteadily, in a drunken version of his habitual dance, and then took a swerving path out of the room and across the hall. I was just wondering whether to follow him, when Ned ran downstairs and strode directly into the room. He stopped short, a little startled, when he saw me.

'Excuse me, Harriet, I thought everyone was next door.'

'Oh, don't mind me – I just wanted to sit quietly, for a moment.'

'As a matter of fact, I've lost my . . .' He glanced around, patting his pockets in that vague, endearing way of his. Noticing his tobacco on the mantel, I got up and handed it to him and then, while I resumed my seat, Ned stood by the hearth, his fingers fumbling inside the soft leather pouch, shredding the tobacco before stuffing it into the bowl of his pipe.

'Are you enjoying yourself, Harriet?' he said, after a moment.

Just as I was about to reply, I sensed a movement over by the door and glanced up. There was Rose, standing in her nightdress, pale-faced, and staring at us, like a little ghost. She raised her arms and reached out to Ned.

'Papa!'

'Oh Rose,' he sighed, wearily. 'Go to sleep, there's a dear.'

'Allow me,' I said, getting to my feet.

'Are you sure, Harriet?'

Waving aside his objections, I took Rose by the hand, then picked up a candlestick and led her back upstairs. Her little room was in darkness, but the glowing candle made the condensation on the skylight window glitter like molten gold. Outside, all was unnaturally dark, as though a blanket had been thrown across the roof – a blanket of fog. I tucked the child into her bed and stepped out of the room. Strangely, the simple effort of climbing the stairs had left me breathless and perspiring, so I paused, for a moment, on the narrow landing. From the river, came the mournful sound of a foghorn, answered, moments later, by another. Sibyl's door lay open. I lifted my candle and peered into the gloom: as far as I could tell, she was fast asleep; at any rate, she lay, mute as a chrysalis, beneath her quilted cover.

Upon my return to the parlour, I was pleased to see that Ned was still there: he was seated on the sofa, smoking his pipe. I told him that Rose had settled.

'How did we ever manage without you?' he said. 'We should get shot of Jessie, have you in residence, upstairs. Not that I'm saying you should be our maid –'

I laughed, retrieving his comforter from behind the cushion

where he had stuffed it, earlier, and passing it to him. He turned it over in his hands.

'You chose this well,' he said. 'I'll certainly need it, if this weather keeps up. That loft is like an icebox.'

Since it was directly beneath the roof, the studio was often too hot in summer, and Ned tended to work in shirtsleeves, but in winter, the temperature plummeted, and he was obliged to add layer upon layer: waistcoat, corduroy jacket, beret, fingerless mittens and, for particularly cold days, he had created a bizarre poncho, by cutting a hole in the middle of an old blanket.

'You could have a better studio if you found yourselves a bigger house,' I told him. 'You could probably afford it, more or less, if you took in a lodger.'

He nodded. 'As a matter of fact, I'm quite taken with Co'path, as a place. If it wasn't for all these blasted portraits, here in Glasgow . . . never thought I'd hear myself say it, but I felt inspired out there. Although, we can't go back yet, because –' He stopped short, as though he had been about to blurt something out.

'What?'

'Ach – it's good news, it's just – I haven't told Annie yet.'

'Oh well – in that case, I shan't pry.'

'I'm telling her tonight, anyway. Just keep it to yourself, for the minute, but – well – I've been offered a solo show, in Hamilton's gallery, in April.'

'In Bath Street? That's marvellous. Annie will be pleased.'

'Possibly not,' he sighed. 'It means I should really get this last portrait done and then work on whatever I'm going to put into the show, and – well – I think Annie had her heart set on us all going back to Co'path, as soon as we could, but –'

His face fell. He looked so gloomy that I had to laugh.

'Oh, Ned – you look exactly like the first time we met. You were scowling then, just like you are now.'

'Was I? Oh aye – because of Hamilton – or Lavery.'

'No – the very first time we met.'

He gazed at me blankly, and then his face cleared, and he nodded.

'Oh, aye. I always forget about that.'

'That dreadful curator.'

Ned laughed. 'Aye, that's right.'

'And you lost your collar-stud, remember, and we looked for it together?'

'Did I?'

While we had been talking, I was dimly aware of some sort of commotion in the hall: the slam of a door; and then footsteps, hurrying to and fro; an urgent tapping; and, several times, the flush of the convenience. Now I heard Annie call out: 'Walter? Walter?' A moment later, she came dashing into the parlour. We glanced up as she appeared, her face stricken and unhealthily pale.

'Dear, there seems to be something the matter with Walter.'

Ned sprang to his feet. 'What is it?'

'He's not well,' said Annie, gulping. 'He's locked himself in – and I need to get in there because – I'm – I . . .' She doubled over, retching, her hands clasped to her mouth, as Elspeth, summoned by the commotion, appeared behind her.

'What's heppened?' cried Elspeth. 'Annie? What's the matter?'

Annie spun around. 'I'm fine,' she said, but scarcely had she spoken, when a stream of purple and greenish vomit, the thickness of gruel, shot, glistening, from her mouth, and spattered in hot jets across the Turkey carpet, and down the front of Elspeth's best frock. Ned rushed to Annie's side, and I was about to dash to the kitchen and fetch a cloth when I realised that I, too, was about to be horribly ill. Barging past Elspeth, I arrived at the WC, just as Walter emerged, wiping his lips with a handkerchief, and I darted past him, and slammed the door – and there, I shall discreetly draw a veil.

Subsequently, there could be no question of us continuing with our Hogmanay celebration. By the time that I had emerged, weak-kneed, but no longer nauseous, Reverend Johnson and the Jewish gentlemen had politely excused themselves, and Annie was lying down in her bedroom, tended by Mabel and Jessie, who were bustling back and forth with bowls and damp cloths. Alas the day, no amount of sponging had been able to save Elspeth's frock, and she had been obliged to leave. Peden was escorted home by the Art School crowd, while Ned had gone in search of a medical man willing to come out on such a night. As for myself, I could have stayed on at number 11 to be examined – and was invited to do so – but, in truth, although I no longer felt unwell, I was exhausted and chilled to the bone. What I needed most of all was rest. Mabel kindly accompanied me, through the fog, to Queen's Crescent, where I reassured her that I was on the mend, and then we said goodnight. She went back to number 11, in order to turn away any further guests, and I crept upstairs to bed, and slipped, thankfully, into unconsciousness, serenaded by a mournful lullaby of midnight bells and distant foghorns.

9

By a stroke of great good fortune, none of us was seriously afflicted that night: the ill effects lasted only a few hours, even in Peden, who had suffered the most. The doctor who examined him initially suspected that simple over-tippling might have been his problem, but amended this diagnosis later, when he saw that Annie exhibited identical symptoms. Concluding that some kind of 'bad food' was the most likely cause, he prescribed calomel and soda powders for both patients. Annie was mortified at the notion that her *cuisine* might have been responsible. However, Peden insisted that there must be some other explanation, for the simple reason that he had not eaten any of the buffet; not one morsel had passed his lips (he claimed) – not even a rissole – since he and Mabel had dined, earlier that evening, at the home of some friends.

This was puzzling news, indeed. Only three of us had suffered stomach pains and biliousness: Annie, Peden, and myself. Annie had sampled almost everything on the table, not during the party – although she had nibbled at a few savouries – but while she had been cooking. The only items that she had overlooked were the black bun and the cake that I had brought as a gift for the family. I myself had eaten only three things: a single vol-au-vent, a dark sliver of black bun, and a slice of the cake. Thus, between us, we had partaken of every dish, but neither of us had eaten exactly the same thing. It made sense, therefore (as I told Annie, the next day, when she called at my lodgings to see how I fared), to rule out the food, and turn our attention, instead, to the drinks.

'I tried some hot ale,' I told her. 'Perhaps the eggs were bad? But then Ned would have been ill. I had a glass of punch. And we had a cup of tea, didn't we, just before Elspeth arrived?'

Annie was pale, and anxious, but otherwise seemed unscathed

by her night of retching. 'I had more tea, later,' she said. 'Apart from that, all I had was punch.'

I thought for a moment. 'Well, it can't be the tea.'

'Walter drank the punch – in fact, that was all he drank.'

We looked at each other.

'And the oranges?' I asked. 'How did they look when you cut them up?'

'They looked fine,' said Annie, perhaps a little tetchy.

'Where did you get them?'

'McLure, the grocer, but there was nothing wrong with them.'

'Do you think it could have been the cinnamon?'

'It looked perfectly fine to me.'

In fact, as we were soon to discover, the contamination had come neither from the oranges, nor from the spices – and nor was it accidental.

When Annie returned to Stanley Street, a little later, at about midday, she found Jessie still engaged in tidying and cleaning. Due to the chaos resulting from our outbreak of illness, most of the housework had been left overnight. Jessie had finished washing the dishes, and was attempting, once more, to scrub out the stains from the parlour rug. Annie retrieved the wine-soaked oranges and spices from the rubbish, but although she turned them over with a spoon, and peered at them, she did not really know what she was looking for and, detecting no visible signs of rot or mould, concluded that whatever had caused us to be ill must be invisible to the naked eye. Thereafter (as she told me, later), she went upstairs. The children had gone across the road to number 14, with Ned, and she had decided to take advantage of their absence by tidying their bedrooms, a task that was always much better accomplished when they were not there to interrupt.

She began with Rose's room and then moved across the landing to Sibyl's, and it was here that she made an unfortunate discovery. Amongst the clothing that lay scattered around the floor, she found Sibyl's apron, which usually hung in the kitchen. Sibyl had worn this garment the previous day. As Annie picked it up, she noticed a slight bulge in the front pocket. The first thought that crossed her mind was that Sibyl had, yet again, stolen the kitchen matches, something that always filled her with a mixture of irritation and woe. Sighing, she reached inside the apron and pulled out – not the expected 'Bryant & May's' but a crumpled ball of card. When smoothed out, this was revealed to be a small packet of stuff that was, in those days, often sold for the purpose of killing rats and mice. The packet was empty, with only a small amount of blue-black poison dust caught in the creases. Here and there, mysterious dark blotches stained the cardboard and label.

According to Annie, her initial reaction was one of confusion because, in the first place, she never bought such products. The apartments in number 11, along with the rest of the buildings in the area, did suffer from an infestation of mice, a particular breed of tiny, dark-furred creatures, most of them no bigger than a puff of sooty thistledown; if one sat very quietly, these little rodents could sometimes be seen darting about the floor and pouncing at crumbs. Annie was of the opinion that it was pointless to try to eliminate them, because they would only return in their dozens, and her policy, by and large, was one of peaceful co-existence. Thus, she found herself wondering where the empty packet might have come from, before remembering that, on the previous afternoon, the children had spent some time at Mrs Calthrop's. Convinced that this must have been where it came into Sibyl's possession, Annie made her way downstairs, intending to call on her neighbour and make enquiries.

Passing through the hall, she noticed the clean punch bowl sitting on a chair, where Jessie must have left it. Annie made a mental note to tidy the bowl away and, by her account, it was only at this precise moment – as her gaze returned to the crumpled packet in her hand – that a terrible thought occurred to her, and she stopped short. So busy had she been, speculating where Sibyl might have acquired the rodent poison, that she had not even made any connection between its presence in the child's pocket and the events of the previous evening.

Of a sudden, Annie realised that her legs were trembling, weak as straw, so much so that she had to step into the parlour and sit down. For a moment, she remained there, in a stunned silence, glancing around the room. On the walls, in several places, were lighter patches on the paper, where she had scrubbed away those nasty little drawings. There, in a corner, was Rose's toy horse, which the child had refused to play with, ever since it had been scorched, so mysteriously. Atop the piano, lay some embroidery that Annie had been obliged to begin again from scratch, after her first efforts had been discovered, ripped to shreds. All this, she took in, with a kind of sick, dull aching in her chest, before staring again at the empty packet in her lap. Later, she told me that she knew then, beyond question, what had made us so ill on the previous night, and who, exactly, was to blame.

Poor Annie! To come to such a realisation, as a mother, must have been horrible indeed. I believe that she may have shed a few tears, albeit quietly, since Jessie was within earshot. (Of course, since I was not present that afternoon, I cannot claim to know exactly what Annie did or thought or felt, but she told me about it, subsequently, in great detail, and I hope to give here a fair and accurate representation of what took place.) Eventually, she dried her eyes, and instead of calling on Mrs Calthrop, she donned her coat, slipped the empty packet into her pocket, and hurried across the road to number 14, the home of her mother-in-law.

There, Elspeth's maid Jean answered the door. The mistress, apparently, had gone on a prison visit to Duke Street, but Ned and the children were in the parlour, with Mabel. Typically, Sibyl was in a sulk, and only scowled at her mother when she appeared at the threshold. Annie called to Jean, who was about to return to the kitchen, and asked her to watch over the girls, for a while, downstairs. Sibyl and Rose liked to play in the basement, which had much to explore, since it contained several intriguing cupboards and presses, the larder and kitchen, and bedrooms: not only Jean's, but that of Mabel and the departed Kenneth. Rose trotted off happily, holding the maid's hand, while Sibyl slipped out of the room in their wake, looking shifty and miserable. Once they had gone, Annie closed the parlour door and, taking the poison from her pocket, she showed it to Ned and his sister, explaining where she had found it, and what she thought it meant.

Her husband's initial reaction was, of course, one of disbelief. He told Annie that she was talking 'damned rot', that such a thing was unthinkable. He poked the packet, which she had set down on the sewing table.

'She must have found it outside,' he insisted. 'Out in the back court or somewhere. She probably realised it was dangerous, and put it in her pocket, to stop the other children getting it.'

Up until this point, Mabel had remained silent, but now she picked up the cardboard packet and, giving it one glance, remarked: 'This is our poison.'

'What?' said Ned, startled.

'I bought it myself, last summer,' Mabel continued. 'D'you not remember? The mice were worse than ever, so Jean and I mixed this stuff with molasses, and spread it on bread, and put it down all over the basement where they'd eat it. But we kept finding dead mice in the bedroom jugs – poison makes them thirsty – and Jean had a heart attack every time she found another one bobbing around in the sink. In the end, we gave up, but we kept the packet in the press, next to the kitchen. At least, that's where it was last time I saw it. There was only a wee drop of powder left in it.'

'That stuff could be anybody's,' said Ned. 'They sell it everywhere.'

Mabel gave one of her scoffing little laughs. 'They do indeed, but I know this packet well. Those stains are where Jean kept dropping the molasses. And the label was ripped in the exact same place. It's our poison, Ned, no doubt about it.'

'So –' said Annie, hesitantly. 'Perhaps Sibyl, at some point, in the past few days, put this in her pocket, and brought it over to our house . . . and then . . . ?'

'What?' Ned laughed. 'Poured it in the punch – to murder us?'

Mabel looked doubtful. 'Mind you, I think I saw it in the press a few days ago, and I'm not sure Sibyl's been over here since then.'

'But all of us that had that punch got sick,' said Annie. 'Now this turns up in Sibyl's apron. You know what she's like, Ned . . .'

'That's enough,' he said. 'I don't want this mentioned again, and not to Sibyl. We can't blame her – she's done nothing wrong. Throw that packet out, and let's speak of it no more. There must have been something the matter with the damned wine, that's all. It's gut-rot anyway: I don't know how you drink it.'

His wife bristled. 'I used a very good wine.'

Ned got to his feet, glancing at the clock. 'Well, I should be getting back . . .'

Annie felt a twinge of irritation: this was typical, that he would leave the room rather than discuss something that he had no desire to face.

Mabel piped up: 'You must admit, it is rather a coincidence.' She widened her eyes at her brother, to drive home her point.

However, he simply ignored her and turned to his wife. 'Are you coming?'

Annie exchanged a final, despairing glance with her sister-in-law, and then, slipping the poison back into her pocket, she followed Ned into the hall. He called to the children, who came running upstairs, and they all trooped back across the street, with Ned striding out in front, so that it was impossible to have a conversation.

The 1st of January is, traditionally, a day of rest in Scotland, and families tend to spend it visiting relatives and friends, or passing the time together, companionably, at home. Annie was hurt, therefore, upon their return, when Ned went straight up to his studio, announcing his intention to put in a few hours of work before dark. This left her alone, with the children, since Jessie had the afternoon off, to visit her family.

Given her suspicions, Annie could not help but feel wary of

Sibyl, whose sulky mood had not abated. The child moped around the place, squabbling with Rose and, from time to time, casting doleful looks at her mother. In due course, by way of experiment, Annie waited until the girls had run next door to the dining room, and then, with trembling fingers, she placed the packet of poison in the middle of the parlour floor. When the children returned, Annie pretended to hem a frock, whilst watching out of the corner of her eye, but Sibyl went straight to her doll, failing to notice the poison. Instead, Rose saw it, and would have grabbed it, had Annie not snatched the box out of reach. Only then did Sibyl's interest perk up.

'What's that?' she asked.

Annie peered, with ostentatious bewilderment, at the cardboard packet.

'I don't know,' she said. 'What do you think it is, dear?'

The child lowered her chin, and made a face, one that she pulled with increasing frequency, a look that Annie interpreted to me, in words, as: 'You may think I'm stupid, mother – but, in fact, it is you who are the stupid one.'

'How am I supposed to know?' said Sibyl.

She peered at the packet, her eyes gleaming. Annie – frightened of the few grains of poison that it still contained – threw it onto the fire, and was relieved to see it blacken at the edges, then curl up and burst into flames. She wondered what to make of Sibyl's reaction: the child had not seemed to recognise the poison, but was this just another instance of her mendacity?

Of course, it was not long before Ned's mother heard about what Annie had found in Sibyl's apron pocket: Mabel told her the story as soon as she returned home, that evening. Evidently, Elspeth had no problem in believing that her granddaughter was capable of putting something nasty in the punch. When I met her and Mabel, a few days later, at Godenzi's, the widow Gillespie was all of a twitteration, adamant that Sibyl must be 'dealt with', once and for all.

'Something must be done!' she kept saying. 'First, my newsletters, then Ned's painting – now this! Heavens – we won't be able to drink a cup of tea without worrying whether it might be our lest!'

Mabel's opinion was that a physician should be brought in to look at Sibyl.

'If she did poison that punch then our lives could be in danger, Harriet. What we need is some professional man who deals with this sort of thing – Dr Oswald, for instance.' As it happened, Oswald worked at the Royal Lunatic Asylum in Kelvinside, and his wife had long been a member of the congregation of Elspeth's church. 'He seems a reasonable man,' Mabel continued. 'I'm sure he could take an informal look at Sibyl, and give us his opinion.'

I must say, I tended to agree with her, but Ned's mother simply shifted about in her seat, looking irritable, and when I asked her what she thought should be done, she gave a shrug of her shoulders, and muttered something about 'more drastic measures' being required. Assuming that she merely meant some form of punishment for the child, I gave little thought to what she had said, until a week or so later, when I learned, from Mabel, that her mother and Annie had fallen out. Apparently, the Reverend Johnson had heard of Sibyl's latest exploit, and had offered to perform an exorcism upon the child. Although Elspeth's church did not condone such practices – sensibly viewing them as questionable and unorthodox – Elspeth had advised Annie to consider the suggestion, since the pastor was very experienced in such matters, having conducted several exorcisms in America.

Upon hearing this, Annie lost her temper with her mother-in-law, for the very first time. Having called her an 'old bag of wind', she demanded that Ned's mother leave the apartment. Elspeth did so, in high dudgeon and, since then, the two women had not spoken. In the immediate aftermath of this disagreement, Ned counselled his wife to forgive and forget. This, however, Annie found herself unable to do, and the fact that her husband refused to take her side, or even reprimand his mother, caused her great sorrow.

To my mind, Mabel's notion of bringing in a physician was eminently more sensible. I believe that Annie did suggest this idea to her husband, albeit tentatively, but Ned would not hear of it. In the first place (he told her), there was no real evidence that Sibyl had done any harm at Hogmanay. In the second place, he believed that, no matter what ailed their daughter (and he did admit that she was, at times, difficult), they should deal with the problem themselves – and that was an end to it, as far as he was concerned.

Perhaps, in an effort to prove something to Ned, Annie became determined to make the child better with no help from anyone else. To this end, she threw herself, whole-heartedly, into motherhood. She stopped attending art classes, and her easel was left to collect dust in the corner of the parlour, for she was too preoccupied with her daughter to spend any time on painting. Unfortunately, ever since Hogmanay, Sibyl had developed a nervous, hacking cough, which showed no sign of abating. We also suspected that she was pulling out her own hair in the night, for clumps of it kept appearing on her pillow. Indeed, her locks had grown very thin and, in places, one could see livid white glimpses of her scalp. Poor Annie spent hours on end rubbing castor oil into the child's head in an attempt to get rid of these bald patches.

By the end of January, the general atmosphere in the family was so unpleasant that Mabel and Walter Peden – having originally planned to hold a large and festive wedding breakfast at number 14 – married in secret, with no guests and only two strangers as witnesses. Not even Elspeth had been forewarned, or invited to the ceremony, and afterwards, when the couple made public what they had done, the blow was compounded by the announcement that they intended to go and live, for a year or so, in Tangier, where Peden had previously spent some fruitful months, painting camels and the like; indeed, their passages were already booked, for a few weeks hence.

Ned's mother took these revelations badly: to be excluded from her own daughter's wedding was something that she found hard to forgive. Relations between her and Mabel had always been strained, but now the widow's feelings were hurt. Her maid, Jean, claimed that the mistress had begun to sleepwalk. Apparently, she wandered the apartment in the middle of the night, lifting things up, only to set them down again, sighing, and once or twice, Jean had awoken with a jolt, to find Elspeth standing in her bedroom doorway, staring fixedly, and yet still deep in sleep.

As the day of the honeymooners' departure approached, there was much discussion about who should accompany them to the railway station, as they set off on the first leg of their trip to Africa. With Annie and Elspeth avoiding each other, there was no possibility that they would both be in attendance. In the end, it was Elspeth who accompanied Ned and the children to the station. Annie and I had said our farewells to the couple on the previous day, and so I kept her company at Stanley Street, that morning, while the others were out. This was the first time that we had been alone in a while, and she took the opportunity to disburden herself. To begin with, she told me how upset she was with Elspeth.

'I don't want her in the house,' she said. 'I'm scared she might drag Sibyl off and submit her to – to – goodness knows what. Can you imagine, Harriet? An exorcism? And Ned hasn't even had strong words with her about it.'

Alas, it seemed that her husband's failure to support her had cut deep. She felt increasingly estranged from him. With the departure of Mabel and Walter, Ned was taking over Peden's evening classes for ladies, at the Art School, and, although the extra money was only to be welcomed, her husband would be busier than ever. 'We hardly spend any time together any more. At least before, we had the evenings. But now, with these classes, he'll be out two more nights a week.'

Moreover, Peden had funded the emigration to Tangier by renting out both his house in Glasgow, and the cottage at Co'path. Of course, Annie was pleased that Mabel and he were to have an adventurous new life together, but it meant that her hopes of staying at his cottage over the summer had come to nothing.

'We can't really afford to rent anywhere,' she confided. 'You've seen the books. Walter's cottage would have been perfect, because he'd only have charged us a nominal rent, if anything. I was looking forward to it – there seemed to be more time in the day at Co'path. We were so happy there. And Sibyl – she seemed so much better, out in the countryside.' She bit her lip, darting a fretful glance at me. 'Harriet, I haven't told you this before, but . . .' Here, she hesitated, and gave me a strange, almost fearful look, before continuing. 'Do you know what she's been doing lately? Just this past few weeks – it's happened two or three times now.'

Unfortunately, there is no polite way of stating what she told me next. It seemed that Sybil had taken to smearing her faeces across the wall of the WC. I hardly knew what to say. I put my arm around Annie, to comfort her.

'Let's try and look on the bright side, dear. It's not all bad.' I racked my brains for some cheerful slant to this new development. 'Perhaps painting on the wall with – with – things other than paint – is evidence of emergent, artistic talent. Perhaps Sibyl will become a great artist, like her father.'

To my gratification, Annie gave a little laugh.

'She'll be fine,' I told her. 'Just you wait and see. Once Ned's show is over, everything will settle down, and all will be well.'

By mid-February, Mrs Urquart – the last of Ned's portraits – was complete, and 'The Duchess' pronounced herself well contented with the result. Now, the artist was determined to spend every daylight hour, toiling and moiling, in his studio and – with single-minded intensity – he began to prepare for his solo show at Hamilton's gallery. His aim was to include recent pictures, not just his views of the Exhibition from the summer, or the portraits that he had been working on of late: he was keen to make a statement, with some new, exciting canvases that he hoped to develop from his sketches of Co'path.

I myself was fortunate enough to be the first person to see one of these new canvases on the very day of its completion. It so happened that I arrived at number 11, one afternoon in early March, only to find that Annie had gone down to the quays with her daughters, because Sibyl had voiced a desire to look at the boats. There was a time, only a few months previously, when Annie might have called upon me at Queen's Crescent and asked me to accompany them on such an excursion. However, it had not escaped my attention that, in her quest to be self-sufficient in looking after the girls, Ned's wife had become less companionable. This was not the first time that I had arrived to find her not at home. Indeed, once or twice, she had – albeit politely, with profuse apologies – turned me away from the front door, saying that she and Sibyl were having some 'quiet time' together (since part of her strategy with the child was to pay her more attention). Of course, as far as I was concerned, anything that made Sibyl a happier and less destructive little girl was to be supported and encouraged.

At any rate, having decided to leave a note for Annie, I accompanied the maid upstairs to the apartment. Jessie went straight back to work, leaving me in the hall, and I had just written the words 'Dear Annie' on a scrap of paper, when I heard Ned's footsteps on the attic staircase, and turned to greet him. We spoke for a few moments, and I could not help but notice that, while we chatted, he kept rubbing at his face with his hands. His general demeanour was so bewildered and distracted that, eventually, I had to ask him if he felt quite well.

'Aye,' said he, with a laugh. 'I'm fine, Harriet. I just – I think I might have finished this thing I've been working on, that's all. I suppose I can't quite believe it.'

'Really?' I said. 'How wonderful – may I see it?'

He hesitated. Presumably, under normal circumstances, Annie would have been the first to view any new painting, but perhaps this was not a binding agreement, for, after a moment, he said: 'Och – why not?'

Upstairs, in the studio, the canvas that he showed me took me by surprise, perhaps because I was accustomed to his pictures of the urban landscape, the Exhibition, city streets, and the like. This, by contrast, was very different: a patch of woodland, with two girls (clearly Sibyl and Rose) scampering between the trees, one some distance behind the other, with the smallest girl glancing over her shoulder, as though there might be something, or someone, in pursuit. No sky was visible, nor any horizon, only the trees and creeping shrubs of a dense wood. The effect was intense and claustrophobic. Ned told me that, whilst at Co'path, he had done some sketches of woods, but the fleeing figures of the children had come from his imagination. He was surprised at how much he had enjoyed painting such a rural scene.

'Well, it is very unusual,' I told him. Indeed, I found it a little eerie, which made me think that it must be a very powerful piece of work.

Ned was gazing at the picture, with a faraway expression in his eyes.

'I'd like to do more like this,' he said.

'You mean – of Sibyl and Rose?'

'No, the landscape.'

'Will you go back to Co'path, d'you think?'

He nodded. 'I hope so. Perhaps for a while, a few months, even more. Do some real painting – not just sketches. Get out into the landscape.'

'Well, yes,' I said. 'That would be an interesting development. Particularly if you're inspired to create pictures such as this.'

'Do you think so?' He turned to me, in earnest. Behind his eyes, I could see a degree of uncertainty. Clearly, my opinion – my approval of his decisions – was important to him.

'Oh yes,' I said. 'There's nothing "tweet" about it, nothing sentimental. It's – bleak and bold. You should definitely do more in the same vein.'

He smiled, apparently reassured. 'Well, you've not given me a bad piece of advice yet.' Then he rubbed his hands together, and glanced at his watch. 'Harriet, if you don't mind, I ought to press on. There's so little daylight, I need to make the most of it . . . I'm so sorry . . .'

'No need to apologise. I'll just finish my note to Annie and be on my way.'

A few days later, I received a reply from Annie, suggesting that we arrange to meet in a week or so. The tone of her message was cheerful, if apologetic. It seemed that her new approach with Sibyl was working. There had been some improvement in the child's moods, and no incidents of vandalism or destruction for several days.

One rainy afternoon, the following week, I happened to be at number 11, helping out, as I often did, with the accounts for both the household and the Wool and Hosiery (having taken over the shop's books, following Kenneth's disappearance). That day, it was Jessie's turn at the washhouse, and she had been up and down the stairs all afternoon, between tub and pulley, leaving me, alone, to get on with my sums. Ned and Annie had been out when I arrived: having left the girls in the care of Mrs Calthrop, they had apparently braved the rain to call at Hamilton's gallery, in order to discuss how Ned might hang his paintings in the forthcoming show.

I had been working quietly in the dining room for about an hour, when I heard footsteps in the close. At first, I assumed that Jessie had returned from the washhouse, but then I heard Ned speak in hushed, angry tones: 'It's breaking her heart. She just wants to see them once in a while.'

The front door – which had been left ajar – was pushed open. The footsteps faltered, and came to a halt, halfway across the hall.

'I'm sure she does,' said a voice that I recognised, at once, as Annie's. Feeling awkward, I was about to alert them to my presence when she continued: 'No doubt she'd like to perform an exorcism on them while she's at it.'

'Och, she hasn't mentioned that in ages. She'd not do anything without our permission, anyway.'

Annie gave a derisive laugh in reply. I began to feel even more uncomfortable, nervous now, lest they enter the dining room and discover me there. I sat motionless, as quietly as possible. I heard Annie mutter something, and then Ned interrupted: 'What's wrong with saying she's proud to have grandchildren?'

'That's not what she said – she said they "run wild".'

'That was in jest.'

'No, it wasn't – it was an attack, on me.'

'She was just making conversation.'

'Anyway, you know perfectly well, Sibyl's much better now. I think it does her good not seeing Elspeth. It certainly does me good.'

'You don't mean that. It's bound to be awkward, meeting her, in the street. With Mabel away, she gets lonely. She just wants to be your friend.'

'Oh, for dear sake,' said Annie, and she laughed bitterly. 'Open your eyes, Ned. You must be blind. Where are you going?'

'I'm away over to see my mother.'

I heard his footsteps echo in the stairwell as he descended. Annie sighed. Then, after a moment, she too went downstairs and I heard her knocking at Mrs Calthrop's door. To my relief, she was invited in, and the door closed, which gave me a moment, at least, before she came back with the girls. I decided to slip away, while I could, to avoid any awkwardness.

Of course, I was upset, for Ned and Annie. The situation was all very awkward, and I was sorry to have overheard their quarrel. I had no idea that such tensions lurked beneath the surface. For some reason, feelings of vague disquiet, and a sense of foreboding, welled up inside me. This skirmish between Elspeth and Annie, and now between Annie and Ned – and all caused, essentially, by Sibyl – seemed destined to escalate out of control. It felt, somehow, pre-ordained, even irreversible.

Tuesday, 18 – Friday, 21 July 1933

LONDON

Tuesday, 18th July. Relations with Sarah continue to be less than amicable, and I still have my doubts about her. There has been no disagreement, no heated exchange, but the atmosphere between us leaves something to be desired. She is cross with me now because I failed to mention the date of my blood test to her, and then I stupidly forgot all about the thing, and missed it. I could easily have telephoned them myself, had she not been so impatient but, for some reason, she wanted to make a great song and dance about booking another appointment, even though all she did was make one telephone call. In my opinion, she has deliberately begun to act as though I am difficult, in order to play the martyr.

This evening, to my relief, she has gone out to see a Marx Brothers picture at the Empire. I sat here, thinking of the past, and trying to remember how, exactly, Elspeth Gillespie used to pronounce and stress her words. Such a strange accent she had: so distinctive. In due course, I looked out my address book and found the telephone number of Miss Barnes, which I copied from Sarah's letter of recommendation before returning it to Burridge's. Then I placed another call to Chepworth Villas. The same polite, breathy voice answered, as before, but this time, instead of asking for Miss Barnes by name, I said (in an approximation of Elspeth's Kelvinside tones): 'May I speak to the lady of the house, please?'

'Yes – speaking.'

This stopped me short, for it was not at all what I had expected. To be honest, I had imagined that the 'Miss Barnes' with whom I had already spoken would – upon being asked for the lady of the house – scuttle off and fetch her employer. I have an idea that this 'Miss Barnes' is simply a friend of Sarah's, someone who works at Chepworth Villas, perhaps as a housekeeper or governess. I have heard and read of such cases: a fake letter of recommendation, including a telephone number; an associate, whose usual duty it is to answer the telephone, and who is primed to adopt the persona of an employer should anyone call in search of a character reference for their friend.

'Hello?' said the voice. 'Is anybody there?'

'Yes, please may I speak to your mistress?'

'I am the mistress. Who is this?'

'Oh, very clever,' I said. 'It's a criminal offence, you know, impersonation. You could go to gaol for some time.'

'What? Who is this? Did you telephone here the other day?'

Doubt seized me. If this person was Sarah's friend, then it was a mistake to have challenged her. And what if she really was the lady of the house?

'Hello!' I cried. 'Hello? Is that – Museum 2186?'

'No, it's not! We're on the Frobisher exchange.'

'Oh, I'm so sorry – wrong number – cheerio.'

Admittedly, I am a little bad-tempered, after events this afternoon. Sarah keeps forgetting to put in an order to Lockwood's and so, while she was at the library, I myself went across the street to the shop. Normally, I would simply place an order by telephone, but I am trying to bear in mind Derrett's words of wisdom about exercise. This has been another sultry day, and by the time that I had reached the ground floor, I was already hot and bothered. As I stepped out into the sunshine, the heat hit my head like a hammer blow. A dray had got itself jammed across the breadth of the road, and a procession of cabs and laden motor buses had drawn to a halt on either side. The drivers were amusing themselves, while they waited, by bandying oaths and sarcasm. I picked my way between the vehicles, which fumed and sweltered under the boiling sun. Despite the awning outside the grocer's, his display of lettuces lay wilting.

Inside, the temperature was a little cooler. The shop appeared to be empty, apart from the delivery boy, who was loitering at one end of the counter, actually scraping marks into the wooden surface with his thumbnail. This particular boy is known to me, as he often complains about the lift in our building when he brings up a box. He greeted me in a way that is, perhaps, peculiar to Cockney lads: an almost imperceptible backward tilt of the head, accompanied by an equally slight elevation of the eyebrows. Then he resumed scraping his initials into the counter. Whilst waiting for Mr Lockwood or his wife to make an appearance, I studied the advertisements that had been pasted to the wall until, of a sudden, through the front window, I spied my neighbour, Mrs Potts, as she lifted a lettuce from the display and approached the entrance. Potts is the most terrible gossip, and I had no desire to be detained by her. Therefore, I spoke up, addressing the delivery boy.

'Excuse me, can you call Mr Lockwood, so that I may be served?'

At that – and just as Potts entered, the boy yelled into the back of the shop.

'Mr Lockwood, sir! You're wanted! It's the whisky lady!'

Stunned by this careless impertinence, I was rendered speechless. I stared at the boy, for a moment, open-mouthed, and then, instead of waiting to be served, made my exit, pausing only to nod stiffly at my neighbour, who smirked and avoided my eye, as I hurried past her into the street, my cheeks burning.

As yet, I have not quite recovered. After all, it is not as though I buy inordinate amounts of whisky from them. The boy must simply resent lugging the cases up the stairs. Bottles, presumably, are much heavier to carry than lettuce and tomatoes. One thing is certain: I shall not be placing any orders with Lockwood at any time in the near future. There is a perfectly good grocer on Marchmont Street, which I have used, on occasion. From now on, I shall take more of my business there. Indeed, after leaving Lockwood's, I went there directly and ordered the few little things that we need.

In the meantime, I must return to the memoir, for I am about to embark upon a description of pivotal events.

Friday, 21st July. Something terribly unsettling has happened. Indeed, my hand is shaking, as I write. I am not quite sure what to think. It is a long time since I have felt this afraid or vulnerable. It all began last night, at suppertime, when I brought up the subject of the piano. Ever since I caught Sarah using the instrument, last month, neither of us has made any mention of it. This mutual silence, or avoidance, has not helped the general atmosphere and so, yesterday evening, in the interest of clearing the air, I decided to try and put her at ease. 'Oh, incidentally,' I said, as she set down my plate on the dining table. 'Please feel free to play the piano, dear, whenever you wish.'

She blushed, and gave her head a shake. 'I'm sorry, it won't happen again.'

'Please! Do make use of it! You play rather well. Where did you learn?'

'Just here and there,' she said, in that infuriating, vague way of hers. She stepped away, towards the door. 'I'm not very good – but thanks for your offer.'

'Well, I do hope you take advantage of it. I so seldom play myself, and it's lovely to hear the instrument in use. Why didn't you tell me you could play, dear?'

She hesitated at the threshold. 'I don't know . . . it just didn't seem –' Her voice tailed away, and then she nodded towards my plate, saying: 'I hope you're going to eat some of that, tonight.'

'Oh, yes – foo foo! How old are you, dear, if you don't mind me asking?'

'Forty-three.'

She produced it without a pause but, for some reason, I got the impression that she was lying. Perhaps it was that deadened look in her eyes, or the fact that her West Country accent had suddenly become very pronounced. She certainly looks older than forty-three. And then, before I could stop myself, the words came tumbling out:

'Now Sarah, do you know any hymns?'

She thought for a moment, lightly slapping the escutcheon with her fingers.

'Well, I suppose I do know one or two.'

'Could I beg you to play one for me, while I eat this lovely supper? Would you be so kind? A hymn would be marvellous.'

The look on her face was what one might call sceptical, but she went out to the hall, saying: 'Well, if you eat something, then I will.'

Tucked away in its alcove, the piano is not visible from the dining table, but I heard her sit on the stool and lift the lid of the keyboard. After a moment or two, she began to play a jaunty tune, which I recognised, within a single bar, as 'Ding Dong Merrily on High': not exactly a hymn, and although she played enthusiastically, she was clearly not very practised in this particular piece, since she kept making errors, and going back to correct them.

As the music bounded along, I picked at my food and gazed across the table towards the birdcage on the sideboard. Layla stood, motionless, on the edge of the china feed bowl, her head cocked to one side, listening, and Maj, bless him, soon began to twitter an accompaniment to the piano notes, although of course, he made up his own melody. The windows were open, and the sound of traffic and smell of fumes drifted up from the street. Sunset had cast the hotel opposite into silhouette, dark against the sky; behind the tall black chimneystacks, the heavens had turned a vibrant shade, somewhere between pink and orange, tinged with violet. It was rather odd to sit there, in the sultry heat of the summer evening, listening to a Christmas carol.

All of a sudden, as though out of nowhere, I was seized by an overwhelming sense of déjà vu: not that I had been in this exact situation before, but there was something terribly familiar about the moments as they unfolded, and something in Sarah's playing that I almost recognised. Not only that, but – far more unsettling – I soon became gripped with the notion that there was a malign quality to the music. The piano has always been boomy, but Sarah seemed to be attacking the ivories far more ferociously than was necessary. Had she simply rammed her foot down on the sustain pedal, to make the noise reverberate around the hall – or was the lengthy, rising and falling, melismatic 'Glo-o-o-r-i-a!' of the chorus always so horribly unrelenting? It was as though the notes – for all their jollity – were vicious spirals, each one of them uncoiling, with furious intent, towards me – towards my person. An evil, creeping fear came upon me, as I sat there – unable to eat, and watching the birds flit around their cage, oblivious – while Sarah stabbed at the keyboard, as if each note was the thrust of a dagger entering my viscera. I began to wonder whether the noise would ever end, or whether I would be frozen there, for all eternity, pinned to the spot by Sarah's hatred, and the din of her hideous music.

But why should she hate me so? Why?

At last, the carol came, clashing, to its conclusion. Having no desire to reveal how dreadfully frightened I was, I managed some polite applause, and called out: 'Bravo! Thanks awfully . . . That'll be all now, thank you.'

The lid of the piano closed; the stool scraped on the parquet. I held my breath, dreading that Sarah might reappear, in all her bulk, at the doorway, but then I heard her slow, plodding footsteps as she retreated down the hall. The kitchen door snapped shut, and then, there was silence.

I sat there, paralysed by fear, feeling the accelerated pounding of the blood in my veins. I cannot say how long, in a state of confusion and dread, I remained in my seat. I only recall that when I stole along the passage to my bedroom, night had crept up to the windows of the apartment.

During breakfast this morning, I watched Sarah carefully. She behaved, as far as I could tell, perfectly as normal. She brought the coffee pot, set the toast in the rack, gave Maj and Layla a glance, and then left the room in her usual lumbering fashion. There was nothing in her behaviour to make me think that she had guessed at my anxiety of last night, and nothing that she did seemed spiteful, in the least. However, I am still gripped by a sense of unease, and am concerned that she might be hiding something. Sadly, I am very alert to mendacity, having been through all that I have had to endure, in life. My experiences – all those years ago, in Scotland – have certainly left me with scars. Moreover, I am well aware that there may be those who will resent that I am writing this memoir, and it would be good to have some reassurance that my companion is to be trusted.

I waited until Sarah had gone out to the shops, then I telephoned to Burridge's and asked to speak to Mrs Clinch. After a slight delay, she came to the apparatus. 'Miss Baxter. What seems to be the problem?'

'Nothing, Mrs Clinch. I simply wish to know, if I may, have there ever been any complaints about Miss Whittle?'

'About Miss Whittle? No! No complaints. Have you got one, Miss Baxter? You must tell me if you have.'

'Not a complaint, exactly. She just seems rather – unhappy. Melancholic.'

'Probably just a bit homesick. D'you want me to have a word with her?'

'Oh no! Please don't. I'm sure it'll be fine. Sorry to have troubled you.'

'Let us know if you do have any problems, Miss Baxter. Cheerio, then.'

'Just a moment – I'd like to know – if I might – the age of Miss Whittle.'

'What, you want to know how old she is now? Can't you just ask her, dear?'

'I'm afraid I can't. It would be – impolite. In fact, she did tell me, but I've forgotten what she said. To ask again would be rude. I'm sure you understand. Presumably you have it written down somewhere, amongst her particulars?'

Mrs Clinch let out a great sigh. 'Hold on a moment,' she said, and the receiver was dropped. I had done well to claim forgetful-ness – Clinch is never happier than when one confirms one's age and infirmity. There was a pause and then various scrapes and bangs from afar, which I imagined were filing-cabinet drawers, opening and closing. Then, closer at hand, there was a rustling of paper. Another sigh, and then: 'Says here she was born in 'eighty-two.'

'Eighteen eighty-two! Are you quite sure?'

'Would it have been better for her to be born in a different year?'

'Ah – no. Except – I believe she told me she was rather younger than that.'

'Well! I'm sure she's not the first to fib about her age. She's perfectly fit and healthy. And you specifically asked for somebody older this time, didn't you – do you remember? . . . Miss Baxter? . . . Are you there?'

'I say – you don't happen to have a note of her place of birth, do you?'

'Birthplace, now? Hold on a moment, please.' There was a muffled sound, as though Mrs Clinch had covered the transmit-ter with her hand. She muttered something to someone. Then she spoke into the telephone again, abruptly. 'Dorset.'

'I see. Dorset . . . is that from her birth certificate?'

'Ooh no! We don't hold them. I've just got a form here, she filled in her own self. Now, will that be all, dear?'

A form she filled in 'her own self'. I wonder how much that can be relied upon for accuracy, given that the girl has lied to my face about her age? Born in Dorset – indeed. I have my doubts. I have been listening to her accent very carefully of late, and have begun to suspect that she may not even be English; the more I hear her speak, the more convinced I am that she might be of Glaswegian origin.

IV

April – November 1889

GLASGOW

Let me deal, briefly, with Ned's solo exhibition, which was staged in the middle of April that year. The show included several of the portraits that he had completed over the past eight months or so, including Mrs Urquart (looking rather glum and severe), a number of Exhibition pictures from the previous summer, and half-a-dozen new paintings. These, Ned had worked up from sketches that he had done at Co'path – windswept, austere land-scapes and rocky coastlines. In similar style to the woodland ren-dering of Rose and Sibyl, the new canvases often had menacing overtones. All the recent emotional disturbances in Ned's life had given these pictures a gravitas, a new weight that set them apart from the work of his peers. The very fact that he had been able to produce six paintings in as many weeks was remarkable: his output had improved, beyond measure. No doubt, in the absence of Mabel, Peden and Kenneth, and with Elspeth now an unwel-come guest, number 11 was a more tranquil household than ever before but, to my mind, it was the continued banishment of Sibyl from the studio that had made the most difference to Ned's abil-ity to work at an uninterrupted pace.

On the first night of the show, Hamilton's gallery was packed with people and all seemed to go well, more or less. There, in force, were the 'Art Club' set: in those days, still a cosy clique of 'hills and heather' mediocrities, like Findlay, who put in an appearance for half an hour. A few of the new breed could be seen amongst the crowd – although not, I noticed, Lavery. The gallery consisted of two basement rooms, and Hamilton had allotted the smaller of these, in its entirety, to Gillespie. I had brought along my landlady, Mrs Alexander, and her daughters, Lily and Kate, who were very excited to be part of the proceedings. Sadly, Ned's wife was not present that evening. The reason given in public, at the time, was that she was obliged to remain at home, because of the children. In fact, I had offered to look after them for her, but Annie had declined. Under normal circumstances, she might have left the girls in the care of her maid, but, unfortunately, the Gillespies had been obliged to dismiss Jessie, the previous week. It so happened that Annie's Christmas gift from Ned – her silver bar-brooch, with the baroque pearl – had gone amissing. Annie wore that particular piece of jewellery only on special occasions, and its disappearance might not even have been noticed for a while had I not, one evening, requested another look at it. Annie left the parlour and returned, bewildered, several minutes later, having failed to find it anywhere in the bedroom. When asked, Jessie claimed not to have seen the brooch for weeks. We were not too worried, initially, but the family possessed few valuables and this silver trinket had been a relatively expensive item. Over the next few days, Annie looked in every conceivable place, but was unable to find the brooch anywhere.

One afternoon, while Ned was out buying wood for a frame, she waited until the girls had gone to the butcher's with the maid, and then undertook a search of Sibyl's room. She half expected to find her missing jewellery there because, unfortunately, whilst little Rose seemed to grow more adorable with each passing day, her sister became only more diabolic, and Annie's earnest hopes that the child was improving had come to nothing. As it transpired, when she looked beneath Sibyl's bed – where the child usually stashed 'appropriated' items – she found only six jam jars, into which her daughter appeared to have urinated. In any other circumstances, such a discovery might have seemed strange but, by this time, we were so habituated to Sibyl's disturbing behaviour that Annie barely remarked upon the jars.

Perhaps it was an intuition that made her decide to look in Jessie's room. Passing the locked door of her husband's empty studio, she entered the little garret at the end of the attic landing and began a quick search. Within moments, she had found the brooch, wrapped in an old stocking, which had been concealed beneath the mattress. Deciding not to confront the thief alone, Annie replaced the jewellery where she had found it and said nothing to anyone until Ned came back, towards dusk. Although the evidence was overwhelming, it was a measure of Ned's kindness that he was reluctant to give the maid notice straight away, and he and Annie spent much of the evening in whispered discussions about what action to take. I know that Ned felt betrayed by Jessie, certainly, but having to turn her out into the street filled him with guilt and regret. In the end, he decided against alerting the police, in case this might condemn her to prison. Dear sweet man! He spent the night in torment, at the prospect of what he was obliged to do the following morning. However, he steeled himself to go through with it, and the girl left Stanley Street before breakfast, with no written recommendation, in case she stole from a future employer. Needless to say, before she went, Jessie protested her innocence, even making a number of veiled accusations, accusations of an outlandish nature, which – as you may know – she was encouraged to elaborate upon during the trial. Since her testimony will be reported later, there is no need to repeat that malicious piece of character assassination here.

Following Jessie's departure, Annie should, by rights, have gone to an agency and found a new girl, but she procrastinated. She seemed to have had enough of unreliable maids for the time being, after her recent bad experiences, not only with Jessie, but also, previously, with Christina. To some extent, I can understand her position. I cannot abide anyone tampering with my belongings, and listening at doors. That is the problem with servants, you see, the lack of privacy. Dusting is mere subterfuge, an opportunity to snoop. In Annie's case, there was the embarrassment of having to conceal Sibyl's eccentric and wicked behaviour, and it must have been awkward, in that small apartment, to have someone sneaking around the place, spying, and eavesdropping. And yet, if only Annie had bothered to hire a maid, then she might have had more time for the children, and things might have turned out rather differently. But, as I have come to appreciate, over the years, there is no point in such regrets: what is done cannot be undone.

The stolen brooch upset Annie more than she would have cared to admit. Previously, she had been looking forward to the opening night of Ned's show but after we learned that her maid was a thief, she seemed to lose confidence, claiming that she did not really care for the clamour of openings.

'You go, Harriet,' she insisted. 'I can't face it. You'll be so much better with all those people. Besides, look at me – my hair's turning grey. I can't go out like this.'

She was right: despite her relative youth, there were now grey hairs, just visible, amongst the gold. I did wonder whether there was some other reason for her reluctance to attend the opening: she and Ned had not been getting on very well, and it was feasible that there might have been some species of tiff. However, if that was the case, she had said nothing to me.

In any event, Ned's show opened without the presence of his wife. Naturally, his mother was there, since Elspeth would not, for the world, have missed an opportunity to bask in the reflected glory of her son's fledgling success. As ever, she made a late entrance. Then she took but a moment to glance around, before protesting that Ned's pictures were 'too familiar', and inviting me to the adjacent room, where the work of Hamilton's other artists was on display. The canvases in front of which Elspeth lingered longest that evening were sentimental, humdrum fare, paintings that told a simple story, assisted by informative nomenclature: a glum urchin, his head swathed in a bandage, had been helpfully entitled *Toothache*; an ancient, smiling beggar, rendered in oils, was known as *Better Wisdom than Gold*; and a picture of farm folk, standing, dejected, outside a quaint cottage was described in the programme as *Tenants' Notice to Quit*. Elspeth sighed, wistfully, as she examined these paintings.

'Och, I wish Ned chose subjects like this – something with a nice message, or a lesson – he might sell better.'

'These pictures are popular,' I replied. 'But they're old-fashioned. Your son's work is more innovative – and I rather like the fact that he avoids moralising.'

But Elspeth had paused, once again, in front of *Toothache*, shaking her head in admiration. 'Marvellous!' she said. 'If only Ned would do something such as that.'

The artist himself was so busy that he and I barely spoke that evening, but I was happy to glimpse him, now and again, through the crowd. In his position as the featured painter, he was much in demand, with Hamilton often at his side, the two of them always at the centre of the conversation, amongst a group of animated persons. Once or twice, when I caught Ned's gaze, across the room, he smiled, or shook his head, as though in disbelief at the situation in which he found himself and, on one occasion, he acted the goat for my benefit, behind Hamilton's back, rolling his eyes, as though overwhelmed, which made us both laugh.

Towards midnight, after the last stragglers had left the gallery, a group of us decided to walk companionably home together along Sauchiehall Street, the western end of which was almost deserted. Earlier rain had given way to clear skies, and the moon was full and bright. With the exception of Elspeth, we had all drunk a little too much sherry. Ned was in fine fettle. As we passed the Japanese curio shop, I happened to glance in at the window display. There, amongst the kimonos and lanterns, I saw, for the first time, the birdcage that is now home to my dear, sweet finches. The moonlight brought out the lustre in the boxwood, making the cage glow. Its shape was so pleasing to the eye; the bamboo slats so fine and delicate; it was a masterpiece of construction. Captivated, I stopped short.

'Look, Ned,' I cried. 'Isn't that birdcage beautiful?'

Whilst Elspeth walked on ahead with Mrs Alexander and the others, Ned paused at my side and peered in at the display. When he saw the cage, he smiled.

'Beautiful,' he agreed.

For a moment, we simply stood there, enchanted, staring in at the window. I could imagine how well the cage would look in the right setting, a cosy, domestic interior, with a bird on one of the perches: one bird – or possibly two.

Next to me, Ned sighed. I turned to look up into his face and saw that his smile had gone, and he seemed thoughtful, even sad.

'What's the matter?' I asked.

'Nothing – I was just thinking about faraway places.'

'I'm so sorry, I didn't mean to –'

'No, it's fine.'

I turned back to the window, mulling over what he had said. Did he mean that he was unhappy where he was, and yearned to go somewhere far away? Was he longing for adventure, the exotic, scorching days and languid nights? Perhaps that was hardly surprising, given his burdensome circumstances, and the dreary Scottish weather. Ned remained silent, and so I murmured:

'Imagine just being able to pack your bags, and go.'

'Like Kenneth,' he said. 'It was him I was thinking about – wondering where he might be – if he is far away.'

'Oh – oh well, I'm sure he's fine, wherever he is. It's probably for the best that he's left Glasgow.'

I suppose that, in saying this, I had Kenneth's secret in mind, but Ned – knowing nothing of all that business – misinterpreted my words.

'You're right,' he said. 'This city – it was no good for my brother, and it's not much good for Sibyl either – the wee soul.'

'Yes, poor dear.'

He was still staring at the window display, but the moon was so bright that, when I turned again, I could clearly see his eyes: they were dark and uncertain, full of pain. Again, I wondered what might be on his mind. My heart was beating strangely; my hands felt suddenly cold.

He was about to speak again when we heard Elspeth, calling from Charing Cross corner, where she and the others were waiting for us.

'Son! Herriet! Are you coming?'

Both of us fell into step, at once, and when I gave him a questioning glance, Ned shook his head again and said: 'Don't pay any attention to me – I've had too much to drink.' And then I watched him as he fixed a smile on his face and strode on ahead, suddenly bold and cheerful, with a quip for Elspeth.

'Mother, you must shout a bit louder, they didn't quite hear you in Carntyne. For your information, Harriet and I were just deciding which kimono would suit you best. We've decided you must wear it to church.'

'Och, son, away with you!' cried Elspeth, delighted to be the focus of his amiable attention whilst in the company of her neighbours.

Of course, we hoped that the exhibition would attract favourable notices and, following the opening, a handful of reviews were published, but, sadly, the reactions were mixed. The most enthusiastic article, in *The Glasgow Evening Citizen*, claimed that although, hitherto, Gillespie's pictures had been tentative, he had now acquired mastery over his own style and, at times, the work showed 'flashes of brilliance'. By contrast, *The Arts Journal* accused Ned of 'cheap cleverism, carelessness and slapdash'. *The Herald* disliked the unflattering, sombre tones of the recent portraits which, it claimed, were unlikely to attract many prospective sitters. And the critic from *The Thistle* confessed that, in the most recent landscapes, the intensity of the style had made his skin 'creep', which could either have been a compliment, or a criticism, depending on what one requires from a painting.

Regrettably, the *Thistle* review was illustrated by a sketch of the gallery on opening night, penned by none other than Mungo Findlay. In his drawing, Gillespie and I were standing close together; I was looking up at Ned, and the caricaturist had made the expression on my face annoyingly rapt. His caption read: 'The Artist in deep conversation with his English friend, Miss Harriet Baxter'. It was all very unfortunate and hardly accurate, since not once, during the course of the evening, had I even stood next to Ned. No doubt, Findlay was making the most of an opportunity to embarrass me. A few tongues were set wagging, inevitably, but only for a brief while.

All in all, in that first week, the critical response to the exhibition was disappointing and, after the initial few days, attendances at the gallery fell away. Gillespie put on a brave face, but I could tell that he was deflated. Later that week, he was even obliged to drop everything and don an apron, to serve behind the counter of the Wool and Hosiery, when Miss MacHaffie fell ill and was unable to work. I, for one, avoided the shop during that period, although I did glimpse Ned, one afternoon, as I returned from a riverside walk. Glancing across, from the opposite side of Great Western Road, I could distinguish him, in the shadowy interior of the premises. He was serving two ladies, showing them rolls of ribbon that he had laid out on the counter; for all the world, he resembled naught but a shop assistant. He looked utterly miserable.

As for myself, perhaps I should just mention that, back in the early spring of that year, I had taken up a new pursuit. In fact, I had been considering trying my hand at drawing and painting for a long time, probably ever since Annie had worked on my portrait. Yes, I believe it was her good example that persuaded me to attempt some pictures, but it took a while for me to pluck up the courage. Eventually, some time after Christmas, I had bought an easel and various other requisites, and I began to practise sketching on paper and daubing at canvases, in secret. My first efforts were frightful, and I kept my new hobby to myself, perhaps because I was mortified to think that Ned or Annie – real artists! – might ask to see the results of my labours. However, it soon became clear to me that I was in desperate need of help, in the form of some sort of tuition, and so I joined the evening group for ladies, at the Art School, which, since Peden's departure, had been taken over by Ned. Of course, it seemed only polite to ask him if my presence in the class, as a friend, would be a distraction, but he assured me that he did not mind in the least. His sole reservation was that it was rather late in the term, and he wondered whether the School would permit me to enrol at such an advanced stage. As a matter of fact, with that very issue in mind, I had already spoken to the Headmaster, who had offered no objection to admitting me as a student. In any case, Ned himself had only just started teaching the class and so, in a way (as we joked, at the time) we would be beginners together.

Annie had seemed a little taken aback when she learned of my plan to attend the classes. But as I told her, I had no lofty aim: it was only ever my intention to dabble in painting and drawing, as a hobby. Perhaps, in an unwitting fashion, she was envious that my time was my own; I was free, in a way that she, as a mother, never could be. There was also the issue of money, of course. Make no mistake, I was all too aware of my fortunate circumstances, *grâce à les bénéfices de mon grandpère,* without whose kind legacy my life might have been quite different. Annie had no such inheritance and, as a woman, in those days, she was in a perilous position, financially speaking. I always felt rather awkward that my small income permitted me to live reasonably well, and without anxiety. Thank heavens, during my lifetime, the world has become a better place: nowadays, we women can own property, whether we are married or not, and I look forward to the day, in the not too distant future, where we can take on the work of men (not only in time of war, mind you), and earn an equal wage, and perhaps even become business tycoons, or magnates – would that not be wonderful?

But where was I? Oh yes, I had begun to attend Ned's classes at the Art School, back in March, and was finding his tuition extremely useful. Not only was he a talented painter, but he also proved to be a gifted teacher. He encouraged everyone as he passed around the room, pausing, from time to time, beside each of us, to comment on our work. Above all, he was a kind man, and no matter how tired he was (and, by then, he often looked tired, his energy depleted by having to teach as well as paint), his criticisms were presented in the most complimentary way: 'A promising start, Mrs Coats. Perhaps you might want to draw the vase lower down, then your flowers wouldn't be crammed into this narrow space at the top of the page . . . but all in all, a very strong beginning.' He showed no favouritism, even to me. Truth be told, he went to the opposite extreme, in the interests of fairness, stopping beside my easel less frequently than he did with the other ladies. I understood, perfectly, his reasons: he was unwilling to make the others feel neglected. Very cleverly, he spotted my main problems, from the start: that, in drawing, I pressed down far too hard on the paper and that, in both drawing and painting, I tended to overwork each detail.

Having embarked upon this new hobby, I soon began to feel the limitations of my lodgings in Queen's Crescent. My rooms were at the front of the house, with dormer windows, which were low, and faced in a southerly direction, more or less, which meant that the quality of light was inconstant. Space was limited, and the ceilings were not particularly high. Given all these restrictions, neither room was ideal for use as a studio. With this in mind, I had written to my stepfather, back in March, to remind him that he had offered me the use of his property at Bardowie. I enquired, politely, whether the house was still available, and whether – with his permission – I might use it, for a while. Whether or not the place was habitable, I did not know, but I had an idea that I might spruce up a few rooms and spend some time there, over the summer, practising my drawing and painting.

Miraculously, I received a reply to this letter: a short reply, admittedly, but a reply nonetheless. Yes, Merlinsfield was available, and yes, Ramsay was happy for me to take up residence there. That, in a nutshell, was as much as was contained in the main body of the letter. However, in postscript, he had added: *Builder still at work on roof. Obliged you would conduct surveillance and inform me at once if he is idle. Suspect he will sleep between the rafters if you let him. Cannot fire brute as he is distantly related to the Tuites by marriage. Took him on as a favour – little did I know! Incidentally, I am off to Switzerland for a few months. You can contact me through my factor, as usual.*

I had absolutely no idea who the Tuites might be: presumably some important local family, with whom my stepfather wished to curry favour.

In any case, a few days later, I went to view Merlinsfield, which turned out to be an old jointure house, close by the shores of a loch. Of the builder, that day, there was no sign, and I was able to explore the place alone, having collected the key from Donald Deuchars, the old retainer, who resided with his wife, Agnes, in the cottage at the gate. The acreage at Merlinsfield was larger than I had expected. At its centre was the main building, a handsome mansion, constructed of stone, with crow-stepped gables. Attached to the house was a large tower, with a substantial room on an upper floor. There were several outbuildings, and the property was perfectly habitable, bar a few damp corners, here and there. I was thrilled, in particular, by the tower room, since it looked out over the countryside, both north and east. From the north-facing window, you could see the wind rippling the surface of the loch, and causing the saplings on its shore to shiver. There was a huge fireplace in the wall, and the ceiling was high. I could not help but think that such a room would make a splendid studio, and I decided, on the spot, to accept my stepfather's offer.

Since then, I had been spending part of each week at Merlinsfield, keeping an eye on the builder, whose name was McCluskey. With Ramsay's blessing, and with a view to staying at the house over the summer, I employed another man to redecorate a few of the rooms. I even gained my stepfather's permission to enlarge the windows in the tower, with the aim of admitting as much light as possible. Provided that I paid for the work, Ramsay seemed to have no objection to any improvements that I might want to make to the structure. Donald and Agnes had been overseeing the builder's efforts, but they were elderly and frail, and could not really be expected to supervise or chivvy him. With my encouragement, McCluskey laboured at a swifter rate, and I had high hopes that the repairs and refurbishments would be finished by the middle of May.

It is perfectly true that I invited Ned and Annie out there, in April. I hired a carriage, and we made a day of it. I wanted them to see the house, with the early daffodils in bloom, and it was also an opportunity to take the children out of Glasgow and let them run around the woods and meadows by the loch. Disappointingly, the day began dull and overcast. Sibyl was fractious: she squabbled with Rose during the journey and then, at the loch shore, threw stones into the water, in rather a spiteful fashion. Annie also seemed unhappy that day. She claimed to have a headache, and even the cawing of the crows seemed to vex her. By contrast, Ned took a liking to the place. He was very impressed, both with the property and with the work that I was having done on the tower and the guest rooms. Most of all, he loved the view from the window of the studio: he kept exclaiming over it, and saying how much it reminded him of some of the countryside around Co'path.

In mid-afternoon, by some miracle, the sun came out. Annie and I sat at the edge of the loch on a blanket, while Ned charged about the meadow, encouraging the girls to chase him, keen that they should make the most of this chance of fresh air and exercise. Rose was always happiest by Annie's side and, presently, she came to join us on the blanket, where she cuddled into her mother, like a little cat, the happy recipient of Annie's kisses. In all likelihood, Annie was unaware that, whenever she contemplated Rose, her favourite child, a particular glow softened her eyes: the light of love – of complete adoration – which never appeared when she looked at Sibyl. A little earlier that day, we had picked some daffodils to take back to Stanley Street, and Rose kept holding the flowers up to her mother's throat, to see the golden light of the petals reflected under her chin. For some reason, this sight tickled Rose, and she kept chuckling away to herself.

Meanwhile, Ned continued to play 'tag' with Sibyl. At one

point, he grabbed her, and spun her around, pretending to stagger under her weight. To my surprise and delight, I saw that the child was laughing: a rare moment.

'Look at Sibyl,' I murmured.

But Annie only rubbed at her forehead, saying: 'What time were you thinking of going back, Harriet? Only it'll start to get dark soon.'

I dare say that we did mention the possibility of us all living there together, over the summer months, but the notion that any serious proposition was made is far-fetched. We all knew that Annie was set on renting a cottage by the sea, or returning to Co'path, should the tenants move out in August, as Peden had intimated that they might. Evidently, Merlinsfield was not what she had in mind. I certainly did not bear her any grudge thereafter, as has been suggested, most recently, with the appearance, earlier this year, of that piece of gibberish, Mr Bruce Kemp's *Famous Travesties of Scottish Justice*. I do not intend to honour that publication with further mention here, since its author would love nothing better than were I to fan the flames of his publicity; but I will say, in passing, that one particular essay therein is nothing but a distasteful flight of fantasy, written by a conceited, embittered person whose mind is severely deranged.

But that is by the bye. People are forever extending invitations, here and there, in the firm knowledge that they will fail to be taken up. 'You must come to tea,' we say. 'Oh, yes, indeed, we must,' comes the reply. But both parties know that such an event will never take place.

11

And now, I must write of difficult things, events that, even all these years later, cause a dull pain of anguish to flare up behind my breastbone. Much has been said and written about what happened on the 4th of May 1889: that warm and, ultimately, wet day. Since virtually verbatim accounts are available – for instance, in Hodge's *Notable Trials* series – I do not propose to tax the limited space available in this memoir by an unnecessary regurgitation of all the details. None the less, I am aware that I have never yet had an opportunity to provide my own description of events. This being the case, I feel that it may be of interest to give some indication of my experience of what transpired.

The 4th of May was a Saturday, and I had spent most of the morning in town, at Pettigrew and Stephens, the department store, looking at glassware. The old sideboard at Merlinsfield contained only a limited amount of mismatched crystal, which was so chipped and cloudy that no amount of polishing would render it hygienic, and thus I had decided to purchase a small stock of new glasses, for my own use, and for any guests that might happen to visit the house.

That morning, the weather was bright and warm, with the promise of summer in the air. Originally, I had no notion of calling on the Gillespies that day. However, while I was arranging for delivery of the new glasses, I happened to notice, on sale, a very elegant parcel-gilt dinner and tea service, complete with plates, entrée dishes, sauceboat, and so on, and I could not help but think of Annie and Ned, who were still using the same faded china that had been produced on the very first afternoon that I had taken tea in their home, almost a year previously. Indeed, the family was forever running short of bread plates and cups, and so, on the spur of the moment, I purchased the dinner set and asked for it to be delivered to the Gillespie residence. Rather than have the crate arrive, unannounced, I decided to call in on my way home, just to let them know to expect a delivery, the following week.

After a cup of tea in the ladies' café at the Panorama, I took advantage of the blue skies, and walked to South Woodside, reaching Woodland Road at approximately half past two o'clock. As I approached number 11, I happened to notice two little figures up ahead: Sibyl and Rose, toddling along towards Carnarvon Street. There was nothing unusual in this: Ned's wife continued, by and large, to treat Sibyl as though she was a normal girl, and left her in charge of her little sister, letting them roam wherever they pleased. Since she had yet to hire another maid, Annie was coping single-handedly with the housework and, now that the weather had begun to improve – and despite Ned's reluctance to let the girls play outside, unsupervised – she often sent her daughters round to Queen's Crescent while she got on with her chores. We were all used to seeing the girls trotting around the neighbourhood, or glimpsing them, at play, in the gardens. At any rate, I hardly gave them a second thought as they turned the corner and disappeared from view.

As it turned out, Ned had also left the apartment that day, at about one o'clock. Annie professed to have no idea where he had gone, and I wondered what this admission might imply about the state of the marriage – although perhaps some couples simply reach a stage wherein each spouse no longer cares to know about the comings and goings of the other. When I arrived, Annie had been cleaning the hall floor: the rugs were up, and her broom had caused what Ned would call a 'stour'. Insisting that I had no wish to disturb her, I told her to expect the arrival of a crate from Pettigrew's, on Monday. I had thought that she might be pleased to hear about the dinner service that I had bought for them. In fact, she seemed almost exasperated at the news.

'That's kind of you,' she said. 'But it's too much.'

'It was a bargain,' I told her. 'Even though there's nothing wrong with it.'

She swiped her broom at the floor. 'I don't mind you treating the girls every so often, but we can't accept it. You must stop buying things for me and Ned.'

'Perhaps he wouldn't mind a new dinner service.'

'No, I think he'd agree with me – you shouldn't be spending money on us.'

'Very well. If you really don't want it, I shall see if I can cancel the order.'

'Please, don't be upset, Harriet. You're just too kind, and – we don't deserve it. I don't mean to be rude or ungrateful, but –'

'Not at all – you're absolutely right. It was silly to buy it without even asking you. Look here, I won't cancel the delivery, I'll just get them to take it out to Merlinsfield, instead. It would be useful to have some half-decent crockery out there.'

'Good idea. Now, if you don't mind, I must get on.' She indicated a pile of dust, and the rugs, in disarray.

'Oh, do let me help!' I cried. Despite her protests, I was more than happy to don a spare apron and wield the dustpan.

To begin with, Annie was quiet, but then, as we worked on, she began to quiz me, as she sometimes did, about my old life in London, with particular reference to any bachelors of my acquaintance. Having established that I harboured no romantic inclination for any Englishman, she moved closer to home.

'How much longer will you remain in Glasgow, d'you think?' she asked. 'Given that London is your home? I suppose if you met somebody here, some nice gentleman – he need not be young, necessarily, perhaps an older man, a widower –'

'Annie dear, do please forgive me for interrupting, but I can assure you that nothing of the sort will happen. There will be no nice widower. One would, in the first place, have to be interested in something more than friendship with a man; and I, for one, am not.'

'But – what about marriage?'

'Good gracious, no,' I laughed. 'Men are all very well, but I would never *submit* to one of them, physically or otherwise. I like them only in the platonic sense. For instance, you know how interested I am in Ned's work, but that is as far as it goes. I have no desire for romance with *any* man!'

'Oh!' said Annie. I could not help but notice the expression on her face; she was not exactly smiling, but she did seem more cheerful.

'Whatever is the matter?' I asked.

'Oh, nothing,' she said. Nevertheless, watching her as she bent to her broom, it was obvious that she was relieved; the very atmosphere had lightened.

We spent the next half-hour or so sweeping the floors, and then I helped her to carry the small rugs down to the street, to beat them. Outside, the town was still in its May mood, the ever-present smoke haze mellowing and softening the rays of sunlight. Dust flew up in clouds as we thrashed the rugs against the metal railings. Few people passed us while we worked, for Stanley Street is a quiet thoroughfare, used only by its residents and a few tradesmen and, perhaps, the odd person on foot, taking a short-cut between the main roads. Across the street, a dog sniffed at the wheels of a stationary cart, while its driver sat dozing at the reins. Over at number 14, Elspeth's maid, Jean, came outside with a bucket and began to scour the front steps. I nodded at her, in greeting, and she waggled her scrubbing brush in response.

My gaze followed the dog as it scampered up the road, and it was then that I happened to spy Sibyl. As yet, she had not spotted us, and was skipping along with her eyes fixed on the pavement, apparently without a care in the world. Beside me, Annie finished beating a rug and turned to follow my gaze, and it was just then that Sibyl glanced up and noticed us. In that moment, as I recall it, the child's demeanour changed. She stopped skipping and her step faltered. Her face underwent a transformation; the quiet contentment was replaced, fleetingly, by a troubled, almost guilty look. Then, she seemed to recover, and as she came towards us, she assumed one of her habitual expressions, a simulacrum of innocent boredom. There was no sign of her sister and I assumed that, soon enough, Rose would come toddling along the street in her wake. Annie, however – with that sixth sense that is peculiar to mothers – was immediately on the alert.

'Where's Rose?' she called out.

'I don't know,' said Sibyl, in a sing-song voice.

'Have you left her round the corner?'

Sibyl shook her head, and drew down her brows, looking upset. Annie tossed the rug that she had been beating onto the steps, and approached the child. 'What's the matter? Where's your sister?' Sibyl stretched out her foot, and drew her toes along a crack in the pavement, muttering something that neither of us could hear.

'Speak up dear,' said Annie.

'Can't find her,' said Sibyl, quietly.

'What do you mean, you can't find her?'

The girl's lip trembled, and tears brimmed up in her eyes. 'I found a – a dead bird, on the ground, and then, when I looked up, Rose wasn't there any more.'

Annie sighed, and turned to me. 'Harriet, I'm sorry but would you mind taking these rugs in? I'll have to go and get Rose. We won't be long.'

'Not at all.'

'Come on,' said Annie to Sibyl, and off they went, hand in hand. Sibyl skipped along the street at her mother's side, seeming to have cheered up once again.

I carried the rugs upstairs and, since I knew exactly where each one belonged, I went around the rooms, laying them on the new-swept floors, having left the front door open for air. After that, I made a pot of tea, since I was sure that Annie would be thirsty upon her return. Twenty minutes later, there was still no sign of any of the Gillespies. Eventually, after almost half an hour, I heard footsteps echoing in the close as someone came running up to the apartment, and then Annie burst in through the parlour doorway, out of breath. She seemed panic-stricken.

'I can't find Rose anywhere. She's not in the gardens, and I've looked all round the Crescent and Cumberland Street, and she's not in the back green –'

'Where's Sibyl?'

'I left her across the road with Jean. Elspeth's out.'

Despite my rising panic, I took a moment to absorb this information. Annie had forbidden her daughters to set foot in number 14, and it was an indication of how worried she now was that she had broken her own rule. I tried to reassure her.

'Perhaps Rose is hiding somewhere. Shall we go and look?'

The back entrances to the tenements were usually unlocked during daylight hours, and the children habitually ran in and out that way, so we left the apartment door ajar, in case Rose returned in our absence. On the way downstairs, Annie paused on the landing to tell Mrs Calthrop that she had left her door open, and asked her to keep an eye out for Rose – or anybody else – going up the stairs. Then, we hurried around the corner to Queen's Crescent.

The gate to the gardens lay open, as it often did. It took just a moment to confirm that Rose was not there – not behind any of the trees, nor under the bench, nor hiding behind the fountain. We walked the length of the Crescent itself, peering over the railings, into all the front areas, and the only unusual thing that we found was a bag of sugar, sitting on a wall. Leaving it untouched, we cut behind the terrace and trudged down the back lane, calling out Rose's name. After that, we stopped in at my lodgings, where all the front rooms overlooked the gardens, and it was possible that one of the Alexanders might have noticed the child wandering off. However, as it turned out, young Lily, Kate and their mother had been at the rear of the house all afternoon, in the kitchen, or the back sitting room. When we told them what had happened, they came outside and helped us to search the immediate vicinity once more, and then we all dashed down Melrose Street and peered along Great Western Road in both directions, but there was no sign of any little girl amongst the passers-by.

'What was she wearing?' asked Lily Alexander, very sensibly.

Annie thought for a moment. 'A blue frock,' she said, at length. 'A short blue frock, with a sort of lozenge pattern, and her apron.'

By that time, the weather had begun to change. Whilst Annie and I had been searching the gardens, dark clouds had crept silently in, from the West. Now, as we stood at the end of Melrose Street, it began to pour – large, intermittent drops at first, and then a heavier shower, with the rumble of thunder in the distance. Too intent on finding Rose to worry about a spot of rain, we decided to split up. Annie gave Mrs Alexander her key and begged her to go around to number 11, and sit there, in case Rose returned to find the house empty, or, should Ned arrive home, to tell him what had happened. Then, convinced that her daughter might have wandered towards the West End Park, Annie made haste, bareheaded, in that direction. Having agreed to look along the main roads, Lily and Kate scurried off. As for myself, I made a close inspection of the smaller streets, near at hand: Arlington, Cumberland, Grant, Carnarvon and, finally, Stanley. I made sure to check all the lanes and back courts, but there was no sign of Rose anywhere, nor of anyone who had seen a girl answering her description. Of course, most children roam far and wide, only to return home safely at the end of their day's adventures, and it might be expected that, left to her own devices, Rose would turn up, unharmed, at some point. However, she was such a clingy child that she disliked to leave Annie's side for long. Even when in the care of Sibyl or anyone else, she tended not to wander too far, because she liked the security of being close to someone she knew; it was this awareness of her character that made us rather worried.

Upon my return to number 11, I glanced up at the parlour windows and saw the pale moon of Mrs Alexander's face, staring down at me. I raised one hand in the air – more a quizzical gesture than a wave – and in response she shook her head, from which I understood that there was, as yet, no sign of either Rose or Ned. Rather than go upstairs, I decided to continue the search.

It occurred to me that – had the child wandered off – there was a chance that she might have gone towards Charing Cross, given that she often accompanied one or other of her relatives on trips into town; she might, out of habit, have trotted off in the direction of the big shops. So it was that I set off towards the east. The rain continued to fall, relentlessly, but an umbrella would have made no difference: having worn no coat that morning, I was already soaked to the skin. I believe that I may have glanced down St George's Road, in passing, but I saw nothing there that drew my attention. On Sauchiehall Street, I stared hard through fences and over walls, into the grounds of all the great villas, in case the child might have slipped through a gateway and wandered up one of the drives. As I reached the Corporation Buildings, the heavens opened and the downpour became torrential enough to empty the landscape of pedestrians, as people scurried towards the shelter of tea shops and doorways. I searched up and down a number of side streets but, eventually, with no sign of Rose any-where, I decided to retrace my steps to Woodside, in the hope that she might already have been found.

At Stanley Street, the main door to number 11 had been propped open, and a few women and children had gathered just inside, to shelter from the rain. In those days – as now – congre-gating at the mouth of the close was frowned upon as 'common', and so it was plain that word must have spread about Rose, other-wise these respectable matrons would not have lingered there, lest they might be mistaken for Jezebels! They were talking amongst themselves, in low voices, as I approached. I recognised one of the ladies as the Gillespies' downstairs neighbour.

'Excuse me, Mrs Calthrop,' I said, 'has little Rose been found yet?'

Calthrop shook her head, dourly. 'But half the street's out look-ing for her.'

I questioned her further. Apparently, my landlady was still upstairs, in the Gillespies' parlour, keeping vigil. Annie had returned, briefly, but when told that there was still no sign of

Rose, she had rushed out again, into the rain, to continue her search. Ned had not yet come home. There was no definite news of Rose, but various rumours had begun to come to light. At half past two o'clock, one of the neighbours had been crossing West Princes Street, and had seen, in the distance, two little girls walking, hand in hand, westwards, in the direction of the River Kelvin. A while later, a small, fair-haired lass was seen passing the old flint mill, alone. Someone else claimed to have been in a grocer's shop on Great Western Road, at about a quarter past three o'clock, when a girl of Sibyl's age and appearance entered and stood in the queue, waiting to be served. And, apparently, young Lily Alexander had spoken to a maidservant who worked on the Queen's Terrace section of West Princes Street. This maid – a girl named Martha – had been returning from an errand, some time after three o'clock, when she noticed a man hurrying along with a bundle in his arms. She had realised that the bundle was human only when it began to cry; it was a little girl, she was almost certain. The man had tried to hush the child, and when that failed, he simply hurried away.

'But you know what skivvies are like,' said Calthrop. 'She's probably made it up, to get attention. More likely it was the man's own wee bairn.'

'No doubt, that's the case,' I said, reluctant as I was to consider any alternative. I had intended to go upstairs and speak to my landlady, but it occurred to me that Calthrop had already told me all that I needed to hear. Therefore, with no desire to stand around gossiping, I hurried back outside, in order to do what seemed to be the most useful thing, under the circumstances, and that was to carry on searching for Rose, while there was still light in the sky.

First of all, I stopped off at my lodgings, where I changed my frock, which was dripping wet. Then I put on a mackintosh and went back outside, armed with my umbrella. Troubled by what Calthrop had said about two girls who had been seen going towards the Kelvin, I decided to head in that direction. Annie and

I had often taken the children along the river, on our walks, and it was quite possible that they might have wandered down there. For all I knew, Sibyl might not have been telling the truth, and I was worried about what might have become of Rose: the paths alongside the water could be lonely; the route often veered close to steep areas of riverbank; the Kelvin was deep in places, powerful and fast-flowing in its lower reaches, and could rise quickly under rainy conditions, such as we were experiencing that day. It was possible that there had been some kind of accident, and that Sibyl was too frightened of the consequences to tell us what had happened.

At intervals, along West Princes Street, tenements were under construction and I peered into the building sites as I went along, but saw no sign of any children. Reaching the river, I headed northwards, keeping close to the water's edge whenever I was able. For the next few hours, I searched the river valley and the strips of woodland along the way. Thankfully, the rain soon stopped. I went as far as the paper works, after which it was too dark to see any more. En route, I was menaced, once, by a dog, and accosted, twice, by solitary men, who may, in the half-light, have mistaken me for something that I was not, but they soon realised their error when I saw them off with sharp words and my raised umbrella. Of Ned's and Annie's missing child, I found not a trace.

It was with blistered feet and aching legs that I returned to Stanley Street, at about half past nine o'clock. Glancing up at number 11, I saw a dim light burning in the Gillespies' parlour, and thought that I perceived someone at the window – possibly Annie, although it was hard to tell. The shadowy figure shrank out of sight behind the curtains as I began to climb the front steps. Now that darkness had fallen, the little group of women and children at the close mouth had dispersed. However, the main door, which was usually locked, had been propped ajar with a large stone. (I later learned that this was at Ned's insistence, in case Rose should return, in the night.) Reluctant to intrude at such a time, uninvited, I rang the bell, rather than going straight up to the apartment, which would have been presumptuous, under the circumstances. After an interval, I heard heavy male footsteps on the stairs, and then on the flagstones of the close. The thwack of leather sole was accompanied by a strange crunching, grinding sound that I could not identify. Presently, the door opened to reveal a tall, thin police constable, a Highlander. I recognised him, from his ginger moustache, as Constable Black, one of the older men who walked the beat around the Claremont and Woodside areas. He brought with him an overpowering scent of peppermint humbugs, which explained the sounds of crunching that I had heard.

'Aye,' he said, leaning down to peer at me, with a blast of cold, mint breath that almost made my eyes water. 'What is it?'

'I'm here to see the Gillespies. Has Rose been found?'

'No yet, missus. But dinna fash yersel', she'll turn up.'

'Oh, I do hope you're right.'

I hesitated, wondering whether he might lead me into the building, but then he said: 'Who are ye, yourself? Likely they'll want tae know who called.'

'Harriet, Miss Baxter. I was here, earlier, with Annie. I've been looking for Rose, these past few hours. I'm a good friend of the family. Do they need any help? I'd be happy to make hot drinks, or anything else that might be required.'

'Naw – nae need. Mr Gillespie's mother's in charge of the kettle.'

'Elspeth? Elspeth Gillespie? Are you sure?'

'Aye, it's Mrs Gillespie, sure as sure. She's making the doctor some tea.'

'A doctor? What's the matter? Is someone ill?'

'Thon wee – Sibyl, is it? – flew up in the snuff and took a wee fit tae herself. She's fine now, but this place has been going like a fair. They need peace and quiet. You'd do better tae come back tomorrow.'

'Oh yes – yes, of course.'

He stepped behind the door, and let it close, gently, against the prop-stone. Then I heard him retrace his footsteps, back up the passageway.

Suddenly exhausted, I returned to Queen's Crescent. The little park lay at the centre, still and quiet, under cover of darkness. I stood on the steps of my lodgings, for a moment. The gardens were desolate and empty. Where was little Rose? And was she safe from harm?

Mrs Alexander had not yet retired to bed, and from her I learned a few more snippets of information. Apparently, she had remained in the Gillespies' parlour until quite late, and had been there, just after six o'clock, when Ned had arrived home, distraught, having been told by the women downstairs that his youngest daughter had been missing for three hours. He asked my landlady if she would mind remaining where she was, in case anyone returned, while he went to the Western Police Office, at Cranston Street. Then he dashed off again, extremely vexed.

Soon afterwards, Sibyl had come leaping upstairs, followed, at a more sedate pace, by Ned's mother, who had just returned from a prison visit and heard the news about Rose from her maid. Elspeth was in a state of near-hysteria and, apparently, it was all that Mrs Alexander could do to calm the woman, fearing (probably rightly) that her raving demeanour might have an ill effect upon Sibyl.

In due course, it seems, Ned reappeared, having been instructed, at the police office, to go home and there await the arrival of a detective who would want to question his wife, in particular. And so, the Alexander girls were sent to find Annie but, as they were on their way out, they met her coming in, accompanied by Detective Sub-Inspector Stirling and the ginger policeman, whom she had encountered in the street. A troupe of neighbours and nosy urchins straggled upstairs in their wake, and Constable Black was obliged to close the landing door, in order to keep them out and maintain some order. In the end,

Calthrop and Mrs Alexander were the only neighbours who were permitted to remain.

'Did Ned's mother stay?' I asked and when my landlady nodded, I remarked: 'I dread to think what happened when Annie saw her.'

Mrs Alexander shook her head, sadly.

'I doubt Annie noticed anybody, she was in such a state, poor thing.'

Evidently, the police conducted their interviews in the dining room, and Annie was the first to be questioned. After several minutes, she emerged, and then Sibyl was summoned into the room, alone. Without the inhibiting presence of her family, and under some clever interrogation from Detective Stirling, the child eventually admitted that she had, indeed, left her sister unsupervised in the gardens that afternoon, but only for a few minutes.

She and Rose had been playing in separate areas of the little park: Sibyl had been inspecting a dead bird that she found lying on the grass, while her sister dug around with a stick beneath the trees. Apparently, at one point, Sibyl glanced up and noticed a woman standing outside the railings, on the West Princes Street side, looking into the gardens. The child was fairly sure that she had never seen this person before. According to her description, the woman wore a shiny blue dress, and a black hat, with a short veil that covered her face to the end of her nose. By the time that Sibyl next looked up, the woman had vanished from her original position, but then she reappeared, soon afterwards, on Queen's Crescent, at the entrance to the gardens. When she caught Sibyl's gaze, she smiled, and beckoned with her finger. Leaving Rose at play, the older girl approached the gate. The woman explained that she had just moved into a house nearby, and needed somebody to run to Dobie's to buy sugar, because she was awaiting the carriers and was unable to go herself. Dobie the grocer's was just around the corner, on Great Western Road, about a minute's walk from the gardens. Sibyl was familiar with the shop, having been there many times with Annie and various others. The woman indicated Rose, who was still playing, a little distance away, beneath the trees.

'Is that your wee sister?' she asked. When Sibyl nodded, the woman took out two pennies. 'Keep one of these,' she said. 'And go and buy me a pennyworth of sugar with the other. I'll look after your sister until you get back.'

Not imagining that there could be any harm in leaving Rose for a few minutes, under these circumstances, Sibyl ran down Melrose Street and around the corner. She bought the sugar at Dobie's, as requested, and – no doubt – felt quite pleased with herself, having never before gone to a shop to make a purchase unaccompanied. However, upon her return to Queen's Crescent, she was vaguely alarmed to find the little park empty, with no sign of Rose or the lady stranger, anywhere. There were few nooks and crannies in the gardens, but Sibyl looked in them all, and then she walked around the Crescent, calling her sister's name. Eventually, when it seemed evident that neither Rose nor the veiled woman were going to reappear, she left the bag of sugar on a wall (where Annie and I saw it, later) and returned to Stanley Street, assuming that Rose had got bored without her and gone home. In the event, realising that this was not the case, and faced with her mother's concern, the child had been unable to admit the truth, fearing that, yet again, she would be scolded or punished for wrongdoing.

As Mrs Alexander explained to me, when the detective conveyed this story to the Gillespie family, and showed them the penny that the woman had given to the child, Sibyl had looked shamefaced. Meanwhile, Elspeth became very agitated. She darted scandalised glances at her granddaughter, but said nothing, for the time being, until Ned and the policemen went out to look at Queen's Crescent, leaving the women alone.

'That was when Elspeth confronted Sibyl,' explained my landlady. 'Saying it was all her fault, as usual, accusing her of wickedness and greed.' Evidently, the child became upset and began to whimper, but the widow persisted, complaining that Sibyl had abandoned Rose. Despite Annie's pleas that she should desist, Elspeth kept ranting on and on until, of a sudden, Sibyl fell to the floor, screaming, and twisting her little body, this way and that, until she seemed to go into convulsions.

'Annie turned quite pale with fright,' said Mrs Alexander. 'She lay down beside Sibyl, and held her, to pacify her.' One of the local lads was sent hurrying to fetch a physician from Woodside Place (a nearby residential street populated, almost entirely, by gentlemanly M.D.s.) By the time that young Dr Williams had arrived, Sibyl had calmed down somewhat, but the appearance on the scene of a medical man seemed to upset her, once again, and the doctor was obliged to give the child a little sedation.

He and Annie put Sibyl to bed and, presently, Ned and the policemen returned, having inspected Queen's Crescent gardens, and found no trace of Rose (by that stage, even the bag of sugar had disappeared). In order to discount the possibility that the child was hiding somewhere, the policemen took lamps downstairs and, with Ned as their guide, they inspected all the back courts, along the lane, and then peered into the basement coal stores of number 11. Thereafter, they announced their intention to search the apartment. Any person who was not a family member was asked to leave and so, along with Calthrop, Mrs Alexander excused herself and came home.

'They won't have found her in that flat,' she told me. 'I was there for hours, and don't think I didn't take the opportunity to look around, just in case.' This admission surprised me, since my landlady was one of the most incurious people I had ever met. I must have looked startled, because she added: 'Och, you know what children are like. I half thought Rose might be playing hide-and-seek to herself. I looked in all the rooms, except one upstairs that was locked, and there was no child there in that place, not in the presses, or anywhere.'

My mind had already leapt ahead, to other matters: 'What about the woman who sent Sibyl to the shop – did the police find her?'

'Not that I know of,' said Mrs Alexander. 'It's a mystery. If there's still no sign of Rose by tomorrow, then they're going to form search parties.'

'Search parties!' In my bewildered state, the very words sounded ominous. 'Let's hope it won't come to that. How did Ned and Annie seem when you left?'

My landlady shook her head, grimly. 'Poor dears, their nerves are shattered.'

'Well, at least they can rely upon each other.'

'Aye, although –'

'What?'

'Well, between you and me, I got the impression they weren't speaking to each other. A few times, she said something to him, he just ignored her.'

Soon thereafter, I bade Mrs Alexander goodnight, and went upstairs to my bedroom. All through the hours of darkness, I tossed and turned, without sleeping, in great distress for my poor friends. There was no question in my mind that Annie would be unable to ignore her own sense of guilt, like a queasy pain, rising in her stomach. Though Ned would never be so cruel as to speak his mind, she must have known that he would blame her for losing Rose, since he had always made it plain that he disapproved of sending the girls outside to play, unsupervised: I had heard him say so, myself, on several occasions. Normally, I tend to take a bright view of most matters, but in this instance, try as I might, I could not be confident of a fortunate outcome. My head was filled with horrible presentiments, and my heart was sick with foreboding.

That night, the police and the doctor left Stanley Street towards half past ten o'clock, with the promise to return in the morning. Ned's mother deemed it wise to make her exit at the same time, having, in the aftermath of her outburst at Sibyl, sensed a degree of animosity from Annie. Thus, she led the men downstairs, leaving Rose's parents alone with their anguish. Detective Stirling had advised the Gillespies to remain at home in case Rose should return, and insisted that there was no point in them going out to search that night. Indeed, it could be hazardous for them to be roaming around lonely places in the dark.

With the apartment empty, Annie was only too aware of the tension between herself and her husband, and (as she told me, later) the atmosphere was desiccate and strange. Earlier that night, while she was explaining, once again, to the detective, how she had sent her daughters out to play, unaccompanied, she had sensed her husband studying her, a sour expression on his face, but when she tried to catch his eye, for sympathy, he had turned away. Now, if she asked him a question, or spoke to him, he would answer, but his replies were cold and abrupt and so, it was almost a relief when, after pacing the floor for five minutes, in furious silence, he threw on his coat, saying that he would rather pull out his own eye than remain there, doing nothing: he was going to try and find Rose. He commanded her to light a lamp at the parlour window should there be any news, and then he went running downstairs, without bidding her farewell, and without any display of tenderness or affection, or any reassurance that they would face this ordeal, together. Moments later, when Annie pulled up the sash and peered out, along the road, she saw her husband turn the corner onto Carnarvon Street, where he was swallowed by the darkness.

Left alone, and utterly miserable, she spent the hours until dawn walking from room to room, every now and then peering out into the murky night, watching and waiting for any sign of Rose, or any news – but none came.

Only at daybreak, did Ned return. The main door was propped ajar, just as he had left it. Pushing it open, he stepped inside the close, and then stopped, of a sudden, in his tracks. There, on the flagstones, lay an envelope. The name Gillespie had been scrawled, in pencil, across the front. Inside, he found a single sheet of paper, which had been written upon, in the same brutish hand. The writing was such a filthy scrawl that it took him a while to work out what it said.

DEAR SIR

BE NOTE AFRAYED YOUR GIRL IS AL WRITE AS WE
GOT HER. MAKE REDY FIFE HUNDERT POUNDS AND WE
WILL DEN TELL YOU WERE TO DELIVER THE MONY. DO
NOTE NOTIFY THE POLISE - OR ELSE! TELL YOUR WIFE
THE CHILD IS IN GUT HANDS.

I myself first learned about this note when Annie described it to me, word for word, just a few hours later. I would not have called upon her so early, except that my landlady had baked some rolls for the Gillespies, and I had offered to deliver them, while they were still warm. Fully expecting to be turned away at the door, I was surprised when Annie almost begged me to keep her company, in the kitchen. Sibyl was still upstairs, sleeping off the effects of Dr Williams's sedation, and Ned had yet to return from the police office, where he had gone, hoping to show Detective Stirling the note. Annie was pale and haggard, and had not changed her clothes since the previous day. When she spoke, her voice sounded strangely flat, without intonation.

'It's a horrible letter,' she told me. 'Big jagged writing, and most of the words are spelt wrong.'

The skin across the back of my neck prickled. There was something sinister about this note with its crude handwriting and bad spelling. However, I was determined not to add to Annie's woes.

'It sounds like a nasty-minded prank to me.'

Her tired eyes lit up, momentarily. 'Do you think so?'

'Don't you? Was it delivered by the postman?'

'No – it must have been brought in the night.'

'But nobody saw anyone approach the building?'

She shook her head.

'What about Ned – has he taken it seriously?'

'I don't know,' said Annie, her voice almost a whisper. 'I did beg him not to take it to the police, but –'

With a frown, she grabbed up Rose's wooden horse from where it lay on the hearthrug. Recently, someone had scraped away the scorched patch on its side, which had left a strange cavity in the belly of the beast, as though it had been mauled. Annie hugged the ruined toy to her chest. She must have spent the entire night chewing her fingers, for the nails were bitten to the quick. She stared into the hearth, hard-eyed and alert. It dawned on me that, for once, she looked older than her years. I glanced out of the kitchen, towards the main door of the apartment, which lay wide open onto the close.

'Where's Elspeth?' I asked.

'Church.' Annie sighed. 'She said somebody ought to pray for Rose.'

So forlorn did she look that I was desperate to reassure her.

'Annie dear – if someone goes to the bother of taking a child, for money, then I'm fairly sure they establish, first of all, that the parents are wealthy. This note is probably just a too silly horrid hoax. Rose will be back, before you know it.'

She nodded, miserably. 'That's what Ned says. She'll come back and . . .' Her voice tailed away.

Perhaps I should point out that, under normal circumstances, I am not much given to lamentation. We adult females do not weep quite as often as some novelists would have one believe; we tend to be made of sterner stuff. None the less, this was one of those rare occasions upon which I found myself becoming emotional. Perhaps it was simply the accumulated anxiety of the past day or so, but I had no desire to break down in front of Annie. There she was, presumably sick with fear, and yet, dry eyed, whilst I, like a prize fool, was ready to blubber. Excusing myself, I tried to gain some composure in the WC, by splashing my face with water. However, as soon as I returned to the kitchen, I was overcome by an urge to weep, once more, and so decided to make myself scarce until I had recovered my equilibrium. I knew that Annie would not be alone, for even as I made my excuses, Calthrop came bustling in to return an egg that she had once borrowed: a slender pretext, since it was quite obvious that she was simply desperate to hear if there had been any developments.

Later that day, when I was sufficiently composed to show my face at Stanley Street once more, events had moved on apace. In my absence, Ned had returned, along with Detective Stirling, and they had escorted Sibyl around the corner to Queen's Crescent, where it was hoped that she might be able to point out the house of the veiled lady stranger. However, it seemed that the woman had simply gestured in the general direction of West Princes Street, and Sibyl was unable to identify any residence in particular. Having failed to be of help, the child became upset, dismayed that she had, yet again, been a disappointment. Poor Sibyl! By this time, it must truly have been dawning upon her that the blame for her sister's disappearance would be seen to rest, largely, upon her shoulders.

By all accounts, she was inconsolable when Ned brought her home, and even though she had not eaten since the previous noon, she showed no interest in any food that was placed before her. Her heartbeat was raging; she trembled and perspired and claimed that she was unable to get enough air, even when her father sat her by an open window, and rubbed her back.

'It's not your fault, pet,' he kept telling her. 'It's nothing to do with you.'

By mid-morning, on the day after Rose's disappearance, two constables had begun to make house-to-house inquiries across Woodside. Detective Sub-Inspector Stirling soon organised a party of volunteers to scour the district. Normally, the police might have waited a few more days to begin an official search but, apparently, the detective wished to take advantage of the fact that this was Sunday, a day of rest, hence more men ought to be available than would be the case during the week. Alas, the weather proved wet and misty, and any participants were destined to have a most uncomfortable and gruelling experience. Moreover, the search had been called at such short notice that there was no time to place an announcement in the newspaper, and the volunteers had to be recruited by word of mouth alone. Consequently, by noon, fewer than thirty local men had convened at the meeting place: the Stewart Memorial Fountain, in the West End Park. A few women and children who attempted to take part were advised to go home, since – with one child lost, or missing – it was deemed unsafe for them to be roaming the western fringes of the city in the fog, particularly those areas wherein the efforts were to be concentrated: the riversides, parks, canals, and waste-grounds.

To cover as wide an area as possible, the men were divided into three sections. The first, led by the park-keeper, Mr Jamieson, concentrated on Kelvingrove and the University grounds; the second – under the command of Detective Stirling, and accompanied by Ned – went northwards by way of the Kelvin valley, past the old flint mill, and as far as the aqueduct; the third, headed by Sergeant McColl, turned east, along the streets and lanes of Garnethill, and then north, through the warehouses and works, towards the wharves of Port Dundas.

In case Rose should return, Annie remained at home, accompanied by various neighbours and friends, and Elspeth and her cronies, many of whom came and went, between church services, during the course of the afternoon. The weather was wet, but not too cold, which was fortunate because the street entrance to number 11 was propped open all day long, and the front door of the apartment simply lay wide open to the landing. When I arrived, at four o'clock, about a dozen women were gathered in the parlour, presided over by Ned's mother, who – reinstated in her old rocking chair – was the focus of much sympathy, now that her granddaughter had gone amissing.

'Oh, Herriet!' was her greeting. 'What have I done to deserve this? What a terrible year it's been!'

Of Annie, there was no sign, and I was led to understand that, some time previously, she had gone upstairs to put Sibyl down for a nap, but had not yet rejoined the company: to my mind, a perfectly reasonable stratagem. I myself was in no mood to pander to Elspeth. That she would cast herself as the prime victim of Rose's disappearance was not necessarily a surprise, but I will admit that I found it exasperating. Thus, I excused myself and went into the kitchen, which no one had tidied or cleaned since the previous day, and thus – to pass the time, while we waited for news – I tried to restore some order.

Presently, I heard the creak of the attic staircase and, glancing into the hall, I saw Annie descend the last few steps. Her face was pale, and even in the few hours since I had last seen her, two vertical worry lines seemed to have etched themselves between her brows. After an initial flurry of greetings from Elspeth and the other women, they left her in peace and when I next saw her, she had taken a seat by the window, a little apart from the others.

Somehow, the day passed. Tea was brewed, and drunk; toast was made, and buttered, but remained, for the most part, uneaten. Every so often, news arrived, carried to us by one or other of the older neighbourhood lads, who had made it their business to run back and forth between the search parties, to gather information. At one point, Sibyl made an appearance, but was so overwrought that Annie was obliged to take her upstairs once again. As time wore on, some of the womenfolk departed, for evening service, or to dine with their families.

Just after dusk, there was a clamour on the stairs, heralding the latest arrival of the neighbourhood boys. On this occasion, all five of them had turned up at once. A few of us, including Annie, hurried to meet them in the hall. The lads were damp, and out of breath, and they spoke at the same time, shouting over each other, but their message was simple enough to understand: no trace of Rose had been found, and the volunteers from all three parties were returning to the meeting point in the park, dispirited and depressed.

I turned to look at Annie. She stood there, stock-still. Her face had a frozen, stunned look. As for myself, I felt rather confused.

The best that could be hoped for was that Rose would turn up, unharmed, having sought shelter somewhere. Of course, it was a great pity that she had not already been found under those circumstances, but at least nothing truly horrific had come to light.

'Thank you for your help, boys,' said Annie, and then, all at once, she turned and stepped into her bedroom, closing the door firmly behind her, without a backward glance, which left us in no doubt that she did not wish to be disturbed.

Forthwith, Elspeth summoned the messengers into the parlour, where she yelped a few questions at them, and exclaimed, excitably, at their responses. So busy was she interrogating the lads, and dissecting every detail, loudly, for the benefit of her audience, that she failed to notice her son's return. I saw him, however, quite by chance. It so happened that I had not accompanied the others when they returned to their seats. Instead, I had lingered in the hall, having not quite decided what to do. Plainly, Annie wished to be left alone, and I could have set an example to the others by discreetly making myself scarce, but I was disinclined to desert her, altogether, and leave her at the mercy of those who remained. At any rate, I was standing, indecisively, at the threshold of the parlour, when I heard a soft footfall on the landing. I turned and – just as I moved forwards to peer into the close – Ned stepped into the hallway. He must have climbed the stairs very quietly, for he had made no sound at all until he was just outside.

It suddenly occurred to me that I had not seen him for a few days, not since our painting class, earlier in the week. I had expected him to be pale, like Annie, but – perhaps because of the shadows in the hall – his face seemed dark; indeed, everything about him had a murky, brooding appearance. His hat was soaked and shone like sable; even his mackintosh was black with the rain. For a moment, he stood, quite still, at the threshold, listening to his mother's voice, as she continued to criticise Detective Stirling. Instinctively, I said nothing. Having stepped away from the parlour door, I was no longer visible to the other women and so would not, by my actions, betray Ned's presence.

Instead of speaking, I clasped my hands together and gave him what I hoped was a look of profound sympathy. At first, he failed to react, until – finally – he looked at me. He looked at me for the first time, as though he had only just noticed me. I saw, of a sudden, how gaunt his face was, how lined and drawn. I stared back at him, into his tortured eyes. They were brimming over, silvered with tears. As I watched him, he raised a finger to his lips, and then he turned, silently, and disappeared into the kitchen. I was about to follow him, on tiptoe – glad that we would, at least, have a few moments alone together – when he closed the door behind him, so gently that it made no sound at all.

Of a sudden, I felt foolish. Having composed myself, I bade the ladies good evening and found my coat. In order to leave, I had to pass the kitchen. Inside, all was quiet. I imagine that, had I pressed my ear to the door, I might have heard some sounds from within: a breath; a muffled sob; the scrape of a chair leg against the floor – or, perhaps, nothing at all. Goodness only knows what I might have heard. As it was, I simply gave the door a sad glance, in passing, as I left the apartment.

12

On Monday the 6th of May, *The Glasgow Evening Citizen* included a paragraph, on page 6, headed: *Suspicious Disappearance of Artist's Daughter.* After a brief summary of the facts of the case, so far as known, the journal asked: *'What has become of little Rose Gillespie? She has not been seen since Saturday afternoon, and there is a growing suspicion that she may have been abducted. Her family and their neighbours have been making anxious search of the local area and their quest is expected to gain momentum later in the week, if she remains unfound.'*

These were very eventful days, as you will be aware if you have ever heard about the case. The mystery of Rose's disappearance was compounded by several other factors: the rumours of a man who had been seen running off with a child; the mysterious veiled lady; and the ransom note. In the meantime, an investigation, of sorts, got under way, and I was able to keep abreast of events during my visits to Stanley Street where the mood was sombre, yet chaotic. I would have dearly loved to have a proper conversation with either Ned or Annie, but the moment never seemed to arise because there was always at least one other person present, if not Elspeth – who seemed to have reinstalled herself in the parlour – then a police constable, or one of the neighbours.

Gradually, as a result of house-to-house inquiries, a clearer picture of what had happened on Saturday afternoon began to emerge. As yet, no trace could be found of anybody who matched Sibyl's description of the veiled stranger. However, the police did manage to track down the servant who had spoken to young Lily Alexander, that afternoon. Martha Scott was employed as a maid in one of the main-door houses on Queen's Terrace, the stretch of West Princes Street situated directly opposite the gardens. She reiterated her story, about a man that she had seen hurrying along, carrying a child. At the time, she was returning to her employer's house, having run out to buy a newspaper for her mistress. She was about halfway up West Princes Street, when she noticed a man on the opposite pavement, heading towards St George's Road. He might have been drunk (Martha thought) because he staggered as he walked. The child in his arms was a girl, it seemed to her, for she caught a glimpse of longish fair hair. Unfortunately, she had not noticed which way the man had turned at the end of the road.

Another witness was found, who claimed to have seen something similar. On the first floor of number 21 West Princes Street, Mrs Mary Arthur, a landlady, had been expecting a parcel, and had been going back and forth to her parlour window, all afternoon, on the lookout for the postman. On one of these occasions, she had noticed a tall, well-built man with a little girl in his arms. Mrs Arthur's account reflected that of Martha Scott, in most respects. She said that the man was bound in an easterly direction and, by virtue of the fact that he was wandering across the street, it looked as though he intended to turn right onto St George's Road. He wore a cap, and seemed drunk. The little girl was stretching out her arms, reaching behind 'her father', which gave the impression that she wanted to go back in the direction from which they had come. The child's frock was of a blue material, with a lozenge-shaped pattern. This description of the garment was particularly chilling, since the frock that Rose had been wearing that afternoon was one that she often wore and it was, indeed, patterned with lozenge shapes.

Witnesses continued to present themselves. On Wednesday night, Peter Kerr, a cab driver, walked into Maitland Street Police Office, saying that, on the previous Saturday afternoon, he had picked up a foreign man in Cambridge Street. The man had been in shirtsleeves, and was carrying a child, wrapped in his jacket. He had asked Kerr to take him across town, and had barely spoken, other than to give his destination. Due to the influx of visitors to the Exhibition the previous year, the driver had become familiar with various foreign accents, and he surmised that the man was either Austrian or German – an immigrant, rather than a tourist. The girl had whimpered during the journey, and something about the drunken foreigner had troubled Kerr, but he had driven them to the Gallowgate, as far as the steel works, at which point, the passenger had called out 'Stop'. Apparently, he paid his fare in full and then, carrying the sleepy child, walked off towards Vinegarhill: a muddy, insalubrious showground site, situated in a singularly foul-smelling spot amongst skin yards, knackeries, and manure works.

One theory was that the veiled woman might have lured Sibyl away by sending her to buy sugar, while her accomplice – the man seen hurrying down West Princes Street – had snatched Rose. The police deemed it possible that this man had later hailed Peter Kerr's cab on Cambridge Street. However, they could not explain why Rose should have been taken, and not Sibyl – nor indeed, why either girl should be abducted for financial gain, since the Gillespies were hardly wealthy. Nevertheless, the police were intrigued by the ransom demand. They were fairly convinced that the person who had written the note was not a native speaker of English. For instance, the use of the word 'gut', in place of 'good', was of particular interest, because this might mark the writer of the demand as a German speaker, which would tally with the opinion of Kerr, the cab driver, that the passenger whom he had dropped off in the East End was of German or Austrian origin.

At dawn on Thursday, a large party of constables and detectives descended upon Vinegarhill. The caravans, works buildings and sheds were searched over the course of the next two days, and the inhabitants – mostly itinerant horse dealers, performers and exhibitors – were questioned, along with the labourers from the various adjacent works. Vinegarhill's residents were mostly of Irish or Romany origin, and they vehemently denied all knowledge of the missing child and any foreign fellow. Disappointingly, the man was nowhere to be found amongst the caravans, and although there were many little urchins running wild about the site, barefoot, none of them bore any resemblance to Rose Gillespie.

Hardly surprisingly, the Gillespies were in a state of grief and horror, agitation and distress. Sibyl seemed to have turned in upon herself, and Annie's eyes were constantly red from weeping. Ned, ever stoical, fought off his sense of helplessness by searching, relentlessly, for Rose. He never settled in one place, and if he and his wife found themselves in the same room together, they barely spoke. Annie was still racked with guilt, and believed that Ned always found excuses to avoid her company.

To make matters worse, the family had come under the terrible scrutiny of the press. Only hours after the first report appeared in *The Evening Citizen*, journalists had begun to pester them for an interview. As an artist, and a public figure, of sorts, Ned was of particular interest. Each day, a handful of ink-slingers congregated on the doorstep at number 11, waiting for him to emerge, and then chased him down the street with their notebooks. Ned (who was only intent on finding his daughter) took to dodging out through the back court, but his pursuers soon foiled that trick, by posting one or two of their number at the rear of the terrace, in Stanley Lane, to give the alarm should Ned appear. In the end, he began to leave home in the early hours, before any of the reporters had taken up their posts. The poor man wore down his shoes, pounding the pavements, each day, while further small-scale searches were conducted by the police and various other concerned individuals and volunteers. Across the entire city, it seemed, groups of men carried out searches of their own districts, all to no avail.

Horatio Hamilton, the art dealer, put up a reward of £20 for any information that might lead to the discovery of the missing child. Ned was excused from his teaching duties at the School of Art that week, in view of what had happened. However, we ladies of the evening class met, as usual, and used the facilities of the School to produce a handbill, with which to publicise the case. Once printed, several hundred copies were then passed to various groups, including Elspeth's church, for distribution at prayer meetings, and so on, and a group of local lads undertook to hand out the leaflets on busy corners, from St George's Cross to the Tron Steeple.

By Friday night – almost a week since Rose's disappearance – no trace of her had been found, and the police were left with no alternative but to go ahead with the organised searches. Thus, on Saturday, the 11th of May, any man fortunate enough to benefit from a half-holiday was asked to meet at the Stewart Memorial Fountain, in the park. Word of mouth, after the distribution of handbills and the publication of several newspaper items, swelled the numbers. Indeed, the unusual circumstances of Rose's disappearance had aroused passionate interest among the population. Men came from all over town and, by three o'clock, despite a deluge of rain, a crowd of a hundred and fifty had gathered. There were only five hours or so remaining until dusk, but it was hoped that, with these greater numbers, the search would be more comprehensive, and that something would come to light. The volunteers searched all the areas that had been covered by the smaller group, on the previous Sunday, but, unfortunately, their endeavours were unavailing, and they returned to the park, disheartened, as night fell.

Another search was planned for the following morning, since Sunday is a day of rest for most men, and even greater numbers were expected to turn out. Ned took part on both days, at the side of Detective Sub-Inspector Stirling, who remained in charge of the case. Annie waited fretfully at home, surrounded by an ever-changing assembly of local women, including myself. Prior to Rose's disappearance, Elspeth and her cronies had been organising a 'Happy Sunday Afternoon' for the canal boatmen, which had been supposed to take place that very day. Instead, about forty boatmen gave up the promise of buttered buns and Psalms, in order to take part in the search. Their involvement swelled the numbers to almost three hundred, and it was thought that the park had not seen such crowds since the previous year, at the time of the Exhibition. The police planned to comb an area of several square miles surrounding South Woodside: from Ruchill down to the Clydeside quays in the south; west, to the grounds of the Infirmary; and east, as far as St Rollox. A dozen large parties set out just after nine o'clock in the morning and the volunteers did not give up until nightfall. But once again, all their efforts were in vain.

One mild afternoon, about a week later, I made my way around the corner, to number 11. It had become my habit, now, whenever I left my lodgings, to avert my eyes from the little park at the centre of Queen's Crescent. In the days immediately after Rose's disappearance, clinging to the vain hope that I might spy her there, my gaze had been drawn, inexorably, to the gardens, much as a tongue will seek out a hollow tooth. Of late, however, the sight of the fountain and trees, encircled by railings, simply pained me.

Thus far, it had been a damp spring, but on that particular afternoon, the sun had managed to pierce the smoky haze that hung, in perpetuity, over the city. At the top of Stanley Street, I shaded my eyes, as I squinted down the road, on the lookout for journalists. This was something else that had become habitual: checking to see how many hellhounds might be skulking about the doorstep of number 11. One intrepid newspaperman from *The Evening Citizen* had even rented a boarding-house room, next door to Elspeth's apartment, which afforded him a direct view into Ned's and Annie's parlour and bedroom. This ink-slinger – the young Bruce Kemp – was a sallow, reptilian creature, with scaly skin, and slanted eyes that were positioned on what seemed like either side of his narrow head, and his horrid visage had become a permanent fixture in the lodging-house window, as he lay in wait, watching for any sign of movement.

Even in daylight hours, Ned and Annie were obliged to draw the curtains, for the sake of privacy.

Today, I could see that Kemp had thrown up the sash, and was brazenly leaning against the window frame as he leered out across the street. Thankfully, it was the luncheon hour, which meant that most of the other penny-a-liners had decamped, as was their habit, to one of the nearby public houses, leaving but two of their colleagues on the pavement, opposite number 11. I put my head down, in an attempt to hide my face, but as soon as the young men noticed my approach, they scurried across the road and fell into step beside me.

'Afternoon, Miss Baxter.'

'Off to see the Gillespies, are we, Miss Baxter?'

Refusing to acknowledge them, as ever, I hurried onward. Thankfully, I did not have to wait to be admitted to the building, for the main door was still propped open with a stone. As I ran up the front steps, one of the reporters fell back, but the other was more persistent, and tried to bar my way, asking: 'How is Mrs Gillespie?' But I brushed past him, and entered the close and – since the occupants of number 11 had made it quite plain that no newspapermen would be tolerated inside the building – there ended the conversation.

Upstairs, I tapped on the Gillespies' front door, and waited. After a long interval, I detected the creak of a floorboard from within the apartment. I knocked again. There was a pause, and then I heard a querulous, childish voice.

'Who is it?'

'Hello, Sibyl, dear – it's me, Harriet.'

I had expected the door to open, but instead I heard only a few more creaks, and then silence. Another minute passed. I was about to knock once again, when heavier footsteps approached and then the door opened to reveal the gloomy hall, and Annie, barefoot, in a shift, her hair in disarray. She looked as though she might have just awoken from a deep sleep. The slight draught, caused by the opening of the door, carried upon it a musty, slightly sour scent, although whether this emanated from Annie herself or, perhaps, from her nightgown, was hard to tell.

'Good afternoon, dear, I'm so sorry, I –'

She shook her head and, without a word, turned towards the kitchen, leaving the door open. I stepped into the hall. There was no sign of Sibyl. In the corner, was a crate, labelled 'Pettigrew and Stephens', inside which, I knew, was the dinner service that I had bought for the family. In the confusion following Rose's disappearance, I kept forgetting to have it sent on to Merlinsfield. In any case, crockery was hardly a priority since the little food that the family consumed during that period was mostly donated by friends or neighbours, and was eaten on the hoof: a buttered roll, nibbled, before being discarded; a spoon dipped, once or twice, into a dish of cold stew; a piece of pastry, broken from the crust of a pie.

The kitchen had acquired the stale, dusty feel of a room that was seldom used, despite a few dirty dishes that were scattered, here and there. For once, however, Annie seemed to be preparing food, for when I entered, she was slicing some cold, boiled potatoes, and the air smelt of hot lard.

'That dreadful man is out there, at the window,' I told her. She nodded, but said nothing. 'How are you, dear?' I asked. 'How's Ned? And Sibyl? Any news?'

She sighed. 'Stirling was here. His boss has taken two men off the case.'

'No! Why on earth?'

'Because there are other cases to investigate.'

'Oh, dear!'

Annie put the potatoes into the frying pan, and then turned to stare at me. In the light of the kitchen window, I saw that her eyes were red and swollen, as ever.

'Listen, Harriet, somebody saw Rose, on a tram, on the Gallowgate.'

'Really?'

'Aye, Mrs Calthrop told me about it.'

'Well, Calthrop –'

'No, but it's true – somebody saw a wee girl, with fair hair. She was on a tram, near the cattle market, with a foreign couple, a man and his wife. The girl was about four years old. Her frock was brown but – well – she might have been given different clothes, by now.' She chewed at her cracked, dry lips, gazing intently at nothing, and then said, almost in a mutter: 'I was thinking of going down there, myself, to have a look.'

'To the East End?'

She nodded, staring into space. Of a sudden, her eyes had taken on a strange, feverish intensity that made me feel uneasy.

'Is that wise?' I asked her. 'What does Ned think? Where is he, by the bye?'

She turned away, with a shrug of her shoulders, and jiggled the frying pan.

'Upstairs. He hasn't come down since Stirling was here.'

There was an edge to her voice that discouraged me from enquiring further, and so I changed the subject. 'I saw Elspeth yesterday morning, briefly.'

'Oh aye,' said Annie, her tone suddenly scathing. She flounced out of the room and returned, a moment later, holding a scrap of paper, which she gave to me. It was a telegram from Mabel, explaining in a few words that she had heard the terrible news and would return to Scotland, if required, as soon as possible.

This came as a surprise to me because, as far as I was aware, the Gillespies had decided against telling Mabel what had happened. When the expectation was that Rose would turn up safely, at any moment, nobody had wanted to worry her and Peden, unnecessarily. Soon enough, it was thought, all would be well, and we would be able to write to them and say: 'You'll never guess what happened here – Rose got lost for a few days! But worry not, she's home now, safe and sound.' Then, as time went on, and the child failed to return, both of her parents were still reluctant to pass on the bad news. I can understand why: writing the words, in black and white, would have been an admission of something; a recognition that Rose might never be found. There had been an agreement between us all, that Ned and Annie would be the ones to decide as and when Mabel should be told. Or, so I had thought.

'Elspeth sent her a telegram,' said Annie, jabbing the potatoes with a knife. 'Old busybody!'

Never before had I heard her call her mother-in-law a name.

'But can you be certain it was her?' I asked.

Annie nodded. 'She admitted it, yesterday. First, she said she didn't think I'd mind. Can you believe it? Then she got all hot and bothered, and said Mabel ought to be told, because Rose is her niece. Did you know about this telegram?'

'Not at all; I'm as surprised as you are.'

'Well, I've had enough of her, interfering. I've sent a telegram to Tangier, telling Mabel that they mustn't come back. It's out of the question! We'll probably find Rose tomorrow, or the next day, and then they'll just have wasted the fare.'

Her face had a brittle look, as though it might fly apart at any moment. She seemed so agitated that I was quick to appease her.

'Whatever you think is for the best, dear. Watch out for those potatoes – they're smoking. Can I be of any help?'

She shook her head, and took the pan off the flame. Then she went to the door and called to Sibyl. I gazed into the hearth, lost in thought, while Annie dished up the potatoes on a single small plate. Presently, Sibyl came in, so silently that she gave me quite a fright when she coughed, and I turned to see her, skulking, at the threshold. Like Annie, she was dressed as though for bed, in a thin, sleeveless shift. Her skin was an unhealthy looking grey-white, the colour of old milk. Her nervous cough was worse than ever and, lately, she had taken to hunching her shoulders, head bent, as though to avoid looking anybody in the eye. She had always been a slender child, but dressed as she was now, in just her shift, I was able to see how scrawny she had become. The hunched posture made her shoulder blades protrude, in a way that looked as though it ought to be painful. Her elbow joints seemed disproportionately large in comparison with her skinny arms, and her collarbones jutted out, far too prominently. She was staring, with what seemed like dread, at the fried potatoes, which her mother had just set on the table.

'Sit down,' Annie told her. Sibyl remained in the doorway, gazing warily at the dish. 'It's your favourite,' said Annie. 'I made them especially.'

'Can't I have them later?'

'No, eat them now.'

The child's lip trembled. 'Can't I take them upstairs? I will eat them!'

Annie sighed. 'Only if you promise.'

'Promise – I do. I promise!'

Sibyl darted forwards, to pick up the food, and then carried it out of the room. Through the open doorway, I watched her scurry across the hall and climb the stairs to the attic, holding out the dish with extended arms, as though it were a collection plate. When I turned back, I realised that Annie had also been watching the child. There were tears in her eyes. She spoke without looking at me.

'They won't get eaten, you know. She's hardly eaten a scrap, since.'

Towards the end of my visit, I heard footsteps on the staircase, and turned to see Ned coming down from the attic. There he was: a dark shadow, crossing the hall, picking up his hat from the stand, approaching the front door – all without even a glance into the kitchen. Unable to catch his eye, I looked at Annie. She was making twists of paper for the fire, and although she must have heard his descent, she paid no heed. I turned back, just as Ned opened the front door and stepped outside. He must have seen us, as he passed, for the kitchen door was wide open and we were both visible from the hallway. But he had simply departed, without any acknowledgement, closing the front door firmly behind him. I heard his footsteps recede, as he ran away, down the close. For her part, Annie seemed intent upon ignoring his abrupt exit.

'That was Ned,' I remarked, but Annie failed to reply.

The tap was dripping, and so I stood up and went over to turn it off. Looking through the window, I was just in time to see Ned dash across the washing green. Two reporters were leaning against the back wall in Stanley Lane, but Ned shot out of the gate so fast that he was almost gone before they had noticed him. They gave a shout, and set off in pursuit. Although I had only briefly glimpsed the artist's face – once as he had passed through the hall, and then when he glanced over his shoulder as he sped down the lane – I could tell that he was exhausted. I turned to Annie.

'Is he sleeping, at all?' I asked.

'I've no idea,' she said, lightly.

Not wishing to pry, I fell silent. Annie's back was turned, and I was unable to see her face. She twisted another length of newspaper, as though she wished that she could throttle it. Presently, she spoke.

'If you must know, he sleeps in the studio, these days, on the chaise.'

I fiddled with the tap, which appeared to need a new washer. To be perfectly honest, I was at a loss for words. Annie seemed to feel the need to explain the situation, because she went on.

'You see, neither of us can bear to be in our bedroom, even with the curtain shut, because that horrible man watches everything. So Ned sleeps in the studio, and I've been spending the nights in Rose's bed.'

'Oh, well,' I said, awkwardly. 'That must be – some comfort.'

All the while, I was wondering whether a marriage that had deteriorated so terribly much could ever be mended or saved.

By the end of May, after nearly four weeks of investigation, the police had failed to unearth a single trace of Rose and had more or less exhausted all possible routes of inquiry. No further ransom demand had been received. The poor child might as well have vanished into thin air. Every witness had been questioned, along with every neighbour of the Gillespies, and all of their friends, including myself. I had hoped that Detective Sub-Inspector Stirling would interview me, since, remarkably, our paths had never crossed, and I was interested to meet him and judge for myself what calibre of man he was. However, as it turned out, along with the Alexanders, I was entrusted to Constable Black, of the ginger moustache, who spoke to us, one after the other, in the morning room at Queen's Crescent. Black offered me a peppermint, asked a few questions about whether I had noticed anything unusual on the day that Rose had disappeared, made one or two notes in his jotter, and thanked me for my time. I gained the impression that I had not been of much help to the inquiry.

Although Detective Stirling had assured Ned that he and his men would not abandon the case, it was unclear how he meant to proceed, unless a fresh witness came forward, or some startling new piece of evidence presented itself. The question remained: what, exactly, had happened to Rose? According to Annie, Detective Stirling had no time for the notion that the child had simply wandered off. His firm belief was that she had been taken, by person or persons unknown; to what end, he could not, or would not say, and he had no explanation as to why there had been no further word from the abductor.

Needless to say, the hunt for the missing child, as daily reported in the newspapers, had brought forth the usual crop of rumours, and various irresponsible correspondents were eager to report that Rose had been spotted, all the way from Dan to Beersheba. There were sightings of a little girl answering her description first at Bridge Street Station, then in Auchenshuggle Woods, and then in Candleriggs. She was also reputedly seen in Kilmarnock, Pittenweem and Oban. Perhaps because of the suspicion that still hung over the denizens of Vinegarhill, most of the reported sightings were in the East End: she was 'spotted' one evening, in ill-fitting clothes, holding hands with a fat Irish woman, on the London Road; the next day, a child drew the attention of passers-by in the High Street, screaming and crying whilst walking with a tall man in a tweed cap; then a lady on the Oatlands ferry, crossing to Glasgow Green, noticed a girl in a blue dress, accompanied by a woman who kept ignoring the child's questions: 'Are we going to see Mama?' and 'Where's Papa?'

The police made every effort to investigate each report – but, unfortunately, none of their inquiries had, so far, led to the discovery of the missing child.

Ere long, we heard speculation that Rose had already been spirited away to some foreign shore (perhaps France or Belgium) where she had been sold, either into a house of ill repute, or to a wealthy Minotaur. There was talk – in the newspapers, and in gentlemen's luncheon bars, like Lang's and Logan's – of White Slavery, and the sordid sexual underworld in which rich men, with the connivance of the police and public officials, brazenly trade in children to satisfy their unspeakable lusts. One further theory was that Rose had not been taken abroad, but was being held captive, in some East End brothel, in Glasgow, where she would be made to fetch and carry for the patrons, until such time – only a few years hence – when she was deemed old enough to be, herself, debauched.

Increasingly determined to speak to the grieving parents, newspapermen began to employ more imaginative tactics. Notes were pushed through the letterbox of the apartment, with various requests and invitations. Would Mr Gillespie consent to an interview? Would he and his lady wife like to have a photographic portrait taken, free of charge? Would he deign to accept the enclosed tickets for *The Scotia*? Would he care to take tea with the editor and his wife? One illustrated journal published a large and very accurate sketch of Ned (penned, of course, by Mungo Findlay), and thereafter, Gillespie began to be pestered in public places by complete strangers: rooms fell silent upon his entrance; people stared at him in the street; and men would approach him, hat in hand, to offer their condolences.

Inexplicably, as if to further deepen the mystery, the sender of the ransom note seemed to have fallen silent. After the arrival of the first letter, there had been every expectation that another would swiftly follow, with instructions about where and when the money should be delivered. Yet, subsequently, the abductor made no further communication, and a month after Rose's disappearance, there had still been no second letter.

One Saturday in early June, I happened to be passing through the Blythswood district: a disciplined grid of streets to the west of the city, crowned by the square on Blythswood Hill. I was returning to my lodgings, having just spent the afternoon helping to distribute handbills, advertising Rose's disappearance. My feet and legs were weary from standing, all day long, at the corner of Buchanan and St Vincent Streets. Only a handful of ladies from the art class had taken part in the distribution of leaflets that day; it was now almost five weeks since Rose's disappearance, and some members of the class had given up hope. There seemed to be a general, unspoken, opinion that the longer Rose remained missing, the less likely it was that she would be found.

I had become ever more concerned about Ned's and Annie's well-being and would have liked to call upon them every day, simply to check on how they fared. However, they had made it known to their friends and neighbours that, after the mayhem of the previous month, they now wished for some degree of privacy. With this in mind, I had restricted myself to visiting only every third day or so, much though I would have liked to call upon them more often. I had seen Elspeth during that period, of course, and was able to keep abreast of developments but, as you may imagine, time weighed heavily upon all of us.

I was in the habit of walking everywhere, taking the opportunity to glance down side streets and up lanes, always in the hope that I might catch a glimpse of a small child in a blue dress. And so it was, that afternoon, that I was about to turn onto West Campbell Street, when I noticed a small crowd of people, standing on the pavement, up ahead. As I drew nearer, I realised that they were queuing outside Hamilton's gallery, where Ned's exhibition was still ongoing. I had heard from Elspeth that attendances had crept up over the course of May, and that Hamilton had extended the show. Several of the recent articles in the press had reported that Rose's father was an artist; a few had mentioned that his paintings were currently on display in a well-known Bath Street gallery; and *The Evening Times*, which had previously ignored his existence, had suddenly decided to send an expert to appraise the exhibition, and an article had appeared in the paper, just the previous day. Evidently, the critic had been struck by Ned's recent paintings of Co'path, particularly the picture of the woods, with two children, who appear to be fleeing from some unspeakable terror or monster. '*Could the bairns in this picture resemble the artist's own?*' asked the reviewer, concluding: '*We are left to reflect that these eerie paintings may well have been hauntingly prescient.*' On the whole, his comments were favourable, which, perhaps, might have accounted for some extra gallery visitors that afternoon.

Curiosity aroused, I decided to wander past Hamilton's. As I approached, I noticed various men slouching around in the queue, some smoking, some spitting, some leaning against the railings with their hands in their pockets. There were several families present, which was a surprise, since children are not often to be seen in small, private art galleries. Some of the boys and girls, clearly bored with waiting, had sat down on the steps, whilst others played at the roadside. A fat, red-faced woman was eating peanuts and throwing the shells underfoot, while her friend tried to calm a screaming baby. As a group, they did not in the least resemble the usual sort who would attend an exhibition; indeed, many of them would have looked more at home on Glasgow Green, amongst the hordes who swarm between the freak shows and whisky booths on a Saturday night.

The queue carried on up the steps, and disappeared inside the front door of the gallery. Since I had last walked along Bath Street, handwritten notices had appeared in Hamilton's windows. One said: 'Gillespie show extended'. The other sign advertised Hamilton's offer of a £20 reward for information leading to the discovery of the artist's daughter.

At the foot of the steps, two amiable-looking women of about my own age stood talking. Simply to see what they would say, I paused and asked them why such a queue had formed. One lady, who was a be-dimpled soul with apple cheeks, gestured at the building. 'It's an exhibition of paintings – did you hear about the wee lassie that got lost, wee Rose?' I nodded. 'Well, her father's the artist, and seemingly, there's pictures he painted of her inside, his daughter, the one that went missing.'

'Indeed?' I replied, before thanking her, and continuing up the street, with a strange, heavy feeling in my chest.

It would seem that, within only a month, Gillespie had become a roaring success.

13

Throughout June, visitors continued to flock to the gallery. Ned's success meant that Hamilton's principal room was also busy, since the public spilled from one space into the next, and there, too, sales had improved. Having first extended the Gillespie show for a fortnight, Hamilton prolonged it for another few weeks, meanwhile mounting a second companion exhibition, of local artists, in the main room. Ned's gloomy style suddenly seemed to find favour, and by the end of month, even his most resolutely grim landscape had been sold. Reviews of his work continued to appear in the press. One gazetteer from *The North British Daily Mail* took a dander around the gallery and, in a subsequent article, he described Ned's canvases as the 'heart-rending work of a gifted but haunted man'. Following the publication of this piece, attendance numbers soared, yet again, as more persons with scant interest in art, but unmistakable ghoulish tendencies, came to ogle the paintings of the tragic father. Perhaps some visitors even hoped to bump into Ned himself, but he had not shown his face at the gallery since his daughter had gone missing.

Ever the man of business, Hamilton wrote to Ned in July, and, after repeating his condolences for the family's recent troubles, tentatively expressed a desire to extend the show yet again. Ned let it be known that he cared not one whit whether the exhibition continued. I happened to see his reply to Hamilton on the hallstand, where it lay, just before it was sent. The note was written on what appeared to be a scrap of torn wallpaper. In it, Ned expressed his indifferent opinion, which was that he had neither the time nor the inclination to take down his pictures, and that the paintings might as well 'hang there until they rot'. Thus, the exhibition was quietly extended, this time for an indefinite period.

Hamilton had also managed to negotiate over a dozen new commissions on the artist's behalf, mostly for portraits, which suggested that Ned's new-found notoriety outweighed any earlier concerns that the public might have had about how sympathetically he might portray them as subjects. Unfortunately, it was not at all certain when he might be in a fit state to resume painting. He had not so much as glanced at a brush in weeks, and his teaching position at the School had been taken over by another gentleman, who was perfectly pleasant, I believe, but not really in the same league as Ned, either as teacher or painter. Needless to say, I had not attended any of the classes that remained before the end of term.

As for Ned, when he was not distributing handbills, or looking for his daughter, he spent the time locked away in his studio, having pinned a black cloth over the skylight to block out any sign of the day. Although he insisted upon darkness, sleep eluded him and (as he told me later), for several weeks, he was subject to hallucinations, in which his missing daughter appeared to him. Once, as he was climbing the stairs to the attic, he thought that he saw her on the landing. It was getting rather dark, but the child seemed to shine out, strangely distinct, in the shadows. She stood up on tiptoe (a posture very characteristic of Rose), smiled at him, and then was gone.

In many respects, Ned appeared to be grieving. His speech and movements had become markedly slow, and – one day, when I happened to be standing near him – I was startled to notice, among his mane of hair, a single strand of white. Then, a moment later, I saw another. As the summer drew on, these white hairs proliferated, until they were too numerous to count.

Tortured by guilt and the belief that she, alone, was responsible for what had happened, Annie took to wandering the streets on the far side of town, in search of her daughter. Try as I might, I was unable to dissuade her from this futile quest. She and Ned would take it in turns to leave the apartment, and, while one of them kept an eye on Sibyl, the other carried out any necessary errands and continued to search for Rose. Ned tended to concentrate on the local area, whereas his wife had fixed upon the theory that Rose was being held captive somewhere in the East End. No doubt various newspaper reports had fuelled this notion, with their salacious references to White Slavery, and the endless sightings of little girls with fair hair. Throughout the summer, no matter what the weather, Annie haunted the side streets along the Gallowgate, flitting in and out of dank wynds and vennels, and searching filthy yards. With a doggedness that became almost mechanical, she would venture inside the closes, and climb the stairs, to question the inhabitants. Sometimes, she was greeted with honest courtesy and compassion; at other times, she had to flee in the face of harsh words; but always, the answer was the same: nobody knew the whereabouts of her child.

With her unfortunate parents lost in their own desolation, poor Sibyl continued to starve herself. Every mealtime was a battle, in which Ned and Annie had to cajole and beg their daughter to consume even a morsel, while Sibyl found ever more inventive ways of avoiding sustenance. Having, in her own mind, contributed to the loss of her little sister, it was as though she wanted to make herself disappear.

Early one morning in August, on his way downstairs from the studio, where he had spent a restless night, Ned happened to detect a change in the quality of light in the apartment. For weeks, in the interest of privacy, the curtains had been drawn at the front of the house, but now, he perceived that the hall was brighter than usual: a half-light spilled out from the parlour. His curiosity aroused, he entered the room, only to see that the curtains were open at one of the casements, and the sash window had been pushed up. Then, to his horror, he realised that Sibyl had climbed outside, onto the sill, as though intending to jump into mid-air. Indeed, as he crossed the threshold, the child rose up and leaned forwards, preparing to leap.

Thankfully, Ned was too fast for her. In one bound, he crossed the floor and, grabbing her by the waist, dragged her back inside, in order to save her from a fall that could only have ended horribly, if not on the pavement or basement area below, then on the railings, which were trimmed, at close intervals, with low, thistle-shaped spikes. Sibyl squirmed and struggled in her father's arms, attempting to lunge across the sill, crying, 'No! No! Let me go!', so that Ned was forced to drop down and cover the child with his own body, in order to restrain her.

This was how Annie found them, moments later. Having spent the night in Rose's bed, she was alerted to the emergency by Sibyl's cries, and ran down to investigate. Upon entering the parlour, she saw her daughter writhing on the floor, pinned down by Ned, who was weeping, and stroking Sibyl's head, to calm her.

'What happened?' Annie cried, and while her husband gave a rapid account of events, the child continued to wriggle beneath him, weeping.

Somehow they managed to lift her onto the sofa. Then, Annie hurried over to close the sash and draw the curtains. Ned clutched Sibyl to his chest, rocking her back and forth, and whispering in her ear. The child sobbed, quietly, but seemed to have calmed down somewhat. Annie sank into the easy chair, and eventually, after what seemed like a very long time, Sibyl fell asleep. Carefully, Ned rose to his feet, and he and Annie carried the child next door to their own bedroom, which had the dusty, petrified atmosphere of a room that is seldom used. Then, while Annie kept vigil over her daughter, Ned went around all the rooms, hammering nails into the sash frames and skylights, so that the windows could no longer be opened.

Following this perturbing incident, Ned finally acknowledged that they needed help with their daughter, and, that evening, he went around the corner to Lynedoch Crescent and paid a visit to Dr Oswald. Ned was shown into his study, where he explained the situation: Sibyl's guilt, and her belief that she was responsible for the loss of Rose; her refusal to eat and subsequent weight loss; the nervous cough; the incident at the window; and then, all the child's previous misbehaviour and wilfulness, a history that ranged back over a period of many months, and included all her various acts of sabotage: the obscene drawings on the walls; the stolen matches; the countless items, burned and destroyed; the unfortunate faecal incidents; and the attempted poisoning at Hogmanay.

Having listened carefully to Ned's account, Oswald asked permission to interview Sibyl alone, and an arrangement was made for him to visit Stanley Street. On the following afternoon, he arrived at the appointed time, and while Ned and Annie waited, apprehensively, in the parlour, the doctor spoke to Sibyl, in private, in the dining room. They emerged after ten minutes or so, and the girl was sent upstairs, while Oswald reported his findings to her parents.

In his opinion, Sibyl was an extremely disturbed and anxious child, in desperate need of treatment, particularly if she was not to starve herself. Given Sibyl's history, there was also the danger that she might not merely cause harm to herself, but also to others. Oswald offered to take her into the asylum, there and then, for a few weeks, to try to encourage her to eat, and to keep her under closer observation than might be possible at number 11.

By that stage, Annie feared for her daughter's life, and was willing to try any solution, whatsoever. However, Ned had a horror of the asylum and would not be persuaded to place his child there, no matter how much Oswald reassured him that the Ladies Department was perfectly humane. After some further discussion, the doctor departed, without Sibyl, leaving the Gillespies with a final word of advice: if they were unwilling to put the child in his care, then they must urgently seek extra help. Both Ned and Annie acknowledged that, for the time being, they did require some assistance but, in their fragile state, neither of them could bear the notion of bringing a stranger into the apartment, and so, any thoughts of hiring a maid were instantly dismissed.

Ned refused to ask Mabel to return from Tangier. Thus, Annie was obliged to swallow her pride, and disregard any antipathy that she may have felt for her mother-in-law, in order that Sibyl might spend the afternoon hours in the care of Elspeth and her maid Jean, at number 14, where all the rooms were at either basement or ground-floor level.

One afternoon, while carrying out a few errands on behalf of my landlady, I happened to wander further east than I had anticipated, and ended up almost at Glasgow Cross. The day was cool and grey, beneath a sky full of hurrying clouds. Perhaps it was a Saturday, for the streets bristled with vehicles and pedestrians, and there was a sense of urgency in the air, as the great tide of humanity swept along the Trongate. I had just paused to admire the archway over the footpath at the base of the Tron Steeple, when the lone figure of a woman came to my attention. She was standing on the far side of the tower, at the edge of the pavement. The hem of her coat had come unstitched, and was stained with mud where it grazed the ground. She wore down-at-heel boots, and her hat had been carelessly pinned. At first, I thought that she was begging, until she turned her head, and I recognised Annie. Here she was, distributing handbills, repeating the same words, over and over: 'Can you help me please? Have you seen this girl? Can you help me please?'

All at once, I felt desolate, and mortified. You see, by this time, any realistic hope of finding Rose had all but evaporated. Even Ned had, more or less, given up the search: since mid-August, he had rarely gone out looking for the child. And yet, still, Annie persisted. It can only have been desperation and, perhaps, a kind of madness that kept her faithful to her quest. I found the situation – her futile persistence – quite upsetting and my impulse, when I saw her at the steeple, was to retreat, before she noticed me. I stepped behind some crates and, at length, when I dared to peek out from my hiding place, I was relieved to see that Annie had turned away without noticing me. I could have made my departure there and then, but found myself lingering behind the crates, to watch her, through the archway. She made such a mournful little figure, holding out her leaflets to passers-by, almost like an automaton.

'Have you seen my daughter? Can you help me please?'

The sight of her engaged in such an earnest yet forlorn quest – was too painful and, in the end, I found myself hurrying away without speaking to her. I headed back along Argyle Street, and then made my way north-west, through the Blythswood District. As ever, of course, I kept my eyes open, but in my heart of hearts, I knew that the search for Rose was futile, and it was only force of habit that made me glance into the face of any passing waif or child. Somewhere, perhaps in Sauchiehall Street, a barrel-organ was playing 'The Lost Chord'. It was an unusually jaunty version of the tune, and yet the stilted, tinny sound of the music that floated across the rooftops was unutterably mournful to my ears.

14

Difficult though it is to imagine, much of life elsewhere had gone on as normal during those terrible summer months. Across the world, people rose in the morning, and went about their daily business. For instance, at St Rémy, in the South of France, Vincent Van Gogh was painting wheat stacks and olive trees. In London, the Novelty Theatre reopened with a production of Henrik Ibsen's *A Doll's House*. Even the criminally inclined were not at rest. There had been reports about the renewal of the Whitechapel murders, and the inquest of another possible victim had begun on the 17th of July. That same month, on the Scottish isle of Arran, Edwin Robert Rose, an English tourist, disappeared and, when his decomposing corpse was discovered, a week later, a manhunt for his murderer ensued. Meanwhile, the British people continued to occupy themselves, once their day's work was done, with entertainments of one sort or another. *Blackwood's Magazine* published a story by Mr Oscar Wilde. The Scottish National Portrait Gallery threw open its doors to the public. In London, diners queued for tables at the new Savoy supper rooms, beneath the blaze of electric lights. The Queen made a short tour of Wales on her way to Scotland, in August. And, in September, Port Glasgow Athletic beat Greenock Abstainers with a final score of 8–0: so much for abstention!

All this carefree activity continued, while in Woodside, Glasgow, at number 11, Stanley Street, there prevailed a suffocating, narrow life of desolation and despair. Only last summer, the family had wandered happily among the crowds at the International Exhibition. Now, in their grief, Ned and Annie had withdrawn from the world, and from each other. Naturally, I did everything that I could to help them during those dreadful months:

nobody can deny *that*. Although we were probably not in each other's pockets as much as we had been, say, earlier in the year, I do believe that recent events had brought us closer, emotionally, than we had ever been before.

In the investigation, there was little progress. Sightings of Rose had all but ceased, and no further ransom demand had been received. The journalists had grown bored by mid-summer, and began to abandon Stanley Street; even Kemp from *The Citizen* eventually packed his belongings and relinquished his 'room with a view'. Then, as August turned to September, any remaining newspaper interest in the Gillespie case was eclipsed by the excitement surrounding the pursuit and arrest of John Watson Laurie: 'The Arran Murderer'. By the time that autumn had us firmly in her grip, not one single area of inquiry had resulted in the discovery, either of Rose Gillespie, or of any single clue that might lead to her whereabouts. The mysterious foreigner who had entered the carnival site carrying a sleepy child had vanished, like a conjuror's rabbit.

The moment that we had all been quietly dreading arrived on the morning of the 17th of September, when Detective Stirling called at Stanley Street, unannounced, to inform the Gillespies that, at the behest of his superior, Detective Inspector Grant, he had been instructed to put aside their case.

Apparently, when Stirling first arrived, Sibyl was hovering in the background, and she was present, in the parlour, when he began to explain the reason for his visit. The child must have slipped out of the room at some point, but Annie realised that she was no longer there only approximately half an hour later, when the detective stood up to leave. Stirling had been very apologetic, and kept insisting that, if it were up to him, Rose's case would have remained open. Of course, both Ned and Annie were disappointed that the police had effectively given up their inquiries, but Stirling's announcement was not entirely unexpected: for some time, we had feared that the investigation would be abandoned due to the very obvious lack of progress. At any rate, perhaps Ned and Annie were prepared for such an eventuality in a way that Sibyl, as a child, was not.

Once Stirling had gone, Ned disappeared into his studio, without a word. Annie went in search of Sibyl and found her curled up on the bed in her attic room. Apparently, the child was in a state of shock that the police had given up hope. When Annie sat down on the mattress, Sibyl threw herself into her mother's arms, with a plaintive cry.

'Will we never find Rose now?'

'Oh, I'm sure we will,' said Annie. She stroked her daughter's hair, which was damp with tears. 'There, now! Shh!'

'But he said the police won't be looking for her any more!'

'No, dear, they have to work on other cases.'

At this, Sibyl wept, as though her heart might break. I imagine that, to Annie, the child felt like a scrap of nothing, wrapped up inside her clothes, all of which now swamped her tiny, bird-like frame. At length, her crying subsided. Annie tucked her into the bed and then sat, holding the girl's hand, until she fell into an uneasy, fretful sleep.

A few hours later, Sibyl came downstairs, looking glum and tearful. However, she insisted that she felt well enough to spend the afternoon at number 14, and so, believing her to be in better spirits, Annie took her across the road. They found Elspeth in the basement, washing the floors, having sent Jean, the maid, to the post office. It was Jean who normally watched over Sibyl, since Ned's mother was often engaged in God's business. However, on this particular day, Annie left the girl in the care of her mother-in-law, and set off for the Gallowgate with a batch of leaflets.

Since the afternoon was fine and dry, Elspeth opened the back door and, after checking that the gate to the lane was bolted at the top, she informed Sibyl that she could play on the grass, provided that she remained within sight. However, the child professed a desire to stay inside and help her grandmother with the household chores, and so they went into the kitchen and sat down at the table, together.

As fate would have it, Ned's mother had decided, that day, to clean her parlour lights: a pair of glass-chimneyed paraffin lamps that she kept for occasional use, preferring their traditional glow to that of the new fangled gaseliers. To begin her task, she tipped the old oil out of the lamps, into a jar. Then, she asked Sibyl to hand her a duster. Elspeth could not be sure what happened next but – somehow – as she took the cloth from her granddaughter, the jar was knocked over, and the old oil spilled across the table. Reluctant to ruin a duster with dirty work, the widow went to fetch rags and, upon her return, caught sight of Sibyl, who was holding out both hands above the pool of oil, as though to touch it, but when she heard her grandmother's approach, she snatched back her fingers and moved away. Elspeth found only a small puddle of paraffin on the table, which was surprising, as the jar had been half full but, thinking little of it, she cleaned up the mess and began to polish the glass chimneys. In the meantime, Sibyl had flitted around the kitchen, from sink, to fireplace, to shelves, finally stepping into the passageway.

'Please may I go out now?' she lisped.

'You may,' said Elspeth, 'provided that you stay where I can see you.'

With that, Sibyl slipped outside and began to skip around the back green, singing to herself. Seeing her thus occupied, Ned's mother returned to her work, confident that if she could hear the child, then it meant that she was close at hand. Presently, however, the singing came to a halt. Peering through the window, Elspeth saw that her granddaughter was crouched down, apparently examining something on the grass. Satisfied that Sibyl was engaged in some innocuous activity, the widow began to refill her lamps. Just then, Jean returned from her errands: Elspeth heard the maid descend the basement stairs and pass the kitchen, on her way to the back door, where she usually hung up her outdoor garment, an old worsted cloak.

Subsequently, according to Ned's mother, everything seemed to happen at once. Something outside the window attracted her attention: a bright light, or a flash, caused her to glance up. Simultaneously, she heard Jean cry out, an unusually offensive expletive. In other circumstances, Elspeth would have had words with her but by then, she was looking out of the window into the back court, and what she saw there seemed, at first, impossible.

Sibyl was in flames. Or, at least, partially in flames: the sleeves of her frock were burning as brightly and fiercely as bonfires. And yet, despite the fact that her clothes were alight, she was walking calmly around the yard, with her eyes lifted to the heavens, her burning arms held out from her body, like the Lord himself on the cross (as Elspeth later described the scene). The child did not scream, or say a word; she made no sound. Within seconds, the flames seemed to spread to her skirts, and leap higher. All at once, Ned's mother became aware of a blur in the corner of her vision, another figure, moving quickly: it was Jean, dashing across the grass, holding out her old grey cloak in both hands, in the style of a matador. She ran at Sibyl and, in one movement, wrapped the child in the garment, and dragged her to the ground. Then she rolled the tiny figure this way and that in the fabric, attempting to smother the flames.

In the same moment, Ned's mother grabbed the bucket of water left over from when she had washed the floor and careened out into the yard, as fast as her legs could carry her. The air was filled with the smell of burning. Her maid was lifting up the child, still wrapped in the cloak. Smoke rose from the scorched material. Sibyl's head lolled back; her eyelids fluttered, then closed. A tin of kitchen matches lay on the grass. All the blood had drained from Jean's face. She turned to her mistress and said something. Her lips moved, but the widow heard not a word, because of a strange rushing sound in her ears. Elspeth threw water over Sibyl, dousing the last of the flames. Then the bucket dropped from her hands and clattered to the ground. Perhaps it was shock, or the unaccustomed burst of physical activity, or a combination of the two, but Elspeth's field of vision shrank to nothing, as darkness closed in. Then she sank to her knees, and fell forwards in a dead faint, landing in a heap in the middle of the back green.

All this took place on the Tuesday. I myself was not in Glasgow on that particular afternoon. I had gone to Bardowie, to oversee the arrangement of some furniture and other household paraphernalia that had been carted out to the house a few weeks previously. However, upon my return to town, I soon heard about what had happened in my absence. Sibyl had been taken to the Royal Infirmary, where she lay on a bed, swathed in bandages and, during the course of several days thereafter, the doctors seemed doubtful that she would survive her injuries and the pneumonia that set in as a result of the accident. We were all very relieved when her eyes opened for a short while, on Friday, and then, again, the following day. For a week, she drifted in and out of consciousness but, thankfully, no further complications ensued. After a further fortnight, the lungs started to heal themselves and, slowly, she began to recover. By some miracle, Elspeth's and Jean's rapid reactions had saved the child. Sadly, Sibyl's burns were extensive, particularly on her arms and shoulders, and the doctors were agreed that she would carry the scars for the rest of her life.

As if that were not tragedy enough, as soon as she was sufficiently recovered, she was taken directly to the Ladies Department of the Royal Lunatic Asylum at Kelvinside, where she was committed for an indefinite period. This time, her actions had been so extreme that even Ned could not deny the truth: the poor girl had completely lost her mind.

It is part of human nature, in such circumstances, to think: 'If only . . .' If only Annie had not taken Sibyl across the road to number 14. If only Ned's mother had not chosen that particular afternoon to clean her oil lamps. If only she had kept a closer watch over her granddaughter. If only the girl had not been so indulged by all and sundry – and so on, and so forth. Such thoughts are useless, inutile, no matter how often one thinks them; it is always too late. Sibyl had forever been a needy and unstable child, whose devious quirks of character put too many demands upon her parents and, ultimately, she had descended into a state of twisted self-loathing and despair. Yet, despite her mental problems, none of us could have foreseen that she would carry out such an act of lunacy. When all is said and done, nobody can be held accountable for what became of her.

15

Thankfully, there was only muted public interest in this latest disaster to strike the family because all of Scotland was now obsessed with the forthcoming trial for the Arran murderer. Only a few short items appeared in the press, and Sibyl's injuries were attributed to a simple, but unfortunate, domestic accident. Some weeks later, when she had recovered sufficiently from her burns, and the time came to move her to the Ladies Department of the asylum, this was quietly done, in the middle of the night, in order to avoid alerting any unwanted attention. As far as I am aware, none of the newspapers reported that she had been admitted to the asylum until it became public, a few months later, during the trial.

Soon after her admission, Sibyl began, once again, to refuse food, and I believe that the attendants found it almost impossible to persuade her to eat. She also became increasingly sensitive to any external stimulus: the sound of a voice could make her wince; at the clatter of a dropped teacup she would cover her ears; a ray of sunlight on her face could cause her to turn up her eyes in agony. Any extremes of emotion caused such agitation in her that it could take hours for the attendants to pacify her. Even the anticipation of a meeting with her parents sent her into a state of anxiety, and she was so distraught after having seen them that the physicians restricted their visits. Ned was instructed that he and Annie should come to see Sibyl only once a fortnight, and that each visit could last no longer than an hour.

Other visitors were discouraged altogether, for the time being. I suspect that Ned's mother was secretly relieved. Although she never admitted to any culpability vis-à-vis Sibyl's current predicament, it is my belief that Elspeth was, in private, consumed by feelings of remorse. One can only imagine how wretched the old lady must have felt: the pangs of dread, churning her stomach; the actual physical ache, in the region of the heart; a tremble in the hands; the bitter taste at the back of her throat; and the ever-present sensation of nausea. These are the kind of symptoms, I suppose, that must have plagued her.

I know that Ned and Annie were set reeling by Sibyl's incarceration in the asylum: it was a devastating blow, and delivered so soon after the disappearance of Rose. In hindsight, I believe that I myself may have gone into something of a depression at around this time. Usually, I have a vivid recollection of the past, but the ensuing weeks are not as clear in my memory as other periods in my life. No doubt, the shock of Rose's disappearance, followed by Sibyl's horrific and unexpected attempts on her own life, and the inevitable repercussions on my friends the Gillespies, all had an effect upon my own state of mind.

The first episode that I can recall with any clarity that autumn was when I visited the Gillespies one Friday afternoon, towards the middle of November. I knew that they had been at the asylum on the previous day, and I was keen to hear any news of Sibyl. That morning, I had picked up one or two things in town for Merlinsfield, and, not wishing to arrive at Stanley Street empty-handed, I also bought an apple pie at the baker's.

The entrance to number 11 was now kept locked, as it had been in the past, since the residents' fears about burglars had prevailed, and the stone that had propped open the door during the early weeks of Rose's disappearance was long since gone. On that particular afternoon, I happened to arrive at the same time as Mrs Calthrop, who let me into the building. We got into conversation on the way in and, by coincidence, it turned out that she had just been to the shops, and had bought some tobacco for Ned. I offered to save her a trip upstairs and, since I was encumbered with parcels, she dropped the twist of tobacco into my carpetbag. Up on the top landing, all was quiet. I knocked, tentatively, and was surprised when the door opened, almost at once, to reveal Ned. Never, in all the time that I had known him, had he answered the door. I must admit that his appearance was startling, even heart-rending. Poor thing: he was unshaven, and his hair stuck up around his head, at all angles. He looked hollow-cheeked and, for the first time, I noticed deep lines around his eyes.

'Oh!' he said, leaning out to peer over the banister. 'I thought it was . . .'

'I'm terribly sorry – were you expecting someone?'

'No, just –' He retreated into the doorway. 'Annie's not here.'

'What a shame. I brought you this apple pie. Oh, and in the depths of my bag, I have your tobacco. I ran into your neighbour, you see. I'd get it out, only . . .'

My hands were full, but I was reluctant to set my belongings on the floor: the landing looked as though it had not been swept in some time. Ned seemed so uninterested in the pie that I wondered whether I was mistaken about apple being his favourite. But, presumably, he had no appetite. Usually, he was chivalrous to a fault, but he must have been in some kind of prolonged shock over all the recent calamities because he did not even offer to take the dish from me. He simply stepped back into the apartment, saying: 'Well, if you want, you can put it on the . . .'

He gestured towards the kitchen, before wandering off down the hall. I put the pie in the larder, and then sought out Ned. He was standing by the parlour fireplace. As I entered, he held out his pipe.

'Do you have that, eh . . .?'

'Oh, yes, of course.'

I set down all my packages and, now that my hands were free, I was able to reach into my bag and give him the tobacco. He put the twist on the mantelpiece and began to cut it, without a word. I took a moment to glance around the room. Even though the newspapermen were long gone from outside, the curtains at the front of the house remained partially drawn, giving the place a funereal gloom. All the windows were still nailed shut, and the apartment had the stale scent of unaired linens, and something else, a sour smell, like rancid bacon.

'Where's Annie?' I asked.

'She's away to Aberdeen for a few days. There was a sighting, of Rose, up there. She's gone to investigate.'

'Oh? I do hope she's not disappointed.'

My gaze fell upon one of my parcels: a large package of stiff brown paper. Inside, was the boxwood birdcage that I had purchased that very morning, at the *japonais* curio shop in Sauchiehall Street. I thought that it might cheer Ned up to see what I had bought, and so I tore off the wrapping paper, and set the cage on the table, exclaiming: 'Look – from the Japanese shop! Isn't it enchanting?'

'What is it?' he asked, with a glance at his watch.

'It's that birdcage – the one we liked.'

'I didn't know you had birds, Harriet.'

'I don't – but I hope to buy some. I was thinking of putting the cage in the studio at Merlinsfield. I've been staying out there some of the time, you know.' I paused, but he made no response, and so I went on: 'Wouldn't that be wonderful – to hear a couple of songbirds twittering away in the corner, whilst one painted?'

'Possibly a bit distracting,' he said.

'Or perhaps not while one worked, but in the evenings, in spring and summer, at sunset. But I wonder what kind of bird? What would you get, Ned?'

'Och, I don't know a thing about birds. A finch?'

'Perfect! And there should be two of them, don't you think, then they can keep each other company: two little sweethearts. Isn't there a bird market in town, somewhere near the Fire Station?'

'I believe so.'

'Oh good. Well, I must go there, perhaps next week. And you're absolutely right, of course, it would be silly to put birds in the studio – although I haven't done any painting, in a while.

Not since your classes, I'm afraid. I just haven't been able to bring myself to pick up a brush. What about you? Have you been able to work?'

'Not really.'

I took a step towards him, intending to pat him on the shoulder, or make some other comforting gesture but, just at that moment, he turned away in order to set his pipe on the mantelpiece and, once that was done, he began moving towards the door, extending one arm, to guide me along with him.

'Thank you for calling, Harriet.'

'Oh, it's a pleasure.'

At the table, I was obliged to pause, in order to pick up the bird-cage. Also, in that moment, an idea had occurred to me. Unsure how to broach the subject, initially, I ventured to ask: 'Don't you find it very gloomy here?'

His only response was to glance around and give a shrug of his shoulders.

'When's your next visit to the asylum, Ned, if you don't mind me asking?'

'Not until the end of next week.'

'Well then! I've had a wonderful idea. Why don't you come out to Bardowie for a few days? It can't be good for you, being here, all alone.'

I could see that the idea tempted him, but he said: 'Oh, no – I wouldn't want to put you to any trouble.'

'It's no trouble. You should get out of town. Then, in a few days, you might even feel like painting. The studio is fully equipped you know.' At this mention of work, he looked so despairing that I went on, swiftly: 'But never mind painting – come out for a rest. It might do you good to focus on something else. I was wondering . . . I thought we might write a book together, about your life and work.'

'A book?'

'Something to inspire young men from similar backgrounds to yourself, struggling artists, to show them that, if they work hard enough, anything is possible. Would that interest you? We could work on it if you come out for a few days.'

He rubbed his face, wearily.

'It does sound like a good idea, perhaps, at some point. But for the minute, I just need to be near Sibyl, and it takes hours to get out to Bardowie.'

'Not hours,' I laughed. 'The train takes no time at all. And believe it or not, there's often a cab to be had, outside the station in Milngavie.'

Ned frowned: of course, he was suspicious of cabs, an attitude that he had inherited from his mother. I did not like to mention that the driver of this particular Clarence was a surly drunk, who drove his horse at such a hair-raising pace that he often overshot the entrance to Merlinsfield.

'You can stay until it's time for your next visit to the asylum. We can just talk about the book, for now – we don't have to write anything.'

'Thank you, Harriet. I'd love to – but I can't at the moment.'

'In a few days, then – or next week? Bring Annie. Bring who-ever you like.'

'Well, we'll see. Can you manage all these parcels?'

As it transpired, he had been glancing at his watch, and so on, simply because he had an imminent appointment in town, and had only a very short time to change his clothes and make himself ready to leave. Apparently, he was going to see Horatio Hamilton. Although Ned refused to be drawn on the purpose of the meeting, I had a feeling that the gallery owner would be eager to know when his protégé intended to resume painting, given that there were over a dozen portrait commissions lined up, all of which would now be long overdue. Hamilton had been sympathetic and supportive during all of the artist's difficulties, but he was also a businessman. I would not have been surprised if he was putting pressure on Gillespie to resume work. At any rate, not wishing to make Ned late for such a meeting, I gathered up my belongings, at once. Ned came with me and opened the front door.

'I'll probably be out at Merlinsfield for the next few weeks,' I told him, as we said our farewells, on the landing. 'So, if you want to come out, on the spur of the moment – you remember how to get there, don't you?'

'I think I remember.'

'It's on the Balmore Road, about halfway along, towards Bardowie, on the left-hand side. You'll see some gates – but the cab driver will know where to come if you tell him you're going to stay at Merlinsfield.'

'Well, let's hope I'm able,' said Ned.

At that moment, I had a thought, and held out the birdcage to him.

'Here,' I said. 'Why don't you keep it, for now? It will be something pretty to look at, if ever you need to cheer yourself up.'

He stared glumly at the cage, and then shook his head.

'No,' he said. 'It's too beautiful for here. You take it.'

'Are you sure?'

He nodded.

'Very well, then,' I told him. 'I'll put it in the studio in Merlinsfield, and you shall have to come and see how it looks.'

'That's probably for the best,' he said, and then, for a moment, his eyes grew very lustrous, and I wondered whether he might be about to weep, but then he said, brusquely: 'Well, if you'll excuse me, Harriet . . .'

As I made my way downstairs, I glanced back over my shoulder. The last I saw of Ned, he was closing the outer door of the apartment, his gaze fixed upon the ground, a preoccupied look upon his face. Poor, dear Ned: so many troubles! Given all that had happened recently, I was fast becoming a believer in the inexorability of Fate. None of the recent catastrophes could have been foretold but, by the same token, it seemed to me that none of them could have been avoided. Try as we might, we cannot escape the inescapable; we are all of us doomed to live out our destinies, like the servant in the fable, who hopes to elude Death by fleeing to

Samarkand, only to find, upon his arrival in the town, that Death is there, waiting for him, after all.

After leaving Stanley Street, I called at my lodgings, briefly, to see if there was any mail for me. A little later that afternoon, I returned to Bardowie with the birdcage and my other purchases. Perhaps, given his circumstances, the time was not quite right for Ned to come to Merlinsfield. However, I did hope that he would take up my offer, in a day or two. A new project, such as our book, was just the thing to divert him. Above all, I was convinced that he ought to spend some time away from that gloomy apartment.

On Saturday and Sunday, Agnes Deuchars, the housekeeper, helped me to finish off some curtains, and on Monday, I began to re-upholster two old chairs that I had discovered in the attic. I also wrote a letter to my stepfather. He had extended his stay in Switzerland but, according to his factor, he was due to return before Christmas. I myself had written to Ramsay a few times, but had not heard from him.

Occasionally, while I worked, I found myself standing at the window of the morning room, looking out towards the road. From time to time, I climbed the stairs to the tower studio. I had placed the birdcage on a table next to the newly enlarged casement, where it looked very well, and where it could stay for the moment, until I had bought my finches.

In fact, I was rather looking forward to having a pair of birds to look after and, eager to visit the bird market, I had decided to go back into Glasgow, on Tuesday. The thought had crossed my mind that I might call at Stanley Street first, to see if Ned would accompany me. He was in need of distraction, and such a trip might help to take his mind off his troubles. There was a chance that I might even stay in town for a while. With Annie gone, it seemed to me that Ned would, perhaps, be in need of company. Having decided to surprise him, my only worry was that he might take it into his head to come out to Bardowie on the very day that I had gone into town. In fact, that night, I had

a dream in which he appeared, wandering up the drive of Merlinsfield, having ignored the Clarence at the station and walked
along the road (which would have been typical of him). In the
dream, I was looking down at him from the window of the studio
as he trudged towards the house, gazing up at me, his eyes shining bright blue, reflecting the light of the sky.

The following morning, I was awoken by the sound of hoofs on
gravel, and the jingle of harness. Rousing myself, I went to peer,
bleary-eyed, out of the bedroom window. In the late autumn and
early winter months, I sometimes find it difficult to estimate the
time of day, since the skies are often gloomy long after the sun has
risen. Looking out, I could see that dawn had broken, but it was
a cloudy morning and the light was still leaden. From the bedroom, I had only a partial view of the carriage drive, but I could
just see the back wheels of an old Clarence, standing at the front
door. Very few callers came to Merlinsfield, and the first thought
that came into my head was that Ned had accepted my invitation
and come to pay me a visit. No sooner had this thought occurred,
than I heard a great clamour at the front of the house, as someone
began pounding the brass knocker. Agnes did not usually come
up from the cottage until eight o'clock and, not knowing whether
she was present, or available to answer the door, I threw a shawl
over my nightdress, and hurried downstairs, almost tripping in
my haste, spurred on by the insistent pounding at the knocker. In
bare feet, I rushed across the flagstones of the hall, crying out, in
excitement.

'Just a moment! I'm coming!'

I rammed back the bolts; opened the door. There on the threshold stood – not Ned – but a stranger, a man of middle years,
dressed in an overcoat and bowler hat. He was perhaps rather
shorter than the average height, a little stout; a plain, ordinary-
looking fellow, with a dark, well-groomed moustache.

'Good morning,' he said, looking me up and down.

For a moment, I was speechless. My heart hammered in my

chest, perhaps because I had run downstairs so soon after waking. Just behind the stranger, stood three other men, two of whom were dressed in police uniform and, in the background, I could see the surly cab driver, leaning against his vehicle. All of them were gazing at me, with frank curiosity. I recognized one of the uniformed men as John Black: the peppermint-sucking constable who had interviewed me, all those months ago. The stranger glanced over his shoulder, as though for confirmation of something, and when Black nodded, the man turned to face me, once again.

'Miss Baxter?'

'Yes,' I replied, recovering myself. 'Good morning, gentlemen.'

'Miss Harriet Baxter?'

'Yes, indeed. And who, might I ask, are you?'

'Detective Sub-Inspector Stirling, ma'am.'

'Oh! Oh my goodness! Is something the matter? Is it Ned? Is he well?'

The detective fixed me with a stare like a gun. 'He's as well as can be expected, Miss Baxter. But I'm afraid Mr Gillespie is not who we're concerned with today. It's my duty to inform you –' He paused, and then went on: '– that I have here a warrant for your arrest.'

I am afraid to say that, after he mentioned the warrant, I hardly heard a word that he uttered. Instead, I became vividly aware of the other men, who were watching the proceedings with great interest, the smoke of their breath rising into the morning air. The flagstones felt like icy metal beneath my feet. I saw Agnes hurrying up the drive, puffing and panting, pulling on her apron, no doubt alerted by the commotion of the cab's arrival.

'Miss Baxter!' she cried, in alarm, and attempted to approach the house, perhaps to come to my aid, but the uniformed constables stepped in front of her, and the other man (who was not in uniform, and who, I now realised, was another detective), led her to one side and began speaking to her in low tones. Agnes listened to him for a moment and then gazed at me, open-mouthed.

Stirling was still talking, his face very close to mine. I remember noticing how densely his moustache grew. Although it was composed, presumably, of thousands of individual hairs, the whole construction moved up and down as one, while he spoke. I wondered how often he must trim the edges. 'Is not the human mind peculiar?' I thought to myself. 'Here I am, being arrested, and all I can think of is moustaches.'

Such was my bewilderment at this turn of events that I did not utter a word or sound until we were inside the Clarence, bound for the city at a steady, but not hair-raising pace. As we lurched along the Balmore Road, heading south, the policemen were silent. Black plucked at his ginger sideburns, while Stirling folded his arms and studied me, with undisguised interest. The other men were, apparently, from the police office in Milngavie, and had remained behind at Merlinsfield, in order to search the house and garden. I stared out across the wintry meadows, struck by the enormous absurdity of this turn of events. Surely they would realise, very quickly – perhaps within a few hours – that they had made a colossal mistake?

I was trying to remain calm, but could not help but feel anxious, and this combination of incredulity and nerves prompted me, of a sudden, to utter a short laugh. I was disconcerted to observe Stirling exchange a glance with Black, who then produced his greasy little notebook, in which he wrote a few remarks with a sharp, three-inch pencil. Sure enough, this nervous laugh of mine was soon to come back and haunt me.

Friday, 25 – Tuesday, 29 August 1933

LONDON

Friday, 25th August. Without wishing to seem too melodramatic, I must record here that I have had a terrible shock. I have been unable to work, either on these notes, or on my memoir, since yesterday morning. This is the first time that I have picked up a pen. Even now, I can hardly think.

For the most part, I have been lying here on the bed, staring into space. There is a burning pain, just below my ribs. The heat is oppressive. Sometimes, I stand at the window, although there is no breeze. Out there, in the world, life continues as usual. From time to time, Daimlers are driven into the court-yard below, and parked. The cars bake beneath the sun, heat rising from their bonnets, rippling the air. Sometimes, young men emerge from the hire garage, rolling up their sleeves. They wash the vehicles and lark about, throwing sponges and water at one another.

Occasionally, I cross my room and hearken at the door, for any sounds from the rest of the apartment. Maj and Layla twitter away, as ever, in the dining room.

Last night, after dark, when I heard the girl retiring to bed, I did consider creeping across the road to book a room in the hotel, but something stopped me, possibly some very rational part of myself, which refuses to believe in my own worst fears. Too nervous to surrender myself to oblivion, I forewent my usual miracle pills. As a result, I lay here, sleepless, all night long, eventually drifting off towards the dawn, for an hour or two, until the gunning of an engine down below awoke me. Before I had even opened my eyes, the terrible thoughts of yesterday crept back into my head, duller after sleep, but only a little less disturbing.

Perhaps I should describe what happened. Perhaps setting it down in writing will help me to put matters in perspective.

Of late, I have been in the habit of taking a bath at least once a day, not through any obsession with cleanliness, but because I find that it clears my head. Our weather has been so terribly hot this summer, with one scorching spell following the next. The heatwaves often last for days on end, to the extent that I find myself becoming quite nauseous and light-headed. This mansion block is terribly stuffy, and submerging oneself in cool water is often the only way to maintain one's composure. More often than not, I lock myself away in the bathroom for up to an hour, both morning and afternoon, in order to reduce my own temperature. It has crossed my mind that, whilst I am thus occupied, and unlikely to emerge, Sarah could use the opportunity to snoop around. Although nothing has ever gone missing, and I have never remarked upon any item that has been disturbed, or caught her in the act, I do believe that, once or twice, upon returning to my rooms, I have smelt traces of her cigarette smoke. Until now, my suspicions have been more of an intuition, rather than anything that I have been able to verify.

Yesterday morning, however, all that changed.

The first event of note was that, amongst the early post, I received a reply from Miss Clay of Greenstead, Essex. She had written her return address in plain view, on the back of the envelope but, fortunately, I had been on the lookout for the postman, and managed to retrieve the mail from the doormat before Sarah had even emerged from the kitchen. In the privacy of my bedroom, I tore open the envelope from Essex, and read its contents. Apparently, Miss Clay has absolutely no complaints about her former employee. According to her, Sarah is a kind and conscientious companion, who left her employ only because she wished to find work in the city, rather than in a sleepy country village.

At first glance, the letter did seem credible. However, the more I examined it, the more I was left in doubt. I could not help but wonder whether – with its lilac ink, spidery hand, and dignified tone – it resembled, almost too perfectly, something written by a genteel spinster from the shires.

Uncertain what to make of this letter, I hid it in my bureau. Then, telling Sarah that I had no appetite for breakfast, I shut myself in the bathroom and drew the water for my morning dip. Having checked the temperature (so cool that it is almost cold, as is the only option, in this infernal weather) I slipped off my shoes and was about to undress when a sudden thought stopped me short. You see, although I had been careful to hide Miss Clay's letter at the back of the drawer, I had dropped the envelope, without thinking, into the waste-paper basket. My worry was that Sarah might notice it – if, for instance, she happened to empty the basket, or if she strayed into my bedroom, for any reason, whilst I was elsewhere. Had Miss Clay not written her return address, then we would have had no problem but, as it was, I felt unhappy that the envelope remained in plain view. Even if the letter were genuine, I did not wish Sarah to know that I had been in contact with her former employer; it might raise unnecessary questions in her mind. Reluctant to leave it to chance, I decided that the envelope ought to be concealed, at once. I left the bathroom and padded back down the hall, still fully clothed, but with bare feet. The door to the sitting room lay ajar and, as I approached, something in there caught my eye.

My companion.

She was seated in my armchair, smoking a cigarette. I was struck, initially, by the sheer nonchalance of her posture. She lay back, low in the chair, as though, by force of habit, she had collapsed into it. Her legs were stretched out, and loosely crossed at the ankles, with one stockinged foot resting upon the other (how unusual it was to see her without shoes!). She looked perfectly at ease, for all the world like a slightly bored *Hausfrau*, taking a moment of leisure in her own sitting room.

Since I, too, was barefoot, I had made no sound as I moved across the parquet in the hall. Sarah was facing the fireplace wall, which meant that she was looking away from the door. Even when I crept up to the threshold, she failed to notice me, and remained, sprawling in the chair. In fact, now that I could see her more clearly, she seemed not bored, but almost transfixed, as though in a deep reverie. At first, I had assumed that she was gazing blankly into space. But then, all at once, I realised that she was staring at the painting that hangs above the mantelpiece.

Previously – at least, to my knowledge – the girl has never shown the slightest bit of interest in art. In my presence, she barely glances at any of the numerous works on display in the apartment; yet, now, here she was, gaping at this picture, as though hypnotised. For some reason, she seemed utterly captivated; staring and staring, gazing up at the wall, like a cat might fix on a bird. The sole movement in the room came from the thin stream of smoke that rose from the cigarette in her hand.

All thoughts of Miss Clay's envelope had vanished from my mind. My legs were shaking. Fearful that Sarah might suddenly turn and see me, I shrank back from the doorway, and returned to the bathroom, one silent step at a time. Safely inside, I closed the door, without a sound, and drew the bolt. Feeling weak, of a sudden, I sat down on the edge of the bath. No longer in the mood for a soak, I pulled out the plug and watched the tepid water swirl away, down the drain.

The sight of that girl gazing up at the canvas had thrown me into perturbation, verging on alarm. I was seized by an overwhelming conviction: not only had she waited until I was out of the way in order to sneak in and look at the picture, but she had done the very same thing on many previous occasions.

The apartment is full of paintings. As well as those in the sitting room, there are pictures in every room, including my own bedroom, where there are about half a dozen. I even have some on display in the kitchen. Why on earth should she be so interested in the one that hangs above the mantelpiece?

All at once, a cloud chased across the sun. The bathroom, with its tiny window, was plunged into shadow, and in that instant, it came to me: this terrible notion that I now cannot seem to shake.

Some time later, I heard the girl in the hallway, calling out to tell me that she was going to the butcher's. The front door opened and closed; I heard the creak and groan of the lift as it began its descent. Only then did I hurry back to my bedroom and lock myself in.

Half an hour passed, and then she was back again, and knocking at my door to ask if I wanted any luncheon. I gave her the impression that I was unwell, and did not wish to be disturbed. Indeed, my indigestion has been rather bothersome; even now, I feel queasy. Later, I rebuffed her offer of tea, and then when she came tap-tapping once more, at around six o'clock, asking if I wanted her to telephone the doctor, I told her that I was going to sleep, and wished to be left alone.

This morning, she has already been at the door two or three times, asking if I am recovered, and whether I want anything to eat or drink. I have no appetite but luckily, there is a jug of water on my bedside table, and I keep a bottle of Scotch in the cupboard, in case my insomnia proves to be irredeemable.

I keep sending her away.

Once, she tried the handle, but the door is still secured.

I shall have to unlock it and emerge at some point soon, if only for practical reasons, which are becoming increasingly urgent. Were it possible to leave this building by some other route than the front door, I probably would. However, there is no way out. I have even investigated my bedroom window as a potential exit. Alas, it has a narrow sill, and then there is naught but a four-storey drop into the courtyard behind the garage.

Is it possible that Sarah is Sibyl? And if so, does she intend to do me harm?

3.30 p.m. She has gone across the road for cigarettes, and in her absence I have been able to make a dash to the facilities. I feel a little better, somewhat calmer, and less distraught.

This weather really does take it out of one.

I had sufficient time to look around the apartment. Everything seems perfectly normal. Maj and Layla are quite safe, thank goodness. The girl has clearly tended to them well during my self-inflicted exile in the bedroom. Their cage is clean; their water bowl full; and they have been given seeds, and one half of an early pear. They are hopping about, as ever, in blithe ignorance.

There goes the lift. It was my intention to lock myself in again before her return. However, one cannot remain behind closed doors, indefinitely. I must be brave, and go out to the sitting room. Oh, but I dare not! No, I must. One ought to have the courage to look her straight in the eye when she comes in.

10.30 p.m. Despite any trepidation that I may have experienced earlier, nothing of an alarming nature has transpired. Sarah, when she returned from the tobacconist, seemed perfectly dull and normal. She poked her head into the sitting room, and expressed concern for my well-being. Thankfully, she appeared not to detect any nervousness on my part. When I told her that I was feeling much better, she asked if I wanted a hot drink, and then trudged off to make tea.

Not once did she glance at the painting above the mantel.

However, now that I have had these strange misgivings, I find that I am unable to look at her in the same way.

This afternoon, when she returned with the tea and biscuits, I watched her closely. If only one could see beyond her middle-aged appearance to tell what she might have looked like as a child – but try as I might, I cannot. Her hair is grizzled; her face sallow and tired; her figure doughy. Time and trouble have moulded her appearance until she resembles ten thousand other women of her age. She does have those neat features that may once have been pretty, but almost fifty years have passed since those days in Glasgow, and I cannot be sure that there is a resemblance between this bloated, faded woman and the girl that I once knew: that thin, frail child, who looked so haunted and guilty in the days after her little sister went missing.

Saturday, 26th August. This morning, simply out of curiosity, I placed a telephone call to the lunatic asylum in Glasgow. Since Sibyl Gillespie has been on my mind, I find myself intrigued to know what might have become of her: was she ever released from that asylum, for instance, or is she, perhaps, still a patient there?

I had hoped to find out some answers straight away but, apparently, they are not permitted to give out such information over the telephone, especially not on a Saturday. It seems that I must put my questions in a letter to a Mr Pettigrew, the Secretary of the asylum, and he will reply, in writing. It all seems frightfully bureaucratic. I did ask the person on the end of the telephone, very politely, a few times, simply to give me a hint: was the Gillespie girl still a patient: yes or no? Even though I explained that I was an old friend of the family, and that we had once been very close, the woman refused to be drawn on the subject. With no other alternative, I have decided to write a letter of enquiry to this Mr Pettigrew.

My sole dilemma is how I am to send it. For various, complicated reasons, I feel just a little awkward at the thought of asking Sarah to take such an item to the pillar box.

A letter came in the morning post, from Derrett. Apparently, the hospital has lost the results of my blood test and he has offered to do it himself. Perhaps I will ask Sarah to make me an appointment. I seem to remember that there is a pillar box outside the surgery. If we take a cab there, I might be able to slip a letter into the posting slot while Sarah is paying the driver.

Sunday, 27th August. This evening, finally, the temperature has dropped. A thin rain has started to fall, coating the sticky windows. Could this be the end of the fine weather, I wonder? Down the hall, the kitchen door is open. Sarah is playing a game of Patience in her sitting room; I can hear the slick slap of the cards as she turns them and lays them out on the table.

I am beginning to allow that I may have been a little hasty. All the girl did was look at a painting. It is, after all, a wonderful work of art. Perhaps she was just daydreaming: perhaps she went into my sitting room to tidy up, and then drifted off into a reverie as she gazed up at the wall. Is that not a much more likely scenario than the one upon which I have been brooding since yesterday?

I will acknowledge that when I saw her staring up at the picture so intently, it did give me rather a turn. At once, everything made perfect sense: her reticence, the lies about her age, even her accent, which I suddenly concluded must definitely be Glaswegian (much disguised, and discernible only because she sometimes shortens her vowels, or rolls her 'R's). There is no question that Sarah's accent is, at times, odd. However, now that I am calmer, I am no longer sure about this theory that she is Scottish by birth. Is it not more likely that her strange pronunciation is merely an unfortunate hybrid, caused by her habit of moving around from one place to another?

She did lie about her age, of course, but then, many women do, and her secretive behaviour may just be due to a natural reserve and desire for privacy. As for her character references, I will admit that I am still a little dubious about their authenticity. However, just because she might have persuaded a few friends to vouch for her does not mean that she is guilty of any larger, more sinister deception.

I have also been thinking about our little 'Ding Dong Merrily' incident, and am beginning to suspect that my anxiety that evening may have been generated by a strange muddle of déjà vu, and the seasonally incongruous music. In writing this memoir, I have been spending a good deal of time locked in my imagination, in memories of the past. It is quite conceivable that, while Sarah was playing, I might have been transported, in my mind, back to another apartment, to Stanley Street, in Glasgow, all those years ago, and to one of the little piano recitals that we listened to in the parlour. Perhaps there was nothing malign in Sarah's playing after all; it might simply have been the case that I got carried away by my own excitable imagination, exacerbated by her unwarranted use of the sustain pedal.

How silly to think that I had envisioned her, creeping in here to the sitting room, whenever she could, to look at the painting above the mantelpiece. Besides, the notion that Sibyl would have tracked me down, after all these years, is inconceivable.

Monday, 28th August. It seems that the rain of yesterday was an anomaly, for the scorching weather has returned, just as punishing as before. I have sent Sarah to Gamage's to see if she can find an electric desk fan. They are bound to stock something of the sort.

In the girl's absence, I have been hard at work. It is fascinating how absorbed one can become in a world that consists merely of ink and paper; I often feel as though I have stepped back in time. There we might be, Annie Gillespie and I, walking through the West End of Glasgow. Or here is Ned, right beside me. If I close my eyes, I can smell him: the sweet reek of his pipe, and the fresh, pine-tree tang of turpentine. Sometimes, if I glance up from the page, it is a surprise to find that he is not actually present, seated in the corner, watching me, his lips curving upwards into a fond smile. Of course, I am dreaming of happier times, when events in the manuscript have taken a gloomy downward turn. I wish it were otherwise.

Tuesday, 29th August 1933. Last night, I lay defenceless on my bed as Sarah pinned me down and injected my arm with a powerful sedative, designed to put me into a permanent state of paralysis and stupor. Although I struggled, she was too strong for me. Her needle pierced my flesh and the drug seeped, inexorably, into my veins. At once, I could feel its deadening effects as it flowed through my body. I knew that, thereafter, I would be entirely within her power. All the strength left my limbs. I could not lift my head. I was inert, immobilised, helpless. For certain, this was the end of me.

Somehow, just as I was about to slip under, I found the strength to fight back. With a huge effort of will, I strained to break free, and then, of a sudden, I awoke, gasping and flailing, my heart hammering in my chest; I was as fearful as a fish hauled from the water and left to perish on dry land.

Of course, it was only a nightmare, probably caused by my visit to the doctor, yesterday, when he took a sample of my blood – but it was too frighteningly convincing, none the less. Indeed, my arm – where Sarah injected me, in the dream, and Derrett stuck his needle – has felt numb and heavy, all day long.

However, this horrid *cauchemar* seems to have reawakened some of my uneasiness about Sarah. I still find it hard to trust her, or take her at her word. My terrors, today, have centred on the birds: I worry that she might harm them in some way. Oh, how I wish that I had never entrusted them to her in the first place, for to relieve her of the responsibility now might risk provoking her: the very outcome that I am at pains to avoid.

Unfortunately, while on our trip to see Derrett, I failed to post the letter to the asylum. I had hoped to slip it into the box just outside the surgery, but barely had I set foot on the pavement before Sarah jumped out of the cab and paid the driver and then, later, on the way out, she had me firmly by the elbow. I shall have to sneak down to the pillar box across the road, at some point.

This afternoon – as a sort of curious experiment – I asked Sarah to dust all the pictures in the sitting room. I had it in mind to watch her while she worked, so that I could gauge her reactions when she came to flick the duster at the one that hangs above the mantelpiece. Would she gawp at it, like she did the other day, when I caught her unawares, perhaps? Or might she, albeit discreetly, treat it with some special reverence? At any rate, I told her to use the small stepladder, with the help of which she could reach the topmost edge of the highest paintings, and then I sat at my desk here, in the corner, to edit my memoir.

The weather was hot – not just hot, as it has been for weeks, but also extremely humid. Sarah, as usual, was dressed in far too many clothes for such sultry temperatures: heavy shoes, thick stockings, and a high-necked, long-sleeved housedress in a muddy shade, reminiscent (if one was being kind) of mulligatawny soup, or (if not) of cattle dung. The material was clingy and unflattering, and dark sweat stains were visible, across her back and under her arms. She dusted with deliberate efficiency, dragging the ladder from one picture to the next, clambering up one step at a time, and running the cloth over each frame with great care. It was simple enough to keep a covert eye on her, under the guise of correcting my manuscript.

There are about a dozen paintings in the sitting room, all of them framed simply; I am not, as a general rule, fond of over-elaboration. The one above the mantel has a delicate, ovolo moulding. Perhaps it was just a coincidence, but I noticed that Sarah left this particular frame until last. By that stage, she was breathing heavily. She mounted the steps, and then drew her cloth across the top of the painting, after which she wiped down the sides. Finally, she descended the ladder and flicked the duster along the lowest edge.

'There,' she said. 'All done.'

Was it my imagination, or had she been a little more cursory with this picture than the rest?

'Have you finished that one already?' I asked.

She gave a strange laugh. 'Yes, it wasn't very dusty.'

'Oh? Well, thanks most awfully.'

As she leaned over to fold the steps, a drop of perspiration rolled down her nose and hung, briefly, at its tip, before dripping onto the hearth. Appearing not to have noticed this wanton cascade of bodily fluids, she simply picked up the steps and lurched away down the hall, leaving her spot of water behind her.

I crossed the room, and peered down at the small, greasy splat on the tiles. For a moment, I was filled with irritation. Why on earth did the woman not dress more suitably for this weather, instead of galumphing about in heavy garments, and sweating all over the place? In this day and age, when females wear practically nothing, why did she always cover herself, from top to toe, in high-buttoned blouses, heavy skirts, and long sleeves?

And then a thought struck me: something so obvious that it has been staring me in the face all along. Of course, I have always assumed that Sarah wears shroud-like garments as a way of disguising her weight. But, of a sudden, Sibyl Gillespie came to mind: Sibyl, who was permanently disfigured when she set herself on fire. According to the doctors, the scars on her arms and shoulders would be with her for the rest of her life. The thought that struck me was this: Sarah Whittle never bares her arms or shoulders – not ever.

V

November – December 1889

GLASGOW

16

In itself, the trauma of being taken into custody might well have affected my memory, but my arrest was not the only dreadful shock that I received on that chill November morning, back in 1889. Before our journey into the city was over, I was to hear tidings that horrified me yet more than my own plight: a revelation, from which I believe that I may never have fully recovered.

Having travelled from Bardowie in silence, I began to come to my senses just as we were drawing up outside the Western Police Office in Cranston Street. It occurred to me that I had no idea what would happen next: I might be locked in a cell, and kept in seclusion for hours; some other officers might assume responsibility for me; Stirling and Black could disappear, never to be seen again. Of a sudden, I was gripped by a desire to learn all that I could about my circumstances, and so I sat bolt upright, and addressed the policemen, with some urgency.

'If you don't mind, I'd like to know exactly why I've been arrested.'

Constable Black paused in the act of opening the carriage door, with his fingers on the handle. Stirling cast a glance at him, then turned back to me. His mouth puckered up, doubtfully, at one side. After a moment, he spoke: 'You don't know?' When I shook my head, the detective sat back in his seat. 'Aye, well,' he said. 'We found the body, you see, on Friday.'

I looked at him, startled.

'It was just off the Carntyne Road, outside the town,' he continued. 'A shallow grave – near an old quarry.'

I had a horrible feeling that I knew the answer, but found myself asking: 'Whose body? Who?'

Stirling widened his eyes. 'Why – Rose Gillespie.'

For a brief interval, I was so shocked that I was aware of no feeling at all: no anguish, no grief, only a strange sensation of numbness, of somehow being suspended in that moment of time. It had grown very quiet inside the carriage. The only sound was the creak of Black's boot leather, as he shifted his feet. He must have been impatient to get inside the police office. Perhaps he was cold. Or perhaps he wanted a cup of tea, or his breakfast. I thought of Agnes, back at Merlinsfield, and wondered whether she would have made my bed and laid the fires, as usual. Such were the banalities that passed through my mind. Strangely, I found myself considering the cast of my own features. I could sense that my face had frozen in a particular attitude, one that might be described as stunned. Tears had pricked my eyes, but they did not fall. For some reason, I could not imagine my expression without contemplating what Ned might think, were he present, staring at me, as the policemen were staring at me now. What thoughts would rush to his mind?

Oh poor Ned! And poor Annie! The horror of it! No doubt, this notion of my friends in torment was too much for me to bear because my thoughts flitted away to trivial subjects, less harrowing to contemplate: Constable Black, for instance. Did he take porridge for breakfast, or a morning roll? Who prepared it for him? And was he possessed of a wife?

Meanwhile, the constable had bent down to retie his bootlace. Stirling offered me a handkerchief, and when I shook my head, he returned it to his pocket, his eyes never once leaving my face. Perhaps half a minute had passed since he had told me the news about Rose. And still, I was numb. I told myself that, eventually, I would feel something. The pain would engulf me; perhaps even crush me; at some point, it would happen. Then, all at once, I flinched, as the door beside me flew open to reveal the driver, standing outside, looking impatient. A blast of icy air swept into the Clarence. Detective Stirling offered me his hand.

'Shall we?' he said, almost kindly, and then he assisted me out of the carriage and into the building.

*

Thereafter, it is hard for me to remember much about the next few hours. At such times, the brain does not function as normal. I had been allowed to dress before we left Merlinsfield, but at the reception in Cranston Street, I believe that they took away my belongings, including some keys, my watch, and a purse containing a small amount of money. Various particulars were noted down, but what they asked me, exactly, I cannot bring to mind. I do have a vague memory of my height being measured but, now, this detail strikes me as incongruous, so perhaps I have invented it. I know that I was put into a cell: a small, dreary room, the stench of which would have sickened a goat. The door was closed and locked; and then, I was left alone.

I recall collapsing, on the ground, in a heap. Stirling's news about Rose must have propelled me into a kind of temporary madness for, as I lay there, on the cold, dusty floor, I felt an overwhelming pressure build up inside my head and body, and so great was this pressure within me, that it seemed as though I might implode, and disappear from the face of the earth. I would cease to exist: such was my state of mind that this unlikely prospect seemed entirely feasible.

Eventually, I crawled over to the bed, where I remained for – perhaps – two or three hours, weeping bitterly, at intervals. Loath to let the policemen overhear me, lest they should think that I was merely lamenting my arrest, I tried to smother these cries by pressing my face, hard, into the coarse blanket. All that I could think of was poor little Rose, and Ned and Annie, and how I longed to be able to comfort and reassure them. Every hour or so, I would hear the turn of the key in the lock, which gave me a few seconds to dry my eyes and recover my composure, before the door would open, to reveal a constable at the threshold, peering in, to ask if all was well. Presumably, he brought me food and drink, and, at some point, I was given a list of solicitors, and told to write a note, requesting legal representation, but of these events I have scant recollection.

In due course, I found that I could cry no more, and the sensation that I might implode or disappear began to recede. That afternoon, I was escorted to an interview room, seated at a table, and told to wait. The table was made of cheap boards, nailed together, the wood so soft that it was possible to mark it with a fingernail, and I passed the time by staring dumbly at the various words that had been scraped into its surface; not all of them were obscene. Eventually, Detective Stirling entered, along with another officer whom I had not previously encountered: a short-legged, curly-haired man with cold little eyes and an insincere smile. Stirling introduced him as Detective Inspector Grant. From this, and from Grant's relaxed demeanour, I gathered that he was Stirling's superior officer. His voice had a drawling, obstinate quality and – perhaps because I distrusted and disliked him on sight – I snapped out of my stunned state, and have a reasonable recollection of what transpired during our interview.

'Now then, Miss Baxter,' Grant began. 'This will be a blow to you, no doubt, to be caught and arrested for the plagium. But the child was found dead, in a shallow grave, so we know there's more to it than that – so you might as well just tell us the whole story, in your own words, and then we can keep this short. I know that you, in particular, won't want to appear foolish, by trying to bamboozle us, or by lying.'

This was his tactic: to imply that he was some sort of Delphic Oracle, well acquainted with me, my character, habits, preferences and aversions, and my supposed crimes. However, Grant was no different from most other know-alls, in that his words were mere self-important swagger; the reality was that he knew precisely nothing about me. One of the words that he had used was unfamiliar to my ears but, unwilling to make myself vulnerable, I declined to ask for an explanation.

Since I had not yet replied, he gave a dry chuckle.

'I suppose you'll be finding all this very trying, Miss Baxter. After all these months, I know you must have thought you'd got away with it.'

Presumably, this conversational style of his was an attempt to fish for some sort of response. However, thus far, the only impulse that his every utterance elicited in me was the desire to slap him. That seems a shameful admission, now, but do bear in mind that I was grieving, and worried about Ned and Annie, and fearful of my own fate, and I am afraid that I found Grant's sly and unctuous manner insufferable. Stirling was gazing at me, calmly, across the table. When I looked into his eyes, something passed between us, and I would be willing to wager that he agreed with my low opinion of his boss. However, with great professionalism, he betrayed no exterior hint of this; he simply picked up his pencil and inspected the point.

'Might there have been a mistake?' I asked. 'Whatever poor soul was in that grave – might it not be – another child?'

My question had been addressed to Stirling, but Grant butted in: 'Rose Gillespie has been identified, by several means. There's no question that it's her.'

The edge of the table had been worn smooth by the hands of countless prisoners. I stared at the greasy wood, lost in futile thoughts. There was no justice in the world: little children lay cold in the grave, while men like Grant, and this cheap, ugly lump of furniture continued to flourish.

'. . . Miss Baxter?'

I looked up. Both men were staring at me.

'What about Mr and Mrs Gillespie?' I asked. 'Do they know about Rose? Is Annie back from Aberdeen? How is Ned? Who is there to look after them?'

Grant gave me a smarmy smile. 'I could have predicted you'd be concerned for the Gillespies, above even your own predicament. Always so selfless!'

'They're my friends,' I told him. 'I'd simply like to know how they are.'

'I'm sure they're as well as can be expected, under the circumstances. But never mind about them now. Tell me about the German.'

'. . . What German?'

'Schlutterhose.'

'Schlutter– ?'

'–hose – Hans Schlutterhose. We know exactly how and where you met him, of course, but I'd be interested to hear some more details.'

'Hans Schlutterhose?'

'Yes – tell me about him.'

'I'm not familiar with any person of that name.'

'You've never met Hans Schlutterhose?'

'I've never even heard the name before.'

'What about Belle?'

'Belle?'

'His wife. You know Belle. Tell me about her.'

'On the contrary, Inspector, I don't know anyone called Belle.'

Grant stroked his chin, and adopted a thoughtful demeanour: all a charade, of course; nothing that the man did was genuine.

'It must have been last year at the Exhibition, I suppose. You were very taken with our Ex., weren't you? You were a frequent visitor. Was that where you encountered Belle and Hans for the first time?'

'I thought you said you knew exactly where and how we'd met?'

'So – you're admitting that you've met them?'

'As I said before, I'm not familiar with these people. I encountered nobody of that name at the Exhibition. Now, I'd like to know more about Rose, if I may.'

'What about her?'

'What happened to her? How did she die?'

Grant leaned across the table.

'That's what we're hoping you'll tell us,' he said. Feeling his breath hot against my neck, I pressed myself back in the chair. He went on: 'Mr and Mrs Schlutterhose have been extremely co-operative, and told us all about your plan, but if you would care to give us your version of events . . .'

I shook my head, exasperated. Grant flicked his eyes at Stirling.

'She doesn't care to tell us,' he said. Then, he took a scrap of paper from the ticket pocket in his waistcoat, glanced at something written thereupon, and replaced it. 'Now Miss Baxter, would you be so kind as to estimate – just so we can keep our records accurate – how much you paid them for what they did? We know that, so far, it's in the region of a hundred pounds.'

'I assure you, Inspector, whoever these people are, they've misled you. I've never heard of them, and I sincerely hope they don't have access to my money.'

'The German claims it was accidental, you know.'

'What was?'

Grant barely paused, as though I had not spoken.

'But something tells me Herr Schlutterhose is only worried about additional charges. Plagium could mean anything upwards of several years, of course, but with the child dead . . .'

This time, I had to ask: 'That word – plagium. What does it mean?'

'Kidnapping, Miss Baxter, abduction – simple enough. Or it would be, if things hadn't got out of hand.' He narrowed his flinty little eyes. 'Make too much noise, did she? Try to run away? Or was it part of your plan, all along? What intrigues me, though, is why you wanted it done, in the first place. Of course, I have my own theories.' He allowed his gaze to run up and down the bodice of my frock in a way that I found disconcerting. 'You're a spinster, no children of your own, you meet this happy family – perhaps that might explain it . . .'

'Inspector, you're talking in riddles. What might it explain?'

He raised his eyes, and looked me in the face.

'Quite simply, it might explain why you paid this German and his wife to abduct and murder Rose Gillespie.'

I stared at him, aghast. He sat back, giving me another of his self-satisfied smiles. Stirling's head was bent over his notebook.

'You think – you think I paid these people to – kidnap and murder Rose?'

'Kidnap her, certainly. As you've been told, that's what you're arrested for, Miss Baxter. For the time being. But as for the murder – how exactly the child died, and at whose hands – that remains unknown, and that's what I want you to tell me about. I can't help thinking you had most reason to want her dead.'

My mind kept going blank: it was as though my brain was controlled by a switch, which was being flipped, on and off, on and off. I half expected to faint. For the first time, I began to feel truly afraid.

'These people must be insane!' I cried. 'It doesn't make any sense. Are you inventing all this, for some reason?'

Grant raised his eyebrows, unable to conceal his delight that he had succeeded in agitating me.

'Not at all, Miss Baxter, we're only interested in what you might have to say. We want to hear your side of the story. Now, I know that you're a friend of Annie Gillespie. What do you think of her? . . . Miss Baxter?'

'. . . Yes?'

'What do you think of Annie Gillespie?'

'Think of her? She's my friend.'

'You do like her,' Grant offered.

'Yes, I'm very fond of her.'

'Yes, indeed. And I know that you're also very fond of Mr Gillespie.'

Here, he left a pause, and simply stared at me, in a provocative manner. The skin across my neck and shoulders began to prickle. I was not exactly sure what Grant was insinuating, but he certainly wished to imply something unpleasant. He turned to his colleague.

'As you may observe, Bill – she doesn't appear to be very pleased.'

Stirling flicked a glance at me, and then returned to his notes.

'Now, Miss Baxter,' Grant continued. 'You've visited the Gillespies' apartment, frequently, and you're familiar with the routines of the household.'

Since this required no reply, I made none. My mind was racing. I had begun to realise that he might pounce on any response that I gave, however innocent, and make it seem suspicious.

'You, more than most, are aware that when the weather was warm enough, Mrs Gillespie often sent her children around the corner, to play in Queen's Crescent. Your rooms, in fact, overlook the street, and if one stands in either window one has a clear view down into the Crescent gardens. Hence, you must have seen the little girls, playing there, many a time.'

It struck me that, perhaps, the only way out of this terrible situation was to say nothing: say nothing and hope that they would soon realise what a dreadful mistake they had made. Although unaccustomed to being deliberately impolite, I forced myself to fold my arms, and then I closed my eyes. This might seem a childish gesture but, at the time, I could think of no other way to demonstrate that I would co-operate no further. Apparently undeterred, Grant blustered on:

'You knew the routines of the household; you knew that the children played in those gardens; you paid money to this German, who has admitted that – acting under your specific instructions – he abducted Rose Gillespie, assisted – possibly, we're not sure – by his wife. Plagium is the charge, as it stands. But what I'm interested in now, is how the child died. Who did away with her? Was it Schlutterhose, Miss Baxter? Or his wife? Or was it you, yourself?'

Keeping my eyes closed, I dropped my head forwards onto my chest. The Detective trotted out a number of other statements and questions, in the interim, all of which were speculative. Difficult though it was not to protest at his ludicrous suggestions, I remained silent. On and on he droned, until I feared that he might never stop. Then, at last, there was a pause, and I heard him say:

'Well, Bill, she doesn't seem to want to enlighten us. That's a pity. We'll just have to see what she says when she goes before the court.'

After a few seconds, Stirling's notebook closed, with a snap. There was a loud scraping of chair legs on the floor, and then the two men left the room.

Hearing no click of the latch, nor any turn of the key, I opened my eyes. The door had, indeed, been left wide open. The passageway appeared to be empty. Just for a second, I contemplated making my escape. I could picture myself tiptoeing along the corridor, slipping through some unguarded exit, and emerging into the street. Where would I go?

But before I had time to consider, a sturdy constable appeared in the doorway, and escorted me back to my cell.

Weary though I was that night, sleep eluded me. My skin itched, and I was gripped by a fear that insects had crawled from the thin mattress, and burrowed into my clothes. Perhaps I was hallucinating, but there could be no doubt that the place was filthy. The stink of the cell was all-pervasive, and comprised a number of foul odours: chiefly, the residual scent of previous occupants, their urine and fearful sweat, together with an undertone of drains. Even the cold air that wafted in through the bars of the tiny window was hardly refreshing, since it carried with it a sulphurous reek from the various works nearby. With every approach of footsteps, or jangle of keys, I prayed that the door would open to reveal Stirling, come to inform me that there had been a mistake: I ought never to have been arrested; I was free to go; moreover, Grant had been dismissed, in disgrace, from the police service. Would I accept the Chief Inspector's humble apologies?

Alas, no such visit came. From time to time, the door did open, but on each occasion, it was only the night constable, lantern aloft, conducting his routine inspection. After a quick glance to make sure that I had not ripped up my petticoats and hanged myself, he would depart, leaving me alone in the cell, with my thoughts. I doubt that they were in any way coherent, given the various shocks that I had received since morning. The interview with Grant had served only to make me yet more fretful and confused, in addition to my grief. I could scarce believe that the police were giving any credence to these wild and unfounded accusations. Whoever these Germans were, presumably they had panicked upon being arrested, and were attempting to foist the blame for their misdoings on some other person – although why they had seized upon me, Harriet Baxter, as their scapegoat, was yet to be revealed. At the time, that they even knew my name was a mystery to me.

I also found it alarming that this man Grant now seemed to be in command. Stirling gave every appearance of being a decent, intelligent fellow. According to Ned and Annie, he was a diligent man, of untiring energy and perseverance, and though he had failed to bring Rose home, they had no doubt that he had tried his utmost to discover her fate. Now that her body had been found, it seemed as though his superior officer had assumed responsibility for the case. Perhaps searching for a missing child was beneath Detective Inspector Grant's dignity: no doubt, only the prestige of a juicy murder inquiry was enough to drag him off the fairway at the Glasgow Golf Club. To my eyes, he was all façade, more concerned with conveying an appearance of sagacity, rather than with the pursuit of real Truth. This was obvious, from the very fact that he had sanctioned my arrest, based on such flimsy – even non-existent – evidence. Indeed, he already seemed convinced of my guilt. My only hope was that whoever presided over the court was a man of superior intellect, who would see, at once, that I was unconnected to these Germans, and insist on a summary dismissal of the case.

Above all, I was concerned about what poor Ned and Annie would make of my being in custody. I could hardly bear the notion that they might, even for a second, see me in a bad light. Another wave of shame passed through me as I imagined my stepfather receiving the news of my arrest. Mercifully, he was still in Switzerland, and I could only hope that – long before he ever got wind of what had taken place – the police would have discovered their mistake, and I would have been released, without charge.

All night long, my mind could only flit from one fretful notion to another and, by the early hours, exhaustion had set in. With no other option available to me, I tried to compose letters in my head. Over and over, I began with the words: 'Dearest Ned, dearest Annie' – but, try as I might, I could not get beyond the first few lines. For all I knew, Ned was already attempting to secure my release. Cranston Street was barely a mile from Woodside, and I wondered whether he might even be present at the Police Court, in the morning. And yet, part of me did dread the prospect of being faced with Ned, in real life, and of discovering how he and Annie might react to the sight of me, in front of them, for goodness knows what stories the police were telling, or what kind of scurrilous picture they had painted of my character.

Perhaps I did fall asleep, momentarily. At one point, I found that I could slip between the bars on the window, and fly out, and up, across the rooftops. In my mind's eye, I flew directly to Stanley Street, where I was able to hover in the air, outside the top floor of number 11. The curtains were open in the Gillespie apartment. I peered through the parlour window – and there sat Ned, alone, his head in his hands. No sign of Annie. Flying closer, I reached out towards the glass. I longed for the comfort of familiar company, the reassurance of talking to him – and yet, I hesitated. I told myself that I had no desire to startle him: he would get the fright of his life, to see me hovering outside, and beating at the window, like a little bird. And so, at the last moment, I shrank away.

As it turned out, the proceedings in the Police Court were a mere formality. The Court was simply a room in the Cranston Street Office, presided over by the Bailie, a rather sinister-looking City Councillor, whose name escapes me. I was given little opportunity to speak and, contrary to what I had anticipated, my case was not dismissed. Instead, I was remitted to appear at eleven o'clock, that very morning, at the Sheriff Court, and was taken there directly, in an enclosed, horse-drawn wagon of dark polished wood. This van was windowless, and possessed only one narrow door, at the rear. As a vehicle, it resembled nothing more than a huge coffin on wheels. The journey was brief, and bumpy, and all that I could see of the outside world, through a tiny skylight in the roof, was a square of grey clouds. At Wilson Street, the two constables who had ridden the footboard helped me out onto the pavement. A few passers-by turned to stare, but otherwise, our arrival seemed to go unremarked.

Inside the Sheriff Court, I was placed in a basement cell, where I had my first meeting with John Caskie, the solicitor whom I had chosen from the list at the police office. I had been assured that all the men named thereupon were expert criminal lawyers but, on first acquaintance, Caskie seemed ill-suited to the legal profession, for he was a mild-mannered gent, of perhaps three and sixty, with the vague, distracted air of a bookseller or, perhaps, an ageing curate. In his hand, he had a piece of paper, a Petition, which laid out the charge against me. There, in black and white, it said that whilst acting with those Germans, I had stolen Rose. Naturally, I impressed upon Caskie my complete innocence of this charge. He looked startled at my hopeful suggestion that the case might be summarily dismissed.

'Heck, no,' said he. 'I doubt that'll happen.'

'Do you have any advice for me, sir?'

'Tell the truth, and dinna haiver.'

'I beg your pardon?'

'Nae haivering,' he said, but when he saw that I was still confused, he clarified: 'Be brief, Miss Baxter. They'll ask you a hantle of questions but dinna worry. This may be your sole opportunity to speak, mind, but say no more than you must. Then we'll see what we can do about getting you bail.'

Presumably, these words were meant to be reassuring, but I am afraid that they afforded me little consolation. As the time approached for my appearance in court, I became increasingly agitated, having no idea what to expect. Caskie had not, as yet, spoken to the Gillespies. He knew not whether Annie had returned from Aberdeen, and was unable to tell me whether the police had even informed Ned of my arrest. Reluctant as I was to have my friends hear about my predicament, part of me felt that it might have been reassuring to see their faces in court but, apparently, the hearing that morning would be held in private, and it was highly unlikely that anyone of my acquaintance would be present. Nor would my Teutonic accusers be in attendance. Caskie had it on good authority that they had already been remanded to prison. Schlutterhose had been sent to the new gaol, outside Glasgow, while his wife was in the North Prison, in Duke Street: a grim, soot-blackened monstrosity that loomed over the city, behind high boundary walls. A few months earlier, I had chanced to pass the main gate, and witnessed several shabby damsels, laughing and jeering, as they were discharged into the street; and I had heard, from Elspeth, the most horrific stories about the conditions inside. The mere thought of Duke Street gaol made my stomach turn over within me.

All too soon, it was eleven o'clock. My solicitor took his leave, and then the constables arrived to escort me upstairs to the Sheriff's chambers. There, behind an enormous desk at the window, sat the bewigged Mr Spence, the Sheriff-Substitute. His Clerk occupied a small escritoire, to one side, while Mr Caskie and Donald McPhail, the beetle-browed Procurator Fiscal, were seated at opposite sides of a table in the middle of the room. Caskie gave me a reassuring smile as I entered, and when the Clerk asked me if I was Harriet Baxter, I mumbled my assent.

After giving the documents in front of him a final glance, Spence opened the proceedings, addressing me in a gentle, refined voice.

'You've had sight of the Petition, containing a charge of plagium against you?'

'I have, my Lord,' I replied.

'Do you understand the charge?'

'I do.'

'Now, Mr McPhail here and I will ask you certain questions.

You're not bound to answer any question, but be aware that your failure to answer will be noted by my Clerk, and could be commented upon at your trial. Remember, this is your opportunity to set out your case.'

Thereafter, the Procurator Fiscal began his examination of me, in harsh, sepulchral tones, and I answered him as best I could. Admittedly, I was nervous, but it was a relief, in a way, to be able to speak, to set out my version of events, which would, hopefully, counter Grant's preposterous theories. As for my testimony that day, I shall not include it. Apart from the fact that I was under great duress at the time, anything that was said has already been described here, more coherently and comprehensively. Besides, the Clerk wrote down every word, and that document, or 'declaration', was read aloud at the trial, and is a matter of public record; it is even reproduced, verbatim, in Mr Kemp's recent pamphlet.

During McPhail's interrogation of me, the Sheriff-Substitute stared, sad-eyed, out of a window, alternately scribbling in a ledger, and tugging at his luxuriant, drooping whiskers, which had surely been grown to compensate for the lack of hair on his gleaming pate, just visible beneath his wig. Once or twice, he scored out some phrase that he had written, and began again. Frankly, he appeared, with Olympian indifference to my Fate, to be using this opportunity to compose some lines of verse! As soon as the Fiscal had exhausted his supply of questions, the Sheriff asked a few more, and then Caskie jumped to his feet.

'My Lord, I wish to make an application for bail on behalf of the pannel.'

Presumably, I was 'the pannel'.

McPhail turned to Spence. 'My lord, as I've already informed Mr Caskie, we're currently conducting further inquiries related to this case.'

'So I believe,' said Spence. He put down his pen and turned to regard me with a searching, melancholy gaze. Although he seemed to have been composing a poem throughout most of the proceedings – which tended to prejudice me against him – in every other respect, he gave the impression of being a perceptive, kindly fellow. Surely he would grant bail?

The Fiscal persisted: 'These inquiries, my Lord, are likely to result in a charge of the most serious nature being levelled against the pannel.'

Spence sighed and looked at me, with regret.

'In that case, I cannot but recognise that another, more serious charge may yet be preferred against you, Miss Baxter, and, accordingly, bail is refused. The pannel is committed for further examination, to appear before me, next Wednesday, and, until then, is remanded in custody.'

So astounded was I at this pronouncement, that I almost missed what he went on to say: that I was to be taken from the Sheriff Court, and housed in the North Prison – the very place that I had pictured earlier, with such dread. The next few minutes are incomplete in my memory. I seem to recall that Caskie hurried over, with various assurances, and promises to visit me as soon as he was able. Then the constables led me out of the building to the coffin-shaped van.

As we rattled northwards towards Duke Street gaol, I felt only numb. All I could think of was that these streets were but a stone's throw from Elspeth's church. Our route to the prison might even take us within sight of St John's, and I kept imagining that Ned or his mother might happen to be passing through that part of town. They might see this sinister van hurtling past, without ever guessing that their friend, Harriet Baxter, was locked up inside.

Prison is a sordid place and there are countless stories that document the sufferings of those poor souls who are unfortunate enough to be incarcerated. To be perfectly frank, I do not intend to dwell on the dismal conditions in the gaol, the lack of hot water and lavatories, the filth, and so on: this is not a manifesto for Reform. Suffice to say, after my initial reception, I was taken to the Head Warder, who informed me that I was to be housed in the hospital. Rather naively, I assumed that this 'hospital' would be a separate building, but it turned out, simply, to be a large 'association' cell on the ground floor of one of the ordinary wings.

Apparently, I was to share this room with two other females, both of whom were already installed when I arrived. Neither woman was sick, as far as I could see, although one was abnormally large in stature, and looked a little dim-witted. The other was a stunning, lively-eyed creature with bright red curls. The Christian names of these two ladies have long since faded from my memory, perhaps because the wardens referred to us only by our surnames. The redhead, Cullen, was a clever piece of work who, as I soon grew to realise, had at least as much power and influence as the warders, and she ran matters in the prison, almost single-handedly, from our cell. The giantess, Mulgrew, was a hefty creature with fists the size of hams. She rarely spoke, but during my first day and night in Duke Street, perhaps as a means of intimidation, she made a point of copying everything that I did: if I sighed, she sighed; if I folded my arms, she folded hers; if I put my hand to my face, she did the same. It was ever so disconcerting, and all that I could do was ignore her, in the hope that she would soon grow bored.

As you might imagine, I was terrified out of my wits. On that first night, I was afraid to close my eyes, although Cullen had assured me that we were quite safe: the door was locked, and neither she nor her associate meant me any harm; indeed, the two women were trustees, of some sort, and I had been housed with them for my own protection. Despite this, I barely slept a wink. My wakefulness was assisted partly by Mulgrew, who snored so loudly, at first, that I began to think that she might be putting it on for comic effect, and partly by the various bangs, crashes, yells and blood-curdling screams that echoed through the dark corridors of the prison.

Once Mulgrew's snores had subsided, I did manage to drift off, but found myself awake at frequent intervals throughout the night and, each time, in the moment that I regained consciousness – not yet sufficiently alert to know where I was – the same phenomenon would occur. For a few seconds, I would lie there, in the limbo between sleep and waking, and then, as I remembered what had happened (Rose dead, myself accused and imprisoned), I would think: 'Oh, what a terrible dream that was!', only, moments later, to jump out of my skin, with a sensation as though my heart and innards had been jerked by invisible hands, and then the sickening sensation of grief, dread and fear would flood through my body, as it dawned on me, all over again, that what I was experiencing was no dream, no dream at all.

Early the following morning, a female warder brought us a bucket of water, and then another arrived with a jug of tea, and later still, a third came knocking, bearing a pot of thin gruel. On the previous day, upon arriving at the prison, I had seen several male warders, but it seemed that this wing was guarded, exclusively, by females. In general, according to Cullen, they were harsher than the males. She was respectful in their presence but, behind their backs, she spoke of them with disdain. Apparently, this particular wing was presided over by a newly arrived Principal Warder, a Mrs Fee, whose authoritarian reputation preceded her.

By mid-morning, Mulgrew, the giantess, had grown bored of mimicking my every move and, for the most part, she sat in silence, biting her fingernails. Cullen, on the other hand, proved to be very informative, and I soon came to realise that she knew more about my case than I did. Apparently, my supposed 'fellow suspects' and I were to be kept separate at all times. Schlutterhose and his wife had been segregated since their arrest; he would remain in the new prison, outwith the town, and to avoid a meeting between his wife and myself, she had been put at the far side of Duke Street, in another female wing. It was unlikely that I would encounter either of this pair of miscreants, since our movements were severely restricted.

'They'll always separate you from your pals, if they can,' said Cullen. 'In case you start fighting about whose fault it is you got nabbed.'

'These people are not my friends,' I told her. 'I don't even know them.'

Cullen exchanged a glance with Mulgrew. 'Even so,' she said. 'Nae doubt they'll be holding a grudge of some sort, so you need to be on yer mettle.'

According to her, the kidnappers were not the only ones who might want to cause me harm. As I soon came to realise, prison was a hierarchical place, with a surprisingly strict moral code. News spread fast and, given the high profile of the Rose Gillespie story, it was only a matter of time before the whole gaol heard that the missing girl from Woodside had been found, dead. I knew that the charges against me were false, but no other Duke Street inmate would have expected so, and many within those walls would not take kindly to someone who was even suspected of having harmed a child. The fact that I was English made matters worse. Thus, Cullen explained, I had been put here, on the quietest wing, and would be watched over, very carefully.

She and the giantess then stood up and proceeded, forthwith, to show me the various ways in which I could protect myself from violent assault by other prisoners. Perhaps, by this stage, nothing would have surprised me, or perhaps I was still in shock; at any rate, I found myself obediently studying them as they demonstrated how to deal with an attack from behind, by striking the assailant in the stomach, with a backward thrust of the elbow.

This extraordinary display was interrupted when the door opened, yet again, to reveal a sturdy female, who simply said: 'Baxter – visit.'

'Thank you, Mrs Fee,' said Cullen, adding, to me: 'That'll be your solicitor.' I interpreted the significant look that she gave me as a warning that this turnkey was the aforementioned new Principal Warder.

'This way,' said Fee, and walked me towards the entrance of the wing. En route, I cast wary glances around me, and up at the landings overhead, but there was no sign of any prisoners anywhere, and I wondered whether they were always kept locked away in their cells. Just before we reached the wing gates, Fee paused outside a half-open door, and gestured that I should cross the threshold ahead of her. I entered the room, fully expecting to see Caskie, and so was shocked to find none other than Elspeth Gillespie standing there, and just behind her, whey-faced and anxious, both Ned and Annie.

'Herriet!' cried Elspeth, rushing forward. 'You poor thing! This must be quite dreadful for you. It's all a terrible mistake, of course. But don't worry – we'll do everything we can to get you out of here.'

Ned looked as though he had not slept in days. His skin was deathly pale, the shadows beneath his eyes almost black. He seemed like a man at the end of his tether. And yet, he gazed at me, steadily and intently, not in an accusing manner, but with considerable sympathy and understanding. It was as though – despite his own fragile condition – he wished to share with me what little strength he had.

'Now you must tell us if there's anything you need,' Elspeth was saying. 'As you're aware, Herriet, I'm on the Visiting Committee, and I know exactly what items you're allowed. But all this shouldn't be for long: there's a hearing next week, and your solicitor will ask for bail, so you should be out soon. Oh! But these past few days, Herriet, it's been terrible, what with the news about Rose, which practically knocked us to the ground, as you might imagine, and then we heard they'd found the awful people that took her, and then, the very next thing, Detective Stirling was at the door, saying they'd arrested *you*! As if hearing about Rose wasn't enough. I don't know what these people can be saying about you, do you? It's patently a piece of nonsense. I told Stirling they've made a mistake, but he says it's out of his hands now. Well, we won't let it rest, don't you worry.'

She went on, but I was only half listening, having become more interested in trying to catch her daughter-in-law's eye. Annie had gone from peering up at the bars on the window, to looking down at the floor. From time to time, she glanced over at Ned, as though to check on his welfare. There were plenty of seats in the room, around the table, and against the wall, but apart from Mrs Fee (who had taken a chair by the door), none of us made the move to sit down; it seemed, in some way, inappropriate. Ned stood by the table, stoop-shouldered, twisting his hat in his hands. His gaze hardly left my face. I longed to say something to him, to speak to Annie, and I found myself interrupting Elspeth.

'It's so good of you all to have come. Thank you. I'm much better just for seeing your faces, believe me. And I just want you to know how sorry I am, about Rose. I only found out yesterday – or, was it the day before? Do forgive me, I've lost track of time. But I'm so terribly sorry. What an awful thing to have happened. If there's anything I can do –'

I looked to Ned for an answer.

'Thank you, Harriet,' he replied. 'But everything is – there can be no funeral until the police have finished with the – the –'

He stared into the crown of his hat, unable to continue. I realised, with a pang of sadness, that he could not bring himself to say the word 'body'.

Elspeth gave his arm a maternal squeeze.

'But in the meantime there are things we must do,' she told me. 'So, Herriet, we do apologise, but we can't stay long. There are arrangements to be made.'

'Arrangements, yes, arrangements – of course.'

I was aware of sounding like a fool, but I could not think of the right thing to say. Had I been an actress on the stage, no doubt I would have made a speech that would have reassured and comforted all those present. But I was not an actress, and we were not in a play. I was just plain old Harriet Baxter and, at the time, I hated myself for my lack of eloquence but, in hindsight, I suppose that any awkwardness is understandable. The circumstances were quite extraordinary, and there we were: everyday, unremarkable folk, thrust into a situation that nobody could have predicted.

'If you don't mind, Harriet,' said Ned. 'We'd rather not talk about – Rose – not at the moment, anyway.'

'Yes,' said Elspeth, swiftly. 'You see, it's best we keep our minds busy. We just wanted you to know we're as baffled as you must be, about why you're in here.'

'You should be in good hands with this Caskie fellow,' Ned added.

'Oh – do you know him?'

He shook his head. 'Yesterday evening –' he began, and then his thoughts seemed to drift, yet again.

'Mr Caskie came to see us all,' Elspeth explained. 'He seems terribly thorough. Hours he was, asking all sorts of questions.'

'That's reassuring,' I said. 'Let's hope he finds out why these dreadful people have picked on me. It's quite beyond belief, really.'

'Yes, isn't it?' said Annie, speaking for the first time. 'Are you quite certain you don't know who they are, Harriet? Perhaps you've forgotten. Could you not have bumped into them on your travels, at some point? Or at the Exhibition?'

I sighed. 'No – I'm sure I would have remembered. Germans! I don't know any Germans in Glasgow. It really is a mystery.'

'Yes, indeed,' said Annie, sharply.

Feeling a little uncomfortable, I turned back to Ned.

'And how is Sibyl?'

'She's doing well,' said Elspeth, before her son could reply. 'We're going up to see her later. Apparently, she's been attending the asylum's Scripture classes.'

'And her burns – poor thing – how are they healing?'

'Very well,' said Elspeth. 'It's quite miraculous, the speed of her recovery, isn't it, son?'

Ned was frowning down at the floor, as though faced with the abyss. Elspeth flushed as she looked at him. She appeared, of a sudden, to be stricken with guilt. There was an awkward silence.

Then Annie said: 'I just find it very odd.'

Ned tore himself away from his private despair to throw her a reproving look. 'No, Annie,' he said.

'Yes, dear, I just want to ask her something,' said she, never once taking her eyes off my face. 'It's very odd, don't you think, Harriet, that these people would be saying these things about you. Total strangers! And they claim you were involved, in some way, with them, with what they did – taking Rose. Why would they say that?'

'I expect they want to pass the blame to some innocent person,' I replied. 'And thereby escape punishment.'

'Oh, aye,' said Annie; she sounded almost scornful.

'Is something the matter?' I asked her.

'Not with me.' She folded her arms and regarded me in what can only be described as a hostile manner. Ned put on his hat and stepped forward.

'Do forgive us, Harriet,' he said. 'But we're all very tired, and this can only be a short visit. We really must be going now.'

He tried to take his wife by the elbow, but she pulled away from him.

'No! I want to hear what she has to say.'

Behind me, the warder rose to her feet, with the words: 'Right then – I think that's just about enough.'

And then, all at once, to my great surprise, there was a rather undignified scuffle. At one moment, Annie was standing there, with her arms folded, then, the next, she gave a cry and lunged towards me. Elspeth shrieked, as Ned tried to grab his wife, and in the same moment, Mrs Fee darted forwards, shoving me aside. Somehow, I lost my balance and toppled, helplessly, to the floor, unable to avoid knocking my head against the table as I fell. I must have blacked out for a short interval – I have no idea how long.

When I opened my eyes, some time later, I discovered that I was alone in the room. The scent of a bonfire had drifted in through the window bars: somewhere nearby, perhaps in Cathedral Square, or at the Necropolis, a gardener was burning leaves. In the distance, the prison corridors echoed with the sounds of a commotion, of raised voices and clanging metal gates, but whatever the disturbance was, it appeared to be happening far away and, as I hearkened, the noises receded even further, until they could be heard no more. At length, still stunned, I sat up and was surprised to see a scrawny young woman standing in the doorway. Never before had I laid eyes upon her. She wore a ragged shawl over a drab frock. In her hands, she held a filthy mop. It was hard to tell whether she was a prisoner, or some sort of char. She gazed at me, dispassionately, then asked: 'What's your name?'

'Harriet,' I told her. 'Harriet Baxter.'

She nodded, and then stepped away, out of sight. I got up onto my knees, and was feeling the bump on my temple, when she reappeared in the doorway. This time, she was carrying an old wooden pail.

'Here,' she said and, without further ado, hurled the bucket, with all her might, directly at my head. I had just enough time to raise my arm, to protect myself, before the hard wood struck my elbow, sharply. Filthy water cascaded everywhere; the pail hit the ground with a clatter, and then the woman ran away, cackling.

For a moment, I was too stunned to move. Then, deciding that I might be less vulnerable on two feet, I got up, and was trying to squeeze the water out of my skirts when jangling keys, footsteps, and the clang of a gate, announced the return of Mrs Fee, who presently appeared in the doorway.

'Aye, well,' she said, sternly. 'You're still alive. They must all be dunderheaded gowks in this gaol! I don't know if those folk should even have been allowed in here at all, whether your woman is on the Visiting Committee or not. Are they witnesses in your case?'

'I dare say they may be.'

'Some silly dummy at the gate ought tae have asked more questions.'

Her stare was so accusing, that I was forced to reply: 'Forgive me, but you can hardly blame me for the incompetence of your colleagues.'

Fee narrowed her eyes, and shook her finger at me, in a warning fashion, as though she had got my measure. Then she peered at my frock.

'You're all wet.'

'How very observant.'

'What are you doing all wet for?'

I indicated the bucket on the floor.

'A woman threw this pail of water at me.'

Fee shook her head wearily.

'Baxter, I hope you're not going to be trouble. I suspect I'm going to have enough to deal wi' here, surrounded by gowks and fools, wi'out you causing fights every five minutes.' She grabbed her key chain. 'Come on now, back to the cell with you, and nae mair of your shenanigans.'

That afternoon, I was once again escorted to the same visit room. This time, I found the solicitor, Mr Caskie, seated at the table. Unfortunately, he had brought with him some disquieting news. He regarded me, gravely, as I entered, and after a few polite enquiries about my health and welfare, he came to the point.

'Miss Baxter, it seems the police have been to your bank with a warrant. They've secured a ledger which suggests that you made some large cash withdrawals, earlier this year, during the spring and early summer.'

'Large withdrawals? I suppose they must have been for Merlinsfield. I've been organising a refurbishment, you see, at one of my stepfather's houses. I had to pay for builders, and materials, and so on. I did withdraw rather a lot for that.'

'Did you keep receipts, or some kind of written record, for these payments?'

'I think so, where I was able. They'll be in my desk, out at Bardowie, or possibly in my rooms at Queen's Crescent.'

'Aye – or the police may have got their hands on them, by now. I'll find out. You see, we might have to produce these receipts in evidence.'

'But – why?'

Caskie sighed. 'Well, I've yet to see this bank ledger, but it seems that the withdrawals recorded there correspond with what the German says.'

'I'm sorry – I still don't understand.'

'Miss Baxter, the amounts this man alleges you paid him, and the dates he says you met in order to hand over the money, bear close approximation to the sums and dates in this ledger. Now, presumably, when he made his declaration, he cannot have known what is contained in your bank's records. But, for example – just an example, mind – say there's evidence you paid him such and such an amount – say £50 – on a Saturday in the first week of April, and, lo and behold, the day before, on the Friday, you'd withdrawn £50 or a little more, then it might not look very good. In other words, Miss Baxter, in court, a clever advocate could suggest you withdrew funds, on one day, in order to pay Schlutterhose, the next. Just an unfortunate coincidence, of course, but one that could prove rather awkward, for us.'

17

Following Caskie's visit, I had a lucky escape on the way back to my cell, when something unspeakable was thrown at me from an upper landing. Thankfully, it missed me by a few inches, but I realised that any excursion onto the wing would be fraught with difficulty, bordering upon danger. I was able to endure the next few days only by keeping busy in any way that I could. Primarily, this involved writing correspondence. For instance, I wrote a long letter to Annie. However, although I drafted several versions, I decided, in the end, against sending it. I did write to both Ned and Elspeth, thanking them for their visit and, after some consideration, I composed a letter to my stepfather. No doubt, sooner or later, one of his lackeys would inform him of my arrest, but I had decided that it would be better that he heard the news from me. I wanted to assure him that it was all a terrible misunderstanding, and that he ought not to return from abroad on my behalf. Fearing that he would be angered by my abandonment of Merlinsfield, and eager not to disappoint him, I assured him that the work on the house had been completed to a satisfactory standard and, in addition, I wrote to Agnes Deuchars, asking her to keep me apprised of any leaks in the roof, or any other matters that might require attention, during my absence. I also sent notes to several others, largely to discourage them from coming to see me, since I had no desire for anyone of my acquaintance to set foot inside that terrible building.

Regrettably, in terms of mail, we were at the mercy of the turnkeys. Letters were forever 'going astray' and, according to Cullen, it was a miracle that we received any post at all. Amongst the early replies that I did receive was a note from Elspeth. She apologised for what had happened on Friday morning, explaining that

Annie was under too much strain for one 'so highly strung' and had, since their visit to the prison, shut herself away in her room. Apparently, the police were still in possession of Rose's remains, but the funeral would take place as soon as possible after the body had been released. With Annie incapacitated, Ned had made a solitary trip to see the undertaker but – overcome by the sheer awfulness of his mission – had fled the funeral parlour before he had even finished explaining why he was there. Subsequently, his mother had assumed responsibility for the burial arrangements, the carriages, and invitations, and so on. She finished by assuring me that she would, of course, come to see me again before the next hearing, if that proved to be possible.

However, for various reasons – not least that their last visit had resulted in a scuffle – there was some question about whether the Gillespies were to be permitted to enter the prison.

Saturday and Sunday passed, with very little to break the monotony. The hours of darkness were the hardest to endure. I tended to jerk out of my slumbers several times a night, my pulse pumping wildly, and – even though my body seemed primed for action and alert, almost as though electrified – it was always several seconds before I was able to recall where I was, or form any rational thought.

My cellmates did their best to buck up my spirits, and I soon came to realise that they were not quite as unsavoury as they had, at first, seemed. Mulgrew, with her great dimpled cheeks and hangdog expressions, was a harmless – even loyal – soul, and Cullen distracted me with stories about her various fraudulent activities, primarily, the dissemination of hundreds of letters wherein she requested donations, claiming to be the victim of an astounding array of strange misfortunes. Of course, her crimes cannot be condoned, but in my embittered state of mind, it seemed to me that anyone stupid enough to be duped by such ploys deserved to be parted from their money. For our entertainment, Cullen performed a dumb-show of the various misfortunes in her begging letters: she froze for lack of a coat; she languished for want of medicine; her father beat her; a horse kicked her in the head; and she fell sick and died. Despite her efforts, time hung heavily upon us, and I often grew close to despair.

On Monday, I received another visit from my solicitor. After he had left me, on Friday, he had attempted to see Belle Schlutterhose, but she had refused to speak a word to him. However, he had since been able to interview her husband, and had also spoken, unofficially, but at some length, to Detective Stirling. Needless to say, I was very interested to hear his account of these meetings. Added to what I had gleaned from Cullen, and from the newspapers that Caskie had brought me, I was able to piece together a half-decent picture of events leading up to the apprehension of the kidnappers. Certainly, this pair had managed to elude capture for seven months, but Schlutterhose and his wife were not exactly masterminds, and they had made a supremely silly mistake, which led the police directly to their door.

It seemed that, on the morning of Friday, the 15th of November, a carrier had been walking in some woodland near the Carntyne Road when he noticed a piece of jute protruding from disturbed ground. Thinking that he might use such a piece of sacking, he pulled at it, and was surprised when it emerged from the earth, along with what appeared to be a set of bones, tangled in rags. The bones were so small that, initially, the carrier thought that they were animal in origin. However, upon closer examination, he saw that the rags were, in fact, clothing – a child's dress, and petticoat – and he realised that he had uncovered a half-buried human body, in some degree of decomposition, that had been partially dug up, perhaps by foxes or dogs.

Within the hour, the carrier had reported his discovery at the police office in Tobago Street. Detectives accompanied him to the woods, and the body was carefully disinterred, and taken to the morgue. As soon as it was confirmed that the bones were that of a small child, the police began to suspect that they might have unearthed the missing girl from Woodside. Eastern Division detectives sent word to their colleagues in the west, at Cranston Street, and Ned was brought, without delay, to the morgue, where he identified his daughter from her clothing, which, although ragged, was still recognisable. At last, more than seven months after her disappearance, Rose Gillespie had been found.

Thereafter, while Detective Stirling escorted the inconsolable Ned back to Stanley Street, police began to examine the new evidence. It seems that, prior to placement in the grave, the child had been wrapped in an old jacket, and then bundled into the jute sack. The sack bore the stamp of the 'Scotstoun Mill' which lay just outside the city, at Partick. Unfortunately for the police, these flour bags were ubiquitous, and almost impossible to trace. The jacket was similarly nondescript: a working man's brown reefer, with no label or other identifying mark. There was a large bloodstain on the chest area, which might have explained why the garment had been buried along with the body. A search of the pockets revealed nothing and, in the absence of any other information, constables were dispatched to question workers at the Scotstoun Mill. Although the discovery of the body was a major step forward in the case, detectives were disappointed not to have more leads.

Once Rose had been identified, the investigation was duly turned over to the Western Division. That evening, the box of evidence containing the jacket and sack was transferred to the police office at Cranston Street, where Detective Inspector Grant subjected it to his scrutiny. Finding nothing of interest, he went home for the night, instructing Detective Stirling to store the box in the evidence cupboard.

And there the matter might have rested, had Stirling simply followed Grant's instructions. However, the Detective Sub-Inspector was a methodical man, who was determined to bring to justice those responsible for Rose's death. This was his first glimpse of the new evidence, and so, upon his own initiative, he carried out a minute inspection of the box's contents. It was during his examination of the bloodstained jacket that he discovered a remarkable 'clue', which was to lead to a breakthrough in the case. Noting that the stitching inside one of the jacket pockets had come undone, he slid his hand through the hole in the lining, and – groping around between the two layers of fabric – discovered an item that had been overlooked, both by his superior officer, and by his Eastern Division colleagues: a thin scrap of paper, worn soft and sheeny by time.

This key piece of evidence turned out to be an 'Account of Wages' issued by the warehouse department of the Dennistoun Bakery, in the autumn of the previous year. The slip itemised, in copperplate script, the dates that the payee's employment had begun and ceased (he had lasted a mere three weeks in his job) and the total amount paid to him in pounds, shillings and pence. To Stirling's delight, inked in a box marked 'Employee' was a name: Hans Schlutterhose.

Even in Germany, Schlutterhose is an uncommon name. At that time, there was only one resident in all of Glasgow thus christened, and, unfortunately for him, he was already vaguely known to the police: Hans Schlutterhose of Camlachie.

Nobody had forgotten the stories of a tall, well-built foreigner, hurrying down West Princes Street, with a little girl in his arms. Schlutterhose broadly answered the physical description of this man, but he had been overlooked in the search for Rose, for several reasons. His misdemeanours had always been of a petty nature – drunken brawls and the like – usually committed outside public houses on the Gallowgate. Moreover, at the time of Rose's disappearance, the police had restricted their interviews to residents and labourers in the immediate vicinity of Vinegarhill. Schlutterhose's home – a single-end (or one-roomed apartment) in Coalhill Street – fell just outside this area.

On Saturday morning, Eastern and Western Divisions joined forces, and a deputation of detectives and constables surrounded the tenement in which Schlutterhose resided. The door to the first-floor single-end was broken down, and the German was apprehended, trying to escape through a back window. He was taken into custody and the police began to search his home.

It soon became apparent that the evidence against him was overwhelming. The wage slip that had been buried along with the body was damning enough, but a search of the tiny apartment revealed samples of Schlutterhose's handwriting, which seemed to resemble that of the ransom note. These samples also showed that he was in the habit of committing several characteristic errors, such as substituting 'gut' for 'good', 'note' for 'not', and so on, errors that were also consistent with the spelling in the ransom demand.

A pawn ticket, found on the mantel, was taken directly to the nearest broker's on the Gallowgate and presented at the counter. In return, the proprietor handed over a small pair of button boots, suitable for a little girl; later the same day, Ned identified these as having belonged to Rose. The proprietor of the shop informed the police that he had received the boots several months previously, from Schlutterhose's wife, Belle. When the dates in the shop's register were checked, it was discovered that she had pawned the boots in May, just a few days after Rose's disappearance. This suggested that Belle might have been involved in the abduction – if not the death – of the child. It also implied that Rose might have breathed her last very soon after she was taken.

A search of the back greens yielded, from almost directly below the window of Schlutterhose's home, a flat stone, stained with a dark red patch of what might have been either rust or blood. The stone had lain for a long time where it was found, for the grass underneath it had faded to yellow. It was thought that this stone might be a possible murder weapon.

Belle had not been at home that morning when the police raided the single-end, but a group of men now lay in wait for her return. Presently, she was spotted, towards noon, weaving her way up the street in a whiskified state. As several police officers approached her from various directions, Belle realised her plight, and was seen to fumble at her throat, and then drop something into the road, just before her arrest. A search of the gutter revealed that she had attempted to dispose of a mother-of-pearl necklace, which bore a strong resemblance to the one that Rose had been wearing at the time of her disappearance, right down to the child's name, engraved upon the silver setting, and Ned was soon to identify it as the pendant that he had given to his daughter the previous Christmas.

Schlutterhose and Belle remained taciturn whilst in police custody over the course of Saturday night and into the Sabbath. On Monday morning, at the Sheriff Court, they were examined, separately, and both refused to speak, at first, other than to confirm their identities. Belle steadfastly maintained that she had nothing to say to the charge. However, when the Sheriff impressed upon Hans that this hearing might constitute his sole opportunity to set out his position, and the Procurator Fiscal went on to inform him that the charges against him might ultimately include cold-blooded murder of an innocent child, Schlutterhose became most agitated, crying out: 'No murder! No murder!' He made a declaration, in which he confessed to having abducted Rose, claiming that she had subsequently died as the result of a tragic accident. According to him, the theft of Rose Gillespie had not been accomplished on his own initiative. Indeed, he would never have dreamed of committing such a crime (or so he said). No – he was a mere auxiliary, a paid lackey, acting upon orders, manipulated into unaccustomed wrongdoing – or, as his declaration put it, to grotesquely comic effect when read aloud, at the trial: 'I was just a prawn in this matter.'

He must have realised that the evidence against him and his wife was overwhelming, and had thus invented a story incriminating someone else, as instigator. And what a story it was! For, according to Schlutterhose, the impetus for the abduction had come directly from none other than myself, Miss Harriet Baxter, an English lady, and personal friend of the Gillespie family.

Why had this loathsome miscreant singled me out, in particular?

Why me? – the prisoner's eternal cry. Make no mistake: I have thought long and hard about why this might have been so. There were times, whilst incarcerated, when I contemplated the tenets of Buddhism, and the notion that I might be suffering punishment for some crime committed, unwittingly, in a previous life. At the time, I was unaware of any connection between the Schlutterhoses and myself and, according to Caskie, the police had been unable, thus far, to link us together, which, according to him, was only to our advantage. I thought that, perhaps, I may have come to their attention at the time of Gillespie's solo exhibition: they might have seen the sketch of me with Ned in *The Thistle*, or heard the silly rumours. Or perhaps I was simply an arbitrary choice on their part, since, in every other respect, they failed to demonstrate one whit of clear, sensible thinking, or good judgement.

Whatever the case, I was easily demonised, and the local newspapers of the day took great pleasure in calling attention to certain of my characteristics that were bound to appeal to the innate prejudices of their readers. Firstly, I was a woman. This may not seem a handicap, in this day and age, now that we have the franchise, but remember that these events took place almost fifty years ago, when the world was a very different place. Not only was I horribly female, but also, I was horribly unmarried; at thirty-six, too old to be of use to anyone, and although the newspapers referred to me as a 'spinster' this was no more than a euphemism for 'witch'. If you are of a certain age, you might even remember the jokes and cartoons at the time of the trial. Gentlemen were advised, in jest, not to read the newspaper of a morning, lest their gaze accidentally fall upon a sketch of my countenance, an image reputed to be so frightful that it would put any man 'right aff his porridge'.

Worse still than my sex and spinsterdom was my unfortunate nationality. With good reason, the Scots despise no race more than the English, and, beneath the façade of colonial co-operation, resentment simmers. It mattered not that my parents were Scottish by birth. I had been brought up down south; my accent was

English; I had what were deemed fancy, southern ways: going hither and thither, unaccompanied, sometimes without a hat – not to mention the cigarette smoking. My final failing was that I was well-to-do, or, comparatively so. Humble origins would have served me so much better, since no species peeves the Scotsman quite so much as an English spinster of independent means: this is a truth, to my mind, universally unacknowledged.

But forgive me; I digress. My point is this: that, in accusing me, Schlutterhose and his wife had selected the perfect scapegoat for their purposes.

My next appearance before the Sheriff took place on Wednesday, the 27th of November. By then, the press was full of stories about the discovery of Rose's body, the capture of the kidnappers, and my own arrest. As yet, Ned had not replied to the letter that I had sent him, and I could hardly bear to contemplate what poisonous rumours he might have heard about me.

For the short trip from the prison to the Sheriff Court, I was, once again, transported in the windowless wagon, this time accompanied by a young female turnkey. I had slept badly, and my hazy thoughts kept drifting to images that I found comforting, such as the studio at Merlinsfield. In my note to Agnes, I had asked her to leave the birdcage where I had placed it, on the table next to the window; I wished with every fibre of my being that I could be there, beside it. Perhaps I would be, soon, for I was hopeful that the Sheriff would, this time, grant Caskie's application for bail. I closed my eyes, and tried to remember how the birdcage felt beneath my fingers, the rough surface of the carvings, and the smooth bamboo slats.

Of a sudden, I heard a din of voices and my eyes snapped open. The horses slowed down and, without warning, the wooden sides of the wagon began to boom and rattle, as dozens of unseen hands banged furiously upon them. The turnkey looked at me, in alarm, as the vehicle came to an abrupt standstill. I heard angry shouts, and more banging. Then, we lurched forwards for another minute or so, before finally coming to a halt. After a brief pause, the back door flew open to reveal a sea of angry faces: about a hundred people had gathered in the street in front of the Sheriff Court. A nervous constable guided us out, while his colleague tried to fend off the rabble. As we stepped onto the pavement, I was met with a hail of rotten eggs, several of which shattered upon my chest and shoulders. The crowd surged forwards, falling over each other, in an attempt to push closer. The policemen were soon overwhelmed. Someone managed to grab my collar, and a fist smashed into my face. The next few seconds are a blur but, somehow, the young warder was able to drag me away, and bundle me, through a side entrance, into the building.

My nose was pouring with blood and, by the time that we reached the basement, I had ruined my handkerchief in an attempt to staunch the flow. Caskie was already in the cell, clutching another Petition in his hand. I had never seen him look quite so grim. Without a word, he handed me the page, and my legs almost buckled when I saw what was written upon it: a second charge, of murder, had now been added to the original one of plagium.

Caskie shook his head.

'This is a bad business – a bad business, Miss Baxter. I havenae a notion what evidence they've got against you on a murder charge, but up there today I'd advise you to say nothing at all, other than to vehemently deny these charges.'

So stunned was I, that I could do little other than nod my head. As it transpired, the proceedings were delayed. We waited, and waited. As the minutes ticked by, and I had still not been called, Caskie looked ever more distracted. I had come to realise that his vague demeanour masked a nature that was exceedingly cautious, almost to the point of pessimism. He tried to hide his anxiety from me, but I noticed that the more agitated he became, the more he hunched his shoulders. Presently, a rumour began to circulate. It was said that the crowd in the street had continued to cause trouble, and even the Sheriff-Substitute himself had been held up outside. Eventually, half an hour late, Caskie was summoned. Then, the constables escorted us upstairs, into the Sheriff's chamber. As I entered, McPhail, the Fiscal, gazed at me, coldly. Mr Spence, the Sheriff-Substitute, was reading a pile of papers that were stacked in front of him. Caskie caught my eye and tapped his finger against his lips, a gesture that might be interpreted as thoughtful, but I knew that he was reminding me to say nothing. And so, when the Fiscal began to question me, I held my tongue.

McPhail soon grew frustrated.

'Is that it?' he demanded. 'Are you going to say nothing at all?'

To which I replied: 'I deny these charges.' But my voice sounded so timid that I had to clear my throat, and repeat: 'I vehemently deny these charges.'

Sheriff-Substitute Spence glanced up and then peered at me, startled.

'In Heaven's name!' he cried. 'What the – ?'

Unfortunately, my nose had commenced to bleed once more. Great crimson drops fell upon my frock, and splashed the parquet floor. Spence appealed to his Clerk and the turnkey.

'Quick – give her something!'

The Clerk gave me a handkerchief, and I did my best to wipe my face and bodice. Meanwhile, His Lordship was questioning my escorts.

'Was this done by these folk outside?' When one of the constables replied in the affirmative, the Sheriff-Substitute shook his head, and then frowned down at the red stains on his parquet, muttering: 'Blood all over the place!'

Alas, 'blood all over the place', was perhaps my undoing, that day, for – with no further ado – Mr Spence set aside his pen and announced that bail was denied. My solicitor was already on his feet, but Spence waved aside his objections.

'Save your breath to cool your porridge, Mr Caskie. You well know that there's no bail on a charge of murder, and your client, sir, looks as though she's gone six rounds with the Boston Strong Boy. We're not about to set her free, only to have her strung up from the nearest lamp-post. Miss Baxter, you are committed for trial, until liberated in due course of law.'

The following day, I received another visit from Caskie. This time, his demeanour was as gloomy as a wet Sunday afternoon. Apparently, he had now seen the warrant that the police had used to examine my bank's records, and the daybook or ledger that they had seized. Thus far, he had been unable to track down the builder's receipts that I had told him about, and he was beginning to fear that this particular argument would prove to be troublesome.

'It's a bad coincidence about these dates,' he said. 'Without the receipts . . .'

'I shall write to Agnes again and ask her to look for them, more thoroughly.'

In the meantime, I ventured to ask him about another matter that had recently been on my mind.

'Surely all these claims that I paid this man money on various dates, et cetera, are of no consequence? There can be no case against me, for the simple reason that I have – or had – no motive. Why would I want to harm Rose, or her family? The very idea is ridiculous. We all doted on her, and I was forever bringing her presents.'

'Yes, so I'm told.'

'Whereas Schlutterhose and his wife presumably *did* have a motive. For example, if they had seen something in the press about Ned's exhibition, might they not have thought – being ignorant, perhaps, of such matters – that an artist who features in the newspaper must necessarily be a wealthy man? And what better way to get his money than to kidnap his child? And why should I send a ransom demand? Financially speaking, I'm much better off than the Gillespies. The police must know that, by now. Is it not patently obvious to them that I don't have a single speck of motive – whereas this man and his wife most certainly do?'

'The trouble is', said Caskie, 'the judicial system of this country doesnae give two hoots about motive. The police and the Fiscal – they're not really interested in "why", Miss Baxter. "Why" is of little consequence to them. What they really want to know is "who".'

I sighed, in exasperation.

'On another note,' Caskie went on: 'I've been investigating an accident on St George's Road, something that Schlutterhose claims happened just after he took the child. Grant and the Fiscal want to disbelieve his story – or at least they want to disbelieve elements of it – but I'm not so sure, and I've yet to speak to any witness. We need to find out exactly what happened that afternoon. That's all for today, except   ' He grimaced 'I'm sorry, but at the risk of upsetting you further, I ought to mention, before I leave, that they're to bury Rose, this afternoon.'

We had been expecting this news for some time but, none the less, I felt quite giddy, of a sudden. My throat was dry and tight.

'You might want to avoid the newspaper for a while,' said Caskie. 'In case one finds its way into your cell. Reading about the funeral might be – painful.'

As it happened, the warders sometimes gave Cullen their discarded newspapers and, sure enough, a few days later, she acquired a copy of Friday's *Glasgow Herald*. She stowed it, out of sight, under her bed, probably to spare my feelings. At first, I followed Caskie's advice, but in the end, my curiosity got the better of me, and I did look at the paper.

'*Gillespie Girl Funeral*' dominated the local news: almost a quarter of a page had been dedicated to the story. A sub-heading quoted a line from the song: '*Ring the bell softly, there's crape on the door*' and, after a brief introduction, the article stated that there could be no sight more melancholy than a tiny white coffin in the arms of a grieving father. Apparently, Ned himself had carried the little casket of remains from the house to the hearse, and from hearse to the grave. It cannot have weighed very much. The article described the artist's clothing: a dark suit, ivory gloves, and a white crape armband. Ned tended to reject conventions of dress and, as far as I was aware, he owned no white gloves but, perhaps, in this instance, he had not had the strength to stand up to Elspeth's demands. Of course, it was even possible that, in his grief, these outward signs of inward sorrow may have seemed important to him, as the last token of respect and affection that he could pay to his daughter.

The child was buried at Lambhill Cemetery. Apart from the inscriptions, and a simple carving of a rose, her headstone was unadorned. At the graveside, her mother, Mrs Annie Gillespie, laid a posy of pale hothouse flowers upon the casket. Then, apparently, she and her husband held hands as the coffin was lowered into the earth. Mrs Elspeth Gillespie, the child's grandmother, was inconsolable, and had to be comforted by her friends, many of whom attended the service. It was noted that Sibyl, the older sister of the deceased child, was not in attendance, since she was currently 'recovering in the asylum' after being 'injured in a fire'. According to a source close to the family, Sibyl had been informed of Rose's death, and was spending much of her time in prayer, or at the piano, playing hymns, in honour of her dead sibling.

The child's mother remained dry-eyed until after the interment, when she broke down in tears. Mr Gillespie had to support his wife as they returned to the mourning carriages and she, in turn, helped him when he stumbled on the path and almost fell. The article said that they gave every appearance of being a devoted young couple who were supporting each other in the aftermath of a terrible tragedy.

Caskie was right: reading the newspaper profoundly upset me. That night, as I lay awake, in sheer misery, I was overwhelmed by a sense of profound isolation. Perhaps because of what I had read in the paper, I found myself lost in the memory of another funeral, that of my mother, which had taken place many years previously. Poor mother had always suffered with her health and eventually died of what was judged, by her symptoms, to be botulism, after having eaten some asparagus that we had preserved, the previous year. I was just fourteen years of age at the time, and beside myself with grief. On the morning of the funeral, I felt utterly alone in the world. Aunt Miriam, who was my mother's unmarried sister, must have been as upset as I was, but she tried to conceal her own grief, for my sake. She gave me some sal volatile just before we got into the carriage, with the result that I felt strangely euphoric and highly strung on the journey to the cemetery.

My mother and Ramsay had been separated for several years, by then, and he had gone to live in Scotland. Aunt Miriam had written to him with news of his wife's death, inviting him to the funeral, but, typically, had received no reply. I remember, above all, as we crept slowly up Swain's Lane in the carriage, the nervous anticipation of wondering whether my stepfather would put in an appearance, and my overwhelming relief when I glimpsed him, standing amongst a line of other black-clad people, inside the cemetery gate.

Ramsay removed his high hat when he saw me, and held it between us as he squeezed my shoulder and murmured condolences. I noticed a few more flecks of grey at his temples, the yellowish eyes, the waxy pallor of his skin. Then, while Aunt Miriam spoke quietly to him, he became very absorbed in replacing the topper on his head, turning it this way and that, altering its angle, to find the most comfortable position. Upon reflection, I believe that he did not care about the hat; he simply wanted some occupation for his hands.

At the graveside, I found a place next to him. The cuffs of our coats brushed against each other, my left against his right. For a moment, I thought that he might take my hand, but he did not and, in my naivety, I assumed that such a thing would have been bad form at a funeral. The gleaming wooden casket transfixed me: the ropes seemed too thin to support its weight, and then there was the impossible thought that a body – my mother's body – was nailed up inside. There had been no rain for days, and the pile of earth before us was powdery, as dry as dust. Everything felt very precarious. As they began to lower the coffin, the ground seemed to shift beneath my feet, and the scent of early lilac was so piercing, that I thought I might faint and topple into the grave.

I had imagined, now that my mother was dead, that Ramsay would take me to live with him in Scotland, since I was too young to reside alone. It was a surprise and disappointment, therefore, after the funeral, when he informed me that he had made arrangements for me to remain, in London, with my aunt. He did drive me back to Eaton Square, later that day, in his carriage, but he had no time to come into the house, because of an appointment in St James's. A few days later, my belongings were moved across town, to the rather more humble circumstances of my aunt's home. My stepfather had a few relatives in the south and, from time to time, I used to be invited to family gatherings, whenever I was remembered, but my connection to the Dalrymple clan was tentative: I was related only by marriage – moreover, by a marriage that had dissolved – and, following my mother's death, the invitations came less frequently. Ramsay did not always make the effort to attend these events and so, until my arrival in Scotland in '88, I had seen him on only three further occasions: once at a christening, once at a wedding, and once at a funeral: an all-encompassing triumvirate of ceremonies.

I had always thought that I would never feel so desolate as I did, after my mother's funeral, when I learned that Ramsay had declined to take me to live with him in Scotland. However, in the days that followed Rose's burial, my spirits sank extremely low, and I will admit that I was as unhappy, then, as I had ever been.

None the less, I would like to make something clear, in this document. At the time, due to my circumstances, I had no means of responding to what was printed in the papers, and thus various inaccurate stories proliferated and were never contradicted. Although it was reported in the press that I attempted to take my own life shortly after Rose's funeral, this was not, in fact, the case. While it is true that I did sustain a slight injury that week, there was a simple enough explanation for the bruises on my throat, which, presumably, were the cause of all the rumours. It so happened that, one afternoon, as the light was fading, Mrs Fee had appeared at the door hatch, bearing a letter. I jumped up and, in my haste to cross the cell, my foot became entangled in a blanket that was trailing on the ground. I tripped so swiftly that I had no time to put out my hands to save myself. In falling, the upper part of my body landed on a three-legged stool. My throat took the worst of it, striking the edge of the seat, which resulted in severe bruising to my larynx. A straightforward, if painful, accident – but not, by any means, the attempt at self-strangulation, or hanging, that was widely reported at the time.

I suppose that I should also say something about the anonymous correspondence that began to be published in *The North British Daily Mail* at about this time. It caused quite a stir and, if you are of a certain age, and resided in Glasgow during that winter, you must certainly remember those letters, or perhaps your parents told you about them, in later years. The first letter arrived at the offices of the *Mail* in early December and was published the following day. Of course, the sender provided no address, but, apparently, the squared circle postmark on the envelope indicated that it had originated in Venice, Italy. As far as it was possible to tell, the spelling and grammar were those of a native English speaker. The writer avoided giving his name, and had signed himself, simply: 'Yours Truly'. This Yours Truly purported to be a friend of Kenneth Gillespie, Ned's brother, who – you may recall – had disappeared, in the autumn of the previous year.

I first learned about this letter from my solicitor, who came to see me on the day after its publication. He assured me that it was probably the work of some poor devil who was desperate for attention. According to him, this sort of thing happened quite often, in cases that had attracted a good deal of publicity. All sorts of crackpots and loons crawl out of the woodwork with unlikely claims. While any sensible editor would have filed such dubious correspondence in the waste paper basket, Mr Ross of the *Mail* had decided to share the ramblings of Yours Truly with his readers. When I expressed surprise that the letter had come all the way from Italy, Caskie reminded me that British residents abroad often have newspapers sent from home; it was even possible that the Italian press (a more scholarly and sober breed than their British counterparts) might have mentioned the forthcoming court case.

Perhaps this Yours Truly had grown bored of living so far from home, in a waterlogged, crumbling city that forever teems with tourists. I can just imagine him, pacing the floor of his lodgings, staring at the damp stains on the stucco walls, or listening to the canal lapping at the sill. Even had this man made friends in Venice, the experience of living in a foreign city can still be lonely, and one has to be careful not to become a nuisance by pestering recent acquaintances with too many social calls. No doubt, he filled his solitary hours with visits to churches and galleries, the Piazza San Marco, the Ca d'Oro, and so on, until – perhaps in a newspaper sent from home – he read about the Gillespie case, and decided to give some meaning to his life, by creating a bit of mayhem.

At any rate, that was the mental picture that I formed of Yours Truly.

I no longer possess any copies of the *Mail* (and, for some reason, Sarah was unable to find any in the library). However, I can recall, more or less, the content of that first letter. Yours Truly began with the claim that he was writing on behalf of Kenneth Gillespie, late of Woodside, Glasgow, brother of the artist, Ned, and uncle to Rose Gillespie, the missing child whose body had only recently been discovered. Apparently, Kenneth would have loved to return to Scotland, to help his family in their time of need, but, for reasons that remained unspecified, this was impossible – both now, and for the foreseeable future.

The letter went on to say that Kenneth had confided in Yours Truly that he was well acquainted with the lady currently being held in connection with the disappearance of his niece. He and Harriet Baxter had become friends (the letter claimed) in the summer of the International Exhibition, a friendship that had developed because of a mutual enjoyment of the theatre. Apparently, Miss Baxter had often given the young man her tickets, if she found herself unable to attend a particular performance. In the autumn, when Kenneth had expressed unhappiness at certain aspects of his situation in Glasgow, the lady – who was financially independent – had encouraged him to leave the city and set up a new life for himself in Venice. Moreover, she had generously paid for his journey, and provided expenses sufficient to cover his first few months abroad. Although, to begin with, Kenneth had been of the opinion that this intervention was only a kindness on the part of Miss Baxter, he had since had time to reflect, and – particularly following recent events – was now beginning to question her motives in assisting him to leave his home town. However, the letter failed to specify what he now considered these mysterious motives to be.

As far as I can remember, Yours Truly concluded with various assurances to the Gillespie family that Kenneth was in good health, along with pleas that they would understand and forgive the young man's inability to return home.

Despite various rumours that Kenneth himself might have been directly involved – that he might have written or, at least, dictated the letter – I suspect that most of its contents could simply have been pieced together from what had appeared in the papers. The part about the theatre was inventive, certainly, and a clever guess: perhaps, it did so happen, once or twice, that I had passed on Princess's tickets to Kenneth, but no more than that. As for the rest, it was complete tosh, and all the more damaging for being so devilishly ambiguous. When I expressed concern, Caskie advised me that the prosecution could not and would not use anonymous correspondence in arguing their case. 'Any fool might have sent it,' he told me. 'It shouldnae have been published at all.'

'Do you think, by the time of the trial, it will have been forgotten?'

His mouth turned down at the corners. 'Well, we can but hope,' he replied.

My other concern, of course, was for the Gillespies. In all likelihood, they would see the *Mail*, for it was Elspeth's favourite journal and she took it daily. Indeed, later that afternoon, there was an envelope from Ned amongst the post that was pushed through our hatch. This was the first time that I had heard from him since he had visited the prison with Annie and his mother. As soon as I recognised his handwriting, my heart skipped a beat. I could have wished for some privacy in which to read what he had written, but Cullen and Mulgrew were both present, engaged at a game of Piquet (or 'Picket', as they called it), the door was locked, and it was impossible to predict when I might next have a moment alone. Thus, I retired to my corner of the cell, sat on my bed, and opened the envelope. The letter is still in my possession and I will transcribe it here, just as it was written:

Dear Harriet,

What a strange and terrible time this is. I don't know what to think. I don't know what to write. No sooner have we begun to recover from one dreadful blow than another is delivered. We've been hearing such unbelievable things. I can't bear to imagine they might be true. Annie keeps going over the time since we met you, almost two years ago now. She pores over every incident and every visit, every wee remark. So far she can't really fault you but seems determined to find proof you have meant us and our children harm all along. She and my mother are continually at odds on this point. Mother will never forget you saved her life that day in Buchanan Street. She keeps throwing this and all your other good deeds at Annie's feet, and insists you are what you seem, an Angel of Mercy, or at least a well-meaning and kind person at heart.

Harriet, this questionable letter in the Mail has caused yet further confusion. I'm to be shown it later this week to look at the handwriting and see if it could have been written by my brother. Annie seems convinced it will be him. She told me, today, the full story of what you and she know about Kenneth. I need hardly say how shocked I am. However, this is one point where Annie can't fault you. Even

[344]

she admits your actions last summer in protecting him were nothing short of miraculous. No doubt you saved us all from a good deal of bother and Kenneth from something far worse. I just wish somebody had told me at the time. Of course, mother knows nothing of this. We intend to keep it that way for it would kill her if she found out. Thank you for guarding the information so carefully, all this time.

At any rate, we're advised to stop sending you letters so this will be my first and last. Mother won't be writing any more either. She says to tell you she would keep up correspondence with you if it weren't for these pestiferous lawyers. They want me to request that you please cease writing to us as well. Sorry about this but it seems we have no choice. I hope you keep in good health until the trial, at which point we will see what we will see.

After much discussion, we have resolved to bring Sibyl home. We need to be a family again and I'm convinced we can care for her here no matter how wrong in the mind she is. The doctors are protesting it's too soon and they mean well, but we've stopped paying our bill, so no doubt that will put an end to their objections. In fact, we're going to collect her this afternoon since we don't want them putting her in the paupers' wing.

Harriet, my mother just wants me to let you know she is praying for you. Also Mabel and Walter are on their way back to Glasgow, due in a week or two.

As for me, I'd like to think that we were right to trust you, and allow you into our home, as our friend. I want to believe you've done no wrong. I don't like to think of you being locked up in that dreadful place. You make a good show of appearing to be capable and robust, but those of us that know you can tell that, underneath all the polish, there are glimpses of someone sensitive, even fragile. In my mind, Harriet, be assured you have the benefit of the doubt unless it's proven otherwise. I can only hope Annie's worst fears are mistaken, and that the true culprits are found guilty (as it seems they must be, given what we've heard about the evidence against them).

Please God you are able to affirm our faith in you, as our friend, that you'll clear your name and be allowed to walk free.

Yours, in great hope and with sympathy for your situation,
Ned

Having read this letter, I replaced it in the envelope. Then I crawled beneath the blankets and lay there, trying to take in the implications of Ned's words. Did this mean that, from now on, the turnkeys would destroy any letters that I wrote to the family? The notion of being unable to contact the Gillespies was terrifying, for as long as I could keep writing to them it seemed to me that I had a chance to remain in their hearts. The trial would not take place for a few months; thus, week upon week was destined to pass without any contact at all between us. The bleak reality of this was just beginning to dawn on me when the door opened, and Mrs Fee appeared, with the words: 'Baxter – somebody to see you.'

It was my solicitor. He was not in the habit of coming to see me two days in a row. Moreover, his shoulders were up, his rather wispy eyebrows down.

'What's the matter, Mr Caskie?'

He sucked his teeth, and stared at me, unsmilingly, for a moment.

'I've just been speaking to the Detective Inspector. You're aware they've been trying to find some connection between yourself and Schlutterhose?'

I nodded.

'Well, they've finally found something – something the German and his wife have been trying to hide. It probably explains a few things, and I can see how, on your part, it's perfectly innocent – but it may hinder us more than it'll help us.'

'What on earth is it?'

'You won't know this, but Belle goes by her married name – has done for several years. But, before she and the German were wed, naturally enough, she used her maiden name, which was Smith.'

I looked at him, expectantly. 'Yes?'

'Does that name mean something to you?'

I thought for a moment, and then shook my head. 'I suppose I've met several Smiths in my time. It's a very common name.'

'Aye, indeed, and that's probably why it's taken this long for the police to make the connection. What about Christina Smith?'

'Christina? The maid? She worked for Ned, and Annie. I remember her, vaguely. They dismissed her, in the end. A very pretty girl, but I understand that she was a slightly dissipated character.'

'Aye,' said Caskie. 'As it turns out, Christina has a sister, and that sister is Belle Schlutterhose. In fact, they are half-sisters, but that doesn't matter: they have the same father.' I gazed at him, unable to absorb the implications of his words. He continued: 'That's why Schlutterhose has been so evasive and unconvincing about how he knew of your existence – and probably why Belle has said so little. It seems likely they were protecting her sister, to prevent her being arrested.'

He gazed at me, dolefully.

'But, Mr Caskie, this is good news, is it not? Surely this must be how they fixed on me as their victim: they'd heard about me from Christina. She and I met many times, when I was visiting the Gillespies.'

Caskie scratched fractiously at his wrist. 'Would that it were that simple.'

'What d'you mean?'

'Well, having finally worked out that the two women are related, the police apprehended Christina yesterday, but they've released her again, this morning, without charge. She was very talkative, apparently, but there's not much they can charge her with – all she did – all she says she did – was set up a meeting between yourself, and her sister and brother-in-law. Inspector Grant is very pleased with himself. He says she'll be much more useful as a witness than as an accused.'

'In what respect, I wonder?'

Caskie stared at the floor for a moment before answering. 'She seems to know more about you than either Schlutterhose or his wife – which would make sense, I suppose. Presumably, you had some dealings with her when you called upon the Gillespies?'

'Only the normal sort of dealings that one has with a maid, no more than that. I may have bumped into her, once or twice, in the neighbourhood.'

'Aye,' said Caskie. 'Well, Grant says she's very convincing. She claims you befriended her, after she was dismissed from the Gillespie household. She says you and she became quite intimate.'

'Good gracious!'

'She says that once you hatched the notion to kidnap Rose, you asked her if she knew anybody who'd be willing to carry it out. Knowing her sister and brother-in-law needed money, she set up a meeting between them and yourself.'

'And she expects people to believe this claptrap?'

'It would appear so. Moreover, she claims to know – mind you, remember all these are only her claims – but she claims to know exactly why you wanted to have Rose Gillespie abducted.'

At this, I almost laughed. 'Really? What on earth does she say?'

Caskie held my gaze. 'Lamentably, Grant is playing games for the moment, dangling the carrot without telling me exactly what her story is. But I'm beginning to think that if they do put her on the stand, Miss Baxter, it could make life very difficult for us. We shall have to secure a very canny advocate.'

'Forgive me for saying so, Mr Caskie, but one would have hoped that such was your intention from the outset.'

In need of air, I rose to my feet and moved towards the window. Of a sudden, the room pitched and tilted. I must have stood up too quickly. The blood had rushed to my head, and I was obliged to drop to my knees, and lean forwards, like a Moslem at prayer, in order to prevent myself from fainting.

18

So intense was the excitement and attention aroused by the case, that it was decided to hold the trial in the High Court of Justiciary, in Edinburgh. Ever since my arrest, the press had continued to pounce on every scrap of gossip; no insinuation – never mind how sordid or unlikely – was beneath them. It had been hinted, variously (and ludicrously), that I, Harriet Baxter, was the female mastermind of an international White Slave operation; that Schlutterhose was not only my minion, but also my paramour; that Rose had been strangled whilst attempting to escape our clutches; and that her corpse had been mutilated and inscribed with Satanic symbols. It is incredible what the newspapers are able to get away with printing.

The trial date was set for Thursday, the 6th of March, 1890. It was decided that I should be moved from Glasgow to Edinburgh at the beginning of the week, early in the morning, and by train, after being taken to the railway station in an ordinary cab. These precautions were designed to avoid attracting any attention, and they did prove successful, in that there was no baying mob awaiting us outside the gates of Duke Street when we emerged on that freezing cold Monday morning.

Three guards accompanied me: Mrs Fee, and two of her male colleagues. Each of them was dressed in everyday clothes, rather than uniform, and so we passed across the concourse of the railway station, anonymously, like four companions, off on an outing to 'Auld Reekie'. The train was already waiting at the platform, and a front carriage had been reserved for our sole use. I had thought that Belle and I might be transported together, but presumably the authorities did not trust that we would be able to refrain from tearing out each other's hair, and so, once again, I was sequestered from my 'co-accused'. She and her husband were to be moved to the Calton-hill gaol later in the week. No doubt, I would see them at the trial, although this would not be my first encounter with them, for I had initially laid eyes upon the pair back in February, on the day of the First Diet. By then, having spent many idle hours in my cell, I had built up a grotesque picture of them in my mind, an image that had become exaggerated, until I viewed Schlutterhose and Belle as barely human. I fully expected them to be filthy creatures, yellow of fang and slack of jaw, perhaps even deformed. It was a surprise, therefore, to see how unremarkable they were, that day, at the Sheriff Court in Glasgow. When I was brought into the chamber, the kidnappers were already in the dock. How dreadfully ordinary they seemed: Belle turned out to be a scrawny creature, pretty, but less prepossessing than her sister, with thinner lips and a harder face, and her clothes were ill-made but clean. Schlutterhose had a square jaw and deep-set eyes. He was dishevelled and bewhiskered, and his frame was lumbering and large. Perhaps it was my imagination, but I thought that there was something of the Frankenstein's creature about him.

Since the First Diet is simply a hearing to confirm that all parties are ready to proceed, the session, that day, took no more than ten minutes. Nothing of note transpired until, just as we were about to be led away, Belle spat in my face, unprovoked, and then let fly with some colourful language, while Schlutterhose drew his hand across his throat, and made various other threatening gestures at me. Mercifully, the guards intervened, and whisked the couple away.

This vitriol, from two complete strangers, took me by surprise. Presumably, their outburst had been some sort of display for the benefit of Sheriff Spence, but if that had been their intention, they failed to impress him, for he merely shook his head as he gathered up his papers: no doubt, he was inured to such goings-on. In my experience, people are able to maintain a façade for only a limited amount of time. No doubt, Spence knew as well as I did that the couple's veneer of respectability had cracked, that afternoon; something of their true nature had been glimpsed. I wondered how the kidnappers would present themselves, later in the week, at the High Court in Edinburgh, before the jury, press and public, and Lord Kinbervie, the presiding judge.

Our train journey was remarkable only for the freezing temperature in the compartment. The turnkeys were ever present, but they talked quietly amongst themselves, leaving me alone with my troubled thoughts. We arrived in Edinburgh just after noon, and took a short cab ride up Waterloo Place to Regent Road. From the distance, at least, the Calton-hill buildings looked like palaces. I doubt that there has ever been another prison located in such spectacular surroundings: it was, indeed, as though I had arrived in my very own personal Athens, complete with Parthenon. Alas – if I may be forgiven an understatement – the interior of the gaol did not *quite* live up to these first impressions. My cell was an incomparably damp and draughty hole. I was kept there, alone, and saw neither hide nor hair of any other prisoner. However, I was always grateful for small blessings. There was some comfort to be had in the sound of the trains, down below, as they passed in and out of Waverley Station at all times of the day and night, and my old view of the blackened tenements beyond Duke Street's perimeter wall was now replaced with a stunning panorama of Salisbury Crags and Arthur's Seat. In order to see these sights, I was obliged to crane my neck and peer through a tiny grate. None the less, it was a dramatic vista, and the grand scale of this austere landscape seemed, somehow, appropriate for the occasion.

On Wednesday morning, I was told that Caskie had arrived, and wished to see me. He had brought with him Mr Muirhead Mac-Donald, the up-and-coming advocate whom he had selected to act on my behalf. In truth, I would have preferred to be represented by the Dean of Faculty but, regrettably, he was unavailable, at the time. I must admit that my spirits sank when I first set eyes upon the youthful MacDonald: at twenty-eight years of age, he seemed hardly old enough to lead the defence in such a high-profile case. He was short in stature, with no neck to speak of; his features were small and squashed, his cheeks ruddy, and he had prominent ears that were set low and far forward on his head. The overall impression was gnomic, to say the least. Caskie had praised him, albeit in typical, muted fashion: apparently Muir-head was uppermost amongst the new young lawyers, possessed of a keen intelligence and cheerful outlook that would stand us in good stead. Yet, to my eyes, he seemed more like a callow legal clerk, and I wondered whether he had enough experience to get the better of the Crown, especially since the team for the prosecution was to be led by James Aitchison: a hawk-like Advocate Depute, notorious across the land for his showy style. I had seen his precise, dramatic gestures imitated a number of times, by Cullen, and a few of the more theatrically inclined inmates of Duke Street. Prison gossip would suggest that Aitchison was not averse to dirty tricks in the courtroom, and it was said that he would use all sorts of ploys to manipulate the jury.

'Are you familiar with Aitchison, Mr MacDonald?' I enquired. 'Have you faced him before?'

'Not as yet, Miss Baxter,' said the advocate. His voice was surprisingly rich and mellifluous. 'But I've studied him many times. Have no fear, Miss Baxter, I have the measure of the man.' And he rubbed his hands together, as though anticipating a jolly, athletic tussle.

'Would that it were only Aitchison that need concern us,' said Caskie. 'Dinnae forget your man Pringle.'

Schlutterhose, Belle and I were the collective 'accused', but the couple were to have their own separate representation, in the form of Mr Charles Pringle, the court-appointed Poor's Roll advocate. He and my lawyers would not be working together: quite the contrary. Caskie had warned me that – given the weight of evidence against the two kidnappers – Pringle could hardly hope to save them from conviction. Thus, his only option was to demonise me, with the intention of making his clients seem like innocent dupes; he would try to evoke sympathy for them in the hope that the jury would recommend leniency in their sentencing, if they were convicted.

'Pringle is bound to be a thorn in our side,' he reiterated to me. 'I guarantee he'll portray his clients as lackeys in your pay – we'll hear that they were mere chimpanzees, turning somersaults at your whim.'

'Yes, indeed,' agreed MacDonald. 'But, of course, fortune is smiling upon us, because of the indictment.'

'In what respect?' I asked.

'Ah well, Miss Baxter, your name appears last upon the written indictment. Schlutterhose is named first, then his wife, then you. So that means that once Aitchison has led his witnesses for the prosecution, Pringle will cross-examine first, and then I'll take the floor, after him.'

'I'm not sure I quite understand your point, Mr MacDonald.'

'You see, my cross-examination of the witnesses will come last; that being the case, I'll be able to negate any damning suggestions put forward by Pringle.'

'All being well,' added Caskie.

His junior colleague gave a laugh and slapped his hands upon his thighs. 'But indubitably, sir!'

After so many weeks of my solicitor's cautious pessimism, the advocate was like a breath of air. Indeed, he even carried with him a refreshing scent, like that of new-washed linens. By contrast, Caskie now appeared to be relishing the role of wet blanket. I ventured to enquire about another issue that I found troubling.

'Mr MacDonald, I gather that the usual day to begin a trial like ours is a Monday, and I wonder why a Thursday has been chosen, in our case.'

The advocate gave a quiet shrug of his shoulders. 'It makes no difference.'

'The Clerk of Court is adamant we're to finish on Saturday,' said Caskie. 'That gives us only three days into which to compress our case.'

MacDonald smiled. 'A reasonable concern, sir. But three days is ample.'

Of course, I was glad to hear that he envisaged no problems, but I still feared that beginning so late in the week might count against us. Just three days to prove my innocence – during at least half of which the prosecution would be at the helm! It scarcely seemed possible.

I also had misgivings about some of the prosecution witnesses that might be called. Back in early February, when I had first seen the list of witnesses for the Crown, there were one or two names that I had recognised as persons who might hold slight grudges against me.

'Not to worry, Miss Baxter,' the advocate reassured me. 'Our character witnesses will, of course, demonstrate that you are a kind, generous and caring person. There'll be no surprises from the prosecution, since Mr Caskie here has been good enough to make sure that all their witnesses have been "precognosed" – which, as you'll know by now, simply means "interviewed" in fancy lawyer's parlance.'

'Parlance that has stood the test of time, for centuries,' said Caskie, quietly, with a glance at his old Geneva watch.

MacDonald looked at him for a moment, and then asked: 'Do you think, sir, that we need concern ourselves about these anonymous letters in the paper?'

Caskie made a sour face. 'They won't be mentioned at the trial, of course, but there's no question that they'll be in the minds of the jury.'

This response gave me little comfort. After the first letter from 'Yours Truly' had appeared in *The North British Daily Mail*, two further pieces of correspondence had been published in the same journal. Although the author continued to remain anonymous, he clearly wished to mislead the police and public into thinking that he was, in fact, none other than Ned's brother, and that he

[354]

possessed information that might throw light upon our case. A detective had been despatched to Italy in order to locate him, and persuade him to return and testify. However, after several weeks in Venice and its environs, the detective returned to Scotland, unaccompanied. Kenneth could not be found, and since, as a matter of law, the trial had to be concluded by a certain date, the Crown was obliged to prosecute the case without him.

A third letter had been published in the last week of February. It reiterated the vague allegations of the other correspondence. Alas, the whole episode had done naught but cast a vague shadow over my character.

'And the Gillespie girl, sir?' MacDonald asked Caskie. 'I'm keen to know your opinion – do you think they'll put her on the stand?'

He meant poor Sibyl, of course, whose name had also appeared on the list of witnesses for the prosecution. It seemed that Ned and Annie had somehow managed to keep the child at home since December and, since she was no longer officially a patient at the asylum, and therefore not classified as being mentally incompetent, she could be called upon to testify. Normally, she would have been a key witness, given that she had been present in the gardens only moments before her sister disappeared, and had (as seemed likely) spoken to the kidnapper's female accomplice. However, I was given to understand that her behaviour was still unpredictable, and thus she would be called upon to give evidence only as a last resort. Naturally, my fear was for her well-being, in that taking the stand might prove too much for her.

'They might call her,' said Caskie, in response to MacDonald. 'That's exactly the kind of dramatic japes to expect from Aitchison. It's a worry, right enough, as she's volatile. But my real concern, as you're aware, sir, is Belle's sister.'

We had known for some time that Christina Smith had been telling the Procurator Fiscal all sorts of 'baloney', as our colonial cousins would now put it, primarily – and crucially, for the prosecution – that she had set up a meeting between myself and the kidnappers.

'Aitchison's case hinges, more or less, on that one statement from her,' said MacDonald. 'That's his masterstroke. And our best hope is to counter her allegations by demonstrating that she's not to be trusted. We know she was dismissed by the Gillespies. And one of the downstairs neighbours is more than happy to confirm that she saw Christina emerging, several times, from public houses in Woodside, while the girl was meant to be taking her turn at the wash-house.' He smiled at me, reassuringly. 'The jury won't approve of that, Miss Baxter, and we can call the girl's character into doubt.'

'Or so we hope,' added Caskie.

Christina Smith's allegation that she had introduced me to her sister and that German was absurd – which you may also have concluded, if you are familiar with Mr Kemp's scribblings on the subject. Of course, very little of his recent essay is true: for one thing, I hardly knew Christina. We were, by no means, friendly, and I was certainly not as intimate with her as Kemp would like to imply. I suppose that Miss Smith must now be in her seventies – younger than myself, though still advanced in years – and I can only imagine that the poor dear has lost her mind in her dotage: there can be no other explanation for the balderdash that she appears to have confided in Kemp when he visited her last summer, in Liverpool (where, it seems, she has resided for many years). At any rate, Mr Kemp ought to be ashamed of himself: bothering a doting old woman, and setting down her addled ramblings in a book, as though they were facts.

Early on Thursday morning, I was taken from my Calton-hill cell to a courtyard at the back of the gaol. There stood yet another coffin on wheels (although, this being Edinburgh, the vehicle was more highly polished, with fancier gilt-painted insignia). I was locked inside with Mrs Fee, and two policemen stood guard on the back step during our bone-shaking journey across North Bridge and up the High Street.

Such was the notoriety of our case that a huge crowd was

expected in Parliament Square, where the public doors would open early, at nine o'clock. I learned later that upward of two thousand persons had thronged the plaza in front of the Court that day. The hordes had already begun to gather as early as eight o'clock and, on the approach to the High Court, the wagon reverberated like thunder. At one stage, some mad fool even leapt from a vantage point onto the roof of the van. There was a thud overhead, and then a leering face appeared in one skylight, whilst a meaty hand came groping in at the other, pulled off my hat, and grabbed at my hair. I gave a shriek, and even the impassive Fee looked startled for a second, before she jumped up and began to batter the intruder's arm with her umbrella, and then the policemen dragged him off the roof. The horses trotted on without delay until, presently, the noise of the crowd abated, the wagon jerked to a halt, the doors flew open, and Fee and I dashed into the building, through a side entrance.

Inside the Parliament House, another policeman led us to a staircase, whereupon we descended one stone step after another, going deeper and deeper into the vaults and cellars of the building. Eventually, we arrived at a strong-door with a wicket-gate and passed through, into the semi-subterranean police offices. There, I was taken into a dark, low-ceilinged room, where we were to wait, under the watchful eye of a corpulent policeman, PC Neill.

The room had a fireplace, but no window, and candles, but no gaseliers. When the door was pulled shut, the atmosphere grew stuffy in an instant. Despite my pre-trial nerves, I soon found myself growing drowsy. One could not help but imagine that the air had been trapped in that cell for centuries, and breathed, ten thousand times over, by scrofulous felons.

Mrs Fee sat, rubbing her raw pink thumbs together. Since our first encounter in Duke Street, she and I had established a tolerable relationship. I had seen a different side to her on the day that the indictment had been served upon me, back in early February. In fact, it was Fee herself who had handed it to me, in the cell.

The sight of my name written down, along with those of Schlut-terhose and his wife, made me realise, of a sudden, that I was now well and truly lumped together with these two miscreants, and presumed, by the Crown, to be no better than them. It was most distressing, and I am afraid to say that the moment got the better of me. Fee was extremely kind that day, although she had since made it clear that she did not intend to befriend me. That morning, as we sat in the Parliament House cell, waiting for the trial to begin, I was surprised to notice a tear on her cheek, as she pressed a bottle of smelling salts into my hands, and said, briskly: 'You might need that.'

As for PC Neill, he barely glanced in my direction. Once, when I did manage to catch his eye, he turned away, the trace of a frown between his brows, his chinstrap biting into the soft flesh of his jaw.

A long interval passed, during which I could hear, but not see, a great deal of bustling to and fro in the offices beyond the door. Presumably, the kidnappers were amongst the arrivals, and I wondered whether they too would be ushered into this same small room. I supposed that there were other chambers in the building, where potential witnesses were being kept in seclusion. Perhaps, at that very moment, the Gillespies, and all the others, were waiting in one such room. Sadly, my stepfather had been unable to return to Scotland for the trial. Poor health meant that he was forced to remain in Switzerland for the foreseeable future: two physicians from different clinics had written to the lawyers, confirming that Mr Dalrymple was suffering from Addison's anaemia, and should not attempt to make the journey home, under any circumstances.

Of course, I should have dearly liked Ramsay to be able to speak in my defence, which we would have asked him to do, had he been able to return. And it might have been comforting simply to have the support of a patriarchal presence. But one must be philosophical. I told myself that one could not always have every-thing that one wanted. Indeed, that was something that Ramsay himself had drummed into me when I was small: 'Compromise, Harriet,' he used to caution me. 'Compromise.' And then, his other favourite saying, which was always the precursor to some form of punishment: 'Sanctions will be brought to bear.'

At any rate, the musings of my weary mind were cut short when a key turned in the lock and the cell door swung open. My breath caught in my throat. Some person outside must have signalled to PC Neill, for he nodded, and turned to me.

'This way, ma'am,' he said, indicating the open door.

For a second, I wondered whether my legs would support me, and I had to lean on the table in order to rise to my feet. Mrs Fee waited for me to pass ahead of her into the hallway, where a few constables stood in sober-faced attendance. PC Neill led us along a dim-lit passage, with Fee and another policeman bringing up the rear. We walked quickly, and in no time at all reached the foot of a narrow, enclosed staircase, with steep, shallow steps, white-washed walls, and an open trapdoor at the top. From beyond the hatch came the sounds of a large assembly of people packed into a cavernous room: coughing, shuffling of feet, and the cacophony of many excited voices echoed beneath a lofty ceiling. Desperate, illogical thoughts came to me: if only I were a soprano, in the wings, about to take the stage at the end of the Overture; if only I were in the Corps de Ballet. Expecting that we would pause, and wait, at the end of the passage, I hesitated, but PC Neill pressed on at the same pace, already mounting the worn, wooden steps. Simultaneously, the turnkey put her hand in the small of my back, and thrust me upwards, towards the light and the clamour. I am no claustrophobe, but I felt trapped in that white stairwell, with Fee shoving me from the rear and Neill's boots and broad serge posterior in my face. I was unable to see past him until, all at once, he stepped aside and I emerged, blinking, from the hatch. A cold draught of air hit me in the face, along with the shocking realisation that I had ascended directly into the well of the court, like a pantomime genie.

At once, a hush fell upon the room, and a sea of inquisitive faces stared at me from all sides, and from the galleries above. I felt my knees go weak. In my panic, my vision blurred. I would, perhaps, have turned back, but with Fee barging out behind me, there was nothing for it but to be guided onto a surprisingly short and narrow platform, where Belle and Schlutterhose were already seated. Unfortunately, we had to share the same bench. To avoid the stares of spectators, I kept my head down, at first, but after a few minutes, I was able to glance at my surroundings.

Directly in front of me, and to the right, was a surprising number of advocates, all dressed in black robes. Like a parliament of rooks, they chattered to each other, in the nest of the court. The three separate groups of legal representatives were present, along with their various associates. To avoid confusion, I will not bother to itemise the names and titles of all the advocates and agents and so forth involved in the case (a list of which can be found in the *Notable British Trials* series); but allow me to simplify matters by saying that amongst these legal gentleman was the notorious prosecutor, the Advocate Depute, Mr James Aitchison: a sleek, auburn-haired figure, with piercing green eyes and surprisingly feminine hands; Mr Charles Pringle: a gentle-faced, grey-haired man, the court-appointed Poor's Roll advocate, who would defend Schlutterhose and Belle; and, appearing on my behalf, Mr Muirhead MacDonald.

For the moment, I was unable to catch MacDonald's eye, as his attention was fixed on a table at the side of the court, upon which were laid out the 'productions', or evidence. Amongst these items were a flour sack, two hefty ledgers, various scraps of paperwork, a flat stone, and a bloodstained jacket. Beside this lay a little pair of boots and a mother-of-pearl pendant and, with a pang of my heart, I recognised these last exhibits as having belonged to Rose Gillespie. I had touched that very necklace with my own hands, and I had fastened those boots many a time. How pathetic and small her belongings looked, lying there, on the table. My vision began to mist over but then, abruptly, the Macer cried: 'Court rise!', and everyone scrambled to their feet, including myself.

The hubbub of voices ceased, as all eyes turned towards the raised platform behind the well of the court, where the judge, Lord Kinbervie, had just entered the chamber. His Lordship made an impressive figure, resplendent in his white and scarlet robes. With a nod to the assembled advocates, he took his place at the bench. His gaze flitted along the dock and paused, momentarily, on my face, but I was unable to glean anything from his expression.

As the initial formalities got underway, I took the opportunity to scan the public gallery for familiar faces. With a twinge of exasperation, I recognised Mungo Findlay, the caricaturist. He was seated in the third row, sketchbook in hand, and when I caught his eye, he saluted me, with a grin. Most other persons of my acquaintance might be called as witnesses, and were therefore forbidden to observe the proceedings until they had testified, but I knew that Mabel might be in attendance, because her name had not appeared on the witness list and thus she was free to spectate if she so desired. Here and there, amid the predominantly male crowd, I could see a few dozen ladies, but there was no sign of Mabel anywhere. Perhaps she had elected to remain with the rest of the family, in the waiting room; no doubt, she would have wanted to keep her brother company. During their empanelment, I chanced a few glances at the jury: fifteen good men of Edinburgh and true. My fate lay in their hands. Amongst their number were a coal merchant and a farmer, a commercial traveller, and a grocer, a fishmonger, a clerk, a saddler, a missionary, and a brewer. The remainder were assorted craftsmen, and all were got up in their Sunday best. I wondered how sympathetic these good gentlemen would be to a comparatively affluent female – and a Sassenach at that.

While the Clerk read the indictment, I was able to get a glimpse of Belle and Schlutterhose. For the present, they were refusing to look at me: both of them kept their faces resolutely fixed, to the front. Their appearance was, once again, disconcertingly genteel. They were well dressed and groomed, commonplace and sober. The German sported a dark, double-breasted reefer with spotless collar and cuffs; his hair had been trimmed, his whiskers shaved. Belle looked almost prim, in a high-necked grey frock. Both she and her husband wore ingenuous, slightly wounded expressions: all in all, very unlike the public conception of kidnappers and killers. To the uninformed eye, they must have seemed hardly capable of scolding a child, never mind abducting or murdering one. It seemed to me that this façade might easily fool an honest jury.

Both Schlutterhose and his wife pleaded 'Not Guilty' to the charges on the indictment: a surprising decision on their part, and no doubt a frustrating one for their lawyers, given what was soon revealed in the German's declaration. However, according to what I had heard from Caskie, their counsel had been unable to persuade them to plead guilty, even to the lesser charge of plagium. Despite already having admitted to snatching Rose, Schlutterhose seemed determined that the lion's share of the blame should fall upon me.

According to the following day's *Glasgow Herald*, I was 'pale, but composed' when I made my plea, and, in pronouncing the words 'Not Guilty', my voice was 'soft and serene'. Pale, no doubt; soft-spoken, perhaps, but I felt neither composed nor serene. Every nerve in my body was alert, my throat was dry, my palms wet. Moreover, I was shivering. The only fireplaces in the room flanked the bench, for His Lordship's comfort. I was cold; but, above all, I quaked with fear. And yet, it seems that I was able to conceal my disquiet, albeit unwittingly, as we humans often do.

There are no opening speeches in Scottish criminal trials, and so, following the preliminaries, Mr Aitchison, the prosecutor, called the first of his witnesses, thus embarking upon his mission to paint as ghastly a picture of events as possible.

The trial had begun.

Friday, 8 September 1933

LONDON

As yet, there is no reply from Mr Pettigrew of the Glasgow asylum. I wonder how long one ought to wait before telephoning again? Another letter could be sent, but my last foray to the pillar box was not an unqualified success. Having failed to post the letter at the surgery, I was obliged to try again, at our local box, the following day. In so doing, I met with a tiny accident – just a slight tumble; luckily, I had already put the letter in the box. Nothing broken, and no fuss warranted but several people ran out of Verrechio's to come to my assistance. They were all very kind, of course, especially Signor Verrechio, although it was all quite unnecessary and a little embarrassing. I could easily have come back up in the lift by myself, but the Signor insisted that I wait for Sarah, and he kept a lookout for her, and called her over to the café when she came plodding around the corner.

Needless to say, she wanted to know why I had left the apartment, and when I told her that I had intended to buy cigarettes, she asked where the cigarettes were – and where, for that matter, was my purse? And then I had to admit that I had left it upstairs. I could tell that she doubted my word. She seems to think that I passed out in the street, although I keep telling her that I simply tripped on a loose paving stone. And no wonder: the pavements in Bloomsbury are in an abominable state.

Then, on Saturday, we had another slight mishap.

I have come to realise that Sarah never emerges from her room in less than full garb: shoes, stockings and all. She bathes, of course, but I have never glimpsed her in a robe: she is always dressed when she enters and leaves the bathroom. If the roof blew off in the middle of the night, in a gale, I do believe that she would appear in the hallway, seconds later, decked out in mackintosh and galoshes.

Having realised that she avoids baring her skin, I tried walking in on her, on Saturday night, after she had gone to bed, hoping to surprise her as she undressed. Once she had bid me goodnight and shut herself away in her room, I left an interval of two minutes, which I judged to be just long enough for her to begin taking off her clothes. However, when I threw open her door and marched in, unannounced, it was to find her seated in the armchair, fully clothed, and stitching her quilt. She looked shocked to see me there, striding into her chamber, as well she might, I suppose. I was then obliged to go through a little pantomime of having mistaken her door for that of the WC.

She now seems to think that I am losing my wits. She keeps asking me if I feel quite well and, this evening, I noticed her checking the level of whisky in one of the bottles.

Yesterday afternoon, I suggested to Sarah that we go for a swim.

'This never-ending heatwave is oppressive,' I told her. 'It's too stuffy. We must get out of here for a while. Have you ever swum at Hampstead Heath?'

She had not. Neither had I, as a matter of fact, but I had read about Kenwood Ladies Pond, several times, in the *Ham and High*, which tends to paint a picture of the place as an oasis of bucolic tranquillity, where scores of women bathe all year round, even in blizzards, when restricted to a mere hole in the ice – and all this a scant few miles from Oxford Circus. Of course, I know the Heath well, and was aware of the Highgate Ponds, but had never ventured, bodily, into any of the waters.

Sarah baulked at my suggestion of a swim, and I could tell that she was reluctant to go, because she kept asking me if I felt well enough, evidently hoping to discourage me. The trouble is, when Dr Derrett telephoned the other day, she was right beside me, trying to get a stain out of the rug, and so she heard every word. Apparently, Derrett does not like the look of my blood sample and wishes me to be X-rayed. I suspect that he is simply showing off and making himself feel important by sending patients for needless, horrible procedures. He offered to book a hospital appointment for me, next week, and I played along with him, but I have no intention of attending. I know all about the consequences of meddling with X-rays: during my time in America, Edison's poor assistant died in agony because of them. At any rate, having overheard the conversation, Sarah has got it into her head that I am poorly, and she tried to use this as a reason why we should not go for a swim. However, in the end, I persuaded her. She toddled off to make sure that the birds had sufficient water and, ten minutes later, reappeared in the hall with a towel folded across the top of her bulging carpet bag.

At my suggestion, we went by tram, rather than cab. Of course, as Sarah pointed out, this would take longer, but it suited my purpose that we should get as hot and bothered as possible, so that, upon arrival at the Heath, we would be longing to peel off our stockings and plunge into the cool waters of the Pond. There was no shade at the tram stop and by the time the right car came along, we were already boiling hot. The staircase presented a challenge, but I wanted to sit on the top deck for the benefit of the view, and the conductor was kind enough not to ring the bell until we were safely installed. Then, off we shot, and rattled at great speed towards King's Cross, before the tram began its long, slow climb out of the city. En route, I pointed out one or two shops that I thought might interest Sarah – Hathaway's confections, for instance, and Zwanziger the baker – but she said little in response.

Presently, behind the panes of glass, we began to bake, like two hothouse plums. Indeed, I was stewed, having, for convenience sake, worn my bathing costume beneath my clothes. As for Sarah, the fabric of her voluminous frock began to emit, ere long, a terrible scorched smell and, assuming that this was body odour, I politely refrained from making mention of it – until we realised that her skirts were, in fact, on fire: either her cigarette or mine (it was impossible to establish which) must have brushed against the cloth and set it quietly a-smoulder, and what with all the other smoke upstairs, we had failed to notice. Thankfully, we were able to smother the flames without too much trouble, and only a small patch of the material was charred.

Sarah caught fire: I cannot help but wonder whether this is a horrible irony.

By the time we got to the terminus, we were both frazzled. Luckily, we found a cab idling outside the Duke of St Albans and although the driver was reluctant to undertake such a short trip, which he claimed was 'not worth his bloomin' candle', he agreed, in the end, to deposit us towards the top of Millfield Lane. From there, we hastened, gratefully, into the green shade of the trees and, after a short stroll, emerged at the Ladies Pond grove, where the facilities are simple: naught but a shed in which to change one's clothes, a deck and pier arrangement of wooden planks, and a few platforms, for diving. A perimeter of thick undergrowth provides bathers with a degree of privacy. On this weekday afternoon, the place was quiet, despite the heat. There were no swimmers in the water, but about half-a-dozen ladies were sunning themselves on the little meadow that slopes down behind the deck. A stout female lifeguard in overalls sat at a metal table by the hut, pouring tea.

Since I had worn my bathing suit, I could undress without having to bother with the changing cubicles. I simply divested myself of my clothes, then combed and repinned my hair, which is very long, these days, and entirely silver. My assumption was that Sarah would go inside to don her costume. However, upon turning to put my comb in my bag, I was surprised to see that she had not, after all, gone up to the hut. Instead, she had spread out her towel on the meadow and was seated upon it, fully clothed, peering warily at the grass on all sides, as though on the lookout for marauding insects.

'Do get ready, dear,' I said. 'We should have a swim now, to cool down, and then dry off later, in the sun.'

As I spoke, I noticed her focus shift towards the deck behind me, and she smiled, as though to greet someone. Glancing back,

I saw, bearing down upon us, the sturdy attendant. Her hair was bobbed: thick, brown and coarse. She came to a halt at the top edge of the meadow, planting her feet wide apart. She had broad, athletic calves, and her shoes were so sensible that they might well have been made for a man. Ignoring Sarah, she looked down at me, sceptically.

'Can you swim, madam?'

'Yes, indeed, thank you,' I replied. 'I've been swimming since I was a child.'

'Well, you shall have to prove it. See that buoy?' She pointed towards one of the floats in the water. 'If you can reach that, you can swim all you like, but I shall have to watch you do it first. Forgive me asking, but you are perfectly fit, are you? We do get a lot of old ladies, so it's not necessarily a problem, but how's your heart?'

I looked at her.

'Any strokes, heart attacks?' she added.

'Certainly not.'

'Good.' She glanced down at my assistant. 'What about you, madam? Would you be able to reach that float?'

Sarah laughed. 'Oh, I'll not be going in the water,' she said. 'I can't swim. I'm just going to sit here, quietly.'

And with these words, she pulled a sewing tin out of her carpet bag, followed by her Kensitas Flowers quilt. From where I stood, I could see that the bag contained nothing else: it seemed that Sarah had brought no bathing costume.

The attendant turned to me.

'Well, madam, if you wouldn't mind, just swim to that float whilst I keep an eye on you, then I'll know you're safe to be in the water.'

'You can't swim?' I said to Sarah.

'No,' she replied.

'But that's why we came here – to get out of our clothes – and swim.'

'Well, I never said I'd swim. But I'm quite happy for you to go

[369]

in, Miss Baxter. You go on, enjoy yourself, and I'll just sit here.'

I stared at her, in disbelief. My armpits prickled, although whether it was with perspiration, or irritation, I could not tell. A fly buzzed, annoyingly, at my ear. I could feel the sun cooking the thin flesh of my scalp to the bone, like meat under a grill. Sarah flipped open the lid of her sewing tin. The lifeguard – who had been following our conversation – cleared her throat, and strode back towards the hut, calling out over her shoulder: 'Whenever you're ready.'

Sarah glanced up at me.

'You can't swim,' I said again.

'No, I've never learned, even though I grew up by the sea – isn't it funny?'

A cloud passed across the sun. From this angle, the Pond looked murky, the colour of Brown Windsor soup. I turned my gaze upon the other ladies, who were seated on the meadow. Some of the younger women's bathing suits were slashed well above the knee, and one girl's costume was designed with a daring, cutaway section, at the midriff. Then I looked at my assistant, who sat there, in her stockings and shoes, and that frumpy frock, now with a silly charred patch in the skirts, and a hole the size of a fist. She had taken a length of cotton and was peering down at her fingers, to thread a needle. Her tight cuffs bit into the soft flesh of her wrists.

'Don't you even want to put on something cooler?' I asked.

'Oh, don't worry about me. Besides, I haven't got any other clothes with me.'

'Well, it's quite private here, you know. I expect you could pull off your frock and sit in your underwear; nobody would take a blind bit of notice.'

Sarah laughed, and shook her head. 'Oh, Miss Baxter,' she said. 'You are a caution, sometimes.'

Then she commenced to sew.

Perhaps it was the heat, but I found myself in the grip of a great agitation. I was seized with a desire to rip open her frock, baring her arms and shoulders to the sun; either that, or stuff her blasted quilt down her throat. To prevent myself from doing anything so foolish, I grabbed my towel and set off, at once, without a word, up to the path, and onto the deck, where I dropped my towel. The attendant had resumed her place on her camp chair, and I nodded at her, in passing.

'Take it slowly,' she said, but before she could give me any further unnecessary advice, I turned, without pause, and – holding the handrail only briefly – allowed myself to topple backwards into the Pond.

Alas, I had not foreseen that the water would be so unspeakably cold. The icy shock of it made my head pound, as though it might explode. I sank, helplessly, through the freezing depths, for what seemed like the course of ages. My lungs began to feel as though they were being crushed. I longed to gasp for air, but I was deep underwater, and still descending. Then, of a sudden, something soft and slimy brushed against my arm. Alarmed, I kicked out, only to dig my foot into a warm greasy substance, and then, in a panic, I swallowed a volume of water. I closed my eyes, feeling myself turn and spin. Perhaps this was what it was like to drown. My ears ached. Opening my eyes, I glimpsed a bluish light, far above me, and began to rise towards it, amid a thousand bubbles. At last, I burst out of the water, scattering a raucous family of ducks. I was choking, half blind and gasping for breath. It seemed that I had all but forgotten how to swim. I lashed out with my arms and paddled my legs, desperate to stay afloat. The buoy lay ahead: much more distant than it had seemed from the shore. I thrashed towards it. The surface of the Pond was green with slime and stank of algae. I realised that it must be very deep: the bottom was invisible and, close at hand, the waters appeared more black than brown.

At last, I reached the float and grabbed onto it for dear life. Mysteriously, my arms were covered with mud. The lifeguard was standing at the edge of the pier, leaning forwards, staring out at me, keenly.

'I can come and get you in the boat,' she shouted.

'No, thank you!' I called back.

And then I caught a glimpse of Sarah, her head and shoulders just visible. She was standing to the left of the deck, where the meadow sloped away, behind the path. Her hand shaded her eyes as she looked out at me. Evidently, she was under the impression that I could not see her, perhaps because I was low in the water and she was partially concealed by the hut and the slope. The expression on her face was cold, unsmiling. She looked – dare I say it – disappointed. It dawned upon me that she must have watched me almost drown, and yet had done nothing to help.

Just as I was absorbing this chilling realisation, I felt a searing pain in my foot, which caused me to scream out in agony. Greatly alarmed, I floundered back to the wooden planks of the deck, and there, was hauled to safety by the lifeguard and a few other concerned women; of Sarah, there was now no sign. Once out of the Pond, it became clear that my toes were gushing with blood. Something had bitten me: a pike, most likely, according to the attendant. I had to submit to the indignity of having her bathe and bandage my foot.

Ten humiliating minutes later, Sarah finally waddled over, claiming to have dozed off in the sun. Absurdly, the lifeguard insisted that I be driven to the hospital. However, the events of the afternoon had unsettled me so much that I only wanted to return home. And so, once we had found the cab, I instructed the driver to take us straight back to Bloomsbury – 'if that might be worth his candle'.

All the way home, Sarah said nothing; not a word. She simply stared out of the window. Sometimes, when she thinks that she is not being observed, she gets a blank, pitiless look in her eyes and, for the first time, yesterday in the cab, I noticed something cruel in the line of her jaw.

In any case, I have – at last – had an idea. It came to me, last night, just as I was taking my little miracle pills in preparation for sleep.

At first, I dismissed the notion, as too extreme. But having racked my brains, I can think of no other way to find out whether or not the girl has these scars. The worst that will happen is that she will sleep late – and a little extra rest never hurt anyone.

Preparation is required; the ground must be laid. I have already begun, this morning, by sending her to Fortnum and Mason's to get a tin of Van Houten's cocoa powder and some vanilla sugar. She will not touch alcohol, but it is to my advantage that she has such a sweet tooth. I still have plenty of veronal, and two or three should suffice, given that she is not habituated to them; perhaps four, to be on the safe side. I am quite certain that no harm can come to her.

Tuesday, 12th September. 11.30 p.m. How annoying! I was all ready to go ahead with it tonight, and did invite her to join me in a cup of cocoa but she refused! In the end, I was forced to drink some all by myself. What is wrong with the girl? I cannot imagine that she suspects anything. Perhaps she was simply not in the mood. Next time, I must find a way to make it more tempting: the addition of a few pieces of real chocolate, perhaps, melted in, and whipped cream piled on the top, like they used to do at the cocoa house, in the West End Park, all those years ago. She used to adore those little glasses of hot cocoa topped with crème Chantilly.

Tomorrow, when she goes to buy birdseed, I will ask her to get me a bar of chocolate and some cream.

Thursday, 14th September. 11.15 p.m. I am almost too thrilled to write. Tonight – at last, after a few attempts, earlier in the week – she finally accepted my invitation and drank a cup of cocoa with me in the sitting room. Happily, everything has conspired to affirm that this is exactly the right plan of action: even the weather seems to approve, because the last few days have been chilly and wet, and much more suited to the drinking of hot drinks at bedtime. I insisted on melting the chocolate myself, which gave me the perfect opportunity to stir in the crushed veronal – three of them (in the end, I decided that four might be too much for one who is not habituated).

She ate the dollop of cream with a spoon. For a brief instant, I worried that she might leave the cocoa – but no, she drank it all down, like a good girl.

Sure enough, not five minutes later, she started to yawn, and then she excused herself and said goodnight. I must say, I did not expect the pills to work quite so quickly.

Now, I am only waiting for her to settle down. For a while, she could be heard, moving around in her room, but her light went out not long ago and all is silent. Another half an hour ought to be enough, and then I shall go in.

VI

Edinburgh

MARCH 1890

19

Since an almost verbatim record of the proceedings is available in the aforementioned *Notable Trials* series, I shall refrain from giving an exhaustive account of the evidence, but will limit myself to certain salient points that merit further discussion, and some matters which, at the time, I was unable to refute.

The first witness, James O'Connell, is worth mentioning if only for the startling effect that his testimony had upon certain members of the assembled crowd. O'Connell was the carrier who had found Rose's body in the woods. He was a florid, burly, bombastic fellow, clearly filled with self-importance at appearing in court. When Aitchison asked him to describe what had happened on that day, O'Connell stated that he had noticed a sack half buried in a patch of disturbed earth, some distance from the road.

'When I pulled on it, I saw it was all tangled up with a body – a child – well, a decomposed body, the bones of a child. I think the flesh had been eaten, by foxes or dogs, but the bones remained.'

At this juncture, the carrier was obliged to pause in his testimony, because of an uproar in court: various people in the public benches began to weep, there were histrionics, and a woman in the gallery actually fainted, and had to be carried out.

Dreadful though it was that a small child had suffered such an abominable fate, this excessively hysterical response was surprising, given that these details must have been known to everyone in attendance, since the whole story had been repeated, ad nauseam, in the press. As far as I was aware, none of these persons in tears, or fainting, were acquainted with Rose or the Gillespies; it was – as Caskie later said – highly suspect. Apparently, some members of the legal profession are not above hiring people to sit amongst the crowds in court and – at certain pre-arranged points – mimic shock, or outrage, or distress (or whatever emotion has been agreed upon), in response to what is said from the witness box. Caskie did not suggest for one moment that the Crown would have stooped to employ such a tactic, but it did make one wonder whether these public outbursts were to be trusted.

During the pandemonium, as the woman who had fainted was carried outside, Aitchison himself stood in the well of the court, with his plump, pink hands on his hips, gazing around and nodding to himself, sorrowfully, as if such reactions were only to be expected.

Once order was restored, and the prosecutor had finished with O'Connell, Mr Pringle began his cross-examination. It was Pringle's tendency to ask questions as though he was a little distracted, and dreamy. Perhaps this was an affectation but, at times (particularly as the trial progressed), it did seem as though his thoughts were, indeed, elsewhere and, once or twice, he was mistaken on points of law, thereby damaging his credibility still further. Mr Pringle was nearing the age of retirement, and he had, perhaps, lost some of his verve. In any case, let us waste no time on him; he elicited nothing of note from the carrier and, thereafter, it was the turn of my counsel for the defence to take the floor.

As he rose to his feet, I pressed my hands together, until my fingers hurt: this was the only means by which I seemed able to maintain my composure, since I was almost breathless with anticipation and nerves. MacDonald took a few paces and then stood perfectly still, with one hand on his chin, as though turning over, in his mind, something of great import. The courtroom fell silent. We waited. Presently, I began to fear that the diminutive advocate had been struck with stage fright but, at last, he levelled a stern gaze at the witness, and posed a question so sharply that it almost seemed like an accusation:

'Mr O'Connell, what, *exactly*, on that day, were you doing in the woods?'

The carrier looked peeved, but replied: 'As I said, it was . . . I was answering a call of nature.'

MacDonald cast a look of mild surprise at the jury. 'A call of nature – couldn't that have been answered, more conveniently, at the roadside? It's a fair tramp from where you abandoned your wagon, to the site of the child's burial, is it not?'

'You might say that,' admitted O'Connell, hauling up his breeches over the expanse of his belly.

'Then why go so far into the woods? Indeed, it appears that you went directly to the shallow grave – almost as though you knew where it was.'

At once, there was a change in the atmosphere of the room: all those present were listening more intently than they had been previously. I wondered where MacDonald was leading us. Could he genuinely think that this man O'Connell was somehow involved in Rose's death?

The carrier had turned pink. 'What – what are you implying?'

'I'm simply curious to know why you went so far into the woods – when you might easily have emptied your bladder behind the first tree.'

The witness muttered something.

'I beg your pardon?' said my advocate, cupping his hand to his ear. 'You shall have to speak up, sir.'

O'Connell blushed. 'It was a more profound call of nature, sir,' he said. 'Best accomplished out of sight of the road. A turd, sir – if I may put it that way.'

From various pockets around the court, there came the sound of ribald sniggers. A few ladies looked affronted.

'Ah. Do forgive me,' said MacDonald, as he backed away from the witness, concluding: 'I shall probe no further into *that* matter', whereupon, the sniggers turned to smutty laughter and Kinbervie was obliged to demand: 'Quiet!'

MacDonald's cross-examination had neither proven, nor disproved, a thing – and yet, with this little opening gambit, he had amused the rowdier elements of the crowd, which did much to gain their favour. Consequently, they felt more at home in the austere surroundings of the High Court, and would now look to the young advocate for their entertainment. Surely this opening would stand us in good stead?

Any mild relief that I experienced, however, was short-lived. When I raised my eyes to the bench, I saw that Kinbervie had turned his head away from the court and was staring into one of his fires with an expression of irritation on his face: clearly, he was annoyed with MacDonald for playing to the gallery. As for the jury, one or two of them were smiling, but the rest, perhaps taking their lead from the judge, remained stony of countenance. All at once, I began to appreciate the degree to which my fate rested in the hands of these gentlemen.

After the theatrical opening afforded by the carrier's grisly account of discovering the body, Aitchison called his second witness, Detective Inspector Grant, who subjected us to the whole terrible story, from the very beginning: the discovery that Rose was missing, the fruitless searches for her, the ransom note, the shallow grave, the bloodstained jacket with the forgotten wage slip in the pocket, the dramatic capture of Hans and Belle, the stone that was found beneath their window, their subsequent statements, the discovery that Belle's sister Christina had once worked for the Gillespies, the seizure of my bank's records, and my own arrest. Somehow, the Detective Inspector made himself seem responsible for every breakthrough in the case. It struck me as duplicitous that he spoke so knowledgeably about events in which his colleague, Stirling, must surely have been more closely involved. Indeed, Grant's main intervention had been to take men off the case. The Detective Inspector had always struck me as a sly, self-satisfied creature, and I was surprised that Aitchison seemed to hold him in great esteem. The prosecutor's respectful manner had the unfortunate effect of making Grant's responses seem plausible, even though, to my certain knowledge, some of them were untrue. I was disappointed that neither Pringle nor MacDonald wished to cross-examine him. Not once, during his testimony, did the detective look in my direction: his intention, I believe, was to make me feel trifling, worthless, beneath contempt; and, as he left the stand, the smirk on his gammon-pink face was like a deliberate rebuke.

No doubt, we would soon hear from Schlutterhose and Belle themselves, when their declarations would be read aloud to the court. I shuddered to think what hideous slanders these documents might contain.

In the meantime, much of that first morning was a battle between Aitchison and Pringle, as the Crown tried to establish Schlutterhose as the primary abductor. To this end, Aitchison called numerous witnesses who had seen him, in the Woodlands area, on the day that Rose had disappeared. For instance, Mrs Mary Arthur, of West Prince's Street, testified that she had seen the German hurrying down the road with a small girl in his arms. According to her, he was drunk.

'Now – hmm – he was drunk, you say?' Pringle reminded her, when he took the floor. 'What made you think so?'

Mrs Arthur adopted a world-weary expression. 'I'm three times married, sir, three times a widow; I know a drunk man when I see one.'

'You said he was unsteady on his feet, and staggering. Did you – looking at him – did you fear for the child's safety?'

'I felt sorry for her.'

'In case he might drop her?'

'Aye – but more that she had such a bad father, blind drunk in the middle of the day – disgraceful behaviour.'

Moving on, Aitchison called Robert Dickson, foreman at the Loch Katrine Distillery, who testified that he had employed Hans Schlutterhose for about two months, during the early part of 1889. He told the court that Hans had appeared at the distillery on the afternoon of Wednesday, the 8th of May, when he had handed in his notice, claiming to have come into an inheritance. Dickson said that this had merely saved him the trouble of firing Schlutterhose, whom he suspected of pilfering, and who had not put in an appearance at work since he had left the yard several days previously, complaining of ill health. Questioned by Aitchison,

Dickson could remember little about Hans's usual clothing, and failed to recognise the brown jacket. However, Thomas Holland, a foreman at the Dennistoun Bakery, was convinced that the garment strongly resembled one that Schlutterhose habitually used to wear. Holland verified that the dates upon the wage slip found in the pocket of the jacket matched the dates that he had employed Hans. He asserted that, despite an initial good impression, the German's behaviour had quickly deteriorated and, ultimately, he had been dismissed after only three weeks, for arriving late, in a state of intoxication. At this statement, Schlutterhose muttered something, and made an obscene gesture at his former employer, behaviour that, I suspected, would not help his case to any great degree.

In his cross-examination, Pringle managed to establish that Scotstoun Mills flour sacks were ubiquitous in Glasgow, and that any citizen might easily lay hands upon one, but this was the sole inroad that he made upon Aitchison's camp.

Laundry owner, Grace Lamont, deponed that, the previous spring, Belle Schlutterhose had worked as an assistant laundress for a few months before giving notice in May, also claiming to have come into an inheritance. Lamont told the court that she had been on the verge of dismissing her assistant, in any case, because of rumours that Belle had another source of employment.

Hearing this, Aitchison raised an eyebrow. 'What other employment?'

Lamont pursed her lips. 'I don't like to say, sir.'

'Please madam, force yourself – what kind of employment?'

'The immoral kind.'

Thereafter, several spirit merchants and publicans testified that Hans and Belle were amongst their regular customers. The couple were well-known drinkers, who were often on their uppers, but in the spring of 1889, it appeared that they had come into some money, and began to spend freely until the time of their arrest, although neither of them had appeared to be in work.

Next, Aitchison called Thomas Wilkie, a dentist, of St George's

Road. On the afternoon that Rose had gone missing, the dentist had heard a commotion down in the street and, upon looking out of his window, he saw a man, sprawled in front of some tram horses, with a child lying beside him on the ground.

'What was your conclusion?' Aitchison asked.

'There'd been an accident,' said Wilkie. 'The man and his wee girl had been knocked down by the horses.'

'Can you describe the child? Her hair? What was she wearing?'

'She had brown hair, I think, and her frock was green.'

'Brown hair and a green frock, you say? Are you sure about that? Not fair hair? Not a blue frock?'

'Her hair was perhaps dirty fair, but the frock was definitely green.'

'And do you recognise the man that you saw that day, here in court?'

Wilkie turned to the dock, and after staring at Schlutterhose for almost a minute, shook his head.

'I'm not sure. The man I saw was about the same size, but he had whiskers and he was more shabby. This man looks different.'

Aitchison pointed at Hans. 'You cannot swear this is the man you saw?'

'No, sir.'

'And did you see any blood, anywhere, on the child?'

'No, sir, none.'

The prosecutor's expression betrayed little, but I could tell that he was delighted with Wilkie's responses. This confused me, momentarily, until I realised what impression this evidence was intended to produce on the minds of the jury. I knew from Caskie that Pringle would call several witnesses from the scene of this same accident who would testify to having noticed blood on the child's head. Since the Crown's murder charge rested upon proving that Rose's fatal injury was sustained later, as the result of a deliberate attack, presumably Aitchison wished to undermine Pringle's forthcoming evidence in any way possible.

Next, we heard from Peter Kerr, a cabman, who claimed to have driven Hans and Rose across town. He told Aitchison that the girl had seemed fine, except for a small amount of whimpering that might normally be expected from a tired child, which had ceased when she fell asleep soon into the journey. He too had noticed no blood, either on Rose's head, or on Schlutterhose's jacket.

'No blood at all?' Aitchison pressed him. 'No sign of any injury?'

'No, sir.'

That seemed clear until Pringle's cross-examination muddied the picture, once more, when Kerr stated that his passenger's garments had been dark in colour.

'Dark, dark,' muttered Pringle. 'And – remind me – where was his jacket?'

'Like I said, he'd it wrapped around the wee girl.'

'Wrapped, you say. Where? Around her legs – hmm? Her body?'

'More like her head.'

'Her head was covered, his jacket dark. Is it not possible, then, Mr Carr –'

'Kerr, sir.'

'Kerr, I do apologise . . . Is it not possible, under those circumstances, that you might not have noticed that the child was bleeding from the head?'

'Aye, I suppose I might not.'

How glad I was that Ned and Annie were not in court to hear all this talk of blood. With this thought, I cast a glance at the public seats and was startled to notice a familiar face in the back row of the gallery: it was Mabel. She must have crept in, at some point, during the morning's proceedings. Currently, she was leaning forwards, listening to Kerr's testimony. She was as slender as ever, and still a beauty, provided that she did not lead with her chin, which gave her a stubborn, pugilistic aspect. As the cab driver was dismissed from the stand, Mabel turned to the dock and, all at once, her gaze locked with mine. I feared that she might look away, avert her eyes. But no – she gave me an almost imperceptible nod, and I nodded in reply, greatly encouraged, for if Ned's sister had not lost faith in me then surely the rest of the family would feel the same?

Somehow, I forced my attention back to the witness stand. Thomas Downie, proprietor of the Carnarvon Bar on St George's Road, identified the couple and testified that he had served them in the early afternoon. He had never seen them before, but he recalled their large capacity for whisky and ale, and the German's distinctive accent. According to Downie, they were both drunk when they left his establishment, and the bloodstained jacket on the evidence table strongly resembled the one that Hans had been wearing that day. Asked about Belle's veil – whether it was down or pinned back – he asserted that she had worn it over her face. Upon hearing this, Aitchison affected surprise.

'How can you be sure that the lady with Mr Schlutterhose was his wife?'

'It was one of those short veils, and you could see through it, a bit. Also, she has the same figure – skinny.'

Aitchison appeared to weigh these words before turning to stare at me in a manner that made my innards lurch with dread. Then, after a theatrical pause, he asked the witness:

'How would you describe Miss Baxter's figure?'

I held my breath, realising, of a sudden, the prosecutor's intention. The publican flicked his eyes towards me with a shrug of his shoulders.

'Thin, I'd say.'

'She is – is she not – as thin as Mrs Schlutterhose? In which case, would you not also describe Miss Baxter as skinny?'

'I might.'

'Therefore – think carefully – could it have been Miss Baxter that you saw, that day, in the company of Mr Schlutterhose?'

Downie winced, but nodded, as he replied: 'Possibly.'

Gracious Heavens! Ignorant as I was of the law, I could see what Aitchison intended. Not only was I to be portrayed as the instigator of this tragedy but, for some reason, he seemed set upon suggesting that I might even have physically assisted Schlutterhose to abduct my friends' daughter – and this was despite the fact that Annie would surely testify that I had been in her company for the entire afternoon. Aghast, I turned to look at MacDonald and Caskie, to see if this line of attack had also taken them by surprise. My solicitor was hunched down in his seat, with his hand clamped over his mouth, but MacDonald was gazing on, scratching the underside of his chin, and yawning, apparently unperturbed.

I prayed that, in cross-examination, he would be able to rescue the situation. However, as it transpired, the damage was done. Doubt had been planted in the mind of the publican and also, presumably, in the minds of the jury, and Downie now claimed that the veiled woman could have been either one of us.

For the first time ever, I allowed myself to contemplate the notion that we might not win our case, and that I might meet my end on the gallows. It may seem surprising that, in all my months in gaol, I had not considered the possibility that I might be hanged, but most innocent prisoners refuse to believe that the worst will happen, and I was no different.

Aitchison's next witness proved equally ambivalent. Miss Florence Johnstone, an elderly widow, who resided at number 63, West Prince's Street, told the court that she was in the habit of sitting at her parlour window and that, on the day in question, she saw a man and woman at the easterly corner of Queen's Crescent, where it meets her own road. The couple had appeared to be disputing something. Miss Johnstone readily identified the man whom she had seen as Schlutterhose.

'He's shaved his whiskers since, but this man here is the very image of him.'

As for the woman she had seen, the widow was less sure: 'Her veil was down, right enough,' she said. 'But it was one of those thin, fine veils. I'm almost certain it was the lady there in the dock.'

Aitchison revealed his teeth, in what, I presume, was meant to be a smile.

'Madam – we have two ladies in the dock. Which one do you mean? Feel free to point to her.' Again, inexplicably, he seemed determined to place me at the scene of the crime. Miss Johnstone raised her hand and, to my great relief, indicated Belle. Yet, the prosecutor persisted. 'Are you absolutely certain it could not have been the other lady – Miss Baxter, here? Take a good look at her. Take your time.'

'Well – now that you mention it, I suppose it could have been her – '

'So you are saying,' thundered Aitchison, 'that this lady in the dock before you, Miss Harriet Baxter, could have been the woman with Mr Schlutterhose that day, in West Princes Street?'

'Well,' said Miss Johnstone, timidly. 'Perhaps.'

This was a catastrophe, especially since, during his cross-examination, MacDonald was yet again unable to eradicate the uncertainty that Aitchison had planted in the mind of the witness – and, at this point, alas, His Lordship decided that he had heard enough for one morning, and adjourned the proceedings for luncheon.

As the public began to scramble for the exits, I glanced up at the gallery, but Mabel must have already slipped out; there was no sign of her. Doubtless, she had hurried to the waiting room, to give a full account of the morning to Ned and Annie.

Mrs Fee and I sat out the recess in the stifling cell, under the watchful eye of Constable Neill. Caskie was elsewhere, closeted with MacDonald, and visited, only briefly, just before we were due to return to court. The Crown's ploy of trying to place me at the scene of the abduction was vexing him, and his bearing was morose.

'We just don't know what that's all about, Miss Baxter. Pure mischief-making, most likely: he wants to plant suspicion in the minds of the jury, to implicate you as much as possible. I dread to think what else he's got up his sleeve – but you try not to worry, Miss Baxter. We know you were with Mrs Gillespie all afternoon, and Aitchison knows we'll show that, beyond a doubt, as soon as we get the chance.'

'Let's hope Annie is clear about the time of my arrival,' I remarked.

'Aye,' said the lawyer, looking, if truth be told, even more pessimistic.

Much of the afternoon was dedicated to medical evidence. We heard from Dr Frederick Thomson, police surgeon, who gave his considered opinion on how Rose might have died. Thomson had inspected Rose's body both at the shallow grave in the woods, and then during the post-mortem examination. It is unnecessary, here, to enter into the many ghastly details of his account. Suffice to say, he had found that the child's skull had been fractured in a way that, in all likelihood, proved fatal, if not at the time of injury, then shortly thereafter. The body showed no other wounds, breakages, dislocations, or marks, and he told Aitchison that the fracture appeared to have been caused by a single impact with a hard, flat surface.

'Might a blunt instrument have caused this wound? A flat stone, say?'

'That's possible.'

From the evidence table, the flat stone was produced: a stone that, according to Inspector Grant, was found 'directly beneath the window of the room in which Schlutterhose lives with his wife'. A dark red stain was clearly visible on one side of this stone but, mysteriously, neither Aitchison nor Thomson made reference to it. According to Thomson, that stone, or similar, could have been used to inflict Rose's injuries – although he thought, on balance, that a heavier stone might be a more likely weapon. Irked by this qualification, Aitchison pressed his witness:

'If not this stone, then – just to be clear – could the child's injuries have been caused if her head were dashed, deliberately, against a hard surface – a wall, perhaps, a table, a hearth – even a floor?'

'That's also possible.'

Under cross-examination by Pringle, and then MacDonald, the doctor confirmed that there was no recognisable pattern or indentation to suggest that the wound had been made by repeated blows with a stone or other blunt instrument. Only a single blow was indicated.

'Hmm,' mused Pringle. 'Is it not the case, sir, that the child's head could have sustained such an impact in some other way – if she was being carried by a tall adult, who was then – perhaps – struck down by something moving at speed – a tram horse, say. The adult is knocked to the ground. The child is propelled into the air and lands a short distance away, hitting the back of her head on the hard surface of the road. In short – an accidental fall.'

'I couldn't rule out that possibility.'

'In other words, Dr Thomson, just to be clear, you – hmm – you agree that the injury could have been sustained by accident – yes or no.'

'Yes.'

Moving on, Aitchison attempted to illustrate that Hans was relatively inoffensive when sober, but to be avoided when drunk. Various local residents had often heard him fighting with his wife. In fact, on the very night that Rose had disappeared, a young apprentice who lived next door to the couple had heard an argument coming from the apartment where they resided. Although no individual words could be distinguished, Belle was heard railing at her husband, then he bellowed at her until, in due course, only the sound of weeping could be heard.

Aitchison ignored this mention of weeping, but it was revisited, later, by Pringle: 'Might I ask, was it male or – hmm – female weeping?'

'Both, sir,' replied the apprentice.

'Both parties were crying? Both Mrs Schlutterhose and her husband?'

'Yes, sir.'

Pringle gave the jury a significant look before returning to his seat.

The proprietor of McGuire's public house on the Gallowgate testified that she had served Hans and Belle on the evening in question, and that later, they had begged her for writing materials, before spending some time, in a corner, composing a letter. We heard from a handwriting expert who had compared various samples of Hans's writing with the letter found in the close on the morning after Rose went missing and, having analysed the writing style and the German's characteristic errors in spelling and grammar, the expert had concluded that Schlutterhose was, in all probability, the author of the ransom note. George Graham, a Gallowgate pawnshop keeper, identified the button boots on the evidence table, and testified that Belle, a regular customer, had pawned them, according to his ledger, on the 7th of May 1889, three days after Rose had gone astray.

'And how did Belle Schlutterhose act upon giving you these boots?' Aitchison asked. 'Was there anything strange in her behaviour?'

'She seemed fine,' replied Graham. 'We even had a laugh about something.'

At this, there were a few gasps of disapproval from the crowd.

And so it went on. Witness after witness gave statements that were undeniably damning for Schlutterhose and his wife. We were encouraged to form a picture of them as not only feckless, dishonest, unreliable, and tempestuous, but also cold-hearted and immoral. Despite Pringle's efforts in cross-examination, Aitchison prosecuted with formidable skill. It seemed an indisputable fact that Hans Schlutterhose had snatched Rose and run away with her, and that his wife had colluded with him. The most ambiguous evidence concerned the tram accident. In pursuit of his murder conviction, the Advocate Depute had done his best to cast doubt on the identity of the man and child who had collided with the tram horses. He had also managed to raise questions about the person witnessed with Hans at, or near, Queen's

Crescent gardens, on the 4th of May, and he had left all those present with just one question in mind: which woman was it – Belle, or the English one?

Towards the end of the afternoon, Aitchison asked for the declarations of Belle and Schlutterhose to be read to the court. Belle had done little more than confirm her identity, and had nothing to say to the charges. Hans, by contrast, had spoken at length. The judge advised the jury that the statements put forward in the declaration would all have been made in answer to questions asked by the Procurator Fiscal or Sheriff-Substitute, and that all oaths and imprecations would have been deleted from the text. In order to elucidate some of what is to follow, I must here include a transcription. Of course, I could easily preface this preposterous document with a thousand caveats and denials. However, let it be noted that I set it here, without comment. No doubt, the reader will be able to judge for himself how silly it is, at a glance.

The Prisoner's Declaration

At Glasgow, the 18th day of November 1889, in presence of Walter Spence, Sheriff-Substitute of Lanarkshire. Compeared a prisoner, who being duly cautioned and examined, declares –

My name is Hans Schlutterhose. I took the child but it was no murder. It was an accident. It was not my idea to take her. We would have looked after her. Dear God, it was only supposed to be for one night.

I am aged thirty-six years. I reside with my wife, Belle, at number 8, Coalhill Street, Glasgow. My wife has nothing to do with this, nothing.

I was born in Bremen, Germany, and have been in Glasgow for seven years. I came first to London in 1879, when I was aged twenty-three years. I came to Glasgow in 1883. Presently, I am not in work. My last employment was about six months ago. I worked at the Loch Katrine Distillery in Camlachie. I did odd jobs, mainly moving barrels. It was horrible work. I was there two or three months but exactly how long I cannot recall. It did not pay well and my health was not so good.

I took the child, in May, the first week, a Saturday. I cannot recall the date. I am now shown a calendar and I can confirm that it was on the 4th of May. To begin with I only went to Queen's Crescent to take a sight. By take a sight I mean get the lay of the land. I was to get the lay of the land first and not take the child until a week or two later when all was ready.

It was about half past two o'clock when I arrive at Woodside. The two Gillespie girls were in the gardens playing. The roads all around the gardens were quiet, there was no man in the street. I saw that it was already a good opportunity not to be missed. The child could be taken and no man would see. We could take her easily, right away. We could carry her as far as the Grand Hotel and take a cab from there.

What I mean is, I could take her. I was alone. My wife was not there. She was at home. She knew nothing of all this. I refuse to continue.

I went to the gate of the gardens and gave money to the sister. I told her to go and buy something for me in the shop. I gave her a shilling. I don't remember what I told her to buy. It was tea perhaps. She ran off. Then I told to Rose her mother is waiting for her at Skinner's and we will buy hokey-pokey to eat. She took my hand and came quite willing. But she walked very slow. In the end, I picked her up and carried her down the street, West Princes Street.

All was good until the main road, St George's. One minute I was crossing the street; the next I was on the ground, knocked down. Some tram horses ran into me. The driver was going too fast. The horses came out of nowhere. It was not my fault. The girl, I could not hold her, she flew out of my arms and landed at a short distance. How far away, ten feet perhaps. I meant her no harm, it was the driver's fault. He jumped down and people came running to see if we were hurt. So I grab the child and ran away with her, up a street.

I am now shown a map and I can confirm that the street I ran up was Shamrock Street. At this point I am still carrying the child. When we are away from the people, I look at her and see some blood on her head at the back. Not much blood. She must have banged her head when she land on the ground. The place where she fell is cobblestones as far as I can remember. I wrap my jacket around her head to stop the blood and carry her until I see a cab at Cambridge Street. She fell to sleep in the cab.

We went to my home in Coalhill Street. When I came home the child is still asleep. Belle was not returned yet so I put the child on a mattress. I have put my jacket under her head for a pillow. There was still some blood, not much. I sat down and I fell to sleep also because I was tired. My wife came home about an hour later. I cannot say where she had been. She goes her own way. When she came in she took one look at Rose, and she tells me the child is dead. At first, I cannot believe her and I try to wake the girl. But she is gone, poor little thing. Oh dear God, I meant her no harm. Excuse me, please, I cannot say further at this time.

I am ready to continue. When we know for sure the child is dead my wife became very upset. I covered the body with a newspaper to hide it but I cannot make Belle calm down. In the end I have put the child in a trunk to get her out of sight. My wife did not want to be in the room with the body so we went out. First we go to the Coffin in Whitevale Street but it's so small there you cannot speak in private and so we went to McGuire's on the Gallowgate. McGuire's is a large house, and we are not so well known there, so we can talk.

Of course my wife was very confused because she knew nothing about the girl, why, because she was not involved. What is she saying? What has she said? She would do better to keep her mouth shut. (Prisoner lapsed into German.)

I am ready to continue. We had just a few drinks at McGuire's to calm our nerves. We were very sad. The child must have split her head when she hit the ground but I could not have stopped it. I was most shocked. I told my wife I would go to the police and tell the truth but she does not want to be left alone. In the end we decide to go to America to make escape. I knew we would need much money if we want a nice life and so because the child was gone I decided to take a ransom from her father the artist. I wrote him a note and paid a boy to deliver it to Woodside. He was just a boy on the street. I paid him one shilling to deliver the note and two shillings for to keep quiet. I never saw that boy since.

I am now shown a letter, it is marked number 1, and I recognise my handwriting and it was written and sent by me to Mr Gillespie.

On the morning after the child died, my wife went out about ten o'clock. She did not want to be there with the body. She will go somewhere else until the body is gone but I must wait until night to hide it somewhere. Soon after my wife is gone I hear a knock at the door. When I open it, I see the lady who paid me to take the child. She knew where I lived because – I cannot remember how she knew. I must have told her. Nobody else told her.

She stood on the landing. She refuse to come in because she thought the child was there and she spoke in a whisper. She tells me Rose is missing and wants to know did I take her, did I write a ransom note. I explain, we had gone ahead because the street was quiet and it was a good opportunity. Then the lady is unhappy. She tells me I should not keep the child there. She wants to know why I had not done as she asked and rented a nice room. She told me I had done wrong. I was to take Rose back to Woodside, at once, and put her at the corner, where she can find her way home.

That was when I have to tell her the child is dead. I explain about the accident and the child hitting her head on the ground. At first the lady did not believe me. So I took her inside and showed her what was in the trunk. When she saw the child dead, the lady is turned very white in the face and she sat down on the ground. She is holding her head like this (prisoner demonstrates). I think she may faint. After some minutes when she stood up, I thought she might attack me. She said some terrible things, not very ladylike, and then she left but twenty minutes later she came back. She was cold to me even though I tell her it was an accident. She tells me to get rid of the body, bury it somewhere deep, outside town. She tells me to say no word to any man. I told her not to worry, Belle and I are going to America. She said, 'I suppose you will want more money', and so I tell her we will take the ransom. Then she is angry again because she never said we should get a ransom. It was not in her plan. She told me absolutely I must not write any more notes to Mr Gillespie. She said she would give me what money I need. We make arrangement to meet a few days later when she will give me more money. Then she left.

That night, I buried the body. I hired a cart and waited until it was dark and then I put the child in the cart and took her out of town along the Carntyne Road. I buried her in the woods, out of sight of the road. May God forgive me!

The lady that paid me, her name is Harriet Baxter. I cannot recall how I know her. I met her somewhere. I remember now, it was at the Exhibition, two years ago. We have had some conversation there. That was how I knew her. I only saw her again, by chance, a few times here and there in the town. One time, last April, I saw her and she told me she want me to do something for her. She says she will play a trick on her friend. She wants this friend to believe that her child is gone missing. Because the child knows her, Miss Baxter needs a stranger to take her. That is why she asks me. She says the child is to be taken for one night only after which I am to return her to her street unharmed. It is for one night only because she did not want her friend to worry too much. The child is to be well looked

[395]

after. We are to give her nice food and toys, whatever she wants. Miss Baxter will pay for all. We are to rent a nice rooms to keep her in and we are to hire a closed carriage so that we can take her, quick and easy and return her, the same. Miss Baxter said we should get a nice quiet rooms so the child would not be frightened and so she would not be seen by our neighbours.

When I say 'we' I mean Miss Baxter and myself. Not my wife. She is innocent.

When Miss Baxter ask me at first to help I said no, because it was breaking the law I think. But she tells me I would not break the law, it was only a little trick on a friend. So I agree to help. After that, I met her three or four times, on Saturdays, when I have a half-day. We met at Lockhart's Cocoa Rooms in Argyle Street. It's busy there always and we won't be noticed. Miss Baxter would not write anything down, and so, many times, she will go over the plan, what had to be done. She had prepared all, she had thought of everything. She said I must recognise the children and so, one Saturday, I had to wait at Charing Cross so she could show me the girls as she walk past with them. Another day she showed me the gardens where they play and the street corner where I must return the child. She would not walk beside me. She walk in front and if she wanted to point to something so I see it, she bend down to tie her shoelace and speak to me quiet as I go past. She told me to take a sight of the area two or three times on Saturday afternoons and work out the best streets to get away with the child. I should also watch the police, how often they walk the street, what times, and so forth. I can't remember dates but it was always a Saturday we met.

I am now shown a calendar for 1889 and I can confirm that the days we met at Lockhart's were the 13th, 20th and 27th of April. On the 20th she also took me to Woodside to show me the area. The 27th was when she took the children for a walk past Charing Cross so I can recognise them. She wants me to take the child in the middle of May or later, when the weather will be warmer. She was sure they would be in the gardens most Saturdays. It was just a coincidence that when I went to take a sight that day it was already warm enough and they were playing in the gardens.

The last time I saw Miss Baxter at the Cocoa Rooms was a few days after the child was buried. She gave me another £25. We had in total £100 from her. But that was six months ago. Now the money is not so much. I was going to ask her for more money.

I cannot say why Miss Baxter wanted this done. I never ask her why. There was not much harm in it, since we were to look after Rose well and return her the next day. If my health were not so bad I would never have done it. It is Miss Baxter who is to blame. As for what happened to the child, it was an accident. It was the horses. They were going too fast. So far as that is concerned that is the driver's fault.

The jacket I buried along with the child was brown. I had worn it for years. There is about £20 pounds left of the money, what was found by the police in the cupboard in my home. We did not go to America because how would we get more money from Miss Baxter? It was always three o'clock when I met her at Lockhart's and always on a Saturday. None of this would have happened if it were not for that woman. I wish I had never laid eyes on her. It was her idea, her fault. I was just a prawn. I was just a prawn in this matter. Since then not a day is gone by but I think of handing myself in to the police. For the record, she gave me £25 on the 13th of April, and £50 on the 20th of April. And on the 11th of May after the child died she gave me another £25.

I deny that I was drunk when I took the child or when I stepped in front of the tram. Before I took her, I was in a public house on St George's Road for a time, but I only had a few. I can't remember the name of the bar. I was not long in there, perhaps a few hours. I was not drunk. Is Belle saying I was drunk? She was the one who was drunk. If she had not gone off and left me to do it I might not have been knocked down. I suppose she is saying she tried to stop me from take the child? Well, she was there. She was with me. She is as guilty as I am. You can tell her to (series of words deleted). (Prisoner lapsed into German and refused to continue the interview.)

During the recitation of this extraordinary declaration, it was only by gritting my teeth, and pressing my back against the rear panel of the dock that I was able to prevent myself from jumping off the bench and causing a scene. Every false accusation, every invention, went through my body like a sting. I wanted to cry out: 'Don't believe him; it's all lies, every word a lie!' All the while, as the clerk read on, I was aware of the jurymen. Every so often, one or other of them would turn his head, to look at me. I kept my eyes lowered, too mortified to glance up, in case I should find myself the subject of suspicious or reproachful scrutiny. Schlutterhose sat there, just a few feet away from me, his expression as mild as milk. How did he dare?

When the clerk had finished reading, Lord Kinbervie explained to the jury that a confession of guilt in a declaration was not, of itself, a sufficient ground of conviction; nor was Mr Schlutterhose's declaration to be considered evidence against any other person, except himself. It was all very well to point this out, but rather too late; for, surely, now, the jury would have countless images in their minds, many of which involved me. I could hardly bear it. I wanted nothing more than to curl up into a ball, and hide myself away, in some quiet corner.

Meanwhile, the slick machine of the court proceedings did not miss a beat; there was no pause to accommodate my trifling emotions, or to allow me to recover; Detective Sub-Inspector Stirling had already been called. As we waited for his arrival, I glanced to my right, only to realise that the kidnappers had been stealing a look at me. Belle turned away, giving me the 'cold shoulder', just as Schlutterhose lowered his fist, and shook it at me: a deliberate, artificial gesture, designed to dramatise, for the benefit of anyone watching, the supposed enmity between us.

[398]

I had thought that Detective Stirling was quite an intelligent man, capable of independent thought but, presumably, there was enormous pressure upon him to corroborate the line of argument being pursued by the Crown. It was a shame that he chose to put a certain emphasis on his testimony. As for what had happened in the Clarence on the way into the police office, I must stress that I was terribly alarmed, not to mention stunned, at having been arrested. Hence, the short laugh that I gave, after a long silence, a laugh that was simply the product of nerves and incredulity, a laugh of exasperation, if you will. There was nothing malign about it, and certainly nothing that was 'chilling' – as Stirling was encouraged to comment, by Aitchison. However, to my dismay, MacDonald failed, once again, to challenge this statement.

After Stirling had quit the stand, and with the hour advancing, Kinbervie suggested that the prosecutor call his last witness for the day. I could tell from the way that Aitchison's fingers were twitching that he was determined to finish on a high note and, following a brief hiatus, he asked for Helen Strang to be called. Miss Strang, a waitress from Lockhart's Cocoa Rooms, turned out to be a doughy-faced woman, with thick, dark eyebrows, uneven teeth, and a blotchy complexion. After a few initial questions, the Advocate Depute asked her whether she had been at work on the 20th of April, the previous year. Strang confirmed that she had.

'And what do you remember from that day?' asked Aitchison. 'Do you remember any customers in particular?'

'Aye, there were three folk in the inglenook, at the side, a foreign man and two ladies. They came in about three o'clock.'

'Did these people arrive as a group?'

'One woman and the man came in together – they seemed like a married couple. And then the other lady arrived about five minutes later.'

'Why do you remember these customers in particular?'

'Well, they didnae seem to belong together. The couple didnae look quite respectable, if you know what I mean. Then the woman who came in, on her own, she was definitely what you might call a lady, and she was English as well.'

'How do you know she was English?'

'She spoke to me. She asked for coffee. Coffee with milk. The other pair had ordered tea. Mind you, the man did ask, before the other woman arrived, if we sold ale, but his wife told him not to be daft.'

'But these people did know each other?'

'I think so, aye. They were huddled over talking, for near enough an hour.'

'Huddled over, you say? Did they talk loudly, or quietly?'

'Quietly, sir.'

'And did you hear anything they said?'

'No, sir, except when they gave their orders.'

'Is there anything else you remember?'

'Aye, sir. After they'd been there about an hour, I went over to ask if they wanted anything else. Well, see as you walk over, you can see into the inglenook. You cannae see the customers very well, and they cannae really see you, but you can see the table in the middle. And while I was walking over, I saw the English lady pass something across the table to the man.'

'What was it?'

'It looked like a sort of package.'

'A sort of package you say? Was it large, or slim?'

'Slim, sir.'

'And what did the man do with this slim package?'

'He put it in his pocket. By the time I got to the table, he'd put it away.'

'Now then,' said Aitchison. 'I must ask you, Miss Strang – can you see those three customers here today?'

The waitress looked around the court, from face to face, for what seemed like an eternity until, at length, her eyes came to rest upon Schlutterhose. She stooped and peered over at him, then slowly pointed her finger, first at Hans, then at Belle, and, finally, at me.

'These three here are very like the customers I saw that day.'

How difficult can it have been to recognise us as the accused, I wonder, given that we were, all three, seated in the dock? I turned to the jury, to see if they might look as scornful as I felt, but, by the expressions on their faces, they all seemed to have treated this identification as valid. It was nothing less than ludicrous. To think that my fate rested in the hands of this crackpot. I am being unkind, of course, but only wish to convey how I felt, at the time. Lives were at stake; not that I cared two figs for Belle and her husband, but all the same, surely someone should have realised that this woman was simply desperate for attention, and prevented her from taking the stand?

Pringle could not resist cross-examining Strang, but he failed to elicit much more from her than Aitchison had already done, and I was glad when he relinquished the floor. I wondered how MacDonald could possibly counter such apparently damning testimony.

'Miss Strang, you say you saw these people on Saturday, the 20th of April last year. How is it that you remember that date, so precisely?'

The waitress gave a shrug of her shoulders. 'I don't know, I just do.'

'Did someone, in the course of your precognition, mention that date to you?'

'I don't think so.'

Aitchison jumped up, but was waved down by the judge.

'Yes, yes,' said Kinbervie. He gave my counsel a warning look and then advised him to continue. MacDonald's next question took me quite by surprise.

'You had a famous customer, a while ago, did you not, Miss Strang? Your colleagues at the Cocoa Rooms are still full of talk about it. Towards the end of last year, I believe it was.'

Strang nodded. 'Aye, sir, it was Miss Loftus, from the Theatre Royal. I served her, sir. We were all very excited to see her, right there, in the room.'

'So I believe. You're a follower of Miss Marie Loftus, are you? You've seen her on the stage in *Robinson Crusoe*, perhaps?'

'Oh, yes, sir, quite a few times. She's one of my favourites.'

'Does she often come to Lockhart's?'

'No, sir, it was just that one time.'

'Do you remember what date it was that you served her?'

'It was December, sir, early in December, I think. We were very busy.'

'Can you remember the date, or the day of the week?'

The waitress paused, and then said: 'No, sir. It might've been a Saturday.'

'And what did Miss Loftus order?'

'Erm – I think it was high tea she had, sir.'

'Anything else?'

'I can't remember anything else.'

MacDonald consulted his notes. 'In fact, Miss Loftus has been spoken to, and she gave us her receipt from that day. Would you mind looking at it?'

A piece of paper from the productions table was carried to the witness.

'Is that the receipt you gave her?' MacDonald asked. 'Is it your signature?'

'Aye, sir.'

'And what does the receipt say that Miss Loftus ordered?'

'Just an aerated drink. I remember now, that's what she had.'

'An aerated drink. Not high tea, then. Yes, I gather that Miss Loftus prefers to dine at home. And what date does it say on the receipt?'

'Monday, the 18th November, sir.'

'The 18th of November – not December, at all – and not a Saturday. So, Miss Strang, it seems you can remember every detail about some anonymous customers you say you served almost a year ago, including the date and time, and what you served them. Yet you have a very poor recollection of a customer you served less than four months ago, a person who is famous, someone –

moreover – whom you idolise. You can't even remember what she ordered. Can you explain this anomaly?'

'Like I said, sir, we were busy that day.'

'No more questions, my lord,' said MacDonald, returning to his seat.

Hardly surprisingly, Aitchison chose to re-examine his witness. In his hands, Strang remembered being so flustered by serving Miss Loftus that she failed to notice what the actress had ordered. However, it was an unconvincing challenge. On balance, I felt that although we had not managed to tarnish Strang completely, a question about whether she had been schooled in her answers must have been raised in the minds of all present.

However, she had pointed at me, along with the other two. I dreaded to think what the jury might make of her story, as they brooded on it overnight and, as I sat in the holding cell at the end of the day, it was difficult not to feel prematurely defeated. When Caskie called to see me, on his way out, I tried to hide my despair.

'Well,' I said. 'At least three-quarters of the day went in our favour.'

'Aye,' said Caskie. 'Bar Aitchison's japes in trying to place you at the scene.'

'And that waitress! And what about that dreadful declaration?'

'Never mind the declaration, Miss Baxter. As the judge said, it's not evidence against you. Our German friend could have said anything about anybody, in his declaration, if he thought it might save his rotten neck, but that doesn't make it true.'

Caskie meant to reassure me; instead, his words only made me consider my own frail neck. Of all my physical attributes, it was the one that I minded least, for it was slender and graceful. How ironic that my one decent feature might be the very thing to be ruined. What, exactly, happened when a person was hanged? Did the neck break from the fall, or was the windpipe slowly crushed until one suffocated? I pictured a noose tightening around my throat, the fibres of the rope cutting into my skin. Or might I be sent back to gaol, for the rest of my days? I strongly suspected that I would not survive a long term in Duke Street.

Caskie was still speaking. 'Now, tomorrow, we must counter the Crown's production of your bank's ledger. If we don't do that, then we're in big trouble.'

'But how are we to do it?'

Although both Agnes Deuchars and Mrs Alexander had been kindly co-operative, neither they nor Caskie's agents had been able to find a single one of the missing receipts that might have exonerated me.

'Well, to be honest, I'll admit, we're currently bereft of ideas,' said Caskie. 'There's also Belle's sister, and she'll treat us to some blatherskite about having set up a meeting between you and that pair of rascals. So we have that to look forward to. Many a lawyer would tell you there's no case against you, Miss Baxter, and I'll admit, there's not much of a one. But unless we manage to tarnish both Christina Smith and the bank evidence, well . . .' He paused, and, perhaps reading the anxiety on my face, tried a different line: 'In my experience, Miss Baxter, it's usually the second day that marks the low point in the case for the defence, but we seem to have gone against the convention and had our worst day first.'

I must say that this reassurance hardly bathed me in relief.

20

The following morning, I was plunged further into gloom when I saw that *The Scotsman* contained the headline 'Gillespie Girl Trial' and proceeded to describe me thus: '*Miss Baxter was dressed in a grey silk frock, dark gloves and charcoal bonnet, with no veil. In appearance, she seems a typical old maid, thin, erect, with fine features, but a Roman nose. While the German's declaration was read aloud, she glanced at him, once or twice, with no visible emotion.*' The Mail had published a sketch of the three prisoners in the dock, featuring Belle and myself most prominently, above the caption: '*Who was the Mysterious Veiled Lady?*' The artist (not Findlay, this time) had been rather unkind to me, I felt.

It was as though the entire country was against me. Noticing that I hung my head, Mrs Fee cleared the newspapers off the table, and chastised Constable Neill for bringing them into the cell. Neil simply gave a shrug of his shoulders, which seemed, to me, an unnecessarily callous gesture.

My mood did not improve as the morning got underway. Once again Mabel was there to monitor proceedings from the gallery. On this second day, I knew that most of Aitchison's volleys would be aimed in my direction. I was only too aware how concerned my lawyers were about the potential testimony of the Crown's key witness, Christina Smith. The bank ledger also loomed large. I felt sure that Aitchison would begin with one of these dreaded pieces of evidence, but the first witness he called was Mrs Annie Gillespie. This announcement caused a marked sensation in the court, as well it might: we were to hear from the dead child's mother. I myself felt very strange indeed, simply at the sound of Annie's name. Here was a prospect that I had been dreading. Ever since her outburst in Duke Street gaol, I was aware that she harboured some unwarranted doubts about me, and I knew not whether she had seen sense in the intervening weeks. No doubt, Mabel would also have told her all about yesterday's events: the German's declaration, and Helen Strang's piffle. Consequently, I found it hard to look at Annie as she entered, and, for the most part, I kept my eyes downcast while she was on the stand.

Here, I find myself pausing, because I am wondering what to say about Annie's testimony. Most importantly, it must be borne in mind that she was a grieving mother, in a fragile state. In some respects, I would argue that her courage was to be commended. Always an unworldly creature, who was, by nature, as vague as a wisp of smoke, she seemed not only distracted, that day, but also frail and, at times, slightly unhinged. Yet, despite this, she refrained from histrionics and shed not a single tear in court, even though, as Rose's mother, she had good reason to be distraught. I have often tried to put myself in Annie's shoes, and can imagine that, for months, all sorts of people had been pouring poison into her ear, misleading her, and distorting her opinion of me. In all probability, she no longer knew which way to turn, who to rely upon, what to believe. In her position, I might well have reacted in the same way, becoming suspicious, distrustful – even delusional, as I must admit that she seemed, at times, on the stand.

Her words are there, preserved for ever, in *Notable Trials*, and in Kemp's pamphlet, if anyone cares to read it. Had I been able to speak in my own defence, during the trial, I would have had something to say about a few of her inaccuracies and misapprehensions. Time is a great deceiver, and Annie's memory had always been notoriously bad. For instance, our main hope was that MacDonald's cross-examination would place me alongside her, at Stanley Street, at the approximate time that Rose was kidnapped. Nobody was sure of the exact hour of the abduction, but the police had calculated that it had taken place at some point between three o'clock, when Miss Johnstone had seen the abductors from her window, and half past three, when Mrs Arthur saw Hans hurrying down West Princes Street with Rose in his arms.

However, Annie was exasperatingly vague about when I had arrived at number 11. She did confirm that I had been with her for most of the afternoon, but could not, or would not, be specific about the exact time of my arrival.

'It might have been about three o'clock,' she told Aitchison. 'But it might have been later. I didn't look at the time.'

'Could it have been four o'clock?' asked the prosecutor.

'Perhaps not as late as four – but I can't be certain.'

She also misremembered the early days of our friendship, deponing that it was on the afternoon that we met that I had engaged her to paint my portrait, which, of course, was not the case.

Aitchison seemed very interested in the portrait. Having established that my father had commissioned and paid for the picture, he asked Annie whether Mr Dalrymple had made the payment in person.

'No,' she replied. 'It was Harriet who gave us the money, on his behalf.'

'So, he commissioned and paid for the portrait, but you never met him?'

'No.'

With a sly glance at me, Aitchison asked her: 'Where was the portrait hung?'

'At his home in Helensburgh,' Annie replied. 'I think that's where he lives.'

'How do you know that – where it was hung, I mean?'

'From Harriet. I think she said he'd put it in his drawing room.'

'I see – in his drawing room. Now, moving on, tell me more about Miss Baxter. She became your friend, I believe, and you liked her?'

'Yes, for some time, anyway.'

'Did your feelings about her change?'

'Yes.'

'Was there an incident that provoked this change in your feelings?'

'Not really, it just happened over time. She became a bit – intrusive. There was this one time I met her in the street and when she asked where I was off to I told her I was going to the shop to buy a bottle of pale ale for Ned, my husband, and Harriet asked me what kind of ale. And when I said I wasn't sure, maybe Murdoch's, she laughed and said: "Oh, don't get Murdoch's for Ned, he's not so fond of that." And I was taken aback, but I found myself asking her what kind of ale I ought to get him, and she suggested Greenhead. And, in fact, she was right because I asked Ned later, and he said he preferred Greenhead Pale Ale. She must have heard him say he liked it or – I don't know. But it made me feel awkward – strange, that she should know his likes and dislikes.'

'That Miss Baxter should seem more familiar with your husband's preferences than you were?'

'Yes, it didn't seem – appropriate.'

'Now, Mrs Gillespie, can you cast your mind back to Saturday, the 13th of April, last year. Can you remember what happened on that date?'

Despite my state of high anxiety, I almost laughed, for Annie could barely remember what day of the week it was, never mind what had happened almost a year ago. However, to my surprise, she replied, immediately, in the affirmative, making me wonder if the question might have been rehearsed.

'Yes, we all went to Bardowie – that is, my husband and children and I went – with Harriet, to a property that belonged to her stepfather. Harriet wanted to show us the house. She was planning to live there, for the summer. She'd made an artist's studio out of one of the rooms, in a tower.'

'An artist's studio? For your husband?'

'No – she'd taken up painting – or that's what she said.'

'You didn't believe her?'

Annie paused for a moment before replying: 'I thought it was a bit odd. She liked art, but she'd never really shown much interest in the pursuit of painting. Not until my husband began teaching at the Art School.'

'I see – and what did she do then?'

'She joined his class.'

'Indeed? And you thought that odd?'

'Well, a bit.'

'Why did you think it a bit odd?'

'I don't know – we saw quite a lot of her, in those days. We thought of her as a friend, I suppose. I was just surprised that she would join Ned's class.'

'And – to return to this day, out at Bardowie – what happened?'

'Well, she invited us to live with her, there, over the summer. We could stay as long as we liked. She had this idea that we could all paint. She said Ned should have the studio, for his work, and she and I could make do, in other rooms.'

'And did you accept this offer?'

'No – not exactly. My husband's very polite, and he finds it difficult to say no. He said something like it was a lovely idea, and I think Harriet may have got the wrong impression, and assumed that we were going to go and stay with her.'

'Did you want to accept her offer?'

'No. We both knew we wouldn't go.'

'Why not?'

'It wouldn't have been right. It would have been too much. Besides, we were hoping to spend the summer on the East Coast. We didn't tell Harriet "no", exactly, but we didn't say "yes" either and we hoped she'd forget about it.'

'And what happened then?'

'Well, we just went home that afternoon. But a few days later, Harriet brought up the house again, when my husband wasn't there. She wanted to know how long we'd stay for, at Bardowie. I didn't want her to be too disappointed. I thought it was better to refuse her, there and then, so there could be no mistake. I told her we wouldn't be going to stay with her.'

Even as I write this, I find myself overcome by exasperation. As I have already made plain, if Annie refused such an invitation, she was perfectly within her rights so to do. I would never suggest that she was a liar, but perhaps this was a little scene that she had conceived, in her mind – perhaps even something that she wanted to be true – and she had somehow convinced herself that it was real. Personally, I have no recollection of the conversation. Yet Aitchison pursued the matter, like a magpie might stalk a fledgling.

'And how did she react?'

'I think she might have taken offence, taken against me. She was angry.'

'Did she lose her temper?'

'Oh no – Harriet would never lose her temper. But I could tell she was raging, underneath. She was holding a teacup, at the time, about to put it on the shelf, and it smashed between her fingers, she'd gripped it that hard.'

Again, Annie must be getting confused here: I did break a teacup at around that time, but by accident, not because I had gripped it hard, but because it had dropped from my fingers.

'Did she change, in her attitude to you, over the next few weeks?'

'Not that I could put my finger on, but she sometimes seemed – I thought I caught her looking at me once, in this funny way. Perhaps it was me – but it made me a wee bit wary of her.'

'You say she regarded you in a "funny" way – how precisely do you mean?'

'I don't know. Something in her eye – not nice.'

This rather unclear statement was left hanging, unexamined, despite the fact that Annie might have meant anything whatsoever by it.

I do intend to refute other parts of Annie's statement to Aitchison, line by line, but am rather too exhausted, at present, for some reason. Perhaps I shall return to this section later, once I have rested. No need to dwell on Pringle's cross-examination: he simply tried to get Annie to corroborate that I had acted strangely on the day of Rose's disappearance, and thereafter. The trouble (for him) was that on that fateful day, the poor dear had other concerns on her mind, and was not exactly paying much attention to me – quite apart from the fact that we must, all of us, have been behaving strangely, faced with the kidnap of a child upon whom everyone doted.

MacDonald kindly refrained from dealing with Annie too savagely but, in his hands, it became apparent that she was not exactly in her right mind. This fact may not be immediately obvious, from the transcripts, for they cannot conjure a visual picture of her, as she stood there, on the stand. I caught stolen glimpses of her, and remember her appearance well. She looked, in all honesty, like a wraith, a pitiful, tortured phantom. The overall impression was of someone who has lost control, someone for whom reality has slipped beyond reach.

Following Annie's testimony, Aitchison called Mrs Esther Watson of London to the stand. Mrs Watson had befriended me, several years previously, when my aunt was still alive, although in poor health. Esther and her husband, Henry, were instructors for the St John Ambulance Association, and I had met them at one of the 'Ladies' classes in 'First Aid for the Injured'. Neither of the Watsons had two pennies to rub together, but they were lucky enough to have inherited a charming old house in Chelsea. In addition to lecturing for the St John, Esther was an operatic soprano. Henry, who had originally studied the law, was something of a briefless barrister. I found them to be amusing company – at least, in the beginning. I dare say that they were rather full of themselves, as people can be, and they did tend to talk exclusively about their own concerns, but they were witty enough, and the three of us spent a lot of time together, and soon became the best of friends.

None the less, faced with Esther Watson on the witness stand, I knew to expect something scurrilous. The truth of the matter was that we had fallen out, rather badly, a few years before I had moved up to Glasgow. In hindsight, I should have known that something was wrong, on the day that Henry took me into the study to show me his stereoscope collection, which turned out to be a set of smutty photographs of some plump, half-clad maids. His expectation, I believe, was that I would find these images arousing, and that looking at them, together, would be the prelude to a steamy encounter on the chaise. A few weeks later, on another occasion when his wife had gone out, he attempted to put his tongue in my ear. It was all very embarrassing, and I was obliged, once again, to cut short my visit. Esther must have suspected something, for she came to see me, later, demanding to know what was going on between Henry and myself. Sadly, she seemed determined to blame me for what had happened, when it was her goat of a husband who was at fault. At any rate, I wondered what slant she might put on events, under questioning, for there was no doubt in my mind that this was the reason behind her appearance as a witness for the prosecution.

Much as it pains me, it should be noted that I give a comprehensive account of this part of the trial. A guilty conscience might seek to conceal allegations such as those made by Esther Watson, on that day. But, as I am sure is evident by now, my only wish is to be open, and honest, and above reproach.

Aitchison lost no time in getting to the crux of the matter.

'You met Miss Harriet Baxter in the year 1883, is that correct?'

'Yes. My husband and I lecture for the St John Ambulance Association. I teach ladies, and Miss Baxter attended my classes.'

'And, outside the classes, how did your friendship with Miss Baxter evolve?'

'Well, we bumped into her, a few times, here and there, at the theatre, and in the street. Then, after the First Aid classes had come to an end, we continued to see her. Usually, she called on us, in Chelsea. She was very curious about First Aid. As time went on, we became friendly, because she was so terribly nice and helpful and accommodating. For instance, she did over all our old sheets, cutting them up the middle and hemming the sides. And one day she went out to the garden, all by herself, and hacked back the shrubbery, where she said it cast too much shadow into the study. Henry was delighted at the difference.'

'She made herself useful, you might say?' remarked Aitchison.

'Yes.'

'Do you have any children, Mrs Watson?'

'No, I'm afraid we haven't been blessed, in that respect.'

It really was too galling. Esther was giving the performance of a lifetime: the soft-spoken voice, the impeccable diction, the neat hat and gloves, the modestly lowered gaze. She must have been forty-five years old, by that stage; still pretty, of course, but somewhat overblown, like a tulip in late May. As far as I was aware, her operatic career had stalled, and she was currently appearing in light musical comedies, something that I know would have rankled with her but, doubtless, she and Henry needed the money.

'And did you and Miss Baxter remain friends?'

Esther glanced at me, and hesitated, before replying. I was dismayed by the coolness of her gaze.

'No – my husband and I were forced to stop seeing her.'

'Please explain.'

But before she could, MacDonald was on his feet.

'My Lord, I must object. The evidence of this witness appears to bear no relevance to the charges Miss Baxter faces.'

The judge turned to Aitchison: 'Advocate Depute?'

'Rest assured, my lord, Mrs Watson's evidence will throw some light upon the direct evidence in the case.'

'Up to the present moment I remain in the dark,' said Kinbervie, with heavy sarcasm. 'But I'll allow you some latitude in your questions, Advocate Depute.'

'Thank you, my lord. Mrs Watson, please tell us why you stopped seeing Miss Baxter.'

With a smile at the judge, Esther resumed her testimony.

'Well, it's hard to explain, but we – I – began to think that she might be trying to inveigle her way into our home. And then I wondered whether she might, in fact, be trying to – to drive a wedge between us, between Henry and myself.'

The long pause that Aitchison then left was undoubtedly designed to allow the significance of this statement to register with the jurymen. Presently, he asked:

'In what way?'

'Oh, there were countless little incidents. I got the sense that, if ever my husband and I had a disagreement, she was secretly pleased. I remember once, when Henry had a headache, and he spoke sharply to me – he said something rather unkind – well, Harriet laughed, and rubbed her hands together, almost with glee. And she had a tendency, when she was with us both, to point out my faults, in front of him. I'm a few years older than she is, you see, and she kept drawing attention to my age. Once, when Henry was there, she stared into my face and said, ever so sadly: 'Oh, Esther, d'you think I'll get horrid jowls, some day, like yours?' But it was always done in the sweetest fashion; she was so charming about it, and amusing, that one couldn't really protest.'

'How long did this continue?'

'Oh, months. Several months. It was all very subtle, you see. Harriet has a way of – she's very charming, and she has this way of wrapping you round her little finger. She can get you to do things, without you even realising. Henry didn't acknowledge it, at first.'

'But, eventually, he did?'

'Well – it was – eh – an incident with some photographs, that finally made him see that there was a problem.'

And then Esther went on to describe what had happened with the stereographs – except that she made it seem as though it was I who had brought them with me to their house, one day, and shown them to Henry.

'So, just to be clear, Mrs Watson: at a time when she knew you would be absent from home, Miss Baxter brought some – let me say, vulgar – photographs, of ladies, to show your husband?'

'Yes, and – as you might expect – it made him terribly uncomfortable, and he told me about it later. Then, we got to talking about Harriet, and when we cast our minds backwards, we realised that there was something – well – not quite right about all those times we'd met her in the street. She lived in Clerkenwell, you see, all the way across London, but we kept bumping into her in Chelsea. She always had a good reason to be in the neighbourhood, but . . . it happened so often. And we began to wonder whether, sometimes, she might have been lying in wait for us.'

'You believe that she had followed you?'

'Not – followed, exactly. But watched us, planned it, in advance, or found out where we were going, so that she could pretend to meet us, by accident.'

'I see. What exactly made you suspect this?'

'Just the number of times it happened. It was too much of a coincidence.'

'And so, you broke off contact with her?'

'Well, we wrote to her, and told her we were going away, and then we pretended to be out, if she called, and we didn't return any of her cards or letters. In the end, she got the message.'

'Mrs Watson, I put it to you that Miss Baxter was infatuated with your husband – was that not the case?'

'I don't know,' Esther replied.

Here, she paused – as well she might have done! I hardly dared to think what preposterous thing either she or the prosecutor might come out with next.

Aitchison prompted her: 'How do you explain Miss Baxter's behaviour?'

'Sometimes – oh, it was all very confusing. It was more as though – more as though she simply wanted to separate Henry and myself – to split us up, to ruin our marriage. You see, she'd always wanted to be her stepfather's little girl – a sort of papa's darling. I visited her once, in Clerkenwell, and her room was like a shrine to him. She'd arranged several daguerreotypes and photographs of him where they could be seen from her bed. Whereas there wasn't a single picture of her mother; you might have thought she hated her mother.'

MacDonald was on his feet to object, but Kinbervie was ahead of him:

'My good woman, what we might or might not have thought is hardly pertinent. Kindly restrict yourself to the facts of the matter. We are perfectly able, here in Scotland, to form our own conclusions, if necessary – although, Advocate Depute, I am not at all convinced that there is sufficient relevance in all this.'

Aitchison apologised to his Lordship, and reminded his witness to stick to the facts. Esther Watson continued:

'Mr Dalrymple, Harriet's father – her stepfather, I mean – he never wrote to her, or visited: a rather distant sort of man. I think it affected Harriet badly. And, it seemed to me that, somehow, in trying to split up my husband and myself, she was wreaking a sort of private revenge – on her mother – or her stepfather – or, I don't know – perhaps, just on Henry and I, simply for being happy together. Although, now that I say all this, I'm afraid it doesn't make much sense.'

She gave the judge her most endearing, dizzy smile.

Kinbervie, who had been listening to her, glassy-eyed and incredulous, raised his eyebrow. Then he cleared his throat and leaned forwards. 'Advocate Depute, fascinating though all this may be – the relevance . . . ?'

'Of course, my lord. Thank you, Mrs Watson – that will be all from me, at the present time. Your witness, my learned friend.'

Once again, Pringle was content to hitch his sled to Aitchison's coat tails, and so the cross-examination passed directly to Mac-Donald. I was aware that my lawyers had something up their sleeves, but in the lead-up to the trial, they had given me no hint of how, exactly, we might counter Esther Watson's radical claims.

When MacDonald rose to his feet, he seemed irritable. In his hands, he held a newspaper, the front page of which he showed to the witness.

'Mrs Watson, do you recognise this publication?'

At the sight of the paper, Esther looked first startled, and then positively dismayed. 'Y–yes, I do.'

'It's an English newspaper. Can you tell the court its name?'

'*The News of the World.*'

'And what kind of publication is it, Mrs Watson?'

'I don't understand –'

'Is it not a newspaper that deals, mainly, in scandals, and titillation?'

'Well – perhaps.'

'Have you ever had any dealings with this newspaper?'

'I – I don't know what you mean –'

'Let me be specific.' MacDonald paused and leaned towards her, impressively. 'Have you ever accepted payment from the editor of this newspaper?'

The entire courtroom held its breath, wondering what significance lay behind his question. Esther hesitated, clearly engaged in some sort of struggle within herself.

MacDonald prompted her: 'Remember, you're under oath, madam. I put it to you that you received payment from this newspaper, only a few weeks ago.'

Esther's face crumpled. 'Yes,' she said, her voice a whisper. 'Yes, I did.'

MacDonald drew himself up to his full height, holding the paper aloft, for all the spectators to see. His outrage was quite awe-inspiring. 'You have signed a contract promising to give *The News of the World* an exclusive account of your friendship with Miss Baxter, and of your appearance, here, in the High Court. This salacious story will be printed for the amusement of those readers who buy this – this – newspaper, next week. Is that not so?'

'Yes.'

'I put it to you, Mrs Watson, that you've embellished your story, and told sensational lies, in order to make your tale more satisfying for readers of this paper.'

'No!' She glanced at me, and then shook her head. 'I may be getting paid, but I've told the truth here today.'

'How much have you been paid, Mrs Watson?'

Esther seemed reluctant to name the sum; MacDonald helped her out.

'Is it forty pounds?'

'. . . Yes,' said Esther, closing her eyes.

There was a gasp from the public benches, for this was a large sum to most of those present, who might never see such an amount of money all at once.

'Forty pounds – let it be recorded – forty pounds – to tell a sordid story, to ruin the reputation of your former friend.'

The advocate turned to the bench and addressed the judge – who could not, at that moment, have looked more surprised had MacDonald thrown up his gown and danced a cancan on the evidence table.

'My lord, not only is the relevance of Mrs Watson's evidence in question, but this is a most flagrant case of a witness being promised a reward for her story. I move that her entire testimony be excluded from the jury's consideration.'

Kinbervie scratched beneath his wig.

'Madam, is this true? You've sold your story to a newspaper?'

Esther looked suitably shamefaced. 'Yes, my lord,' she said, and then added, with a girlish simper: 'I didn't think it would matter.'

'Well,' said Kinbervie. 'It does – and you needn't flutter your eyelashes at me.' Then, he turned to address the jury. 'Gentlemen, I must ask you to disregard the evidence of this witness.'

Subsequently, he took Esther to task, most sternly, for wasting the time of the High Court of Justiciary. I scarcely heard a word that he said to her. It was such an overwhelming relief that my former friend had shown herself to be an out-and-out liar (as well as a non-entity). And yet, I wondered how effective the judge's instruction to the jury could be. After all, whether he told them to disregard her or not, the fact remained that they had listened to every word of her scurrilous account, and it seemed inconceivable that they would not have been swayed, in some degree.

Caskie was preoccupied when he came to see me, during the recess. He and MacDonald had been discussing Aitchison, and the way that he had conducted his prosecution thus far. MacDonald was convinced that the Advocate Depute would leave his key witness, Christina Smith, to the very last, in order to produce her, with a flourish, and end on a dramatic note, with her testimony that she had, at my request, set up a meeting between her sister and brother-in-law and myself.

'Aitchison's clever, you know,' Caskie told me. 'But it's a risky strategy. He's saved all his most damning evidence until the very last few hours. He wants to swirl his cape and leave the stage with a bang, for he only has this afternoon to wheel on his linchpins: Christina, and this blasted bank evidence.'

'I do wish we'd been able to trace those builder's receipts,' I muttered.

'Aye well, we didn't, and I don't doubt Aitchison will make it look as though you went to the Bank of Scotland in St Vincent Place to withdraw money which you then paid to our German friend.'

'I certainly did no such thing. In fact, I don't believe I've ever set foot in the Bank of Scotland.'

Caskie looked startled. 'But, Miss Baxter, there's no question you've withdrawn money from there. Your name appears in the ledger, many times.'

'I doubt that it features in the Bank of Scotland's ledger, Mr Caskie. I use the *National* Bank of Scotland.'

He thought for a moment, and then clicked his tongue. 'Of course,' he said. 'Foolish of me, but the names are so similar, and everyone knows that Bank of Scotland.'

'Yes, but it's such an ugly lump of stone. The National is just up the street, and has a very charming façade, which is why I chose it.'

'Hmm,' said Caskie, frowning, as though trying to remember something. Certainly, this conversation had troubled him, but he simply hurried back upstairs, without saying anything further.

Later, as I resumed my place in the dock, I glanced up at the spectators. A terrible sense of foreboding was growing within me, not helped by the possibility that Ned's wife might decide to join Mabel in the gallery, now that she had testified; I did not relish the notion of spending the next few hours beneath her gaze. However, there was no sign of Annie, as yet.

While the court waited for Kinbervie's return from luncheon, I noticed that Caskie had drifted over to the evidence table. He was examining the bank ledger and some paperwork, with a puzzled look on his face. Before long, he hurried over to MacDonald, document in hand, and began to whisper urgently in his ear. The advocate frowned as he took the sheet of paper from Caskie and peered at it, but there was no time for me to fathom what the matter might be, because, just then, the judge returned, and the proceedings got underway.

As it turned out, Aitchison's first move, that afternoon, was to summon one Neil Ennitt, bank clerk. Mr Ennitt was a gangly young man with pimples, and I must admit that I felt inordinately apprehensive as he was sworn, given Caskie's concerns about the bank evidence. Thus, as the prosecutor approached the evidence table and introduced the ledger, I braced myself, only to see my advocate surging to his feet, at once, with the words:

'My Lord, I have an objection.'

The judge looked startled. 'Are you sure, Mr MacDonald?'

'Yes, my Lord, there's a matter I must bring to your attention, and it would require a recess.'

Kinbervie gave a sigh. 'Is that really necessary?' He indicated the jury. 'These good gentlemen have only just resumed their seats.'

'Apologies, my lord, but I've an objection to the line of evidence.'

With visible irritation, Kinbervie adjourned the jury and the witness. As they filed out, we all waited, on tenterhooks, to hear what my counsel might have to say.

MacDonald nodded to the Macer, who handed up a piece of paper to Kinbervie – the same document that appeared to have troubled Caskie.

'If Your Lordship would have before you Production Number 17,' MacDonald began. 'Your Lordship will see that it is a warrant. This was issued last year when detectives at Cranston Street undertook to examine Miss Baxter's finances. As you'll see, the document has been issued in the name of the Bank of Scotland, in Glasgow, at number 2, St Vincent Street.'

'Yes, yes,' said Kinbervie, impatiently, glancing at the warrant.

'My lord, in the first place, the correct address is number 2, St Vincent *Place*: at the George Square end, St Vincent Street becomes St Vincent Place.'

'May I see the warrant?' Aitchison interjected, coldly.

The judge passed it to him, saying: 'Mr MacDonald what's your point?'

'In fact, my lord, Miss Baxter doesn't even possess an account at this bank, nor at any branch of the Bank of Scotland. Her bank is the *National* Bank of Scotland — which, you'll be aware, my lord, is a separate institution. The National is further up the road, on St Vincent Street itself, a smaller building. Now, it may be that, in filling out the details on this warrant, an understandable mistake was made: most Glaswegians, asked to name a bank on St Vincent Street, would immediately think of the Bank of Scotland, although it is, in fact, on St Vincent Place. Understandable or not, a mistake has been made and an inexcusable mistake at that. This warrant has been made out for the wrong bank.'

'My lord,' interrupted Aitchison. 'The evidence from the ledger will show clearly that Miss Baxter withdrew large sums of money upon certain dates. It's an integral part of the case against them.'

'No doubt,' said the judge, who seemed scarce able to believe his ears. 'Mr MacDonald, what of the policeman who went to fetch this ledger? Surely he should have checked the details on his warrant?'

'It appears he didn't, my lord, and this is definitely the warrant that was presented at the National.'

'By some miracle, the fellow went to the correct bank,' said Kinbervie, drily.

MacDonald nodded. 'My Lord, he was probably acting on verbal instructions from a superior. And then, the bank staff, no doubt flustered by the police presence, also appear to have failed to check the warrant properly.'

Kinbervie raised a scathing eyebrow. 'One tends to assume – naively, it seems – that police documents are beyond criticism.'

'Indeed so, my lord, but the upshot is that the ledger was seized without any legal authority and therefore is inadmissible as evidence in this trial.'

Aitchison affected boredom. 'My lord, it's hardly an egregious error,' he said. 'What matters is that we have the correct ledger.'

'Pray give me a moment, Advocate Depute, in order to consider,' said Kinbervie, and he fell to perusing the warrant, in silence.

And so, I had been right in thinking that something had bothered Caskie, during the recess. Having checked the paperwork, he must have realised what had planted the notion in his mind that I was a customer of the Bank of Scotland: it was the warrant, which (I later learned) he had glanced at, only that morning. Being an old stager, versed in the technicalities of the law, he hoped that this tiny mistake could be exploited in our favour, and that there was a chance that we might be able to have the bank evidence disallowed. But would the judge be persuaded?

Presently, after due consideration, Kinbervie looked up.

'Advocate Depute, your production – the ledger – is from Miss Baxter's bank, the National Bank, in St Vincent Street, is that correct?'

'Yes, my Lord. It's from the correct bank, and it's the correct ledger and can be spoken to by Mr Ennitt, the bank employee.'

Disappointment began to sink through my stomach, as Kinbervie continued:

'You'd agree with me, Advocate Depute, that this warrant relates not to the National Bank of Scotland, but to the Bank of Scotland.'

'Yes, my Lord, but –'

'Advocate Depute, there are rules to be followed in these matters, as you well know,' said the judge and then, with a nod, to MacDonald, he raised his voice for the benefit of the general assembly. 'This evidence was erroneously acquired, and is therefore inadmissible in this court, and must be withdrawn. I'm assuming, Advocate Depute, your witness was only going to speak to the ledger, in which case, no need to recall him.'

It took me a moment to realise that we had won our point.

Aitchison knew when he was defeated. With a curt nod, he returned to his table. There was a pause, as he stared down at his papers, one absent-minded hand fiddling with the ties at the back of his wig, the muscles in his jaw twitching and grinding, as though his face was changing gear.

Well – that was, indeed, a highly unexpected stroke of luck. The prosecutor's first real setback: we had won a crucial battle, one of two that we would have to win that afternoon, if we were to have even a chance of success. For the first time since the previous day, I felt a glimmer of hope.

We had not long to relish the moment, however, before Aitchison galvanised his forces and resumed the offensive, with the reading of my declaration. I cannot say that it was worth his while, for there was nothing therein that helped his case: I had simply told the truth and, in listening to my own statement, read aloud, I felt that I had given a fair and eloquent account of myself. Perhaps the prosecutor agreed, for he moved on, swiftly, by calling Ned Gillespie, an announcement that knocked the wind out of me as surely as though I had been punched in the pit of my stomach. Here was a moment that I had been anticipating for weeks. Of course, prior to the trial, it was impossible to know exactly whom Aitchison might put on the stand. Witnesses have no choice in whether they appear for the prosecution or the defence and, although being summoned by the Crown does not necessarily imply that a person will speak ill of the accused, it had wounded me to see Ned's name so casually recorded on the witness list of 'the opposition', alongside the likes of Esther Watson. I had attempted to ascertain whether my lawyer thought that Ned was likely to be called, but Caskie had seemed uncertain, saying: 'Your man Gillespie wouldnae be at the top of my list, if I were prosecuting – but he wouldnae be at the bottom either.'

As we waited for Ned's arrival, a curious unreality seemed to creep into the High Court. I had a sense of being at unbearably close proximity to everybody in the room, and yet, simultaneously, I felt very far away. For the first time, I noticed a few peanut shells on the floor, near my feet, and an unaccountable whimsicality made me wonder who on earth, whilst in the dock – what murderer, what baby-farmer, what brute – would have been so cool-blooded as to munch on nuts whilst watching their own trial unfold before them, with the casual interest of a circus-goer, picnicking at the ringside? I began to feel dizzy. The faces of spectators in the public gallery swam before me. They seemed harsh and inhuman, as though they had been carved in wood. Were they really shouting? The clamour of voices was so loud that it drowned out the approach of Ned's footsteps, but silence fell as soon as he entered the court.

If I close my eyes now, I can still picture him. Had his name not been called out, I might not have recognised my dear friend. His complexion had as much life and colour as cold ashes in a grate. His hair was almost entirely grey. Despite the chill in the Parliament Building, a sheen of perspiration lay clammy upon his skin. He walked slowly, deliberately, and looked neither right nor left as he crossed the room, towards the stand. A clerk passed him the Bible, and Ned gazed at the floor, grimacing every so often, while he was sworn. For anyone who knew him, it was most disconcerting to watch. It occurred to me that he might actually be physically ill, in some way.

Aitchison was asking him a question.

'Yes,' answered Ned. 'At the Grosvenor Gallery. I had a painting in an exhibition there. We met only briefly.'

'And then you encountered her again, in Glasgow, at the International Exhibition, in the May of 1888.'

'Aye. By then, she'd become acquainted with the women in my family.'

'Where was she residing, at this time?'

'Round the corner from us, in Queen's Crescent.'

'The very same Queen's Crescent from where your daughter was snatched?'

'Aye,' said Ned.

'And when did Miss Baxter's visit to Glasgow become permanent?'

'I don't know. I think, to begin with, she only meant to stay for a few months, but as time went by, she talked less and less of going back down south.'

'And you became close to her.'

A frown creased Ned's brow. 'Well, the women in my family did. My wife painted Harriet's portrait, and – eh – she was often in our home, or across the street, with my mother and sister. And, of course, that first summer, we all spent time together, at the Exhibition.'

'So, if I may repeat the question, you became close to her?'

'Only in the sense that she was a friend of my wife.'

Here, of necessity, Ned was being cautious and discreet. Of course, we were close friends – as many men and women are, nowadays – but it would have been inappropriate to advertise the fact, back then. Moreover, there had been all those rumours, after Findlay's sketch of us had appeared in *The Thistle*.

'And – you would sometimes bump into Miss Baxter, in the park and street?'

Ned thought for a moment before replying: 'Yes, we did.'

'How often did that happen?'

'Quite a lot. Harriet's lodgings were only a few minutes from our building. Where we live, you can't walk down the street for bumping into people you know.'

'I see. And did you bump into Miss Baxter rather more frequently than might be explained by simple coincidence?'

'No. As I said, we were neighbours. It was perfectly normal.'

Aitchison cast one of his looks of mild disbelief towards the jury box, and then remarked: 'You personally must have bumped into Miss Baxter from time to time, when you were alone?'

Ned scowled. 'What do you mean to imply, sir?'

'Nothing at all. I simply would like to know whether you ever bumped into Miss Baxter, accidentally, when you were unaccompanied?'

As though it were an effort to contain his temper, Ned set his jaw, and replied, tersely: 'Aye.' His manner was brusque, but I could tell that he was simply in a highly emotional and anxious state.

'How often? Once – twice? Half-a-dozen times? Fifty?'

'I would say in the region of a dozen.'

'A dozen times? Does that not seem rather a lot to you, Mr Gillespie?'

'Is it your intention to ask further questions on this matter?' Ned snapped. 'Or shall we talk about something more pertinent to the death of my daughter?'

Taken aback – as we all were – the judge coughed and spluttered, then intervened.

'Mr Gillespie. We all realise you must be very upset, but be so kind as to answer the Advocate Depute's questions. I shall be the one to dictate the pace, in this courtroom, and I do not require your assistance.'

Ned looked somewhat chastened. 'I beg your pardon, my lord.'

Poor Ned! It was only the strain that made him sound so impatient and irritable. In other circumstances, I would have applauded his riposte to Aitchison, for I was sick of seeing witness after witness treat the man with fawning deference.

Kinbervie gestured to the prosecutor. 'Please continue.'

'Thank you, my lord. Now then, Mr Gillespie, did you not think it coincidental that you met Miss Baxter in London, and then, a few months later, she turns up in Glasgow, residing not three minutes walk from your home?'

'It was a coincidence – but coincidences do happen.'

'And you never felt bothered by Miss Baxter, or pestered by her?'

Ned pursed his lips, and frowned again. 'Sometimes we did. My wife began to tire of her visits, at one point. But Harriet was always so very kind and helpful. To shun her, or avoid her, would have been awkward, even churlish. And she is an unmarried lady, living in solitary circumstances. Our feeling was that she was, perhaps, lonely, in Glasgow, and we tried to make her feel welcome.'

'It was around the time that you befriended Miss Baxter, was it not, that the behaviour of your eldest daughter, Sibyl, began to deteriorate?'

'About that time, aye, although she's always been a high-spirited child. She went through a difficult period, but she's now much better behaved.'

'And this improvement in her behaviour dates from when?'

'Eh – she's been getting much better these past few months.'

'A period that coincides, rather neatly, don't you think, with Miss Baxter's incarceration in prison?' Ned simply looked troubled, and so Aitchison continued without waiting for an answer. 'How did Sibyl and Miss Baxter get along with each other?'

Ned gave a shrug of his shoulders. 'Sibyl is a child. They got along well enough. Harriet was always kind to her, and brought her presents.'

'Ah, yes – the many presents of Miss Harriet Baxter. And you yourself, Mr Gillespie, how do you feel about your daughter – about Sibyl?'

A shadow passed across Ned's face. There was a pause, and then, when he spoke, his voice was cracked, gruff with emotion.

'She means everything to me.'

Aitchison acknowledged Ned's grief with a deferential bow of his head.

'Understandably so, Mr Gillespie, understandably so.' Here, the prosecutor paused, and took a sip of water, before resuming: 'But sir, did it ever seem to you that your affection for your daughters or your wife might have vexed Miss Baxter?'

'I don't follow what you mean.'

'Let me put it more plainly – did you ever suspect that Miss Baxter might be jealous of Sibyl, or jealous of your wife or, indeed, of anybody who might have been close to you, or the recipient of your affection?'

Here, I turned to stare at MacDonald, expecting to see him rise to his feet but, to my dismay, he did nothing. He just sat there. Aitchison continued with his questions, in a coaxing manner, his voice full of spurious concern.

'Mr Gillespie, on the 31st of December 1888, you held a Hogmanay celebration at which Miss Baxter was one of the guests, is that correct?'

'Yes.'

'And I believe that punch was served that evening, and everyone who drank that punch fell ill, is that so?'

'Yes. To my mind, it was bad wine that caused the trouble.'

'Indeed? Please tell us what was found, the following day, in your daughter Sibyl's room, in the pocket of her apron.'

Ned coughed, before replying: 'An empty packet of rodent poison.'

'And did Sibyl get the blame for what had happened, with the punch?'

'Not from me, anyway. My wife and mother thought different.'

'On the night of the party, did Miss Baxter have access to Sibyl's room?'

'Aye.'

'And would she have had an opportunity to put the packet of poison in your daughter's apron?'

'She had the opportunity, but you can't blame Harriet. She herself got ill that night. If she knew there was poison in the punch, then why would she drink it? Like I said, it was just bad wine.'

'Did you see Miss Baxter drink the punch, Mr Gillespie?'

'I think so. I saw her with a glass of it, at one point.'

'Did you see her take a sip from the glass?'

'I can't remember.'

'Did you see her being ill?'

'Not exactly. But she looked terrible, and complained of a stomach ache.'

'And was she seen by a doctor, like the others who became ill that night?'

'No. She didn't want to make any fuss – very typical of Harriet.'

Aitchison raised his brows and widened his eyes.

Really, I need hardly interject here to defend myself, or make any justification, for Ned said it all. His stubborn refusal to believe that I could have been responsible for any of Sibyl's crimes speaks volumes. Realising that he was on a hiding to nothing with this folderol about the poison, Aitchison moved on.

'Did it never cross your mind, Mr Gillespie, that Harriet Baxter might have had some malign intent with regard to certain members of your family – that she could, for her own complicated reasons, have been trying to punish Sibyl, or cause a rift between you and your wife?'

Ned hesitated before replying. 'Harriet – Miss Baxter – is so kind, she seemed like a good friend to us. My wife may have her doubts. But nothing of the sort ever entered my mind, until –'

'Until when, Mr Gillespie?'

Why did MacDonald not do something? He was just sitting there, as though he had been glued to his seat. His expression was as calm as ever, but his eyes had glazed over in a way that made me suspect, of a sudden, that he had lost confidence.

Turning back to the stand, I was shocked to realise that, for the first time since he had entered the room, Ned was looking directly at me. It quite took me by surprise, for I had been glaring over at MacDonald, trying to will him, by dint of brainpower, to leap up and intervene. And now, Ned's eyes were upon me: staring, questioning, wanting to know. He seemed, almost, to be pleading with me, in silence. The seconds ticked by: how many, exactly, I could not say. What oceans of meaning can be contained, within one look! Held in his gaze, I stared back at him, for as long as I was able and, in the end, it was not any sense of guilt on my part that made me glance away (put that in your pipe and smoke it, Mr P. E. Dant – or whatever your name was – of *The Scotsman*); quite the contrary. It was simply that Ned looked so tortured, so haunted, so wounded, and I could not bear to see my dear friend in such a wretched state, knowing all the horrors that he had gone through. It cracked my heart in two. I bowed my head and stared at the floor beneath my feet, the waxy green linoleum of the dock.

'Mr Gillespie?' Aitchison prompted.

I heard Ned clear his throat and then, after a moment, he continued.

'I suppose, after Harriet's arrest, once we'd got over the shock of it, I did begin to wonder, and think back. I remembered that one of our maids, Jessie, had said some vile things about Harriet, when she was dismissed, about a year ago. Of course, we didn't believe a word then, because Jessie had stolen something from us and we thought she was just trying to worm her way out of a tricky situation.'

'And now?'

'I'm not sure what to think any more. I don't know what to think about anything or anyone, including Harriet Baxter.'

After that, I could not look at him again. It was as though something very heavy had landed on my heart, squashing it, and crushing all the breath out of me. Of a sudden, I ceased to care what happened. They could find me guilty, if they wanted. They could tear me, limb from limb.

Too late – too late. Outside, the bells are ringing. Christ Church, St Giles in the Field, St George's. And all of them say, too late.

The next few witnesses are but dim in my memory. As I came back to my senses, I was aware of Aitchison summoning the dreaded Christina Smith to the stand and then a lull, as we waited for her inevitable arrival. Everything around me seemed dull and dampened. It was as though I was shut away from my surroundings. Straight ahead of me, Aitchison had puffed himself up in preparation for his star witness. As he turned to survey the court, his gaze met mine. His green eyes glinted. Unable to bear the sight of him, I bent my head and focused on the little vial of smelling salts in my hand. At some point, I came back to my senses, when the hiatus was broken by the return of the Macer. He entered alone, and shook his head in response to a questioning look from Aitchison. There was a pause, whilst the prosecutor carried on whispered conversations, first with the Macer, and then with various legal colleagues. Presently, he turned to address the judge.

'My Lord, for the moment, I'm afraid we're unable to locate one of our key witnesses. We hope to produce her, at any minute. She did answer her citation this morning, and we believe she's in the vicinity, somewhere.'

Kinbervie slid a sideways glance at the clock. It was ten minutes short of seven. 'Might I remind you of the hour, Advocate Depute? Have you no one to produce, in the meantime? If I'm not mistaken, you're in no position to delay, for this trial must conclude tomorrow.'

'You are never mistaken, my lord,' said Aitchison. 'If I can just beg your patience in waiting for Miss Smith.'

Kinbervie clucked his tongue. 'It's now ten minutes to seven. You have until the hour to place her in the witness box.'

'Very good, my lord.'

Gathering his assistants and the Macer around him, Aitchison whispered urgently to them, and then they hurried out of the chamber, one after the other. The judge sat back in his chair, pulling at his lower lip, with one eye on the clock. I myself watched the minute hand as it made its slow progress upwards, towards, and then beyond, the number 11. In the interim, the public remained remarkably quiet, aware that the court was still in session, and that Kinbervie would tolerate no more disruptions. Aitchison's demeanour appeared calm, and it was only by careful study that one could see how he betrayed his nerves in the twitch of his fingers. As the minute hand reached the hour, footsteps were heard scuttling along the corridor towards the court. The door flew open, and the Macer practically skidded into the chamber. Aitchison, as beady-eyed and irascible as an owl, stared at him.

'Well?' he demanded.

'I'm sorry sir,' replied the Macer. 'I spoke to Miss Smith myself, this morning, in the waiting room, but it seems that one of the caretakers noticed her leave the building soon afterwards – and she hasn't been seen since.'

Aitchison turned to the judge. 'My lord, if I may –'

'Advocate Depute,' interjected Kinbervie. 'Can you produce your witness?'

'No, my lord.'

'Do you have another witness whom you wish to present?'

Aitchison was seen to bow his head, a fraction. Then, he looked up, his expression so full of bile that I thought he might spit.

'Call Jessie McKenzie,' he announced.

You may or may not remember that Jessie had worked as the Gillespies' maid for about six months. Aitchison produced her as though he had just turned over a winning card. However, I saw MacDonald nod to himself, and smile. Evidently, he felt capable of dealing with McKenzie. It was no shock to learn that she was a witness: her name had been on the original list, and she had been precognosed, but I suppose that it was a slight surprise that, in the absence of Christina, Aitchison had called her. I had warned Caskie that Jessie had taken a dislike to me, simply because I was English, and I had told him about an incident that had turned out to be a misunderstanding on her part, but he was confident that, no matter what she said, we could discredit her testimony, because she was a thief.

Led by Aitchison, Jessie began to describe certain events that she claimed took place in the March of 1889: the aforementioned misunderstanding. MacDonald was soon on his feet.

'My lord, I object to this line of questioning.'

The judge peered at him. 'On what grounds, might I ask?'

'On grounds of relevance, my Lord. This alleged incident took place weeks before the abduction, and appears to have little or nothing to do with this case. My learned friend is simply grasping at straws, to fill the gaping hole left in his case by his absconded witness.'

The judge glanced at Aitchison. 'Advocate Depute?'

'My lord, I assure you that Miss McKenzie's evidence will cast light upon the direct evidence in the case.'

'Very well,' said Kinbervie. 'Let's hear what the young lady has to say, and then we can decide whether or not it's relevant.'

Since Jessie's testimony is printed verbatim in Kemp's pamphlet, I will skip Aitchison's examination of her – which was interrupted continually by objections from MacDonald – and simply take the opportunity to make my denials here: for instance, if what she said was true, then why did she not challenge me, at the time, like any sensible person would?

MacDonald put this very question to her during his cross-examination, but she was evasive, saying that she had not wanted to confront me.

'Miss Baxter was a friend of the family, sir. It would have been awkward.'

'If, as you say, you spied upon her that day, can you explain why Miss Baxter failed to see or hear you?'

'Well, sir, I didnae make any noise. Like I said, she went in the dining room, and I wondered what she was up to, so I crept across the hall, and the door was half open, so I peeked through the crack between the door and the frame.'

'And afterwards, what did you do?'

'Afterwards?'

'After you'd spied on her.'

'Just went back to the kitchen. And then later, when she'd went home, I had a look to see what it was she'd done.'

'Ah yes,' said MacDonald, peering at his notes. 'And please tell us what you found, exactly.'

'I already said –'

'Yes, but I'd like you to be more specific. What did you find on the wall?'

Thus far, both Aitchison and Pringle had dealt with the issue in quite general terms, though I cannot decide whether this was due to prudery on their part or a desire to avoid, in the minds of the jury, association with something so crude.

Jessie's cheeks had flushed. 'It was – I'd rather not say in public, sir.'

'You've already told us, have you not, that it was an obscene drawing?'

'Yes, sir.'

'Done in red and black crayon – low down – on the wall.'

'Yes, like I said.'

'Anatomical?'

'Sorry, sir – I don't understand the question.'

'You said the drawing depicted a part of the human body – the male body?'

'Aye, sir.'

'Let's be clear – what you are claiming is that Miss Baxter – this lady you see before you now in the dock – got down on her hands and knees and – with a child's crayons – defaced the wall of her friend's dining room with an obscene drawing of the – excuse me, my lord, ladies, for this coarseness of terminology – the male private parts, executed in red and black?'

'That's right, sir.'

'The red crayon, presumably, used to draw the outline of the male organ – is that correct?'

'Yes.'

'And the black?'

'For the – for the hairs, sir.'

'In your opinion, Miss Baxter would do this for what reason?'

'Like I said before, sir, I don't really know, but she must have wanted to get Sibyl into trouble, because Sibyl was always in trouble, at that time, for doing things like drawing on walls, and hiding things and breaking them.'

'You didn't confront Miss Baxter, at the time, and you didn't express any concern to your employers?'

'No, sir.'

'Why did you not tell them? Surely that would have been the thing to do?'

'Miss Baxter was their friend. She was always at the house. They spoke well of her – I didn't think they'd believe me.'

'Miss Baxter was helpful to your employers, wasn't she?'

Jessie gave a shrug of her shoulders. 'She certainly made herself useful.'

'And she was fond of the children?'

'Rose, aye. Poor Sibyl, she's not an easy bairn – you have to indulge her.'

'Did Miss Baxter indulge her?'

'Sometimes.'

'And the children liked Miss Baxter?'

'I suppose so. She gave them lots of presents.'

'Were you jealous of Miss Baxter, Miss MacKenzie? Of her friendship with the family, her relationship with the children?'

'No, not at all. I'm not jealous of her, no, I'm not, I'm quite happy, so I am.'

MacDonald raised an eyebrow, eloquently conveying the thought that must have been going through the minds of all present. He might have remarked: 'The lady doth protest too much', but instead, he simply asked: 'You're sure of that?'

'Aye, sir.'

'Now, tell me – think very carefully, back to that day – did you see the crayons in Miss Baxter's hand, at any point?'

'. . . No, sir.'

'Did you see her, in fact, make any mark on the wall with a crayon?'

'No, sir, she had her back to the door, and I couldn't see, exactly. I just saw her crouched down in the corner, and then, after she left, I went and looked at what she'd drawn.'

'That was your assumption – that she'd been drawing on the wall.'

'There was a drawing, where she'd crouched down. It wasnae there before.'

'Prior to that afternoon, how long was it since you entered the dining room?'

'I don't know – a day or so? The previous night, it might have been.'

'And the children had access to the room in that time?'

'Well – yes.'

'Could one of the children, then – could Sibyl not have done the drawing?'

'Well – I suppose so. But I saw Miss Baxter right there.'

'Yes, but you didn't actually see her make any marks on the wall, did you?'

'No, sir.'

'Your own action, at the time, once Miss Baxter had gone, was to wipe away the drawing. Why did you do that?'

'Because I knew Sibyl would get in trouble for it. She was always getting into trouble, and it wasn't her that done it – not this time, anyway.'

'Did it not occur to you, at any point, that Miss Baxter might have been trying to do exactly the same thing – that she might have been trying to wipe away the drawing, to get rid of it, in order to protect Sibyl, just like you'd done. Did that not occur to you?'

'No, sir.'

'Was the drawing smudged at all?'

'Not much – a wee bit.'

'You mentioned that you wiped away the drawing with a scrubbing brush, and soap and water. Could you have wiped it off with your bare hand?'

'I don't think so – not very well.'

'You've stated that, a few days later, you spoke to Miss Baxter, in private, and asked her what she'd been doing in the dining room. How did she respond?'

'Well, like I said, she denied it.'

'Denied?'

'That she'd even been in the room. Then when I said I'd seen her crouching down, she said that she remembered.'

'What did she remember?'

'She said she'd seen the picture on the wall and kneeled down to try and clean it away, with her hand, but it wouldnae come off.'

'With her hand?'

'Aye.'

'Did she seem angry, that you had accused her?'

'No really, sir, not on the surface, but she was always very nicey-nicey.'

'And, moving on – as you told my learned friend, the Advocate Depute – you were dismissed a few weeks later, for stealing a brooch.'

'I never stole it.'

'As you told the Advocate Depute –' The lamps had been lit, long since, and MacDonald had to peer down as he consulted his notes. 'You said: Miss Baxter must have stole it and then went and put it under my mattress, so I'd get the blame. She wanted shot of me, in case I told about what I'd seen.'

Now, I knew that Jessie had never been terribly keen on me, because I was from 'down south' and so on, but I had no idea that she harboured such a low opinion of me that she would give voice, on the stand, to such terrible falsehoods. As if I would even conceive of doing anything that might result in Sibyl getting into trouble: the notion was preposterous. Of course, my lawyers had hoped that we could discredit Jessie's testimony with the revelation that she was a thief, but we little expected Aitchison to preempt us, rather cleverly, by introducing the subject of the stolen brooch himself, along with this far-fetched allegation that it was me who had hidden it in Jessie's room, deliberately, in order that she would lose her job. Pringle, in cross-examination, had fortified this picture of me as some sort of malign mischief-maker, and Kinbervie did nothing to stop this specious line of evidence.

MacDonald did his best to demonstrate that Jessie was motivated by ill will. Alas, her artless, couthy manner and lack of sophistication tickled the crowd, with the result that he was hard pressed to undo the damage that she had wrought.

'Miss MacKenzie, what did you think of Miss Baxter?'

Jessie gave a shrug of her shoulders.

'Did you like her?'

'She was fine – a bit stuck-up, I suppose, that's what I thought anyway, until she done that drawing and dropped me right in the skink with thon brooch.'

The laughter which greeted this remark was immediately suppressed by His Lordship. MacDonald continued:

'What about folk from England, in general – the English – do you like them?'

Jessie thought about this for a moment, and then resolutely shook her head. 'No really, sir.'

This delighted so many of the spectators that Kinbervie threatened to clear the court, following which he turned to address my advocate.

'*Tempus fugit*, Mr MacDonald. If you'd be so kind as to make haste.'

'Certainly, my lord.' MacDonald turned back to the witness. 'Miss McKenzie, if I might summarise, then: in your mind, this English lady – whom you admit to having disliked – drew an obscene picture on the wall, for which she knew Sibyl Gillespie would get the blame.'

'Yes.'

'And then, later, after you had confronted her, she engineered your dismissal, by stealing a brooch, and hiding it in your room, where she ensured that it was found by your employers. Would that be an accurate summary of what you believe to be the case?'

'Aye, sir.'

MacDonald cast a disbelieving glance in the direction of the jurymen.

'Is it not true that you're simply jealous of Miss Baxter, particularly her relationship with the Gillespie children whom you liked and who were fond of her?'

'No, sir.'

'I put it to you, Miss McKenzie, that there is nothing behind these claims and stories of yours.'

'Oh, but there is, sir.'

'I put it to you that they are nothing but a fiction: they are simply the product of your imagination.'

'No, sir,' protested Jessie. 'They cannae be the product of my imagination, because, you see, sir, I havenae got an imagination.'

Even His Lordship was seen to chuckle as he gathered his papers, preparatory to adjourning the proceedings for the day.

Thus ended the case for the prosecution. Christina's failure to appear was certainly fortuitous, as was the prohibition of the bank evidence, but so much else had gone wrong that I was in no mood for rejoicing. Back in the gloomy depths of the Parliament House, I sat, numb, and close to despair. Jessie's final comment had endeared her to the crowd. The only person who did not seem at all amused was Ned's sister. She had frowned as she stood up to fasten her coat, and I found it impossible to catch her eye before she turned and hurried out of the chamber. As far as I was aware, Mabel had heard all about Jessie's various accusations at the time of her dismissal but, presumably, she had scuttled off to tell her brother everything anew. My fear was that Jessie's words would now carry more weight, having been spoken from the witness box. In truth, the incident that she described never happened; or rather, it did happen, but Jessie misinterpreted what she saw.

The notion (as put forward by Kemp, in his pamphlet) that Jessie's testimony illustrated something profound about my nature – and therefore merited inclusion in the trial – is erroneous. Kinbervie should have interrupted Aitchison's examination, and dismissed the witness, since her evidence did not refer, in the least, to the abduction of Rose. As it was, the Crown was able to use the girl – her muddled mind and mistaken conclusions – to blacken my character, pure and simple.

But would Ned and Annie now be persuaded that I had, in fact, done something to victimise Sibyl?

21

The prosecution having taken two days over their case, Messrs Pringle and MacDonald were obliged to share the last day of the trial. The morning began badly, in the holding cell, when Caskie arrived with the startling news that MacDonald might call Sibyl Gillespie to the stand. This had not been part of my lawyers' original strategy. However, they were keen to counter Aitchison's suggestions that I was the veiled lady who had sent Sibyl running to the shop.

I could not help but be alarmed.

'Is she well enough?' I asked Caskie. 'I thought you said she was volatile?'

'Aye,' said he. 'It's a risk, but if we can get her to positively identify Belle instead of you, then that'll be a real feather in our case.'

How I wished that he had said 'cap'. It seemed a terrible omen that he would have so mangled a cliché on the most important day of my life.

Upstairs, the courtroom was crammed to suffocation. I scanned the gallery as I took my place in the dock and found Ned, in one of the back rows. He was staring at the floor, his pale face betraying the traces of acute mental suffering. There was no sign of Annie, and I was unsure what to deduce from this fact, for surely his wife could have joined him, had she wished. Mabel was also absent.

At long last, Kinbervie took his place at the bench. It was after ten o'clock, and I was already impatient, acutely aware of the shortage of time remaining. Thankfully, Pringle called comparatively few witnesses. According to Caskie, the situation was not looking good for Schlutterhose and Belle. Pringle seemed to have persuaded them that their only hope was to try and evade the murder charge, because he addressed his efforts, in the main, to demonstrating that Rose had died as a result of injuries sustained in the tram accident in St George's Road.

John Wheatley, the driver of the vehicle involved, said that on the afternoon in question his tram had been proceeding along St George's Road at the normal pace, when he noticed a man with a girl in his arms, attempting to board the tram in front. After this tram failed to stop for him, the man had turned to look down the street, apparently startled by the sound of a wagon dumping its cargo of stones. Then, seeming to forget where he was, the fellow stepped forwards, without warning, directly into the path of Wheatley's horses. The driver claimed to have applied his brakes, at once, and hauled the reins, but it was too late: one of the horses reared up, and its collar caught the man's shoulder, knocking him to the ground, and causing him to drop his little girl. When Wheatley jumped down from his platform, the man was already on his feet, scooping up the child, and saying: 'All is good, all is good.' His accent sounded foreign to the driver's ears, possibly Italian, but Wheatley could not be certain. According to him, the man in question was a tall, powerfully built fellow, with a beard and whiskers. The driver verified that the man had seemed intoxicated, saying that he 'stank like Dundashill'. When asked if he was able to identify the man, that day, in court, Wheatley stared long and hard at Hans, before replying: 'The prisoner is about the same size and build. He looks neater, but that might be because he's cleaned himself up. I'd say the prisoner is very like the man I saw.'

In cross-examination, Aitchison was keen to emphasise any shred of doubt.

'And, in your opinion, the man you saw that day was an Italian?'

'Well, he sounded Italian to me.'

'Not German?'

'Well, sir, I don't know much about it, but I thought he was Italian.'

Aitchison avoided asking Wheatley about whether or not the child had been bleeding, and for good reason: examined by Pringle, the driver had been absolutely certain on one point: that he had seen blood on the little girl's head.

'She was definitely bleeding,' he told Pringle. 'I reckon she gave her skull a crack when she fell. The blood was at the back of her head.'

Several other witnesses who had seen the incident also attested to having noticed blood on the child's head immediately afterwards. All but one of them identified Schlutterhose as the man who had picked her up, after the collision, and hurried away. Each witness was shown one of Ned's paintings of Rose, and all were unanimous in stating that the girl in the picture resembled the child that they had seen that day. Most of the spectators craned forwards in their seats to get a glimpse of Rose's portrait, but Ned's gaze dropped to the floor, as though he could not bear to contemplate the image of his daughter, painted by his own hand. For the rest of the time, he kept his eyes fixed on the witnesses.

Miss Celia Stewart was a neat, well-gloved little person of about sixty years of age, with wispy white hair and a dry, precise manner.

'The prisoner was clearly in a state of inebriation,' she told the court. 'He stepped onto the tramlines without checking that there was nothing approaching, as one does, or should do, almost by instinct, these days.'

'And – eh – where was the – eh – the tram at that stage?' asked Pringle.

'The horses were about eight feet away from him, coming on at a fair clip – not too fast, mind you, but the usual speed. They were on him in an instant. The child was knocked out of his arms as he fell.'

'Did he let the – eh – the child go in order to save himself?'

Miss Stewart shook her head.

'No, it was unavoidable. He couldn't have saved her from falling. He was sent flying and she was knocked from his arms and landed several feet away.'

'You are saying that he couldn't help dropping the girl?'

'No – he had no time to react – although he could have had the good sense not to step in front of the tram in the first place.'

'But when all's said and done, it was, in your opinion, an accident?'

'Without a doubt.'

During cross-examination, Aitchison was keen to quash any notion that Rose might have perished as the result of this collision. Despite a lack of evidence to the contrary, he wanted us to believe that Rose had been 'done away with', at some point following her arrival at Coalhill Street. Yes, there might well have been an accident in Woodside on the afternoon in question, but the prosecutor was determined to dispel any belief that Hans and Rose could have been the man and child involved or, at any rate, that the child could have been hurt by such a fall. I found Aitchison's manner with the defence witnesses uniformly supercilious, and his attitude to Miss Stewart, in particular, was sneering. He seemed almost affronted that he was obliged to question an ageing biddy whose opinions he clearly considered to be irrelevant. For her part, the witness refused to be bullied, and lost not a feather.

'Miss Stewart, you said you were forty feet away at the time of this accident. And you are asking us to believe that you can identify this prisoner, this stranger, when you were at such a distance from the tram?'

'Oh, I was only that far away at the moment of the accident. As soon as it happened, I hurried over and, when he stood up, I was as close to him as you are now, only a few feet away. The prisoner is definitely the man I saw that afternoon.'

Perhaps wisely, the prosecutor dropped this angle and moved on.

'And what happened to the child when she fell?'

'She hit the ground; her head hit the ground first. I saw it clearly.'

Aitchison gave her his most disbelieving look.

'From forty feet away – you're sure of that, are you?'

'Yes, I am, because I remember being quite horrified at the time. Had she fallen another way, on her behind, for instance, she might have fared better, you see. But as it was, her head took the impact. The road is cobbled there, and cobblestones are extremely hard. I thought, at the time, that it would be a wonder if she did not sustain a severe fracture of the skull, if not some trauma to the brain.'

The Advocate Depute widened his eyes and turned slightly, so that the jury would be able to appreciate his mocking smile.

'I take it, dear lady, you are an expert in skull fractures and brain trauma?'

'Not exactly,' replied Miss Stewart. 'My speciality is midwifery, which I've practised all my life but, as a younger woman, I did study medicine in Pennsylvania, when I lived in America.'

Aitchison turned a deep shade of pink, and his eyes glazed over.

'Indeed, so you did, indeed,' he muttered, looking down and leafing, busily, through his notes. Such a slip was unusual for the prosecutor. Whether he had been aware of Miss Stewart's medical background, and simply forgotten it, or whether the subject had never come up during her precognition, I have no idea; at any rate, this was a noticeable error and I believe that it betrayed how much he had been rattled by Christina Smith's failure to appear, the previous day.

Following Miss Stewart, we heard extensive testimony from Pringle's three physicians: Dr Heron Watson, Dr Charles McGillivray and Dr Alexis Thomson, all of whom were highly regarded experts in the fields of medicine and surgery. Various gruesome experiments had been carried out on animals and skulls, and the doctors reported the results, which suggested that the head fracture was caused by an accidental fall onto a hard surface, probably stone.

Shown the flat stone from the evidence table, all three physicians agreed that it was probably too light to have inflicted the wound on Rose's head. Mr Pringle asked Dr Heron Watson about the dark red stain on the stone.

'These marks here – eh – resemble blood, do they not?'

'There's no blood on that stone,' said Heron Watson. 'I tested it myself.'

Pringle affected surprise. 'Indeed? And if it's not blood, then what is it?'

'Rust, sir. Just rust. This stone, at some point in its history, must have lain up against a piece of metal – a chain, or perhaps a nail was sat upon it, or an old buckle. You add the Scottish weather to metal, sir, and what do you get, but rust?'

All this went in our favour, showing the supposed 'murder weapon' for what it was: a damp squib. Realising this, Aitchison changed tack, in cross-examination. He compelled each doctor to admit that – although they preferred the notion that Rose had been hurt as the result of an accidental fall – her fatal injury could have been caused had she been deliberately flung down onto a hard floor or hearth, or had her head been bashed against something solid.

I felt terrible that Ned was subjected to all these grisly details, particularly since it was a pointless waste of time: not one of the physicians, either for the Crown or for the defence, had been able to rule out the opposite view.

Pringle went on to wheel out a number of witnesses who claimed to be friends and neighbours of the accused couple. In a stark contrast to what we had heard two days previously, these persons testified that Hans and Belle were nothing but good, simple, kind-hearted folk who lived a quiet and abstemious life in the poor but respectable district of Camlachie. One could not help but wonder where all these accommodating acquaintances could have been dredged up: in the Moray Arms, no doubt! As the time dragged on, and one bosom friend after the other took the stand, it was almost impossible not to lose patience. The morning was almost over; Pringle was just wasting the court's time with flim-flam. I was beside myself, particularly at the thought of Sibyl's impending appearance. Whenever I glanced at the clock, the hands appeared to be moving around its face at an accelerated rate.

At one point, Nelly Smith, Belle's mother, was called to the stand. She assured Pringle that Belle and Hans had been with her, in her home, from morning until night, on the day in question. Despite Pringle's meaning looks at the jury, I doubt that any one of them took her testimony seriously, for she was not a terribly convincing liar, and one tends to assume that a mother will do anything to protect her offspring. Moreover, what she said was in contradiction to Schultterhose's declaration.

MacDonald elicited the sole inescapable fact of her testimony.

'You have another daughter, do you not, Mrs Smith?'

'Aye – Christina.'

'Christina Smith. And can you tell me where Christina – Belle's sister – worked, during 1888, from about February to October?'

'Aye, sir, she worked in Woodside, for Mr and Mrs Gillespie.'

There was a murmur in the crowd.

'Your daughter Christina, Belle's sister, worked for a period of several months, for the Gillespies, the parents of Rose, the child who went missing.'

'Aye.'

'Presumably, Belle knew Christina worked there, and knew of the Gillespies?'

'Aye, I suppose.'

'Did she or didn't she?'

'She did.'

'And, presumably, Belle had heard, through Christina, of Miss Baxter, the Gillespies' friend, the well-heeled English lady?'

Nelly looked shifty. 'I don't know anything about that.'

'Really? Most interesting – thank you, Mrs Smith.'

At long last, Pringle called his final witness, Jem Wright, a gin-blossomed, bewhiskered character. In cross-examination, my counsel got the better of him in a way that overshadowed the testimony of the other 'friends'.

'How long have you known the accused?' MacDonald asked Jem.

'About three years, sir, two three years.'

'And you say Hans Schlutterhose is a teetotaller?'

'That he is, sir.'

'And of good character?'

'Aye, sir, very good, very good,' said Jem – helpfulness itself.

'Where did you first meet Mr Schlutterhose?' MacDonald asked, casually.

'Eh – I cannae mind, exactly. Probably in the General Wolfe, sir, or the Coffin, or the Moray Arms, or mebbe the Sarry Heid.'

The crowd managed to stifle their laughter. MacDonald appeared to reflect for a moment.

'The General Wolfe, the Coffin, the Moray Arms, the Sarry Heid,' he repeated. 'These are public houses, are they not, in Glasgow's Gallowgate area?'

'You've got it, sir.'

'But, Mr Wright, did you not just tell us that the accused doesn't drink?'

'Aye – naw – he doesnae – he doesn't touch a drop.'

'In that case, what, might I ask, was he doing, in all these public houses?'

'Oh, he wasnae drinking, sir. He was eh – most likely – sir, he was just – eh – just –' Here, Jem struggled for a moment, until inspiration dawned, and his face brightened. 'Knowing the big fella, he was maist likely just looking for a fight.'

The resulting hilarity provoked the judge to warn spectators that he was minded to clear the court, a threat that quelled the racket at once.

Still buoyant from his exchange with Jem, MacDonald opened our case for the defence by calling Elspeth Gillespie. Elspeth! How strange it was to hear her name, to see her walk into the court. Her eyes sought me out as she crossed the room and, to my relief, she acknowledged me with a look of sympathy.

'Mrs Gillespie,' MacDonald began. 'How well do you know Miss Baxter?'

Elspeth blinked. She seemed somewhat nervous. She kept clutching at the fabric of her garments, and wringing her hands.

'I'd count her as a friend. In fact, Herriet Baxter saved my life.'

'Saved your life? How did that happen?'

Elspeth appeared delighted to have been asked. I myself had heard this story several times, in the past. 'Well, it was almost two years ago —' she began, but Aitchison had already sprung to his feet.

'Really, my lord, I can hardly see the relevance of this story, especially if it took place so long ago.'

'Indeed?' said Kinbervie, scratching his ear. 'Well, Advocate Depute, you yourself have given us some fairly antediluvian evidence.'

'My lord, if I may continue,' said MacDonald. 'I believe there can be no better indication of my client's nature than what you are about to hear.'

Kinbervie sighed.

'Aye, well, let's hear what this lady has to say, and then we shall see how relevant it is.' He peered at the witness. 'If you'd be so good as to continue, madam.'

'Thank you, my lord,' said Elspeth, and gave him a curtsey.

She went on to describe what had happened on that hot afternoon, in the late spring of 1888, when she had fainted in Buchanan Street and swallowed her dentures. Inevitably, there was amusement at this revelation; even Kinbervie was seen to chuckle. Questioned further, Elspeth testified that, had it not been for me, she would have succumbed to melancholia towards the end of the previous summer, after the abduction of her granddaughter which was swiftly followed by the departure of the Reverend Johnson, who (as it transpired) had only been masquerading as a preacher, and who had stolen the proceeds of Elspeth's Penny Orphan Fund. She also itemised various other good deeds that I had done, here and there, about the neighbourhood, including some financial support that I had given to her maid Jean, when Jean's father had been ill. In all her responses, Elspeth portrayed me as a veritable paragon of virtue. No need to record her many kind words verbatim; however, one thing was plain: her trust in me was absolute, and she was convinced of my innocence. What a dear, sweet person she was! As MacDonald brought his questions to a close, I almost wept with gratitude, and shame: to think that I had, on occasion, harboured uncharitable thoughts about Ned's mother.

'Mrs Gillespie, to summarise, how would you describe Miss Baxter?'

'Oh, she's such a kind and generous person, I've always thought of Herriet as a Good Samaritan, perhaps, or an Angel of Mercy.'

'Thank you, Mrs Gillespie.'

Pringle rose for his cross-examination, looking rather more sprightly than he had done all week. He seemed to be staging a late rally – either that or he was anticipating the end of the trial with some pleasure.

'Did you see anyone on the afternoon in question?' he asked Elspeth. 'When Rose went astray. For instance, did you see any of your neighbours out in the street?'

Elspeth hesitated. 'Well,' she said. 'I did see Herriet.'

Mr Pringle made a display of surprise.

'You saw the accused, Harriet Baxter? Where did you see her?'

Elspeth turned her gaze towards the dock and, for a second, our eyes met. I was unable to gauge anything from her expression, apart from the fact that she was clearly in torment. She turned back to Pringle.

'On Stanley Street. I was on Woodlands Road, on my way out to a church meeting. I'd just bought some scones to take with me, and I was passing the end of our street again, on my way to the tram stop.'

This, I had not realised: that she had seen me, that afternoon.

'Let me establish this beyond doubt,' said Pringle. 'On the afternoon in question, you did not once see Mr Schlutterhose or his wife?'

'No,' admitted Elspeth. 'I've never seen them before.'

'But you did see Miss Baxter in the street?'

'Yes, I think she was going to my son's house, at number 11.'

'Although – she could have carried on to Queen's Crescent, could she not?'

Evidently, Pringle had decided to ape Aitchison's technique, by attempting to imply that I had been up to no good, in some way, perhaps that I had been heading for a rendezvous with Schlutterhose. I doubted that anyone would give credence to such a scenario. However, when I glanced at the jury box, I saw, to my alarm, that the gentlemen therein were following the proceedings with great seriousness.

'Perhaps,' Elspeth admitted. 'She may have been going home. She does live in that direction, after all. But I just assumed she was going to number 11.'

'Thank you, Mrs Gillespie.'

Returning to the advocate's table, Pringle gave the jurymen a long glance, the meaning of which was plain enough: believe this silly woman, if you will, but if you have any sense at all, you will realise that she has been duped.

Before Pringle had even reached his seat, Aitchison had launched into his examination of the witness.

'Going back to Buchanan Street, when you fainted,' he said. 'Is it not correct, Mrs Gillespie, that you'd seen Miss Baxter before that day?'

'I don't know,' said Elspeth. 'I thought I might have seen her, the week before, going into Assafrey's tea rooms, as my son and I were coming out.'

'How strange that Miss Baxter always seems to pop up somewhere in the vicinity of you and your family. Mrs Gillespie, may I just clear up one point? You keep referring to your son's "house", and yet . . .' He paused for a moment to check his notes, then continued. 'It is my understanding that your son lives in a top-floor apartment – not a house.'

'Oh, excuse me,' said Elspeth. 'It's just I'm in the habit of saying "house". You see, I reside in a main-door house – one of only a few in our neighbourhood.'

Alas, this sounded preening. The prosecutor gave her a smile of contempt.

'Indeed – how nice. Moving on again, how often would you

say Miss Baxter visited your son's "house"? Once a week? Twice? Five times?'

'Perhaps three times a week. Sometimes more, sometimes less.'

'Three times – sometimes more. And this, in addition to the many occasions that all of you seem to bump into her in the street. Rather a lot, is it not?'

'Well – not really. We were – we are friends – neighbours.'

'How would you describe Miss Baxter's relationship to your son?'

And so, relentlessly, his questions continued. Away from her own domain, Elspeth had little guile, and Aitchison was skilful enough to draw out her less appealing qualities. It was not difficult to portray her as a vain, prattling, silly woman, with a tendency to brag, and only a slim grasp on reality. I watched, in dismay, as he made her appear to be so blinded by her own self-importance that she was incapable of seeing the truth – or, at least, his truth, which was that she had been taken in by a clever, manipulative person, a lonely spinster, who had inveigled her way into the heart of the Gillespie family. Poor Elspeth. As she left the stand, she attempted to raise my spirits with a watery smile, but there was no hiding the anxiety in her eyes as she was ushered out of the courtroom.

MacDonald looked unusually grave as he watched her depart. I saw him rub his forehead, as though, momentarily, he was at a loss. However, he was quick to call his next witness, Walter Peden. Caskie had assured me that Peden would be a good witness for us and Walter did, indeed, look very respectable in his Sunday best. Much to my relief, he refrained from dancing about like a Hottentot on the stand. His learned demeanour was well received, and – by some paradox – his refined English accent seemed only to augment his credibility. The spectators listened to him, quietly, with respect. One could sense in the atmosphere of the court that they put their trust in him: here was a proper gentleman, a Galahad, a brick.

MacDonald encouraged him to confess that he would never

have married Mabel, had I not been instrumental in bringing them together.

'The same thing happened a few times,' Peden told the court. 'The three of us had arranged to meet but, for some reason, Harriet failed to make an appearance, which rather threw Mabel and myself together, alone.'

'Was this a deliberate piece of matchmaking on the part of Miss Baxter?'

'I wouldn't be surprised. It would be just the sort of thing she'd do. Harriet likes to be helpful. Some might call it interfering, but her intentions are good.'

Aitchison took him to task on this point during cross-examination.

'You say that Miss Baxter brought you and your wife together?'

'That's right.'

'Do you believe that matchmaking is always a selfless activity, Mr Peden?'

'I suppose so; I've never thought about it.'

'In your opinion, then, Miss Baxter was only acting generously in attempting to act as matchmaker for you and your wife?'

'There was nothing in it for her, other than to make Mabel and I happy.'

'You were a good friend of Mr Gillespie's, were you not?'

'I still am, sir.'

'And you are also an artist – you and he spent a lot of time together, before you were married, did you?'

'Yes.'

'And your wife – she and Mr Gillespie were close, as brother and sister?'

'Oh yes – practically inseparable. Mabel was always in his studio – as I myself was, from time to time.'

'But not so much now that you're married?'

'I suppose not. When one is married . . . one has other things to do.'

'Being married to each other has, effectively, removed your

wife and yourself from Mr Gillespie's life, has it not?'

'Well – perhaps not removed, but we see Ned less. And, of course, when we were living in Tangier, we didn't see each other at all.'

'Whose idea was it that you and your wife go to live in Tangier, I wonder?'

Peden looked puzzled. 'It was my idea, sir.'

'Not Miss Baxter's?'

'No.'

'How far is Tangier from Glasgow, Mr Peden?'

'Several thousand miles, I should think.'

'Several thousand miles – and presumably, Miss Baxter encouraged you to go and live several thousand miles away?'

'Well, she was enthusiastic about the idea, yes.'

'Enthusiastic – I have no doubt. No further questions, my lord.'

Next, MacDonald called several witnesses who spoke favourably of my character, including dear old Agnes Deuchars. She was in her best frock, and what looked like a new hat, and she had a little cry on the stand as she told the court what a 'nice lady' I was, and how well I had looked after her husband and herself at Bardowie. After Agnes, two ladies from the art class deponed that I was a well-liked member of the group, who was always encouraging of my classmates' efforts, and who had been at the forefront of the leafleting campaign at the time of Rose's disappearance. In turn, the Alexander girls, my landlady's daughters, claimed that they had never catered for a more pleasant or uncomplaining lodger.

If only we had been able to call these witnesses earlier, there might have been more balance to the trial. Unfortunately, the judicial system gives precedence to the prosecution, and arguments for the defence are only heard late in the day. In my case, the jurymen had heard so many defamatory aspersions since the trial had begun that it would be a miracle if their judgement had not been swayed.

Even our character witnesses came under attack from Aitchison.

My landlady, Mrs Alexander, gave a perfectly lovely account of me: no problems there. However, as the prosecutor rose to his feet for cross-examination, he wore an expression that I had come to recognise. I have seen a similar gleam in the eye of a fox, just before it pounces.

'Mrs Alexander, can you please tell the court what was found beneath Miss Baxter's bed, when the police searched her rooms.'

'Yes, they found a painting – a portrait of Miss Baxter – rather a good portrait, I thought. I don't know why she kept it under the bed, except – well – one doesn't always want to look at oneself.'

'Quite. And was there a signature on this painting?'

'Yes, in the bottom left corner. It was signed Annie Gillespie. Miss Baxter used to go round for the sittings, to the Gillespies' apartment.'

'Were you aware that the portrait was originally commissioned by Miss Baxter's stepfather, Mr Dalrymple – that he had asked for it to be done?'

'No, I didn't know that.'

'Annie Gillespie was under the impression that Mr Dalrymple had the painting on display, at his home in Helensburgh. And yet it was found under Miss Baxter's bed. Why did Miss Baxter never give this portrait to her stepfather?'

'I'm afraid I don't know. Perhaps she wasn't pleased with it.'

'Did it ever occur to you, Mrs Alexander, that Miss Baxter's stepfather might not even have asked for the portrait to be done, in the first place – that Miss Baxter might have lied about the commission in order to gain access to the Gillespie home?'

MacDonald was on his feet, immediately.

'My lord, I must object. My learned friend, the Advocate Depute, is simply up to mischief – trying his luck, my lord, and hoping to mislead the jury.'

Yes, indeed. Of course, there was a perfectly good explanation for why the painting was still in my possession. Quite simply, I was too embarrassed to give it to my stepfather. Oh, it was all very well, at the time, while I was sitting for it, and even, at first, when it was completed. I thought that Annie had done a marvellous job. But, once I had taken the portrait home, the more I looked at it, the more I grew to dislike it. Laid out on canvas, my image was only a constant reminder that my looks were far from the physical ideal. Ramsay had always teased me about my appearance, particularly my nose. The more I examined the portrait, the less I could bear the notion of him seeing it. Consequently, I stopped referring to it whenever I was in contact with him and, after a few months he, in turn, seemed to forget about it. He never mentioned it again, and I was extremely glad of the fact. I simply put the canvas under my bed, and ignored it. Regrettably, nobody else was aware of what I had done, for I would never have let Annie know that I had failed to pass on to Ramsay a picture that she had taken such care in painting. Of course, at the trial, had I been given the opportunity, I would have testified to this effect, as would Ramsay, no doubt. However, the matter was left hanging, unresolved.

Kinbervie was peering over the rim of his spectacles, at Aitchison.

'Sir, do you have a genuine question for Mrs Alexander?'

The prosecutor bowed his head, in what seemed like an apology.

'My lord, I have finished with her.'

'In that case,' said the judge, turning to my advocate, 'Mr Mac-Donald, if you'd be so good as to make haste. Time is fleeting, as I'm sure you're aware.'

'Yes, my lord.'

As Mrs Alexander left the chamber, MacDonald stood at the advocate's table, staring down at his paperwork. Thus far, he had been quick to summon each witness, but this time, there was a long pause. Eventually, he raised his head, and turned to the Macer.

'Call Sibyl Gillespie.'

I shot a glance at Caskie, to see how confident he looked, and was dismayed to see that his shoulders were up around his ears.

When his gaze met mine, he pursed his lips, and gave his head an almost imperceptible shake, gestures that I found myself unable to read: was he telling me not to worry? Or was he indicating that he himself was worried? It was impossible to say.

Meanwhile, Ned had leaned forward in his seat, and was holding his head in his hands. He only looked up when the Macer returned, leading Sibyl into the courtroom. Every person present watched her cross the chamber. She looked more frail than ever. Her eyes were dull, her hair a few pale wisps hanging down below her plaid hat. She wore a matching coat, on top of a high-necked velveteen frock, trimmed with crape. The clothes swamped her and, beneath them, one could tell that her limbs were mere bones, draped in skin. Of course, the weather was still cold, and it was appropriate that she should be bundled up for warmth, but I could not forget that the layers of plaid and velveteen also helped to conceal her scars. When she climbed into the witness box, only her hat and the sallow little face beneath it were visible above the top rail. To begin with, she kept her eyes fixed upon the ground, and the cast of her countenance was so wary and full of foreboding that Kinbervie leaned forward and spoke to her, reassuringly:

'Now then, young lady, be not afraid. These good gentlemen here just wish to ask you some questions. Then you can return to your mother. Is that understood?'

Sibyl looked up and nodded, timidly, her eyes huge in her pinched little face.

'Good girl. Now you must tell the truth, dear. Do you understand what I mean by the truth? For instance, if I said I was wearing a wig on my head, would that be the truth, or a lie?'

Sibyl regarded him, dubiously, as though she feared that he might play a trick upon her. 'The truth?' she said, at length, in a small, uncertain voice.

'That's right. And if I said I was wearing – oh, let's say – a haggis on my head, what would that be – truth or lie?'

The child simpered, then said, with more confidence: 'A lie.'

'Very good. And why must we tell the truth here, in court?'

Sibyl considered this question for a moment, before speaking.

'Because we're to find out what happened to Rose, and it's important because if it's proved then the people that took her can be punished, but if it isn't proved, they won't be punished – nor should they be.'

Inwardly, I could not help but smile, because it was as though Ned was speaking through her; no doubt, he would have seen it as his duty to try and explain to his daughter some principles of justice and the law. I glanced up at him, but his gaze was fixed, intently, upon Sibyl. Evidently, she had impressed the judge.

'I've known, in my time, one or two lawyers who could not express it so succinctly,' he said. 'Thank you, young lady.' He turned to my counsel. 'Mr MacDonald, sir, if you would – be brief.'

MacDonald approached the witness box.

'Now then, Sibyl,' he said, in soft, yet audible, tones. 'I won't ask too many questions, and I just want you to answer each one as you see fit. Do you think you can do that for me?' She nodded. 'Good girl. Now then, I want you to think back to the day when your sister Rose went missing, last year. Do you remember that day? You can tell me "yes" or "no", if you would?'

'Yes,' lisped the child.

'Very good. Now, you and –'

'Rose is dead,' Sibyl said loudly, interrupting him.

'Yes, that's right – and we're trying to find out how it happened. Now, Sibyl, you and your sister were playing in the gardens that day, weren't you, at Queen's Crescent? Do you remember playing in the gardens? You can answer "yes" or "no".'

'Yes.'

'Good girl. And can you remember what else happened that day?'

Sibyl thought for a moment. 'There was a dead bird on the ground – but I didn't touch it.'

'Good – and did you see anyone else at the Gardens? Any other person?'

'There was a lady came to the gate.'

'I see – a lady. And did she speak to you?'

'Yes.'

'What did she say?'

'She asked me to go to the grocer to buy some sugar.'

'And did she give you some money?'

'Two pennies. One for the sugar and one for me, but – but – but I would have shared my penny with Rose – I would have.'

'Of course you would. Now, Sibyl, I want you to think carefully, and tell me what the lady looked like.'

'She had on a blue dress, and it was shiny.'

'Anything else?'

'She had a hat on, with a veil.'

'And was she thin, fat, or average in size?'

'I think she was quite a bit thin.'

'Now then Sibyl, I want you to look over here.' MacDonald came and stood in front of the dock. 'Look at the two ladies sitting behind me. Now, does either of them resemble the woman you saw that day?'

Sibyl flicked a glance at us and then immediately turned back to MacDonald.

'Please may I go closer?'

The advocate glanced at Kinbervie, who nodded assent. MacDonald hurried to the stand and led Sibyl down into the well of the court, bringing her directly in front of the dock, so close that I could see the downy hairs that grew along her jawline. The child was quaking. She stared, solemnly, first at Hans, then at Belle. It was all very unnerving. MacDonald tried to put her at ease.

'Take your time,' he said. 'Tell me if you see the lady you saw that day.'

Sibyl tilted her head to one side and looked directly up at me, for the first time. Her eyelids narrowed and I saw her lips move, but she made no audible sound. I believe that she might have said my name to herself, under her breath. Then she smiled at me. I cannot tell what made me shudder: perhaps it was just the look in her eyes, a kind of cold deadness. Her gaze passed back along the dock to Belle, whose countenance showed plainly that she was sick with dread at this turn of events.

'Take your time,' MacDonald was saying.

The child looked from Belle to me, and back again. My entire body was rigid with anxiety. Every person in the room was silent and still, as we all gazed at Sibyl.

'Look at the ladies, and if you recognise the one you saw at the Gardens, just tell me "yes" or "no".'

'Yes,' said Sibyl, at length, her voice flat and expressionless.

'Perhaps it would be easiest if you pointed. Just raise your arm and point at the lady who asked you to go and buy sugar. Which lady did you see?'

Sibyl raised her arm and extended her finger. To begin with, her hand hovered, so that she was not pointing at anyone in particular, except Schlutterhose or one of the policemen. I held my breath. Of a sudden, it was as though I could see more clearly. Everything in the courtroom was radiantly defined. Everything was brighter, more vivid. I could see the stitching in the seams of Sibyl's coat. The colours of the plaid threads were lush to my eyes. Strangely, I felt that I had been granted supernatural powers, and that I understood, innately, how those threads had been woven together. Sibyl's trembling hand became the focus of my newly razor-sharp mind. Her skin was so pale that it seemed to glow. Her nails were short and ragged but I knew, beyond doubt, that, at some future date, she would cease to bite them. Her bony little fingers trembled, but I was seized by the conviction that, one day, she would wear a wedding ring, and her hand would be held, and caressed, by her husband. She might seem fragile now, but, in the end, she would get well again, and lead a normal life.

The moment seemed to last for ever. Then, at length, Sibyl swivelled, and pointed directly at Belle.

'Her there, in the middle. That's the lady I saw.'

Out of the corner of my eye, I could see Belle dropping her

gaze to the floor, scowling, as though disgraced. The entire court-room seemed to exhale, as one.

'Good girl,' said MacDonald. 'Now you can –'

He was about to help the child back to the stand when Sibyl suddenly hunched over on the spot. She opened her mouth, as if to speak, and then her head ripped forwards. In a flash, she reached out and grabbed the dock, right in front of me, her hands gripping the bars of the balustrade, next to my feet. In the same moment, she made a faint whining noise, then her head jerked back again, and she stared me right in the eye.

'Harriet!' she cried.

Of a sudden, I heard a strange sound that I could not place. At first, it made me think of heavy cloth being ripped, and then I thought it might be rainwater, from a broken gutter, thundering on the roof. It was only when I glanced down to Sibyl's feet, and saw the pool of liquid beginning to spread out from beneath the hem of her coat and across the floor, that I realised, exactly, what was happening.

MacDonald saw it, in the same moment, and took a step back-wards. Aitchison sprang to his feet, with a horrified look on his face.

'By thunder!'

'Harriet!' cried Sibyl. 'Harriet!'

She gazed down at the pool of urine spreading out around her skirts, and her face crumpled. Having lost control of her bladder, she now seemed unable to marshal her emotions. She began to whimper, and the whimper soon turned into a wail. All of the advocates had frozen to the spot in horror. Kinbervie was peering down into the well of the court, bemused. Then, he saw the pud-dle on the floor.

'Oh dear – no,' he said.

There was a commotion in the crowd and, looking up, I saw that Ned had jumped up, and was craning his neck, trying to see what had happened. I could hardly bear the thought of the misery and mortification that he would feel, once it dawned upon him. Of a sudden, I discovered that I was on my feet; I could not help myself. I was speaking aloud, intervening, taking charge. According to the following day's *Glasgow Herald*, my voice was commanding but full of compassion, my face 'the very glass and image of sympathetic concern'. In the opinion of the reporter from *The Scotsman*, my rapid and kind-hearted actions put the entire assembly of learned gentlemen to shame. *The Mail* wondered whether those gathered in the court had finally glimpsed my 'true character'.

'Gentlemen,' I found myself saying. 'Please be so good as to look after this poor child – can't you see she's unwell?' I reached out across the balustrade, and leaned down to rest my hand on Sibyl's shoulder, to reassure her. 'Don't worry, dear. These good gentlemen are going to look after you now.'

Thank Heavens, at these words, MacDonald suddenly snapped to his senses, and appealed to the judge: 'My lord – may I beg your permission to remove this witness from the court, at once.'

'Granted,' said Kinbervie. 'Take the poor wee thing away.'

The Macer hurried forwards and he and MacDonald led the child towards the exit, supporting her between them. Poor Sibyl was inconsolable, no doubt overcome by shame at the display she had made of herself, in public. As soon as the door had closed upon her, Kinbervie spoke, in aside, to his clerk.

'A brief adjournment, I think, while we clear up this mess.'

I glanced up, but Ned was no longer in his place. Turning my head, I caught sight of him, just as he dashed through one of the exit doors of the gallery. However, I felt sure that he must have witnessed what had happened. I had helped his daughter, by coming to her rescue, boldly and without hesitation. Even if his faith in me had wavered of late, it seemed certain that this incident would help him to see me, once again, in a better light.

Friday, 15 September 1933

LONDON

Friday, 15th September. In hindsight, the problems yesterday were partly my own fault. I should have thought things through more carefully, even though, to begin with, all seemed to go well. The girl was fast asleep by the time that I entered her room. Her curtains were drawn, but I could see well enough to creep forwards in the light that spilled in from the hall. The air smelt faintly of talcum powder. Her breathing was shallow, but regular. Softly, softly, I tiptoed across the carpet, relieved to see that she was lying on her back. I reached out and – ever so carefully – undid the top button of her nightgown. She did not stir. Taking confidence, I unfastened another button. Even then, she did not wake. As far I could tell, her throat and upper chest were free of scars, but further down, in the shadows of her bosom and at the tops of her arms, it did look as though the texture of her flesh changed, and the skin appeared darker. To make absolutely sure, I had to take a closer look. I undid a third button successfully enough, but my mistake was to switch on the bedside light, in order to inspect her properly, for as soon as I did so, her eyes popped open.

I realise now that I should have used at least four pills. The three that I gave her appear to have had a negligible effect. She lay there, momentarily, blinking at me, in confusion. I lifted my hands, in a gesture of appeasement.

'Shh!' I whispered. 'Go back to sleep.'

Instead of doing as I said, she glanced down at her chest, seeming to register, only then, that her nightgown was open, her bosom naked. An explanation was required, and quickly.

'Don't worry,' I told her. 'I'm just on the hunt for something.'

She looked up, and stared at me in a manner that is hard to

describe. No doubt, she loathes me now, for having found her out.

'You're not so clever as you thought,' I told her.

That was when she screamed and hit out at me. The violence of it took me quite by surprise – but then, I had always thought that Sibyl had the potential to be violent. As she sprang up and out of bed, she knocked over the lamp, which fell to the floor, and smashed. I grabbed the sleeves of her nightgown and there ensued an undignified scuffle, in which she manhandled me towards the door, whilst I grappled with her, attempting to disrobe her further, for I wanted to get a proper look at her arms, simply to confirm what I already knew. However, the act of reaching out to push me had yanked the nightgown back up over her shoulders, and the lamp was broken, with the result that I could see very little.

Of course, she is a good deal younger and stronger than I am and, in the end, she succeeded in thrusting me out of the room. Not content with that, she continued to shove me down the hall to the kitchen, where – to my great indignation – she shut me in, as though I was no more than a child. I threw myself at the door a few times, but she held fast from the other side and so, after a while, I gave up.

There happened to be a bottle of Scotch by the sink, and so, just to calm my shattered nerves, I poured myself a small glass, and then I started talking to the girl, through the door. I hoped to persuade her to let me out, but no matter what I said, she made no reply. After a few minutes, I tried the handle again, only to find that the door opened straight away: she had made herself scarce. In fact, she had gone back to her room. I could hear her in there, moving around. She had flicked on the ceiling lamp: a chink of light was visible around the door frame. Perhaps she had pushed the chest of drawers against the door on the inside, for it would not budge. As far as I could tell, she was dragging the furniture around and throwing things. In a rage, no doubt, that I had out-foxed her.

Off I went, into the sitting room. Various bangs and crashes could be heard, and then, after a few minutes, she emerged, wearing a coat over her nightgown, and carrying her cardboard suitcase. I remained where I was, looking at her through the open doorway, determined not to betray that I was afraid. She had put on her shoes but, for once, she wore no stockings. Her hair was in disarray. The Kensitas Flowers quilt dragged behind her; she was trying to fold it as she went, with one hand. When she caught sight of me, she paused.

'I'm going – I have to go.'

'Going where?' I asked. 'The lunatic asylum?'

With a sigh, she headed for the door, pulling at the quilt. I realised, all at once, that I wanted her to stay. We could talk about old times; I never get to talk about old times. Perhaps I could detain her by pretending that nothing was wrong, by making it seem as though I had not, after all, guessed her secret.

'Go back to bed, Sarah,' I told her, careful to use her fake name. 'Get some sleep. In the morning, everything will be back to normal.'

'I can't stay here. I'm giving notice.'

'Strictly speaking, you aren't giving any notice at all, not if you go now. It's just a misunderstanding. Let me explain –'

'No – no explanations. Don't you say nothing! Talk the hind leg off a horse, you would. You could make anyone do anything, just by talking to them.'

'What on earth d'you mean, you silly?'

She glanced around, and then pointed to the barometer.

'That thing there, I bet you could make me take it off the wall, even if I didn't want to. If you just talked at me for two minutes, you'd have me doing it.'

'Why on earth would I want you to take the barometer off the wall?'

She made a strangled, agitated sound and, abandoning her attempt to fold the quilt, she bundled it under her arm.

'I don't care what you say. I'm leaving. It's not right here, not right at all.'

'But Sarah, dear, what about the poor birds? They'll miss you terribly.'

That hit the mark: her face fell.

'I can't help that,' she said, presently. 'You'll have to look after them again.'

'And what on earth are you going to say to the registry – to Mrs Clinch?'

'I'll just tell her I'm leaving, and I need another job.'

'Perhaps you can go and work for your friend Miss Barnes again. She seems to be your greatest supporter. Why did you stop working for her, by the bye?'

'Miss Barnes? If you must know, Miss Barnes could no longer afford me.'

'Ah yes, very plausible,' I said. 'But what about Clinch? She'll think it odd if you leave me. We're both going to look quite strange, you know. You, in particular, are going to look very strange. They'll wonder about you – you can guarantee it.'

'Well, I don't care!' she retorted. 'I don't care if I look strange. You're the one who's strange. I just want away from you – you bloody mad bitch!'

Yes – those were her exact words. She was in such a heightened emotional state that she no longer knew what she was saying. I should have disregarded her cruel name-calling, but still, such things can be hurtful.

Then she was at the door, grabbing at the handle, stepping outside. The thought of her, charging out, at midnight, in such a vulnerable state, alarmed me. I followed her onto the landing, and found her frantically pushing the button for the elevator. Several floors below, the machinery clunked into life, and the lift began its usual lament as it ascended, squealing and groaning.

The girl gave me a ferocious sideways glance. 'You're not crying, are you?'

'No, dear, not really. I'm just concerned. You're acting so strangely.'

'Oh, blood and sand!' she exclaimed, and then (although I was nowhere near her): 'Get away from me!'

Instead of waiting for the lift to arrive, she grabbed her suitcase and quilt, and started running down the stairs. I called out after her:

'Don't be so contrary, dear! It's after midnight. Come back when you've calmed down. I'll leave the door open for you, just in case! Don't you want to say anything to the birds – Sibyl? Sibyl?'

I only called her by her real name as a kind of last-minute test, to see if it would make her turn back. But there was no reply, only the scuttling of footsteps, fading away, as she sped down wards, towards the street, the quilt glimmering in the darkness, as it trailed on the steps behind her.

VII

March 1890

EDINBURGH

22

With Sibyl's testimony, the case for my defence came to an end. For almost three days, the jury had listened and observed as dozens of witnesses had appeared before them. Some of those called to the stand had told the truth, and some, for their own reasons, had given a version of events that might not have been entirely honest. Various medical men had testified at length and yet, despite their knowledge and eloquence, and all their scientific experiments, they had succeeded only in confusing matters further. The advocates were now obliged to draw this muddle into some semblance of meaning in their closing addresses to the jury. These speeches are, by nature, lengthy, and I have no intention of typing my fingers to the bone in an effort to duplicate them here, particularly since the texts of the statements are in the public domain, but I shall attempt to summarise.

Aitchison was first to take the floor. He spoke for almost ninety minutes, and never once referred to his notes, which, in my opinion, may have accounted for a few of his many lapses and errors. However, I do not scruple to say that he knowingly made what might be called a 'naughty' speech, which included many matters that he should not even have mentioned. Frustratingly, at the time, I was unable to intervene or point these out, and so will now take the opportunity.

In order to gain attention, the prosecutor began in hushed tones, so that all present had to strain to hear him. Only as his argument progressed did he become more animated. His face turned pink, his green eyes gleamed and, the more his passion grew, the more spittle gathered in the corners of his mouth. Every so often, to emphasise his point, he would strike his right fist into the palm of his left hand. He told the jury that never before had he conceived that any person could commit such a dastardly outrage against a pure and innocent child. Equally shocking to him was the notion that any female could have had a hand in such crimes – and yet (according to him) this had been proved, without question, to be the case. He had no hesitation in asserting that the three persons in the dock had committed these hideous atrocities.

The motives for the crimes were not, initially, obvious, he told us. Why, he asked, had this particular child, this particular family, been chosen? If a ransom was the goal, then why had the abductors not selected one of the wealthy Glaswegian families who lived not a stone's throw from Stanley Street in the grand terraces near the park? But financial gain had never been the primary motive; as it was, the ransom note was a mere afterthought, born out of panic, and never pursued. In that case, why Rose? Why the Gillespies? The answer was plain, according to Aitchison: 'These two ne'er-do-wells did not choose their victim: she was chosen for them.'

Here, he had the audacity to gaze at me, long and hard, before continuing.

'What do we know of Harriet Baxter?' he asked. 'We know that, only a few years ago, she inveigled her way into the London home of Mr and Mrs Watson, and – for complex reasons that perhaps she herself does not even understand – attempted to reduce their marriage to rubble.'

By rights, at this point, what should have been reduced to rubble was the prosecutor's statement. Here was his first infraction: he should not even have mentioned Esther Watson, given that the jury had been instructed to disregard her testimony. I felt that Kinbervie ought to have stepped in to reprimand him, but it seemed that closing speeches were permitted to unfold, without hindrance, no matter how improperly an advocate behaved, and Aitchison was allowed to continue, uninterrupted.

'We know that she met, in London, a handsome Scottish artist and, a few months later, she was found to be living in Glasgow, just around the corner from this artist and his family. Gentlemen, what a coincidence it was that she kept popping up, wherever the Gillespies happened to be. And how useful she made herself, how indispensable: solving problems, even saving the life of Mr Gillespie's mother.'

This, according to Aitchison, was the beginning of a stealthy process of inveiglement. 'But the real abomination was that, as Miss Baxter wormed her way into the bosom of the family, she simultaneously began to destroy it. Any person close to Ned Gillespie was her target, particularly anyone with whom the artist had a special bond. His favourite daughter, a mischievous child, became – mysteriously, by degrees – an apparently dangerous child. Could it be any coincidence that the deterioration in Sibyl Gillespie's behaviour began soon after the arrival upon the scene of Harriet Baxter? Who really was responsible for all the mayhem that was created in the Gillespie household: belongings gone missing or found destroyed, a bowl of punch laced with poison, obscene drawings appearing on walls. We have heard from Jessie McKenzie who witnessed Miss Baxter in suspicious circumstances, in association with one of these drawings. Was this an isolated incident? Was Sibyl really a disturbed child, or had she simply been persecuted and then wrongfully accused, time after time, until she was driven beyond reason, out of her wits?'

On and on, the prosecutor went, suggesting that I had, by various devious means, conspired to rend the family asunder. I must say that I barely recognised the picture that was painted of me. 'What began as a few spiteful little actions grew in scale, until Miss Baxter sank to the lowest depths, all moral sense in her destroyed.' Aitchison asked us to imagine a painting, a portrait of family and friends, with all the children and adults gathered together. 'And then, one by one, the figures in the picture begin to disappear. A brother vanishes, destination unknown, possibly Italy.' (Again, since Kenneth had barely been mentioned during the trial, I feel that some objection should have been raised.) 'A sister and friend are married off, and sent packing to Africa. A child is victimised until she loses her mind. And, finally, gentlemen, the ultimate wickedness, another child is abducted and murdered.'

Here, he paused to contemplate me, with distaste. I was seized with a wildly inappropriate urge to make a face at him: if he could be ridiculous, then so could I. Thankfully, I quelled the impulse, and averted my gaze. On he went with his diabolical lies, the meat of his argument. According to his theory, I had spent months trying to make my 'lair' (Bardowie!) attractive to the Gillespies, and when they declined to live there with me for the summer, I became incensed beyond reason. Fixing upon Annie as the person to blame for refusing my invitation, my rage rankled and grew, and I devised a ploy to take a hideous revenge upon her, by making her favourite child disappear. Not only would this cause her grief, it would be yet another opportunity to prove myself indispensable to the family.

'But how could this lady accomplish such an abduction? Certainly not alone: the puppet master requires his marionettes. And so Miss Baxter was obliged to find accomplices, persons already so submerged in sin and iniquity that they would barely hesitate to do whatever they were asked, as long as they were well enough paid. Where to find such persons? It is a matter of fact that Belle Schlutterhose's sister, Christina, was a former maid of the Gillespies – we heard as much from Nelly Smith, Belle's and Christina's mother. In the spring and summer of 1888, while Christina was working in the Gillespie home, we know that Miss Baxter was a frequent visitor. Christina and Miss Baxter were well acquainted; this is a fact, indisputable, gentlemen, and here is the connection between the three prisoners, a connection to which Christina Smith would have testified had she taken the stand. She would also have thrown some light upon other matters, including a meeting that she set up, between Miss Baxter and her co-accused.'

Need I point out that none of this evidence had actually been produced in court? Yet again, Aitchison was on thin ice. Hurrying on, he reminded the jury that a nefarious meeting had taken

place between the three prisoners, each of whom had been identified by Helen Strang, the waitress. Moreover, Strang had witnessed Miss Baxter handing over a slim package. 'Could this have
been a bundle of notes? We've heard evidence to suggest that it
was, for, soon after this date, there was a change in the fortunes of
Mr and Mrs Schlutterhose. They both gave notice at their places
of employment – and yet, they began to spend more freely. This
money must have come from somewhere. What sort of person
has such resources? Presumably, those of independent financial
means. And what is Miss Baxter but a woman of independent
financial means?'

At this point, it would not have surprised me had he brought
up the disqualified bank evidence, but perhaps even Aitchison
felt that he had already chanced his luck enough. Instead, he
advised the jury to disregard any testimony which placed Hans
and Rose as victims of the accident on St George's Road. As far as
he was concerned, this tale was unrelated: 'Most of the witnesses
to this incident have testified that Mr Schlutterhose looks nothing like the man who was knocked down by the tram. Indeed, it
seems more likely that he was an Italian.'

Now this was a cavalier piece of chicanery, for at least half of
the witnesses had said, under oath, that Hans did resemble the
man that they had seen, and only one had supposed him to be an
Italian! It was all that I could do to stop myself from jumping up
to challenge Aitchison.

Next, he had the barefaced cheek to dredge up his notion about
the veiled woman, still determined that the jury should believe
me to be the person who had sent Sibyl to the shop. 'Who was this
mysterious female?' he asked – ludicrously disregarding the fact
that she had, that very afternoon, been pointed out to the court,
quite unambiguously, when Sibyl had identified Belle.

Turning his focus to the supposed murder, Aitchison pro-
claimed: 'We can be sure of one thing: some time after her arrival
at Coalhill Street, Rose Gillespie died. Did someone lose patience
with her? Did she try to escape? Or was it always Miss Baxter's

plan that little Rose should be silenced, once and for all?'

Yes, he allowed, no spatters of blood were found in Coal-hill Street, and no sign of a struggle. He dismissed these trifles, reminding us that the killers had many months in which to cover their traces. Perhaps the flat stone produced in evidence had not, in fact, caused Rose's injury, but the lack of an obvious weapon should be no hindrance to the jury in their deliberations. 'Look around you,' he extolled them. 'In the right hands, anything can become a murder weapon: a wall, a cast-iron hearth, a floor. And any one of these prisoners could have caused the wound that killed Rose Gillespie.'

Here, Aitchison came to stand beside me, close to the balustrade of the dock.

'But, gentlemen, did not Harriet Baxter have the most reason to silence Rose, for she was the only one of those involved that the child knew, and would recognise. She was the one most at risk, should Rose remain alive. Do not be fooled by Miss Baxter's genteel demeanour here in court. Beneath her clothing, she has a strong and unnaturally vigorous frame.'

Raising his arm, he held his hand in the air, like a claw. 'As we've heard, she is so strong that she can smash a china cup, like that.' And he snatched at the air, closing his fingers with a snap that reverberated around the chamber.

'Harriet Baxter could easily have overpowered a child of Rose's size, and dashed her brains out on the floor.'

At this, there was a murmur amongst the crowd, a few gasps, and one shriek (which, to my mind, must have been rehearsed in advance).

Bish bosh eyewash. I cannot bear to write down any more of the man's false and hysterical accusations. He closed by submitting that the prosecution had established, beyond reasonable doubt, that the prisoners were guilty of the crimes charged, and he asked the jury for their verdict accordingly. By the end, he had worked himself up to a perfect pitch of outrage. I can still see him now, as he took his seat, his eyes burning with intensity, his hands a-tremble as he adjusted his wig. Had I been able, I might have torn it from his scalp and dashed it in his face.

Next came Pringle, the absent-minded Poor's Roll advocate, who might well have had his own doubts about his prospect of success in defending the kidnappers. He was hampered from the first by his clients, who had insisted on pleading not guilty, despite the extent of the evidence against them. Since Aitchison had done his best to tarnish me, Pringle devoted his efforts, in summing up, to saving Hans and Belle by casting scorn upon the murder charge. He reminded the jury that no real weapon had been found, and there had been no witness to murder. The red stain upon the flat stone was not blood, but rust; the stone itself too light to wield as a convincing weapon. He insisted that the balance of the medical evidence showed that Rose's injuries were in keeping with the theories of the defence, and had been sustained at the scene of the tram accident. Lastly, he emphasised that it was incumbent upon the Crown to prove murder – and that had not been done.

Finally, it was the turn of Muirhead MacDonald, my counsel. I can still hear, to this day, the rich, honeyed tones of his voice as he paced the well of the court. He might have been small in stature, but his voice possessed great authority. His main argument hinged upon the lack of evidence pointing to any link between the kidnappers and myself. Helen Strang had supposedly seen us together – but had not her memory been proved to be imperfect? She could remember, in every detail, waiting upon three strangers, a year ago, and yet failed to recall the first thing about serving a famous actress, only in November. What might be concluded from this anomaly? Why did she recall one occasion better than the other? Was her memory faulty? Or had person or persons unknown helpfully provided Miss Strang with a date and various other details?

'It would also appear that the Crown would have you speculate as to a link between the accused couple and Miss Baxter, in the form of Christina Smith, sister of Belle and former maid of the Gillespies. Well, gentlemen, the only real link which exists in the evidence is that between the accused couple and Christina Smith. Would that not explain how the kidnappers knew of Miss Baxter, and why they plucked her name out of thin air when they found themselves in a tight spot? The Advocate Depute might pretend to hint at revelations that might have been made, had his final witness taken the stand. But, gentlemen, his pretences are not evidence. This former maid has not even deigned to appear as a witness at this trial. There is no evidence whatsoever of any direct link between the accused couple and this lady, Miss Baxter, who sits in the dock before you.'

The truth of the matter was simple, MacDonald told us.

'These two lazy ne'er-do-wells decided to try and make some easy money – an old story – a familiar tale – and one that seldom ends well. In this case, the escapade indeed had a sorry end. This wretched couple stole Rose Gillespie. Here in court, this very afternoon, young Sibyl identified Belle Schlutterhose as the veiled woman who sent her to the shop that day. What happened next is unclear. Perhaps, the couple argued; it seems likely since – according to the owner of the Carnarvon bar – they were both in a state of inebriation. Let us assume that Belle Schlutterhose staggers off, leaving her husband to snatch Rose and carry her across town. Alas, Herr Schlutterhose had not the sense to refrain from drinking that day. In escaping with Rose, in his befuddled condition, he stepped directly into the path of a tram, with tragic results.

'Once it became clear that Rose was dead, this pair of miscreants panicked. They buried the child's body and – overwhelmed by guilt at what had happened – even these despicable characters could not pursue their initial intention, to claim a ransom. Therefore, having sent their first note, they let the matter lie. Yes, gentlemen, they may have handed in their notice at work, whilst continuing to spend money freely – but the testimony of laundry owner Grace Lamont explains where and how that money was earned: immorally, on the streets, by Belle Schlutterhose.

Knowing only too well that they might, one day, be tracked down and arrested, Belle and her husband concocted a story about the abduction, trying to shift the blame onto someone else. Gentlemen, they picked upon somebody whom they knew might be easily demonised: an English lady, unmarried, who, to their certain knowledge, was a friend to the Gillespie family. If they could only make Miss Harriet Baxter seem responsible for their failed plans, they might be able to inculpate her, and thereby escape punishment.'

Lord Kinbervie began his summing up at five o'clock. To his credit, he did direct the jury to ignore some of what had been mentioned by Aitchison: 'Reference has been made to what Christina Smith might, or might not, have said, had she given evidence. I direct you, gentlemen, to disregard all such references, for the simple reason that you have not heard any evidence whatsoever from Miss Smith herself.' Thrice, during the course of his speech, the judge advised the jury to use their 'common sense', an opaque piece of guidance, which mystifies me to this day, and which I am convinced that the jury found unhelpful, for is one man's common sense not another man's folly? I studied His Lordship's face as he spoke, trying to tell whether he meant what I hoped: that they should find me innocent, on both counts. Kinbervie gave every appearance of being a reasonable fellow, unruffled, tolerant, and squarely in the camp of decency and discernment, but it was impossible to tell whether, in his opinion, I was also in that camp.

Throughout his address, I was painfully aware that we inhabitants of the dock were under the close scrutiny of all those present in the courtroom. From time to time, during the course of the past few days, the focus of attention had wandered away from us, but now it had returned, and at greater intensity than ever. With all eyes upon me, I felt as fragile and exposed as a seedling that withers beneath the scorching gaze of the noonday sun. However, there was little I could do about it; I could not bow my head, or creep away to hide in a shady corner. I simply had to bear it, and maintain my composure. No matter what the outcome, I was determined to keep my dignity.

At ten past six o'clock, Lord Kinbervie sent the jury away to consider their verdict. As they filed out, he stood up, as though to stretch his legs, and then quietly left the room. Advocates, deputes and agents began to drift away through various exits. The custom in Scotland, at that time, was for prisoners to remain seated in the dock during the jury's final recess, and so there we remained, the three of us, between our guardians, the policemen, and turn-keys, sitting in silence, and avoiding each others' eye, whilst all around us, whispers became mutterings, and mutterings swelled into conversations, some of which became heated, until the buzz and hum of voices filled the panelled chamber. Hardly anyone remained in his seat, as the spectators began to roam about the public gallery, to speak to their friends.

Perhaps I was in a state of extreme agitation, but I found the torrent of noise almost insupportable. I wondered how long we would have to wait for the jury to reach a decision. Would it be a good sign if they returned after only a short interval – or would it be better if they toiled at length over their deliberations? Presumably, they would not need long to work out who was responsible for the abduction, given that Sibyl had identified Belle, and various others had recognised Schlutterhose. They might argue, for a while, about the tram accident: Pringle had worked hard to establish that Rose, and the child who had been seen to crack her head, were one and the same, but a few of Aitchison's witnesses had also been convincing. The jury's final discussion would almost certainly concern myself, and whether or not I had been involved. Surely, this issue would provoke the most discussion, given what we had heard during the course of the trial. On balance, I concluded that, as far as I was concerned, the longer they were out, the better.

In the event, less than half an hour had passed when the tinkle of the bell was heard. I tried not to feel dismayed. There was a rush, as the spectators clambered back to their seats, and advocates and agents melted in from the wings and settled around their table. At the sight of Kinbervie approaching the bench, an awed hush fell upon the court. The jurors filed in, and I could not stop myself from staring at them, looking for some sign of my fate in their expressions. However, none of them even glanced in the direction of the dock, and their faces were as impassive as ever. They neither smiled, nor frowned, and said nothing to each other as they took their seats. To my surprise, I felt Mrs Fee grab my hand. Perhaps she knew better than I did – was the jury's lack of visible emotion a bad sign? Ned had been absent from the chamber during the advocate's speeches, no doubt tending to Sibyl with Annie, but I spotted him, perched at the end of one of the back rows, just as – in the corner of my vision – I became aware of a figure, rising to his feet. It was the Clerk of the Court, who asked: 'Gentlemen, have you agreed your verdict?'

One of the jurymen, the foreman, rose to his feet and replied: 'We have.'

'In respect of the first charge, of murder, do you find the prisoner Hans Schlutterhose, guilty or not guilty?'

'Not guilty, sir.'

'Do you find Belle Schlutterhose, or Smith, guilty or not guilty?'

'Not guilty, sir.'

'And the prisoner, Harriet Baxter, guilty or not guilty?'

'Not guilty, sir.'

There was not a breath in my body. I could feel Fee's hand tightening around mine; I thought she might squash me. For a few seconds, a deathly hush reigned over the chamber. Then the Clerk spoke again:

'And in respect of the second charge, of plagium, do you find the prisoner Hans Schluttherhose guilty or not guilty?'

'Guilty, sir.'

'Do you find prisoner Belle Schlutterhose, or Smith, guilty or not guilty?'

'Guilty, sir.'

'And the prisoner, Harriet Baxter, do you find her guilty or not guilty?'

'My lord, we find this charge against Miss Baxter –' Here, he paused for a moment, before announcing the words: 'Not proven.'

Not proven.

So intent had I been on outcomes of guilty or innocent, that I had all but forgotten this idiosyncrasy of the Scottish Law, the not proven verdict. For a moment, I struggled to remember what exactly it implied, and whether it always resulted in acquittal. The only example that I knew of was from over thirty years previously, in the case of Madeleine Smith. Her not proven verdict had allowed her to walk free. Was that to happen, in my case? All this rushed through my mind as, here and there, throughout the court, gasps could be heard, along with a few cheers, some shouts, and a smattering of applause, although whether any of this was to congratulate me, or to celebrate the conviction of my co-accused, it was hard to tell. I looked up at the gallery to try and gauge Ned's reaction, but almost half of the spectators had surged to their feet and I could no longer see any sign of him amongst the crowd.

As Kinbervie and the officers of the court attempted to regain some order, I scanned the chamber for Caskie, but he, too, had disappeared. Afterwards, I learned that he had gone off, immediately, to confirm various arrangements that he had put in place, to ensure my safe passage from the court. Meanwhile, MacDonald was at the advocate's table, with his head in his hands – a reaction that was misinterpreted, of course, by some commentators, who chose to ignore how hard he had worked to save me from conviction.

With order restored, Kinbervie looked me squarely in the eye and announced: 'By verdict of the jury, you have been acquitted of the charges against you. Miss Baxter, you are dismissed from the bar.'

The trap door opened. I was ushered from the court, down into the engulfing darkness of the stair, leaving Schlutterhose and

Belle to wait for Kinbervie to pronounce sentence upon them. I understand that he gave them each ten years' imprisonment, a fairly stiff sentence for plagium, which makes me suspect that he was unable to disregard the fact that the stolen child had died.

Caskie had circulated a rumour amongst the crowds in Parliament Square that I was to be driven from thence to Waverley railway station. Instead, his plan was to escort me out of the back of the building, through a gate in the wall, and thence to a cab, which would take us, by a quiet route, via Lauriston Place, to Haymarket station. His plan seemed to have worked, for when we came outside, twenty minutes later, there was no mob at the rear of the court, and on the far side of the gate, the lane was empty. We emerged onto the Cowgate, a low, shabby street of tenements that ran beneath a high bridge, and it was a surprise to see people, dully and drably, going about their ordinary business. Indeed, the street was quite busy, with groups of men and women milling about, here and there. To our right I saw the cab, waiting on the nearside of the arch beneath the bridge. Stools and chairs, and a few whatnots were spread out on the greasy cobblestones, where a woman was selling furniture on the street. As Caskie guided me between her wares, my eyes were drawn upwards, to the parapet of the bridge, high above. A lone figure stood behind the stone columns; a wan face framed by pale masonry. It was Ned. He was gazing into the distance, along the Cowgate towards the east, so lost in thought that he was unaware of Caskie and me, far below him, in the street. Perhaps the crowds in Parliament Square had been too much for him, and he had fled to this spot, around the corner, for a moment alone. Or had he guessed that this might be the route that Caskie would use to whisk me away to the station? Had he, in fact, come to the bridge to try and get a glimpse of me, or speak to me? Was it even possible that he wanted to thank me, for having come to Sibyl's rescue?

Caskie failed to notice Ned; his gaze was fixed on the cab, and as we approached the vehicle, he hurried ahead to speak to the driver, and instruct him to avoid the Grassmarket, or any road where a crowd might have gathered. The figure on the bridge had still not moved. Left alone for a second, I called out:

'Ned!'

The sound of my voice dragged him from his reverie and he came to his senses. He leaned forwards and peered out between the columns of the parapet, but he was still looking beyond me, at a point further along the street. I waved my arms, to attract his attention.

'Here, Ned. Here I am.'

And then, he saw me. His expression changed from bewilderment to realisation. There was no colour in his face. His skin was livid white. He stared down at me in a way that he had never looked at me before, a way that I did not recognise. His gaze was icy cold. It chilled me to the bone. And then he turned away from the parapet, and was gone.

Sunday, 17 – Saturday, 23 September 1933

LONDON

Sunday, 17th September. Incredible though it may seem, I am almost at the end of my memoir. In the beginning, I had no conception of how long it would take to write; six weeks, perhaps, might have been my guess. However, here we are, over five months later, and I have not yet quite finished. I cannot say why it has taken so long, given that I have been working at it, diligently, every day. I dare say that I may have been carried away in certain sequences, by including, at times, such particulars as the spoken dialogue and so on, but I did find that once I had begun to remember my time in Glasgow, I found it hard to stop. Everything just came back to me, and it seemed a missed opportunity not to relay each and every nuance. 'Le bon Dieu est dans le détail', as they say (or should that be 'le Diable'?).

My emotions, upon approaching the conclusion, are mixed. Today, I am tired and drained, with a touch of bile; perhaps I am running out of steam. In the main, I feel sadness: not simply because of the tragic nature of what happened, but also because – the trial and the tragedy notwithstanding – I have enjoyed revisiting my time with the Gillespies, and now it seems that I must set them adrift; the cord of my memories must be cut. I am not bidding farewell to the family, for ever, of course. They are still here, with me. If I sit very still, I can almost sense their presence.

To my regret, I have only a few keepsakes from that time. I used to keep these mementoes in my jewellery box, but lately I have found it helpful to have them here, on my desk. I like to turn them over in my hands, while I am thinking. Two trifling objects: a single collar-stud, that once belonged to Ned, and a scallop shell. The stud is a plain old thing, in brass. The scallop shell is the kind that ice-cream vendors sometimes still use as a dish upon which to serve their wares. I saw Ned discard it, one day, in the West End Park, after he had finished eating some hokey-pokey. At the time, I was bringing up the rear, perhaps with Mabel, or Annie. Ned was with Walter Peden. They were strolling along, talking, and it made quite a lovely picture of two friends passing the time together (of course, Peden was only annoying after one had got to know him). When Ned had eaten his ice-cream, he glanced around, trying to decide what to do with the shell. Many visitors to the Exhibition simply used to fling their empty 'escalopes' into the river, or toss them into the bushes, but Ned placed his upon a wooden fence at the riverside. There it sat, gleaming white and pink against the dark wood as he continued on his way, and I approached in his wake. Of a sudden, Rose and Sibyl bolted past me, babbling, as usual, in their reedy voices. They skimmed along the fence and, for a moment, I thought that they might accidentally knock the hokey-pokey scallop into the river – but no, they scampered on, and it remained, untouched. As I drew abreast of the fence post, almost without thinking, I picked up the shell and slipped it into my pocket. It was cool, and a little damp, perhaps from Ned's tongue.

11.30 a.m. I have just had the most marvellous little snooze and awakened very refreshed. I must contact the registry tomorrow and request that they send me another assistant. Having thought it over, I feel only relief that that person has gone. When she attacked me, I saw her for what she really is: a cold, cruel person, with an unexpected capacity for violence. The whole business has been very upsetting. Indeed, it has made me quite nauseous and feverish. I have been sick to my stomach several times since she left. For a while, I did wonder whether the girl might have been up to her old tricks and poisoned me, somehow. Without going into detail, it appears as though I have been swallowing coffee grounds, although I have no memory of doing so. Perhaps this is simply a reaction to the upsetting events of last night. It almost feels as though I am vomiting out all the fears and bad feelings that have accumulated over the past few months. But what are these dark specks, if not coffee grounds? They look like dried blood. Are they some sort of crystallisation of every horrid thing that has been building up inside me because of that girl's presence in my home? Could anxiety have caused my innards to bleed?

Perhaps it is a good thing to have purged myself of these foul accretions, to flush out all the badness that she brought with her into this apartment.

Monday, 18th September. Well, that was a waste of time. I shall not be using Burridge's ever again. Clinch has never been terribly polite, but today her discourtesy bordered on insolence. I can scarce believe all the piffle that she came out with, about her girls being reliable souls who can do no wrong, et cetera. I was obliged to remind her that – in the not-too-distant past – two of her 'reliable souls' simply vanished in the night, without a word, for that is what happened with Marjory, and then with Gwen, the first and third candidates that she recommended to me: two girls who seemed perfectly fine to begin with, but in both cases, they packed their bags and walked out within a few weeks, giving no reason or explanation. As for Dora, the second girl, the less said about her, the better: had I known that she possessed such a filthy temper, I would never have taken her on in the first place. Quite simply, the vetting procedure at Burridge's is not stringent enough. How did Sibyl even get onto their books? Presumably, they know nothing of her real history.

As far as I can tell, nobody at Burridge's has actually spoken to her. I believe that there was a letter from her, lying on the doormat, when Clinch opened the office, this morning. I gleaned the impression that it was only a short note, in which 'Miss Whittle' handed in her notice, not only to me, but also to the registry. Clinch tells me that it is Miss Whittle's intention to return to Dorset. Ha! I tried to explain that Miss Whittle is not who she claims to be, but Clinch refused to listen. When she threatened not to send me any more girls, I stopped her in her tracks.

'Do you think I would want any more of your egregious employees? I only telephoned to inform you that I shall certainly be taking my business elsewhere.'

'Do what you like, dear – see if I care.'

'I most certainly shall!' I told her. 'Oh – and the word is register.'

'Beg your pardon?'

I spelled it out for her: 'R-E-G-I-S-T-E-R. Register – not "red chester", as you are so ridiculously fond of saying.'

That is the end of Clinch; I have seen her off.

Frustratingly, I must now start all over again with yet another firm. Every single one of the supposedly 'first-rate' registries has turned out to be nothing of the sort and, in recent years, I am reduced to Clinch and her ilk. Extremely tiresome and inconvenient, but it must be done. I have eaten nothing since yesterday, except a stale Oval Osbourne, and yet, although I have not cooked any meals, the place is beginning to smell a bit whiffy, and all the ashtrays are full, and these flies are becoming a blasted nuisance. I cannot understand where they creep in, for I have closed all the windows. There are flies, everywhere, I now realise, everywhere I look, those lazy flies that swirl and dart beneath the lampshade in the centre of the room, and also, droning in and out, big buzzers, bumping against the windowpane. They make my skin crawl.

Dr Derrett telephoned, this morning, rather cross, wanting to know why I had failed to attend hospital for my X-ray. He insists on booking another appointment, but that will have to wait, for I have quite enough to do, in finishing my manuscript. As well as revising everything that I have done so far, I have yet to describe what happened, following the trial. The final part – the aftermath – is still completely unwritten. Indeed, I have not even planned what to include in that section. I suppose that I should say something about what happened to me: the initial return to London, and so on, and the discovery that, even here, the penny press would make my life a misery. In the days that followed the trial, I lived in constant fear of reprisals, and after a few nervous weeks here in London, I had had enough. My stepfather was still suffering from ill-health, and unable to leave Switzerland and, thinking that I might find some sanctuary there, with him, I sent a telegram, proposing that I travel out to join him. However, the reply that I received was from his factor. It informed me that all visitors were being discouraged for the foreseeable future, and suggested that I write again, in a few months, when, perhaps, the situation might have changed.

Thereafter, on something of an impulse, I booked my passage to New York. One afternoon, a few days before my departure, I found myself on Piccadilly with a few hours to spare. I ended up wandering through the park, and by the time that I had reached the other side, I had resolved to continue westwards, and bid farewell to Eaton Square, to my childhood home. Ramsay kept the house closed up, and it was opened only on the rare occasions when he visited London, but I had no notion of going inside: I simply wanted to look at the old place.

Dusk was falling as I turned off the King's Road and approached the terrace, which seemed much taller than I had remembered. I walked down the narrow pavement along the edge of the gar dens. Up ahead, across the road, I could see the house, halfway down the terrace, the ribbed columns of the portico, and, on the first floor, the shallow balcony spanning the drawing-room windows. There was an empty Victoria sitting beneath one of the plane trees; the horse, a stallion, had been tied to a railing and the driver was leaning against the fence, smoking his pipe. I paused to stroke the animal's nose, while I gazed across the road, at the windows of our house, particularly those on the third floor, where the nursery used to be. To my surprise, while I was watching, a few lights went on, here and there: in the hallway, the front sitting room, and a few rooms upstairs. It occurred to me that, perhaps, Ramsay had loaned or rented the place to someone – although that seemed unlikely.

I was still standing there, wondering about the lights, when a Hackney drew up in front of the portico. Imagine my astonishment when I saw Ramsay descending from the cab. He paid the driver and then walked briskly up the steps, and entered the house. A few minutes later, he appeared in the window of the front sitting room, closing the shutters.

I believe that I may have stood there for several minutes. The next thing I knew was that the driver of the Victoria was at my side, speaking to me.

'Is something wrong, madam? You look ever so strange.'

'What? No – no.'

'Only I thought you was going to faint, you gone so pale.'

'No, I'm fine . . . Do you work here, in one of these residences?'

'Yes, ma'am.' He indicated the house beside my stepfather's. 'There.'

'Does – does anybody live in that house, next door?' I asked him. 'Who was the man who went in there, just now?'

'Oh, that's Mr Dalrymple. Usually, he's up in Scotland, but he's been here now, several weeks.'

'. . . How many weeks?'

The man rubbed his chin. 'At least a month, I'd say. It was a while before St David's, he arrived, I reckon. But we've hardly seen him – he hasn't been out in daylight since he got here.'

I could well imagine. Doubtless, he had no wish to advertise his presence in the country, since both the Scottish authorities, and myself, had been under the impression that he was on his deathbed, in Switzerland. He could have spoken in my defence, and yet he had chosen to dissociate himself from me, to feign illness. Of all the slights and hurts and rejections that I had suffered at his hands, this was surely the worst. And yet, the strange thing was, I felt very little – very little at all.

A few days later, I sailed for New York. There is not much to say about my time there. Apart from one minor misunderstanding – so minor that it never even came to court – I was able to exist in relative obscurity in America.

*

More importantly than myself, of course, I must decide and plan out what I am to write about all the Gillespies and what became of them.

I gather that Mabel and Peden had intended to return to Tangier soon after the trial, but were obliged to remain in Glasgow when it became clear that the Wool and Hosiery was about to fold. Ned, who was nominally in charge, was not in any state to run things, and he had been unable to keep the shop in profit. As the proceeds now constituted the family's major source of income, Mabel and Peden took over, and attempted to save the business. Peden evicted his tenants, and he and Mabel moved back into his old house, in Victoria Crescent Road. In an effort to create more income, Elspeth was obliged to take in lodgers at number 14, which gave her a few extra pounds. However, the role of landlady did not sit well with her, and she was never entirely content with these new arrangements.

As for Sibyl, her dramatic appearance as a witness seemed to have been her undoing: it had tipped her over the edge. There is no clear account of what happened immediately after the trial but what I do know is that she was readmitted to the Glasgow Asylum later that week. Apparently, Ned made several attempts to bring her home over the months that followed, but his efforts were to no avail, because, this time, Sibyl really was beyond help, and the decision to release her now lay outwith her father's control. Ultimately, she became catatonic, and refused to acknowledge anyone she knew, including both of her parents.

Shut out by Sibyl, Annie resumed the peripatetic way of life that she had adopted whilst searching for Rose and began, once more, to tramp the roads around the city of Glasgow, becoming a common sight to those who recognised her. As time went by, she began to travel further afield, until eventually she stopped returning home altogether, and became a sort of vagabond. She did not go mad, exactly, but she developed an aversion to being indoors. At some point – alas – the relationship between her and Ned came to an end. I was not there to see it; by that time, I was settled in America, but I did hear rumours that they were no longer husband and wife. Eventually, Annie disappeared from notice, and I have been unable to find any record of what happened to her, nothing in the papers, no obituary, no gravestone. Perhaps she is still out there, tramping the highways and byways of Scotland: for some reason, I picture her as an old crone, in ragged, blackened garments, with dirty grey locks, and down-at-heel shoes.

As for Ned's mother, she died of apparently natural causes, in the winter of 1891. In fact, by a strange coincidence, at around about that time, I had a dream in which Elspeth choked to death on a bacon rind, but later, I learned that the post-mortem ruling was that she had suffered a massive heart attack.

Following his mother's death, Ned went further into decline. Before the trial, he had resumed painting, but it is my understanding that he stopped again, after Sibyl returned to the asylum. The door of his studio was locked; he never entered there again. In order to live, he was obliged to resume work as an assistant in the Wool and Hosiery, although I gather that Mabel and Peden kept him on more as an act of charity, since he was not much use as a salesman. As far as I know, he never painted again. Having been on the verge of making a name for himself, at the time of the Exhibition, he drifted into obscurity. Nowadays, one hears talk of 'the Glasgow Boys', Lavery et al., but Gillespie's name is never associated with that loose alliance of painters. I believe that Walter Peden did encourage Ned to go back to painting, and even persuaded Mr Whistler to write him a letter, full of compliments, urging Ned to resume his work, but all was to no avail. Meanwhile, Peden's own sentimental animal portraits became infernally popular.

Instead of painting, Ned became obsessed with reclaiming all of his work, even pictures that had no meaning for him, such as the portraits that he had done, on commission. I believe that he invented non-existent exhibitions, and 'borrowed back' canvases, which he then never returned. His aim, in recouping these pictures, was unclear, at the time. He never exhibited them, but kept them stored in an old mews workshop at the back of Peden's house.

In the spring of 1892, Ned moved into the workshop, while continuing to try and reclaim his paintings from their owners. I personally never heard from him, although he must surely have remembered that I was in possession of his picture of *Stanley Street*, which hangs in my bedroom. As already mentioned, when Euphemia Urquart refused to lend him her portrait, he attempted to burgle her home, only to be thwarted by her butler. It is my understanding, from someone who was acquainted with one of the Urquarts' maids, that Detective Sub-Inspector Stirling was called to Woodside Terrace and asked to investigate the attempted burglary. The contents of the pockets of Ned's jacket, left behind in his escape, revealed his identity. However, Stirling was sympathetic to the artist; perhaps he felt guilty at having failed, for so long, to solve the mystery of what had happened to Rose. At any rate, he persuaded the Urquarts not to press charges, and the matter was forgotten.

After the rumours about the Urquart painting had subsided, I heard very little more about Ned, until late in 1892. In October, on the third anniversary of the date that Sibyl had first entered the asylum, it is my understanding that Ned made a huge pile of all — or, should I say, almost all — of his canvases, inside the workshop in Victoria Crescent Lane, and then set them alight. The building soon became an inferno. It was thought, at first, that Ned had become trapped, by accident. There was only one exit from the workshop, on the ground floor, but any person imprisoned inside could have escaped, either through there, or by climbing out of an upstairs window, for it was only a mews, and the first storey was not very high. However, investigators found that the door had been bolted from the inside, and Ned had not made any attempt to escape from the building, by either route.

By the time that I heard of Ned's death, his funeral was long over. My grieving had to be done in private, as was the case with my stepfather, who also died in my absence, in 1895, when his latest gadget, an imported shower-bath, exploded with him inside. Ramsay's funeral was carried out so swiftly that there was no time for me to return to England. I never saw him buried, and the next time that I set foot on these shores was in 1913. By then, the trial of Hans and Belle Schlutterhose and my part in it were forgotten. My father had bequeathed his land and properties to Glasgow City Council, but, with my small income, and the sale of my aunt's house, I was able to settle here, in Bloomsbury, in some approximation of tranquillity. That is, until the publication of a certain provocative little pamphlet.

For ever and a day, this murky, ambiguous 'not proven' has hung above my head. Alas, 'the Scottish verdict' is unclear, saying neither one thing, nor the other. In fact, I believe that when a Scottish jury return a verdict of 'not proven' what they mean is not so much: 'We don't think you did it', but more: 'We think you probably did do it – but, luckily for you, the prosecution didnae prove it well enough.'

They might as well have found me guilty.

Kemp's theory is that I escaped conviction only by foul means and one of the main contentions of his pamphlet is that I managed to bribe Christina Smith and prevent her from appearing at the trial. His supposition is that I contacted her, from prison, and persuaded her to disappear from court on the day that she was due to give evidence. Of course, I barely knew Christina Smith. I doubt that I even knew where she resided, at the time. Even had I known her, and wanted to communicate with her, it would have been almost impossible, for all my mail was inspected and read before it was posted. Kemp fails to realise how very difficult it is to smuggle letters in and out of gaol, a feat possible only if one has friends in high places within the prison hierarchy, and if one is willing to bribe and cheat and lie. One would have to be very clever indeed to dream up a way of secretly carrying on illicit correspondence with someone in the outside world.

*

Tuesday, 19th September. Yet more evidence to uphold my theory that I am purging myself of all the badness and anxiety engendered by that girl. This involves a somewhat indelicate revelation. Lately, I am called to stool in the middle of the night. This happens, several times a week, and wakes me from sleep, at about four o'clock in the morning. Today, it was half past three o'clock when I awoke, and stumbled down the hallway to the WC. I had turned on the light and, as I pulled the chain after using the lavatory, I happened to glance back, and was alarmed to notice that my elimination, instead of the usual colour, was as black as tar. Upon reflection, I expect that this is a sign that I am expelling the last of all the horridness and vexation that I have been feeling over the past few weeks. However, momentarily, I was quite disturbed.

I have been awake ever since, hard at work on planning the last part of this memoir. It is now almost nine o'clock in the morning. I do wish Lockwood's would open, as I want them to send over a few necessities, but I have rung their number several times, and nobody answers the telephone. I am nearly out of Muratti's and a few other things. Perishing for a cigarette.

Friday, 22nd September. Now, this is interesting, and a little confusing. A letter has arrived, in the middle-day post, from a Mr William Cuthbertson, who claims to be the newly appointed Secretary of the Glasgow Asylum. Apparently, the previous secretary, Mr Pettigrew, passed away at the end of last month, leaving a large amount of unopened correspondence. Mr Cuthbertson apologises for the long delay. He has now consulted the appropriate files, and is able to inform me that, according to the records, a Sibyl Gillespie who was first admitted to the asylum in the autumn of 1889, and released in the December of the same year, was readmitted in March 1890, and continued to be a patient there until the July of 1918, when she died of influenza.

1890 to 1918. It hardly seems credible. I wonder how accurate this information can be? People were dropping like flies that summer of 1918. Is it possible that adequate records were maintained during the epidemic? Could this person whose file has been found even be the same girl? The dates of admission are similar, but there must have been some administrative error. It surely cannot be the same person, for it would mean that Sibyl spent almost thirty years in that abominable place, and then died there.

It does not bear contemplation.

Besides, I saw her scars. I am almost certain that I saw them.

Saturday, 23rd September. Yesterday afternoon, when I walked past the dining room, I noticed that the birdcage was on the table, rather than on the sideboard, where it should be. Presumably, that is where the girl left it. Or perhaps I moved it when I was seeing to the birds, which I must have done, earlier this week. I cannot seem to remember. Things move around in here, apparently of their own accord. There are black splashes down the wall next to the piano; I have no idea what they are or where they came from; and there appear to be mushrooms growing in the bathroom. At any rate, one of the finches – possibly Maj – was making rather a lot of noise: a short, sharp cry that I have never heard before. A few hours later, I happened to pass the room once again and, as soon as he saw me, Maj started to make the same insistent sound. I thought it over, whilst rinsing out my glass, and decided that this would be the sort of noise that a bird would make were he suffering. The cry was too urgent, too piercing, to be anything else. Maj wanted me to notice him; he wanted me to pay attention. I suppose that I have been rather busy, these past few days, with my planning.

When I returned to the dining room, and approached the table, I saw, at once, why he was upset. Layla was lying on her side in the bottom of the cage, completely still. She looked very small, and very dead. Her feathers were ruffled and grubby. Her one visible eye was half shut, and her little legs were curled along the length of her body. She was partially covered by something rubbery and reddish-green in colour. At first, I thought it might be her little insides all exploded outwards. Then I realised that it was an old – very old – dried-up piece of apple skin, from one of the half-apples that we pop into the cage, from time to time. The skin seemed to have been draped across the lower part of her body. Maj was still making his 'alarm' sound, frantically flitting from perch to perch. Every so often, he would alight on the floor of the cage, beside Layla, and then cry out sharply, and look at me: as though he wanted to ensure that I had seen her.

Not knowing what else to do, I tried to talk to him in a soothing voice. I moved closer to the cage and peered inside to get a good look. It was impossible to say how long Layla had been dead, but in this muggy weather it would not take long for her to begin to rot. The cage floor was filthy, covered in seed and droppings. The water dish looked as though it contained some sort of foul, thick broth. I tried to think of a way of extracting Layla without touching her. In the end, I simply removed the base from the cage, along with the droppings, the water tray and the dead bird, and set it in the corner.

Then – with Maj still clinging inside, to one of his perches – I took the upper part of the cage next door, to the sitting room, where I placed it on some sheets of newspaper. Maj seemed unperturbed by this change of location. I gave him clean water and fresh seed. Finally, in the kitchen, I poured myself a stiffener. A huge bluebottle was buzzing around some of the rubbish in there, and so I closed the door on it and took my drink through to the sitting room.

Here I sat, contemplating Maj, and wondering how the apple skin had come to be draped over poor dead Layla. Had he dragged it there to cover her body? And if so, then why? Was he acting on instinct, as best he could, to bury his mate, and protect her from potential predators? Had he draped the skin over her as some sort of tribute, or mark of respect? Or was the sight of her corpse simply so painful to him that he wanted to hide it? These last two explanations seemed unlikely – and yet, given his frantic behaviour, perhaps not impossible.

There is also the question of what might have caused Layla to die. She was quite old, for a finch. But could that horrid girl have done something to harm the bird, before she left? She could have done it while she had me trapped in the kitchen.

Poor Maj. The love of his life, his only sweetheart, exists no more. Now, he will have to live alone, in his boxwood cage. No more can he sing to his lady love, or groom her feathers; no more will he feed her while she begs, open-mouthed, like a chick. Having said that, he seems to have adapted well to his new environment, here in the sitting room. He has drunk the clean water that I gave him and, every so often, he throws some seed out at me from between the bars of the cage. He seems less traumatised, and no longer makes that sharp, warning cry.

Next door, Layla must be decomposing. I shall have to get up soon, and dispose of her body, for it has begun to smell. Her death has had a surprisingly profound effect on me. I feel quite overcome this evening, and am incapable of working on my manuscript. I shall have to make a start on the final section tomorrow, or in a few days. Perhaps something about the bird's death, or the loneliness that Maj must inevitably feel, has struck a chord in me.

From time to time, as I write these notes, I lift my head, and glance around the room, at Maj, or out of the window, across the road to where the shadows are thickening against the gable wall of the hotel. Every so often, I let my gaze rest upon the picture that hangs above the mantelpiece, a canvas that is always a comfort to me, for it is Ned's painting, of course, the first of his that ever I saw, and my dear favourite, *The Studio*.

Acknowledgements

Tom Shankland: I cannot thank you enough for your help, support and advice, at every stage of the writing of this book; I definitely couldn't have done it without you. I am eternally indebted to Petra Collins for her patience, wisdom and expertise in Scottish Law; any legal errors herein are mine. Heartfelt thanks to Lucy Mulvagh, Jamie Milne and Andrew Binnie for their encouragement and helpful feedback on early drafts of the novel. I am much obliged to Catriona and Stewart Murray and Amanda McMillan for allowing me to have a nosy around their 'Stanley Street' homes. For kind advice, many thanks to Alastair Dinsmor, of the Glasgow Police Heritage Society and Theo Van Asperen, of the Glasgow Art Club.

Thanks also to the following: Dr Jonathan Andrews; Jimmy Powdrell Campbell; David Lister; Dr Mark Godfrey; Professor Gordon; Robin Campbell; David Stark; Reverend Kenneth Stewart; Brian Stewart; Ronnie Scott; Kevin Brady; The Mitchell Library; University of Glasgow Library; The British Library; www.hiddenglasgow.com

I am also very grateful to Jonny Geller and Angus Cargill, and all at Curtis Brown and Faber and Faber.

Of research materials the following indispensable publications deserve mention: *Public Lives: Women, Family and Society in Victorian Britain*, by Eleanor Gordon and Gwyneth Nair, Yale University Press, 2003; *Glasgow's Great Exhibitions*, by Perilla Kinchin and Juliet Kinchin, White Cockade Publishing, 1988; *The Glasgow Boys*, Roger Billcliffe, John Murray (Publishing) Ltd., 1985; *Glasgow Girls*, ed. by Jude Burkhauser, Canongate Books Ltd., 1993; *Sir John Lavery, Photography, Glasgow International Exhibition of 1888*, by Brian Thom McQuade, published by

TH.A.H.M. van Asperen, Glasgow, 2006; *Trial of John Watson Laurie*, edited by William Roughead, Notable British Trials, William Hodge and Co. Ltd., 1932, Reprinted Gaunt, Inc. 1995; *The Oscar Slater Murder Story*, by Richard Whittington-Egan, Neil Wilson Publishing Ltd., 2001; *Glasgow in 1901*, by James Hamilton Muir, William Hodge and Co. Ltd., 1901, reprinted by White Cockade Publishing, 2001; *Tea and Taste, The Glasgow Tea Rooms, 1875–1975*, by Perilla Kinchin, White Cockade Publishing, 1996; *Glasgow Pubs and Publicans*, by John Gorevan, Tempus Publishing Ltd., 2002; *The Buildings of Scotland, Glasgow*, by Williamson, Riches, and Higgs, Penguin Books, 1990; *The Godfrey Edition Old Ordnance Survey Maps*, especially that of Hillhead, Glasgow (Lanarkshire Sheet 6.06), published by Alan Godfrey Maps, 1998; The National Library of Scotland Ordnance Survey Town Plan of Glasgow @ http://geo.nls.uk/maps/towns/glasgow1894/openlayers.html; *The Kenwood Ladies' Bathing Pond*, by Ann Griswold, York Publishing Services Ltd., 1998; *First Aid to the Injured*, by Dr. Friedrich Esmarch, Smith, Elder and Co, 1882, (from Archive CD Books); *Lying Awake*, by Catherine Carswell (1950), reprinted by Canongate Books Ltd., 1997; *Open the Door,* by Catherine Carswell (1920), reprinted by Virago/Penguin, 1986.